Seasons in Paradise

Other books by Barbara Cameron

The Quilts of Lancaster County Series

A Time to Love
A Time to Heal
A Time for Peace
Annie's Christmas Wish

The Stitches in Time Series

Her Restless Heart
The Heart's Journey
Heart in Hand

The Quilts of Love Series

Scraps of Evidence

The Amish Road Series

A Road Unknown
Crossroads
One True Path

The Coming Home Series

Return to Paradise

SEASONS IN PARADISE

THE COMING HOME SERIES

Barbara Cameron

Abingdon Press
Nashville

Seasons in Paradise

Copyright © 2016 Barbara Cameron

All rights reserved.

The persons and events portrayed in this work of fiction are the creations of the author, and any resemblance to persons living or dead is purely coincidental.

Macro Editor: Teri Wilhelms

Published in association with Books & Such Literary Agency

Library of Congress Cataloging-in-Publication Data

Names: Cameron, Barbara, 1949- author.
Title: Seasons in Paradise / Barbara Cameron.
Description: Nashville : Abingdon Press, [2016] | Series: Coming home series ; book 2
Identifiers: LCCN 2016009636| ISBN 9781426771927 (softcover) | ISBN 9781501827341 (ebook)
Subjects: LCSH: Amish—Fiction. | Man-woman relationships—Fiction. | Paradise (Lancaster County, Pa.)—Fiction. | GSAFD: Christian fiction. | Love stories.
Classification: LCC PS3603.A4473 S43 2016 | DDC 813/.6—dc23 LC record available at https://lccn.loc.gov/2016009636

John 14:2 in chapter 17 is from The Authorized (King James) Version. Rights in the Authorized Version in the United Kingdom are vested in the Crown. Reproduced by permission of the Crown's patentee, Cambridge University Press.

16 17 18 19 20 21 22 23 24—10 9 8 7 6 5 4 3 2 1

MANUFACTURED IN THE UNITED STATES OF AMERICA

For my cousin Deb

Acknowledgments

To everything there is a season...

The farm my mother and her eight siblings grew up on in Indiana has been the inspiration for the farms I write about in my books. I vividly remember watching my Uncle Harvey, the youngest in the family, ride his tractor in his fields. His wife, my Aunt Delores, made the family welcome whenever they visited, and that can't have been easy given the number of family members who descended on the farm for vacations. She has often been the inspiration for the female characters who make a home so welcome, who make family keep wanting to go home. Aunt Delores made a little bedroom under the eaves of the second story so welcome for the many nieces and nephews who visited. She even kept a small toy chest that had belonged to my mom and her twin sister stocked with toys and let us choose one each time we came.

I was sitting on the grass near the road one day when I saw my first Amish buggy and became fascinated with the Amish.

Memories of how that farm looked so different from season to season inspired this story, the second in the Coming Home series. It starts in spring and ends up in winter, at Christmas, the holiest of holidays.

When people think of Christmas they usually think of home. But I got to wondering what happens if home is a place you've had to avoid? What happens then? My hero, Sam, has had to leave his Amish home and live in the *Englisch* world. Mary Elizabeth, the woman who loves him, believes he needs to return to his community and his faith—and her—and it will take her seasons to do so.

Thank you to my editor, Ramona Richards, for continuing to believe in my stories, and thank you to Teri Wilhelm, my macro editor, and everyone at Abingdon Press who helps produce beautiful covers and proofread and distribute...oh, so many people and so many jobs, I'll never be able to thank everyone.

Thank you, dear reader, for choosing my books.

And thank You, God, for taking my hand and helping me tell a story of faith and love.

1

Mary Elizabeth always thought there was nothing lovelier than springtime in Paradise, Pennsylvania.

Today the sky was a rich blue, not the gray it had been for too long this winter. The clouds that scudded overhead were soft clumps and a pure white, not heavy and dark and spitting snow or rain.

A warm breeze carried the scents of flowers and plants and...

Manure and fertilizer.

Her nose wrinkled as she stood on the back porch of her *schweschder* Lavina's big old farmhouse and watched David, Lavina's *mann*, working with his *bruders,* Sam and John, fertilizing the fields.

Well, to be honest, she watched Sam, not the other men. Sam and John came nearly every weekend now that spring planting was taking place in Lancaster County. It took all three of the *bruders* as well as occasional help from their *dat*, Amos, to do the planting, as would the eventual nurturing of the crop. It would take the four of them and some of the men from the community to harvest come November.

Mary Elizabeth had begun to think Amos would never turn the farm over to his eldest *sohn*, David, and her *schweschder* Lavina. David had finally despaired at fighting with his *dat*. Amos had been so difficult he'd driven David, then Sam and John away.

David had returned to Paradise to help his *mudder* take care of his *dat* when he got the cancer. No one had been more surprised than David and Lavina when Amos had a change of heart after recovering and decided to turn the farm over to his *sohn*.

Mary Elizabeth knew she would never forget this Christmas past when Sam and John walked into her *haus* and surprised both families after an absence of more than a year. But that return was brief and temporary.

It was a miracle, she'd thought, when they came to celebrate the birth of the Christ child that night. But her hopes that Sam would stay had been dashed just hours later. The two *bruders* went back to their apartment in town that night.

Both Sam and John said it was *wunderbaar* that their *dat* had recovered and they were thrilled that David would take over the family farm. But they refused to return home or to the Amish community the *bruders* had grown up in.

Mary Elizabeth had thought her heart was broken when Sam followed David out of the community, but that Christmas night she'd found it was possible for her heart to be broken a second time.

So now she watched Sam working in the fields she knew he loved but would leave after supper at day's end. And she knew she had to stop yearning and find someone else. She didn't feel like an old maid at twenty-three, but she wanted to make a home with a *mann* she loved, have *kinner*. Be loved and be happy.

"Mary Elizabeth, *kumm* and have some iced tea with me."

She turned and smiled at Lavina. Whenever she looked at her two *schweschders* it was like looking in a mirror. The three of them could have been triplets with their oval faces, round blue eyes, and blonde hair. They'd been born just a year apart so they'd grown up close.

Her oldest *schweschder* seemed to glow these days. She'd married David after the harvest in November and now, several months later, was obviously enjoying being a new *fraa* and making a home.

Mary Elizabeth wondered if there was a reason her *schweschder* glowed besides being a new bride...many Amish started their families early. And Lavina and David had lost a year of being together when he had lived away from the community.

So far Lavina hadn't said anything and with a voluminous apron tied over her dress, looked slim as ever.

"See if Waneta would like to come have some iced tea," Lavina said as she poured the tea over ice in tall glasses.

Mary Elizabeth knocked on the door of the *dawdi haus*, and Waneta opened it. "Would you like to have some iced tea with us?"

"*Danki*, that would be nice." The older woman smiled, walked into the kitchen, and took a seat at the kitchen table. "It's *gut* to see you, Mary Elizabeth."

"You, too."

Had Waneta noticed how often she came to visit—and so often on the weekends? Mary Elizabeth wondered.

The three of them chatted easily as they drank the tea and ate some chocolate chip cookies Lavina had baked earlier that day. Waneta talked about making some curtains for the *dawdi haus* and seemed happy to be living there now that Lavina and David had taken over the main part of the *haus*.

"Don't you love the color of the kitchen paint Lavina chose?" she asked Mary Elizabeth. "Yellow is so cheerful. It reminds me of the daffodils that are blooming in front of the *haus* now that it's spring."

Lavina smiled at her. "I'm glad you like it." She looked at Mary Elizabeth. "We painted the kitchen in the *dawdi haus* the same color after Waneta saw how it looked in here."

Waneta took a sip of her tea. "Amos never thought we needed to paint in here, but it had been years since we did it and it really brightens up the room."

Mary Elizabeth was glad to see how well her *schweschder* and Waneta got along. The two had always been close, and she knew

Waneta was grateful that Lavina had talked David into returning when Amos had gone into chemotherapy more than a year ago.

Amos walked in a few minutes later, hung his wide-brimmed straw hat on a peg near the door and washed his hands at the kitchen sink. Waneta jumped to her feet and hurried to pour him a glass of iced tea as he took a seat at the table.

"It's warm out there," he said. "Warm, but there's a breeze."

"Maybe you should take a little rest. You don't want to overdo."

He frowned as he took a long swallow of tea. "I'll see how I feel after I have this."

"Is the planting going well?" Mary Elizabeth asked him.

He nodded. "After all the arguing about trying new crops and fancy new methods David's planting exactly what I'd planned." He looked smug.

Mary Elizabeth exchanged glances with Lavina and her *schweschder* warned her with a shake of the head not to say anything. But Mary Elizabeth knew better. David was planting what his *dat* had planned because the order had been placed months ago and because he was grateful that he'd been given the farm. Without that gift, without Amos softening, David would have had a very hard time buying a farm in Lancaster County.

"Is David coming in for a break?" Lavina asked Amos as she pushed the plate closer to him.

He picked up a cookie and bit into it. "*Nee*, no one wanted to stop yet. Rain's coming later this afternoon, and they want to get as much done as possible."

Lavina looked at Mary Elizabeth. "I'll take some cold drinks out to them."

"I'll help," Mary Elizabeth said.

"*Danki.*"

"I think I'll take a rest after all," Amos said. "*Danki* for the tea and cookies, Lavina."

"*Ya, danki.*" Waneta said. "I think I'll go get some mending done. *Gut* to see you again, Mary Elizabeth."

Amos nodded to her and the couple went into the *dawdi haus* and shut the door.

Lavina and Mary Elizabeth filled glasses with ice and tea. "Are you sure you want to do this? Sam's out there."

Mary Elizabeth sighed. "I know. I want to talk to him."

"I see."

"I'm probably *ab im kop*, but I'm still in love with him."

"I know that feeling. I couldn't forget David after he stayed away for a year."

"Don't tell David what I said."

"You think he can't guess after you and Sam dated?"

"*Nee*, I guess you're right."

They put the glasses on a tray with a plate of cookies and carried them out to the edge of the field the men were working in. An old table had been placed there so trays could be set on it to serve workers in the field.

Lavina waved to them and the men stopped working and walked over.

David was the first to reach them. He took off his straw hat and wiped his forehead with a bandanna before he accepted a glass of iced tea. Mary Elizabeth saw the love in David's eyes as he gazed at her *schweschder* and looked away, feeling it was a very private moment between the two of them.

Her eyes met Sam's. He reached for a glass of tea and gulped down half of it. She watched the muscles move in the long column of his tanned throat as he swallowed.

"It's warm today," she said as she held out the plate of cookies to him.

"Hey, do I get some tea?" John demanded as he stepped up to the table.

"*Schur*," Mary Elizabeth said, handing him a glass with barely a glance.

"Talk about making a guy feel welcome," he muttered when she continued to look at Sam.

"What?" Mary Elizabeth turned to John.

13

"Nothing."

The three *bruders* looked so much alike they could have been triplets—tall, square-jawed, with dark blue eyes so often serious. Sam and John wore their brown, almost black hair in an *Englisch* cut because they still lived in that world.

"Where's Rose Anna?" John asked.

Mary Elizabeth tore her gaze from Sam and gave John a chilly glance. "She wasn't feeling well," she said shortly.

He set the empty glass down on the tray. "Well, that was cooling," he said. He picked up one of the cookies and walked over to sit on the back porch.

Mary Elizabeth couldn't help it. The three Zook *schweschders* had always loved the three Stoltzfus *bruders*. So far only one of the *schweschders* had married one of them.

When she glanced back at Sam, she was surprised by a look of sadness in his eyes before he set the glass down. "*Danki.*"

He glanced up at the sky, beginning to cloud over and turned to David. "Ready?"

David nodded. "I'll be in soon," he told Lavina and set his glass on the tray.

Lavina glanced at the sky. "Watch for lightning."

"I will."

Lavina picked up the tray and they walked back to the *haus*. "Do you want to stay for supper? Sam and John are eating with us before they go home. It's the least I can do when they're helping David."

Mary Elizabeth bit her lip. "It might give me a chance to talk to him for a few minutes afterward." She took a deep breath. "I'm just thinking that it's time we either got back together or…" she trailed off.

"Or?"

"Or I need to move on and find someone else. I want what you have, Lavina. Oh, I'm not coveting what you have," she rushed to say. "You know that. I just want to be with a man I love. Make a home, a family."

"I know. And I understand. Maybe we can find a way for the two of you to have a moment alone to talk."

Mary Elizabeth grinned at her. "Playing matchmaker?"

Lavina returned her grin. "Just returning the favor, dear *schweschder.* Just returning the favor."

"You're welcome," Mary Elizabeth said.

She set the tray on the kitchen table. "Why don't you help me make supper?"

"*Schur.* What do you need me to do?"

"The men will be hot from working in the field. Let's find something that will be lighter. Maybe something cold. I already made two pies for dessert. Peach."

"Sam's favorite."

"David's, too."

Mary Elizabeth walked over to the refrigerator and perused its contents, perfectly at home in her *schweschder's* kitchen.

"We could make a big bowl of potato salad and add cubes of this leftover ham and maybe some cheddar cheese," she said. "Add some rolls and the pies and that's a nice meal."

"You're right. Get the potatoes and we'll start boiling them."

The two of them made fast work of chopping celery, onion, ham, and cheese. Lavina swayed when she turned from washing the potatoes at the sink. Mary Elizabeth grasped her shoulders and pushed her down into a chair.

"Are you *allrecht?*"

"Fine, fine." Lavina took a deep breath. "Just moved too quickly."

"Maybe I should get David." She didn't like how pale her *schweschder's* face had gotten.

"*Nee*, it's nothing. I mean it, I don't want him to worry."

"You stay put," Mary Elizabeth insisted when Lavina started to rise. "If you don't sit and rest for a few minutes, I'll call David."

"*Allrecht, allrecht.* Get the potatoes and let's get them peeled."

They peeled the potatoes and cubed them. Mary Elizabeth put them in a pan filled with water and set it on the stove.

She sat down at the table. "Lavina?"

"*Ya?*"

"Are you—?"

"Am I what?"

"You know."

"*Nee*, I don't know." She looked innocently at Mary Elizabeth.

"Having a *boppli!*" Mary Elizabeth hissed. Honestly, how dense could someone be?

"Sssh," Lavina said, glancing at the door of the *dawdi haus*. She frowned and looked thoughtful. "Oh my, do you think . . . ?" she trailed off.

"I don't know. Do you think?"

A smile bloomed on Lavina's face. "Oh my," she breathed. "Maybe."

They sat there for a long time grinning at each other until they heard the rumble of thunder. Mary Elizabeth jumped up and poked at the potatoes. Done. She drained them and put them in a bowl over another filled with ice to quickly cool them. Once they were cool enough, she added mayonnaise, the chopped vegetables, ham, and cheese. A quick stir and it went into the refrigerator to chill.

She looked out the kitchen window. The men were still working in the fields, casting glances up at the sky as they did. She set the table and made sure they had two pitchers of iced tea waiting in the refrigerator.

She couldn't wait until supper was finished and she could talk to Sam.

One way or another, she'd know what to do after this evening.

2

Sam didn't want to run into Mary Elizabeth again, but there was no avoiding it.

He opened the screen door and sure enough, there she was sitting at the kitchen table talking with Lavina.

She glanced at the clock. "Finished for the day?"

"No. I cut my hand, and David insisted I come in and take care of it." He strode over to the kitchen sink and turned on the tap.

She got up and came to stand beside him. "That looks deep."

"It's not bad."

Lavina poked in a kitchen cupboard and brought over a first aid kit. "You don't want to risk infection." She set it down on the kitchen counter beside the sink. "See that he takes care of it," she told Mary Elizabeth. "I'm going to go change."

"No need to fuss," he told Mary Elizabeth. "I know to be careful. We get minor cuts on the construction job site all the time."

She snapped open the lid on the kit. "It's not fussing."

He soaped the cut, wincing as it stung, then ran water over it until the suds ran down the sink and the cut stopped bleeding. She handed him a paper towel to dry his hand and then squirted a line of antibacterial ointment on the cut and wrapped it with gauze.

"There," she said, taping the gauze to hold it in place. "But how are you going to keep it clean and dry out in the fields?" she asked, tilting her head to one side to study his hand. "Hmmm."

Then her expression brightened. She reached into a cupboard and pulled out some plastic gloves. "Here, wear this over it while you're working."

He started to object but she was right—no point in cleaning and bandaging the cut and then going out and exposing it to more dirt and manure in the fields.

"Thanks," he said, avoiding her eyes.

"*Wilkumm.*" She busied herself putting the gauze and ointment back into the first aid kit and snapped it shut.

The sound seemed loud in the quiet kitchen.

Sam stood there awkwardly. He'd returned home for Christmas and had had to tell her that it was temporary, that he wasn't back to stay like David.

He'd never forget seeing the hurt he caused. Tears had welled up in her eyes, and she'd rushed from the room. He hadn't seen her again until David asked for his help with the spring planting today.

And he'd walked into the kitchen and there she sat talking with Lavina. The hurt was still there in her eyes...Mary Elizabeth had always been more assertive, more outspoken than her *schweschders.* So he wasn't surprised when she'd stayed after Lavina left the room to change, obviously giving them some time alone.

He turned to leave.

"Sam?"

"*Ya?*" He regarded her warily.

"I want to talk to you."

He glanced out the window. David and John were still working in the fields, more quickly now. "Now's not a *gut* time. We're trying to finish before it rains."

A rumble of thunder sounded overhead as if to confirm what he said. Her gaze shifted to the view out the kitchen window. Clouds scudded overhead.

"*Allrecht*," she said. "After supper."

It was a statement not a question. Ordinarily he might not have liked that but he figured he owed her that.

"After supper. I'll give you a ride home." He left and walked back to the fields. David agreed to give John a lift home when Sam explained he needed to talk to Mary Elizabeth.

Farming was hard work. He didn't mind hard work, but it was difficult to be here doing what he loved when he now had to work in town. And working on a Saturday wasn't his idea of fun. A guy liked to have a weekend off once in a while. During the week he worked construction building new homes, so he was tired and ready to relax by Saturday.

David hadn't asked for his help. But Sam knew he needed the help and what were *bruders* for? He hadn't looked forward to seeing his *dat* again even after David had said he'd changed a lot. He'd seen that he seemed different Christmas night but couldn't help being cynical. Could any man change that much? And could it last?

He and his *dat* were wary of each other. They'd barely spoken since he started helping David when spring planting began. It helped that Amos still tired easily after he'd been told he was in remission. He often had to go into the house to rest so they didn't have to spend too much time in the fields together. The two of them hadn't had a lot of opportunity to talk.

Today, Amos hadn't been out in the fields long and had done little more than supervise. And share his opinion about how things were being done.

Over and over.

David was taking it very well. He had a lot more patience with the old man than Sam did that was for *schur*.

Rain began falling an hour later. Resigned, they led the horses back to the barn, unhitched the plow, and fed and watered the stock.

The workday was shorter than usual, but Sam and his *bruders* had worked hard and the three of them headed in to supper, running when it began to pour. They pounded up the steps to the porch. John was the first.

"You old men can't keep up!" he teased and laughed and elbowed them as they tried to enter the house at the same time.

"Here come the rowdy Stoltzfus *bruders*," Lavina remarked dryly.

David grinned and advanced on her, shaking raindrops on her. She swatted at him with a kitchen towel, her cheeks reddening as she warned him to behave.

"Boys will be boys," Waneta said, watching her *sohns* with a fond eye. "Go wash up."

They jostled each other a bit more just for form, but after they washed up, they settled into their chairs at the table and were on their best behavior. It might be David's *haus* now, but Amos had walked into the room and sat there at the table, watching Sam with what he felt was a critical eye. If he looked at John that way Sam didn't notice, but John looked unconcerned.

As soon as the meal was blessed John busied himself filling his plate. He handed Sam the bowl of potato salad. Sam served himself several big spoons of it. As he passed the bowl to David he saw the pies sitting on the counter. Well, well . . . he was tired and sweaty and his muscles ached.

But there was pie for dessert.

Since there was a big bowl of ripe peaches sitting near them, he had a suspicion what kind his sister-in-law had made. And she had a fine hand with baking pies.

There was little conversation as the men of the family ate hungrily.

Sam polished off two helpings of the potato salad, a couple of rolls, and a piece of pie. Not to forget several glasses of iced tea that finally cooled him off.

Once or twice, he caught Mary Elizabeth watching him, her expression unreadable. But as much as she guarded her expression he'd guessed from the way she'd told him she wanted to speak to him that it wasn't going to be pleasant.

So he had to admit to himself that he lingered over a second piece of pie and yet another glass of iced tea. He wasn't in a hurry to talk to her.

"*Gut* pie," Amos said, and Lavina beamed at him.

"Not as *gut* as Waneta's, but I hope I'm getting better," she told him modestly.

"I don't want to say how many years I've been baking pie." Waneta smiled at her.

"Didn't take you long," Amos said, giving his *fraa* a fond look.

Sam couldn't believe his eyes and ears.

Supper done, he thanked the women and joined the men outside as they talked about what they'd do the following Saturday. A short time later, Mary Elizabeth came out of the *haus* and gave him a questioning look. He excused himself and pulled keys out of his pocket.

The rain had stopped but storm clouds hung over the area.

They walked without speaking to the pickup truck. He opened the passenger-side door and she slid inside.

As he started the truck, he gave her a cautious look. Seemed to him that when a woman said she wanted to talk, it usually wasn't a good thing.

———— ∞ ————

Mary Elizabeth glanced around the interior of the truck. "Looks familiar," she said simply as she snapped her seatbelt into place.

"Bought it from David," he told her. "He's letting me make payments."

He put the truck in gear and backed out onto the road. "So, what did you want to talk about?"

Tension fairly radiated from her, as palpable as the storm clouds overhead. Her body was stiff in the seat, her chin thrust out. She cut her eyes at him, and the hurt and anger in them blazed at him.

"Are you ever coming back?"

"Well, that was blunt."

And cold. The rain had chilled the air, and now her tone seemed to make the interior of the truck even chillier. He switched on the heater.

She folded her arms across her chest. "That's me. Blunt Mary Elizabeth."

True, he wanted to say. But he didn't. She wasn't beating around the bush, so he knew he needed to hear her out.

"I told you at Christmas I was just back for that night," he said carefully. The roads were wet and slick, and he didn't relish a confrontation driving her home.

"You've been back since then. So I thought maybe..."

"I'd want to come back to stay?" he finished for her. The meal he'd enjoyed felt like it was turning to lead in his stomach. Why couldn't she let this be?

"Ya."

He tried to think what to say. As the silence stretched between them she fidgeted.

"Never mind. I guess I have my answer."

He looked for a place to pull over and after he found it, turned to face her.

"Where would I go, Mary Elizabeth?" he asked, feeling pinned between a rock and a hard place. "If I moved back to the community, where would I live?"

He heard the bitterness in his voice but he couldn't hold it back.

She stared at him, speechless.

"Don't say I could move in with David and Lavina. That wouldn't be fair. And I don't have the relationship with my *dat* that David does."

"But you could."

He shrugged and turned his gaze to look forward. "We talked about this months ago when you got David to drive you to talk to me. We didn't get anywhere then and we're not going to now."

"Because you're too stubborn."

"Me? Not my *dat*?"

"He's changed."

"With David. Not with me."

"It's not that you don't want to come back," she said quietly. "You don't want me."

She opened the door and slipped from the truck before he could stop her.

"Mary Elizabeth! Where are you going?"

"What do you care?" she shot over her shoulder as she ran across the street and started walking back home. "Go home, Sam. Go home and have a happy life."

Frustrated, torn, he glanced back at the truck. He wanted to follow her, but he'd left his keys in the truck. He ran back to it, started it, and after checking for oncoming traffic, did a U-turn and followed her.

"Get in. I'll give you a ride," he called through the open passenger window.

"*Nee, danki,*" she said stonily, refusing to look at him.

"Mary Elizabeth!"

He slammed on the brakes, and the truck slid a little before gaining traction. Pulling over on the side of the road, he shut the engine off and yanked the keys out of the ignition. She had a head start on him, but his legs were longer and ate up the distance. He grasped her arm, and she spun around and tried to smack it away.

"Listen, be reasonable."

Her mouth worked but no words came out. "I don't want to be reasonable," she said finally, glaring at him.

"Like that's news," he blurted then was instantly sorry when he saw the shock on her face.

Lightning flashed.

"Look, be mad but be reasonable and get back in the truck," he demanded. "It's not safe out here for you."

The sky opened up then, pouring rain down on them.

Her shoulders slumped. "*Allrecht*. But I'm not talking to you anymore."

She stomped back to the truck and climbed inside.

Sam got back in and realized she was shivering. He reached into the back, found a blanket, and tossed it at her. "Use this so you don't catch a cold."

"*Danki*," she said between clenched teeth as she wrapped it around herself before fastening her seatbelt.

And that was the last she said as he drove her the short distance to her home.

He barely had a chance to stop before she was yanking free the seatbelt and sliding out of the truck.

Sam watched her run up the walk, then the stairs to the front door of her house. She went inside without a backward glance.

Furious with himself for the way things had gone, he slammed his hand against the steering wheel then yelped with pain. Of course he'd hit it with his injured hand. It started bleeding again. He grabbed a bandanna lying on the seat beside him and wrapped it around his hand and gingerly drove home.

John sat in the recliner, dozing as the television blared. Two beer cans sat beside the chair. They'd talked about his drinking before.

But as he stood there he realized he just didn't have it in him to deal with another scene today. He walked on into the kitchen to take care of his hand.

A few minutes later John wandered into the kitchen to poke his head into the refrigerator. He plucked out a beer and popped the top while he watched Sam running water over his hand.

"So how'd it go talking to Mary Elizabeth?"

"Not so great."

"How's the hand?"

"Fine."

John took a gulp of beer and peered at his hand. "Doesn't look like it."

He shrugged. "I must have banged the cut open driving home." He pulled a couple of paper towels from the roll and wrapped it around his hand. He opened a kitchen drawer with his uninjured hand and rooted around in it. "Have you seen the antibiotic ointment?"

John shook his head. "Maybe in the bathroom? First aid kit?"

Sam went into the tiny apartment bathroom and found the kit. Inside was a half-empty, old tube of ointment and a roll of gauze. He squirted it on the cut then bound it with the gauze and taped it.

"Need any help?" John called from the other room.

That was just like John...always asking if you needed help after the job was done. Oh well, at least he hadn't had to have him breathing beer fumes all over him as he did first aid. "No, I got it. Thanks."

He wandered back into the living room and stretched out on the sofa. Maybe watching the rest of the game on television would take his mind off the disaster with Mary Elizabeth that afternoon. He considered the beer John sat sipping as he relaxed in the recliner.

No, he wasn't going to start drinking when he'd had a bad day. That was the way to an even bigger problem. Feeling a little depressed, he focused on the screen. "So who's winning?"

—∞—

Mary Elizabeth hurried into the house. "Got caught in the rain," she said as she rushed past her parents sitting in the living room. "Going to change."

She raced up the steps to her room, grateful to see Rose Anna's bedroom door was shut. Her youngest *schweschder* would be curious about what had happened at David and Lavina's farm today, and she just didn't want to talk.

Tiptoeing past her door, she slipped inside her room and quietly shut the door. What a relief to be home, in her room, where she could regain her composure. Peeling off her sodden bonnet and *kapp*, she pulled off her dress and underclothes. She turned on the shower, stepped into the tub, and felt the tears start.

She'd held them back during the drive home, determined not to let Sam see how much he'd hurt her. But now she let them fall. They were tears of hurt but of anger, too, and she never got angry. *Gut* Amish *maedels* didn't get angry, she chided herself. They were supposed to be above such behavior, to serve God and family and community and above all, forgive those who hurt and angered them.

Even men like Sam who'd abandoned them so close to the time after harvest when they'd expected to marry.

She swiped at the tears on her face. When would she feel less hurt? Less angry? When would she forgive?

Feeling defeated, she stood under the spray until the water ran cool before she shut it off and stepped out to dry herself. She pulled on her nightgown then sat on her bed and drew a comb through her still-damp hair.

There was a knock on her door. "*Kumm*," she called and her *mudder* opened the door. "I thought you might like a cup of tea. You looked cold when you came in."

Mary Elizabeth smiled as her *mudder* slipped into the room. Sometimes she thought her *mudder* didn't look old enough to be the parent of three grown *dochders*. She was still as slender as a *maedel*, her complexion smooth and creamy, her hair the same blonde without a strand of gray.

She set the comb aside. "*Danki*, I was," she said as she took the mug from her. "The shower helped me warm up some."

Linda sat down next to her on the bed, took the comb, and began drawing it through the long blonde tresses. "Did you have a *gut* day?"

How could she answer that? She nodded. It *had* been *gut* until she had the quarrel with Sam. "The men got everything done they wanted to just before it began raining."

"Sam brought you home."

She must have heard his truck. "*Ya.*"

Her *mudder* touched her cheek and made her look at her. "You've been crying."

Mary Elizabeth blinked rapidly. She didn't want to cry again.

"What kind of tears were they? Hurt or anger?"

She found herself smiling wryly. "Both. I'm afraid I argued with him."

"I'm not surprised."

"You know me."

"He hurt you. I'm *schur* he wasn't surprised that you were angry with him."

"He was, a little."

Amish couples didn't often share with their parents that they were dating but after Sam left, her *mudder* had found her crying and Mary Elizabeth hadn't been able to hold back why.

"But I shouldn't have said the things I did. I should forgive him."

Her *mudder* kissed her forehead. "It'll come, dear one. It'll come." She rubbed her back. "Why don't you put on a robe, go sit by the fire in the living room and dry your hair?"

"I think I'd rather just climb into bed."

"*Allrecht.*"

"*Mamm?* Before you go, tell me the story again, the one about you and *Daed.*"

Her *mudder* laughed softly and gathered her into her arms like she was a little *kind.* "You always loved that story, you and your *schweschders.*" She fell silent for a moment and gently rocked Mary Elizabeth.

"Once upon a time there was this boy, this tall, handsome blond boy with the most beautiful gray eyes, who went to the same *schul* with me but he never really saw me. It was the last year of *schul*—I think we were about thirteen or fourteen. All the other *maedels* thought he was so handsome, too, but he didn't seem interested in any of us. He was so serious about his studies, you see. He wanted to learn everything he could. At recess he'd even sit there on the sidelines and read these big books about farming while we were playing volleyball or just talking and laughing.

"And then one day this big dog came running on the playground outside the *schul*. I don't know where he came from, but he ran into a group of us and all the *maedels* went running, screaming, and before I could run away the dog knocked me down and I thought he was going to bite me. Your *daed* chased him away and helped me up, and he pulled out a bandanna and wiped away my tears. And he looked at me, really looked at me. And we couldn't stop looking at each other."

"And one day when you were old enough he asked you to marry him."

"He did. And we had three beautiful *dochders* and lived happily ever after."

Mary Elizabeth smiled. How could she not believe in love after hearing that story all her life? "I love that story."

Her *mudder* hugged her, and Mary Elizabeth inhaled the scent of lavender her *mudder* grew and liked to tuck into her dresser drawers.

"Sweet dreams, *lieb*. See you in the morning."

She smiled. "See you in the morning. Tell *Daed gut nacht*."

"I will."

"And *Mamm*? *Danki*."

Her *mudder* smiled and left the room. Mary Elizabeth climbed into her bed and pulled her quilt up around her shoulders. And slept.

3

A vase full of sunny daffodils sat on a nearby table, but it looked like Christmas in the Zook sewing room.

When you sewed authentic Amish quilts for a shop patronized by tourists visiting Paradise, Pennsylvania, you started sewing them days after the last Christmas and worked on them up until the week before the next one.

The Zook women didn't mind. All of them loved working on the quilts whether they were traditional Amish quilts or more modern Christmas-themed ones.

Linda, their *mudder*, was humming a Christmas hymn to get them in a festive mood. Lavina and Rose Anna joined her but Mary Elizabeth wasn't feeling particularly joyful today. Matter of fact, she thought it better suited her mood to work on an Old Maid's Puzzle quilt. But they didn't have an order to make one so for now, she needed to work on one of the quilts Leah had commissioned.

She watched Lavina sewing a quilt with big, bright scarlet poinsettias. Before she'd married David Stoltzfus, she'd sat with them sewing every day. Now that she had to run her own home she couldn't always join them every day, but she managed three or four days a week.

Their sewing room was an explosion of color in fabric and yarn set on shelves her *dat* had built. He often chided them that they had enough fabric to start their own store but they knew he was teasing them—especially when he just built more shelves without being asked.

Each of them had chosen a Christmas quilt pattern. Mary Elizabeth stitched on the snowflake quilt, her *mudder*, a log cabin pattern with Christmas touches of holly leaves and berries, and Rose Anna cut pieces of fabric for a wall hanging with a family of snow people.

Mary Elizabeth found her thoughts wandering back to the conversation she'd had with Sam several days ago. She frowned as she remembered how she'd gotten so frustrated—*nee*, angry— that she'd gotten out of the truck and tried to walk back home. He'd followed her, trying to persuade her to get back into the truck. If it hadn't been raining, if lightning hadn't slashed across the sky, she'd never have gotten into his truck.

She knew it was childish of her, but she'd needed to work off her anger. Pacing her bedroom after she got home hadn't helped.

He was never returning home. And he hadn't asked her to follow him into the *Englisch* world.

It was time to think about seeing someone else. There was a singing this Sunday after church. She'd be going…

"Time for a break," Linda announced. She stood and put her quilt down on her chair.

Rose Anna, always ready for a break, jumped up and followed her from the room.

"Do you want to talk about it?" Lavina asked her quietly.

"About a break?"

"You know what I mean."

"I guess it's no secret that Sam and I went for a drive to talk about us, is it? Or talk about how there isn't an 'us'?" Mary Elizabeth frowned as she set her quilt down.

Lavina shook her head and looked at her with a sympathetic expression.

"Well, too often people say they know how someone feels, but you really *do* know." Mary Elizabeth said.

"When David left the community he was gone a year. It was a very long year."

"At least he came back. Sam doesn't want to. And that seems to be his last word on the subject."

"I'm so sorry."

Mary Elizabeth found herself blinking back tears. Determined not to cry, she took a deep breath and rose. "Well, now I know. So, I've decided I'm going to the singing on Sunday. I'm not moping another minute over Sam Stoltzfus."

Lavina hugged her. "I'm happy for you if that's what you want."

"It wasn't what I wanted, but it's what I have to do."

"Lavina? Mary Elizabeth? Are you coming down?" their *mudder* called.

"Be right there!" Lavina called back. She turned to Mary Elizabeth. "Do you want me to bring some tea up to you?"

Mary Elizabeth shook her head. "*Mamm* or Rose Anna would just ask what's wrong. You won't say anything?"

"Of course not."

They went downstairs and Mary Elizabeth found to her delight that her *grosseldres* were joining them for tea and cookies in the kitchen. She'd missed them so much this past winter when they visited Pinecraft, Florida.

Miriam, her *grossmudder*, was scolding Abraham, her *mann*, for piling a half- dozen cookies on his plate. "You'll spoil your supper," she chided and she tried to look stern, but her blue eyes twinkled.

"*Gut* to see you, *Grossmudder, Grossdaadi*." Mary Elizabeth leaned down to kiss the top of his snowy white head. She giggled as he drew her into a hug and rubbed his beard over her cheek. She'd always loved the way it tickled.

Bending, she kissed her *grossmudder*'s wrinkled cheek. "Don't worry, *Grossmudder*. You know he'll be hungry for supper when it's time."

Abraham bobbed his head. "Never missed a meal. Especially the ones my *fraa* cooked for me." He gave Linda a fond look. "Not that you're not a *wunderbaar* cook."

She smiled as she poured tea. "You'd best say so since I'm cooking supper tonight."

Mary Elizabeth took a seat at the table and watched her *gross-eldres* as they exchanged loving looks, pats on the hands resting on the table between them. What must it be like to love like that? she wondered. Love for so many years?

"Cookie?" Lavina asked, holding them in front of her to get her attention.

She took one. They were her favorites—her *mamm's* oatmeal cookies with butterscotch morsels. Her *mudder* would ask her if she wasn't feeling well if she didn't eat one or two.

But it tasted dry and bitter in her mouth.

As soon as she could, she escaped upstairs to the sewing room, claiming she had quilting class tomorrow and didn't want to get behind. She was able to sit with her own depressing thoughts and sew for some time before the others joined her.

When she found herself sighing and feeling sorry for herself even after her *schweschders* and *mudder* joined her to sew, she gave herself a stern talking to.

She had a wonderful life whether or not she had a *mann* in it—or even someone dating her at the moment—a warm, wonderful family, a safe and secure home. And a job that was fun and endlessly creative. Every day she could stay in her home and be with people she loved and do something that paid well.

Time for her to do what she'd heard an *Englisch* friend say to herself once: "Get over yourself."

So she sewed until she needed to stand and walk around a bit, and then she decided to help her *mudder* make supper. And after supper was eaten and dishes were washed, she turned to her *mudder.*

"Would you mind if I took some fabric in to donate to the shelter tomorrow?"

"*Nee,* that's fine."

"Got enough of it," her *dat* muttered as he ate a second piece of pie. Then he glanced up and grinned.

She'd started volunteering at a shelter for battered women along with Lavina months ago and thought at the time she was doing it for others. But along the way she wondered if she was supposed to learn that life wasn't supposed to be just about yourself.

After she gathered enough fabric to stuff a shopping bag, she carried it downstairs and left it by the front door so she wouldn't forget it when Kate came to pick her up the next day.

She was used to making something beautiful out of little scraps of fabric sewn together with care and attention and imagination. It was time to look at her life that way.

No one could make you feel more like a jerk than a woman. Not your boss, not your *mudder* or *dat.*

No one.

In a foul mood, Sam hammered a nail into the wooden window frame, glad he had something to vent his temper on. He had feelings for Mary Elizabeth. It seemed like he always had. But like his two *bruders,* he'd left the Amish community when they felt they just couldn't handle the way their *dat* treated them.

He should have known that once Lavina, his new sister-in-law, had persuaded his *bruder,* David, to return home that Mary Elizabeth would start thinking that he should, too.

Were all women born romantics?

He hadn't been able to return to the Amish community as David had. Maybe it was wrong not to forgive his *dat* for the way things had been between them, but that was the way it was. When he returned for Christmas he saw that his *dat* had changed a lot, but there was still a problem between them, one that a visit didn't fix especially when Amos acted stiff and wary of him and John. They'd been back a number of times since then helping on the farm on Saturdays, and he and John hadn't felt any lessening of the tension.

Schur, their *dat* didn't shout at them or belittle their efforts at farming the way he used to. And he treated their *mudder* better than he had before.

But there was still this prickly reserve…

So that left Sam with his apartment he shared with John, the youngest *bruder,* and the job he'd worked for more than a year now with an *Englisch* construction company. He didn't mind not being given the farm as David had. After all, David had returned home and put up with their *dat's* unpleasant behavior while he underwent chemotherapy. Neither of his *bruders* had.

Sam wasn't sure how much of Amos's change in behavior had been realizing God had given him a second chance or how much David had forged a new relationship with him. But David deserved the farm. He'd always loved it.

Sure, he was lonely sometimes. He missed Mary Elizabeth, his friends, his church. John had been enjoying the time away from their *dat,* had viewed it as his *rumschpringe.* Several times Sam had found John partying with his friends in their apartment and had worried over his drinking and dating women who seemed…rather forward compared to the women in the Amish community.

Although, Mary Elizabeth was not a traditional sort of Amish *maedel.* She'd always been more confident, more outspoken than other women. He'd liked that. Too often the *maedels* pretended to be everything they thought the man they were interested in wanted. They deferred to him to the point that they weren't themselves.

He didn't want someone who did that. He'd seen his *mudder* spend her life so desperate for her *mann's* love that she'd accepted treatment that wasn't *gut* for her. Maybe now she'd gotten the kind of marriage she'd hoped for. Maybe he didn't have to worry that Amos behaved harshly to her. Or worse, raised his hand when no one was around to see.

Sam was so lost in his thoughts it took a moment to realize that a shadow had fallen over the window in front of him.

"Time for lunch."

"Right. Thanks."

The job foreman looked at what Sam had done, nodded with satisfaction, and moved on.

He walked out of the house they'd been working on for the past two months. They were making *gut* progress. He'd parked his truck under the shade of a nearby tree. He let down the tailgate and sat on it with his lunch box.

"Hey, how are things going?" Peter asked him. He hopped up on the makeshift seat.

"Pretty good. Nearly finished with the windows. You?"

"We have another day on the roof." Peter looked up, shading his eyes from the sun. "Weather should hold up."

Tall and lanky, Peter took off his straw hat and wiped his forehead with a bandanna.

They bent their heads and said a prayer of thanks. Sam might have left the community, but he hadn't forgotten the way he'd been raised.

"How's Sadie?" he asked Peter as he unwrapped his sandwich.

"*Gut,* but she's pushing to get married." Peter unwrapped his sandwich but didn't immediately bite into it. He sat there looking at it.

"What's the matter? You love ham and cheese."

"Lost my appetite." He looked at Sam. "Why is it *maedels* are so interested in rushing to get married?"

Sam thought of Mary Elizabeth. He shook his head. "They're ahead of us in a lot of ways. *Schul.* Thinking of marriage. Of having *kinner.* They're raised that way."

He bit into his own deli turkey sandwich. "They don't do the crazy risky stuff we do," he said with a full mouth.

"I think jumping into marriage too soon is pretty risky. I mean, there's no divorce." He shuddered.

"True. The *gut* thing is that we know the *maedels* pretty well growing up with them. It's not like the *Englisch* who don't often know the one they're marrying as long."

Peter nodded. "You've got a point." He ripped open a bag of chips and offered it to Sam.

He took a handful and munched thoughtfully. "Mary Elizabeth and I had a talk the other day. She wants me to come back home. And she wants the same thing as Sadie. She didn't say November specifically, but I know it's on her mind."

With a sigh, he took another bite of his sandwich. "I don't want this repeated but the Zook *schweschders* have been interested in the Stoltzfus *bruders* for some time."

"*Ya?*" Peter dug out more chips and chewed them. "One's been caught so far."

Sam winced. "I wouldn't call it caught."

"What *would* you call it?"

He had him there. "Well, David is very happy. Marriage is fine for some. I'm just not ready yet."

"Me, either."

"I'm happy single."

"Me, too."

Sam finished his sandwich and opened a baggie of store-bought cookies. He offered it to Peter, but he shook his head. "*Mamm* made brownies. She sent one along for you."

He brightened. "*Ya?* I always liked your *mudder.*"

"She likes you, too." He finished his sandwich, tucked the wrapping in his lunchbox, and brought out the brownies. He handed one to Sam and bit into the other.

The foreman stopped in front of them. "Man, you guys always have the best lunches."

Peter held out the plastic baggie containing another brownie. The foreman took it with a grin, thanked him, and moved on.

"Brownnoser," Sam muttered.

Peter laughed. "You're just jealous."

"*Ya.*"

"You know, I don't have any reason to brownnose the boss. I'm thinking of starting my own business."

"Really?"

Peter nodded. "It's time."

Sam thought about that. Peter was two years older than him.

"I want to work for myself, not someone else," Peter told him. "Don't tell me you haven't thought about the same thing."

"Who doesn't?"

"So what do you think? Want to join me?"

"Join you?"

Peter nodded and pulled a bottle of iced tea from his lunch box. "Think about it. We can talk some more tomorrow."

Sam nodded and pulled out his bottle of lemonade. "Maybe you can bring some more of those brownies."

"Wouldn't that be considered brownnosing?"

"Not unless you're making me boss."

Peter laughed and clapped him on the back. "Partners, Sam. Partners."

"What's in the bags?" Kate asked Mary Elizabeth when she picked her up the next day.

"*Mamm* said we could donate some extra fabric. Lavina'll be here in a minute."

"No hurry." Kate drummed her fingers on the steering wheel.

Mary Elizabeth studied her. She'd known Kate, an *Englisch* police officer, for several years but she'd never seen her in a state of . . . suppressed excitement like today.

"Are you okay?"

Mary Elizabeth looked at Kate. She was a petite woman with enormous energy, only perhaps ten years older than her, but she had eyes that looked like they'd seen so much. Mary Elizabeth supposed that was because before she was a police officer she'd been in the military. She worked, took care of her two young children and her husband, and still found time to start then run a quilt class at a local women's shelter.

Lavina hurried to the car and got in the back seat, apologizing profusely for holding them up.

"You feeling okay?" Kate asked her as she looked in the rearview mirror. "You look a little pale."

"I'm fine," Lavina said as she buckled her seat belt.

Something in her tone made Mary Elizabeth turn and stare at her. Lavina was indeed looking pale. And she'd dashed into the bathroom just as they were supposed to walk out to Kate's car. Once again she wondered if her *schweschder* might be going to have a *boppli* . . .

Kate started the car, backed down the driveway, and then pulled out onto the road leading to town. "I'm glad both of you could come today. We have a special guest visiting this morning."

"Oh? Who?" Mary Elizabeth wanted to know.

"You'll see," Kate said mysteriously.

The room they used in the upstairs of the women's shelter was full of women chatting and sewing when they arrived, but there was no visitor yet. It was a happy place where Mary Elizabeth and Lavina enjoyed volunteering once a week. Mary Elizabeth took the fabric out of the shopping bags and placed it on shelves built into one wall of the room and immediately some of the women had to look at it. Most of them didn't get into town to shop at the stores, so it was the treat that she'd thought it might be to have something new to use in their quilting and sewing projects.

Kate passed out the week's quilt block, and the three of them walked around saying hello and checking to see if anyone needed help.

Carrie, one of the women staying at the shelter, walked in and smiled. Mary Elizabeth couldn't help thinking the woman looked so different these days. Back when Mary Elizabeth started volunteering less than six months ago, Carrie had come into class with a black eye and a sullen attitude. She had made it clear she didn't think there was any point in attending the class. Later, when she'd seemed to change, it hadn't been for a good reason. Like many of the abused women here, she'd been persuaded to see her ex-boyfriend. Apparently, he was as abusive as her ex-husband had been.

Their relationship hadn't ended well. Carrie's innocent remark to him that some Amish women were teaching quilting at the shelter had led him to steal a quilt from them. The quilt had been recovered with Kate's help but not before her ex-boyfriend had hurt her for helping with the investigation. Carrie had apologized and started attending classes, where she actually began enjoying learning how to sew with the other women who lived here.

The class was nearly over when Mary Elizabeth glimpsed movement out of the corner of her eye. She looked up and saw Leah, the owner of the Stitches in Time shop in town, walk in.

Kate jumped up from the chair she'd been sitting in at the front of the room and rushed to greet her. The two stood chatting at the back of the room. Leah nodded at Mary Elizabeth when she saw her looking in her direction.

After a few minutes, Kate and Leah walked to the front of the room.

"Why do you suppose Leah's here?" Lavina whispered to her.

"I have no idea."

"I'll be right back."

Mary Elizabeth grabbed her hand. "Where are you going? They look like they're about to say something."

"I have to run to the restroom. I'll be right back." She rushed from the room.

"Ladies, please stop sewing for a minute," Kate raised her voice to get the attention of the class.

The sewing machines stopped and everyone looked at her expectantly. Mary Elizabeth marveled at how quiet it got. You could have heard a pin drop.

"Some of you may know Leah here. She's the owner of Stitches in Time in town. Leah has been very generous to us. She's donated fabric and supplies from her shop because she believes in what we're doing."

Spontaneous applause broke out. Leah blushed. A spry, white-haired Amish woman in her seventies, she wasn't used to being acknowledged like this.

"Leah has more energy than anyone I know," Kate continued. "She came to me with a very interesting proposal she wants to talk to us about today." She gestured at Leah to speak.

"I'm so happy to be invited to meet all of you today and to see what you've been doing," Leah began, smiling as she looked around the room. "I've been sewing all my life, and there's nothing I love doing more. But, I also love seeing others enjoy sewing, so Kate and I have come up with an idea that we'd like you to consider."

A ripple of excitement ran through the room. Mary Elizabeth glanced at the doorway, wondering what was taking Lavina so long. She was going to miss Leah's announcement.

"The store next to mine came up for sale recently, and I've decided to buy it and open another shop," Leah said. Her blue eyes sparkled. "I like to encourage creativity in others, and I want to have local crafters sell their work there. I've seen some of the work you ladies have been creating, and I want to offer you the opportunity to sell your work there."

There was a ripple of excitement in the room. Leah paused and let the women chatter for a few moments before going on. "I thought I'd call it Sewn in Hope, and I'm planning to be open in two months, so there will be plenty of time to sell crafts made for Christmas gift-giving."

She smiled and stepped aside for Kate.

"I want you to be thinking about what you'd like to make and sell, and we'll take one or two samples to Leah to approve for sale," Kate said. "I think this is a wonderful way for you to make some money to save up for when you're ready to move into your own places. And Pearl has said she'll see to child care a few hours each day so you can work right here."

Lavina hurried back into the room and took her seat next to Mary Elizabeth. "What did I miss?" she whispered.

"Wait until you hear what Leah's planning!" Mary Elizabeth whispered back.

4

It took a long time for the room to empty.

As the women filed out of the classroom, they chattered excitedly. It did Mary Elizabeth's heart *gut* to see them this way. In the months she'd been volunteering here at the shelter with Lavina she'd seen so many of these women come in scared, sometimes bruised and beaten...beaten down, in Kate's words. Often they had only the clothes on their backs. And the *kinner*...if they had *kinner*, those poor little ones were even more scared.

Gradually they began to feel safe. Protected. Supported. Some of them drifted into the classroom and became interested in the quilting and sewing crafts. Some of them drifted out after they said it really wasn't for them. The *kinner* clung to their *mudders* and looked too old for their years. Velcro kids, Kate called them, desperate to hold onto the only security in this scary world they knew. Gradually, as they saw their *mudders* relax and felt the love and support here, they smiled and played and went back to being *kinner* again. Ellie lingered with her *mudder* and chatted with Leah about how she'd sewed the tiny quilt that covered the doll she carried in her arms and never let go of.

Mary Elizabeth waited with Lavina—actually, Lavina had slipped from the room again in a pretty big hurry—and watched Carrie approach Kate.

"I want to apologize," she said.

"For?"

"When I came to this class the first day, I said it was a waste of time. Why should we bother with it? No one was going to hire us to sew a quilt. We're not Amish."

"Well, you were right," Kate said, unoffended. "Leah's not asking anyone to sew a quilt and pretend it's been done by an Amish woman. But the shop will offer quilts, and there are plenty of things the women here can make to sell there. And they'll take the same skills everyone's learned in the class."

"Well, anyway, I'm sorry for the attitude I showed. You've been great to start the class and show up here each week when you could be home putting up your feet."

Kate laughed and tucked the quilt she'd been working on in her tote bag. "Thanks. I love doing it. And sometimes I put my feet up here and sew."

She paused and looked up at Carrie. "Actually, what you said stayed in my mind and when I was in Leah's shop recently we got to talking. A few weeks later she called me and wanted to chat about her idea for the new shop. So you might say what you said to me that day led to this opportunity for the women here at the shelter."

"Wow."

"Yeah. Wow." She settled the strap of her purse on her shoulder and picked up her tote bag. "I'm thinking maybe you could help me get everyone organized with what they're going to do. I figure you were pretty good with people working at the bar like you did."

"Yeah, I could do that. Yeah." Carrie grinned.

"See you next week."

"See you." Carrie walked over to put her project box on the shelf.

"Sorry things took so long today," Kate said as she walked downstairs and on out to the car with Mary Elizabeth and Lavina.

"We wouldn't have missed it for anything," Lavina said.

"You were out of the room a lot of the time," Mary Elizabeth reminded her.

"Everything okay?" Kate asked Lavina as she unlocked the trunk of her car and put the tote inside.

Mary Elizabeth saw Lavina blush, but she nodded and got into the back seat.

Kate dropped them at their house, and Lavina hurried ahead of Mary Elizabeth. When she walked inside, Lavina was closing the door of the downstairs bathroom.

Mary Elizabeth walked into the kitchen. Her *mudder* was slicing a loaf of bread.

"Did you stop for lunch on the way home?" her *mudder* asked.

"*Nee*, Kate wanted to talk to us—the class—about something. *Mamm*, listen, I'm worried about Lavina. I think something's wrong with her."

Linda looked up. "What is it?"

"I swear, she's been running to the bathroom every ten minutes. That's where she is now."

"*Nee*, I'm not." Mary Elizabeth jumped guiltily and spun around to see Lavina standing in the doorway.

"Are you *allrecht, kind*?" Linda asked. She hurried to press her lips to Lavina's forehead to check for fever.

Lavina laughed and hugged her. "Don't treat me like a *boppli, Mamm*. I'm just going to have one."

Linda drew back and stared at her, then she threw her arms around her *dochder* and hugged her. "Oh, I'm so happy for you!"

Mary Elizabeth hurried to her side and hugged her. Worry turned to joy in a moment.

"What's going on?" Rose Anna wanted to know as she walked into the room.

"David and I are having a *boppli!*"

Rose Anna screamed and joined in on the group hug.

Their *dat* found them like that, bound in a group hug in the middle of the kitchen.

"What is going on?" he asked approaching a bit warily.

Linda pulled away, wiping her eyes on a tissue. "Jacob, we're going to be *grosseldres!*"

"Lavina?" he asked, looking at her for confirmation.

"*Ya, Daed.*"

He held his arms wide and all the Zook women piled into them.

Mary Elizabeth knew she would remember this moment for the rest of her life.

Her journal slipped out from under her pillow when she climbed into bed.

Mary Elizabeth stared at it for a long moment. She hadn't written in it for a long time, but something made her tuck it under her pillow every morning anyway.

She pulled the quilt up around her and flipped to the last page she'd written on. The page was blotched and in places the ink had run. No wonder. She'd been crying as she wrote about the visit she'd made to see Sam. All the hurt came back now as she stared at the page. He'd refused to return to their community, said he was sorry that she was upset but he wasn't returning to the community.

She'd cried that day. She'd cried as she wrote in her journal. And she felt tears welling up now as she held it in her hands.

Did it matter that he hadn't met her gaze that day and avoided looking at her every time he saw her at his *bruder* David's farm since then?

She blinked away the tears, determined not to spend one more second, one more tear over him. Closing the journal, she turned to put it on the bedside table, but the moisture in her eyes caused her to misjudge the distance and the book fell on the floor. Leaning over, she picked up the book and the slip of paper that had fallen from it. She set the book on the table and leaned back to look at the paper. "My wish list for my *mann*," she read.

She remembered when she'd written it. Katie, a friend of hers, had told her she'd made such a list once. Mary Elizabeth had thought it was silly at the time—the kind of thing that daydreaming *maedels* did. And it was actually a little arrogant. After all, she'd heard all her life that God set aside the right person for you so telling Him what you wanted was telling Him how to do His job, wasn't it?

But she'd sat down and composed such a list. And a short time later she'd found herself looking at Sam Stoltzfus one day and realizing he was everything she'd put on her list.

So she put the list in the journal and forgot it. After all, she had the real thing.

But everything had changed. She sat up in bed, reached for a pen on the bedside table.

And took a deep breath and began a new list.

"So did you hear the news?"

Sam sat on the grass in the shade of a tree and pulled a bottle of iced tea from his lunch box. He drank half of it down and recapped it before he looked at Peter. "What news?"

"Leah is opening up a second shop."

Sam grinned. "I had no idea you'd taken up quilting."

Peter scowled at him. "Don't be a jerk. She needs help doing some renovations on the shop—it's next to Stitches in Time."

"How do you know?"

"Heard it from my *mudder*—who heard it from Fannie Miller who heard it from—"

"Never mind. In other words, from the Amish grapevine."

"Right. Anyway, Leah's *mann* died last year, so he can't help her like he used to. So I stopped by to see what I could do." He took a big bite of his sub and chewed. "If you're interested, this could be our first project together."

Sam looked at him. Peter sat there looking so calm, eating his lunch and talking about making the renovations on Leah's shop the first project.

Of the company, he'd asked Sam to think about joining him just two days ago.

"You're serious."

"Very."

"You'd give all this up." He waved his hand at the controlled chaos of the construction going on around them.

"Dead serious."

"You move fast."

"Got to jump on opportunities, you know?"

"You sure do. You talked about starting your own company just two days ago."

"Told you, been thinking about it for some time. Then this came along. I'm thinking it's a sign. God's giving me the go-ahead."

"It's one job."

"And then we'll get another."

"You can't know that."

Peter just looked at him. "You can't know we won't."

Sam didn't have any answer to that. He kept eating his sandwich even though he was getting pretty tired of eating bologna. It had been on sale, and pennies counted when your budget was as tight as his was.

"So why'd Leah decide to open another shop? Seems like she's pretty busy already with Stitches."

Peter finished his sub and started on an apple. "She says it's a craft shop. Women from a local shelter are going to sell their stuff they sew there."

"Shelter?"

"Yeah."

Sam searched his memory. It seemed to him that the last time he'd seen Lavina and Mary Elizabeth, they had talked about teaching quilting at a women's shelter.

"So, you in? Leah wants us to get started next week. We can do it a few afternoons a week after we get off here. Then we can see how it goes with other work, quit this job when we have enough business coming in."

Sam stared at the sandwich in his hand, at his patched work pants. Things had been tough since he'd moved into an apartment with John. Rent was high, then there was gas and insurance and the payment he made to David on the truck. Some extra money would come in handy. It wasn't the farming he loved, but it was work.

"That sounds reasonable."

"We'll make a great team," Peter told him, clapping him on the back. "I come up with the ideas, you rein me in a little."

"And your girlfriend reins you in the rest of the way?" Sam asked him with a grin.

"*Ya,*" Peter said, chuckling. "Say, she sent along some oatmeal cookies. Want one?"

"Are they any better than the last batch?"

"She's getting better." Peter held out the bag. ·

Sam took one and bit into it. Or tried to. It was hard as a rock. "You're right," he mumbled around a bite. He hoped he hadn't chipped a tooth. "Look, Boss is waving us back to work."

When Peter glanced over, Sam tossed the cookie aside and hoped a squirrel had better luck.

"So anyway, I told Leah I'd see if you could stop by with me after work today to take a look at things."

Sam had known Peter for a long time, but he'd never seen him move so quickly on anything.

"*Schur.*"

"Maybe you can give me a ride there?"

"How would you have gotten there if I hadn't said yes?"

Peter set his lunch box in the front seat of the truck. "Knew you would." He loped off to the ladder set against the house, climbed up, and moved out of sight.

Chuckling, Sam put his own lunchbox into his truck and returned to work installing windows. Like many of his fellow Amish men, Sam had never been inside Stitches in Time, Leah's quilt and crafts shop. Peter led the way and seemed a lot more at ease in the land of fabric and crafts and...the bustle and chatter of women.

Two of them, very familiar, stood at the front counter. To his utter shock, one of them was Mary Elizabeth.

"Peter! Sam!" Leah cried. "So glad you both could come by today! I want to get started quickly on the new shop. Mary Elizabeth, do you want to walk over with us? She'll be helping us coordinate with the women sewing the crafts we'll sell in the new shop," she explained.

Sam stood silent, absorbing the information. He wondered how much they'd see each other while he and Peter did the renovation.

"*Schur.*" Mary Elizabeth looked at Sam. "I'd like that."

Leah took them next door, a whirlwind chattering nonstop the whole way. Leah had granddaughters, but Sam had always thought she had enough energy and drive to run circles around much younger people.

"As you can see, the last tenant left quite a mess."

Sam looked around at the broken shelving, the holes left in the walls by fixtures being pulled out.

"First thing I want to do is put an entranceway into Stitches so customers can move back and forth through both shops," she began and then she was on a roll.

Peter took notes and Sam took measurements. Mary Elizabeth observed and said nothing—new behavior for her. Sam didn't think he'd ever known her to be quiet this long. An hour later, Peter and Sam had what they needed.

"I'll have an estimate for you in two days," Peter promised.

"Remember I need to be open by September 1."

Sam felt his stomach clench. How would they get everything she wanted done by then if they were working part-time? But when he glanced at Peter and got a warning look, he kept his mouth shut.

"*Allrecht*, I know what you're thinking," Peter said as they climbed into Sam's truck.

"So now you read minds as well as think you're Superman and can work two jobs?"

Peter fastened his seat belt and leaned back in his seat. He tapped his notebook on his knee. "How about we go for a pizza and work up a bid and a work schedule?"

"Pizza?" It was days before the next payday.

"I'll buy. You can get the next one."

"'Cause we'll be rich then, right?"

Peter laughed. "*Ya*." He opened his notebook and started jotting something down.

Sam drove, concentrating on the traffic, a mixture of people heading home after work and tourists who weren't always paying attention to driving but were instead checking out the scenery.

And all the while he drove he wondered if they got the job how he was going to handle coming into contact with Mary Elizabeth at the new shop.

⚬⚬⚬

"You're up early," Linda said when Mary Elizabeth walked into the kitchen the next morning.

She went straight for the percolator on the stove. "I spent a lot of time at the quilting class yesterday, then with Leah at the new shop. I don't want to get behind in my work."

Her *mudder* flipped pancakes onto a plate then set it in front of her. "You won't. You sew quickly."

"*Ya*, but I'm working on making my stitches smaller. That takes time."

Linda sat down at the table with a cup of coffee. "You always were impatient. Why, you were even born a month early."

Mary Elizabeth grinned as she cut into a pancake. She'd heard that many times. "Mmm, these are *gut*."

"Don't talk with your mouth full," her *mudder* said automatically. But she smiled.

The back door opened and Lavina walked in.

"Two early birds."

Lavina clapped a hand over her mouth and ran for the bathroom. When she emerged a few minutes later her face had a slight greenish tinge. "You had to mention…well, let's just say you mentioned early birds and I thought of what they eat."

A funny expression flashed over her face and she bolted for the bathroom again.

When she returned to the kitchen a second time she had a damp washcloth in her hand. She sat and held the cloth to the back of her neck.

"Is there anything I can get you?" Linda murmured, reaching over to rub her back. "Maybe some crackers and a glass of ginger ale."

"You have ginger ale?"

"I bought some right after you told us you were going to have a *boppli*." She rose, filled a glass with ice, and brought it and the bottle of ginger ale to the table.

"If I'm half the *mudder* you are, I'll be happy," Lavina told her fervently.

"You'll be a *gut mudder*. You always helped me with your *schweschders*. Some other *mudders* warned me sometimes the oldest *kind* can be jealous of the other *kinner*, but not you. Once I found you giving Rose Anna her bottle when I walked into her room. She'd woken from her nap, you saw she was awake and got her bottle out of the refrigerator." She smiled at the memory. "Well, time to wake Rose Anna," she said, and she got up.

"Do you want me to take her a bottle?" Mary Elizabeth asked, grinning.

"You know she'd stay in bed all morning if she could," Linda said. "If you took her some food, she'd stay there longer." She walked to the stairs and called up.

Mary Elizabeth and Lavina winced. Their *mudder* had quite a carrying voice when she called up the stairs.

"She must have a pillow over her head," Linda muttered as she started up the stairs.

"So, you'll never guess who Leah's getting to do the renovation on the new shop."

Lavina stared at her. "*Sam?* Really?"

"Who told you?"

"No one. I could just tell by the look on your face. Does that mean you'll see more of him since you're helping with the things the shelter ladies are sewing?"

Mary Elizabeth nodded.

"Well, well." Lavina took another sip of her ginger ale, then picked up a cracker and bit into it. She looked thoughtful. "This is interesting. David left the community and didn't intend to return, but then he did when his *dat* got sick and we got back together and got married. Sam refused to return and said he didn't want to get back with you and now the two of you are going to be tossed together—"

"We're not going to be tossed together," Mary Elizabeth said flatly. "I don't want him anymore." She ate the last bite of her pancakes and set her fork down on her plate with a snap. "You and Rose Anna are welcome to the Stoltzfus men. I've had enough of Sam."

Lavina reached to touch her hand. "I'm sorry he hurt you so much. I know how that feels."

"I know you do. David hurt you a lot. I'm glad the two of you got back together, but I don't have as forgiving a heart as you do."

"If you love him, you find a way to forgive him," Lavina said simply. She touched her abdomen and smiled. "And if you do, there's a lovely reward."

Mary Elizabeth felt a lump form in her throat. She'd never seen Lavina look so happy.

"Sam's not interested in me, so I have to move on." She got to her feet and set her plate in the sink. "I think I should start looking for someone else. I'm not wasting any more time. I want a *mann* and *kinner.*"

"I felt that way, too. But then you remember what happened. God had other ideas."

"Well, He hasn't had them this time with Sam and me."

"*Nee*? Then why do you suppose He's got Sam working on Leah's shop and you're helping coordinate the crafts she'll sell there?"

They heard footsteps descending the stairs. Their *mudder* entered the kitchen followed by a grumpy looking Rose Anna still in her house robe.

"Someone decided to get up for pancakes," Linda said cheerfully as she walked to the stove and turned the gas flame up under the cast iron skillet.

Rose Anna sank into a chair and yawned. She frowned at her plate and appeared half-asleep. Mary Elizabeth took pity on her and rose to get her a cup of coffee. She set it in front of her *schweschder*, stirred in two teaspoons of sugar then sat again. Rose Anna thanked her. At least Mary Elizabeth thought her grunt was a thank-you.

She perked up some when their *mudder* placed a plate of pancakes in front of her.

"Lavina, how are you feeling? Want to try a pancake?"

Mary Elizabeth studied her face. Lavina had lost the greenish tinge.

"Maybe a small one."

"See you upstairs," Mary Elizabeth said as she rose and left the room. She couldn't wait to get sewing. Working on a quilt settled her as nothing else did. She sat in her favorite chair and began working.

Lavina came upstairs a few minutes later.

"How'd the pancake do?"

"The *boppli* seems to like it." Lavina patted her abdomen and sat in a nearby chair. She didn't pick up her quilt in the basket next to it right away. "So what are you going to do now that you've decided not to be interested in getting together with Sam?"

"I mean it."

Lavina nodded. "I know you do. I know you."

"There's a singing Sunday evening. I thought I'd go to it."

"You're going to the singing?" Rose Anna asked as she walked into the room. "We can go together!"

"That's right." Mary Elizabeth realized she was stabbing her needle into the fabric and relaxed her fingers. She was going to the singing, and she was going to have fun. She'd meet someone and forget all about Sam.

Why, she had put him totally out of her mind. Totally.

Sam who?

5

Mary Elizabeth looked around at the group of young people at the singing. It was the second one she'd attended with Rose Anna and while she was having fun, she hadn't met anyone new.

And it felt like Noah's Ark tonight. So many people had paired up with someone or come with them. Although couples who dated kept their relationship secret, it didn't take a genius to figure out who had already decided who they wanted to spend the evening with. Some had already left early, deciding it would be more fun to go for a long buggy ride home.

While everyone took a break and enjoyed snacks, Mary Elizabeth took a careful inventory of the available single men. She knew all of them. Had grown up with them, attended *schul* with them. None of them had attracted her then. None did now.

Like Lavina and Rose Anna, she'd fallen in love with a Stoltzfus man and couldn't seem to find anyone else she liked.

"Stop frowning, you'll scare men away," Rose Anna hissed.

Mary Elizabeth shrugged. "It's not like there's anyone here this evening that I'm interested in."

"I know what you mean, but you have to give it a chance."

"I saw you talking to Mark Troyer."

Rose Anna grinned. "He's sweet. And fun. But he's no John Stoltzfus."

"So you're just flirting?"

"*Schur.* Why not? John's off enjoying himself in the *Englisch* world. He may never come back the way David did. So I may as well keep my eyes open, enjoy someone interested in me." She glanced over at the refreshment table, met the gaze of Mark. He grinned at her. "Gotta go," she said and headed over to the table.

Mary Elizabeth shook her head. Rose Anna had been moping around about John just weeks ago, but now she was flirting with Mark.

"*Gut-n-owed.*"

She turned and stared into the face of a man she'd seen earlier that day in the church service but hadn't met.

"I'm Ben Miller," he said. "I just moved here from Indiana."

"Mary Elizabeth Zook. Nice to meet you."

She stared up at him. He was at least six inches taller than her, and she was the tallest girl in her family. It was kind of nice, she thought. And he had the bluest eyes and nicest smile. She couldn't remember the last time she'd seen Sam smile.

"I moved here a week ago from Indiana. Luke Miller is my cousin."

"Luke mentioned you were moving here last time we spoke," she told him. "You'll be joining him and his *dat* making furniture."

"*Ya,* I'm looking forward to it." He took a deep breath and glanced around. "I smell honeysuckle. It's already summer here."

"We have ridiculously short spring seasons in Paradise," she said. "They're over in a blink."

"Want something to drink?"

"*Schur.*" They walked over to the refreshment table. There was still a little time before the singing began again.

"You sing many of the same hymns I grew up with. Not everything's the same in this community, though."

"Sometimes the *Englisch* think the Amish are all alike no matter what state we live in." She picked up a plate of brownies and offered it to him.

He took one and bit into it. "*Gut.*"

"*Danki,*" she said with a smile.

"You made these? They're great. I think I'll have another."

She held out the plate just as Anna called everyone back to the singing.

Ben grabbed a paper napkin, wrapped the brownie in it, and stuck it in a pocket. "Talk to you after? Maybe give you a ride home?"

"I can't tonight," she said. "I came with my *schweschder*." When she saw his disappointment, she felt her spirits lift. "But we could take a ride tomorrow if you like."

"*Ya*, I'd like."

Rose Anna lifted her eyebrows in question as Mary Elizabeth joined the others to sing, but she could hardly talk to her now.

The minute the singing was over, Rose Anna made her way to her side. "So, tell me about the new guy."

She didn't have much to tell. They hadn't had long enough to talk. But her mood was light as they rode home.

The next day Mary Elizabeth knocked at the back door of Lavina and David's house, then walked inside.

Waneta turned from the stove where she was cooking breakfast. "Well, *guder mariye*. What brings you here this morning?"

"I thought I'd help Lavina in the garden before it gets too warm."

"I've been helping her some since she's not feeling *gut* in the morning," Waneta said. She turned off the flame under the frying pan. "I'll go get her."

"I'll be outside."

Lavina came out a little while later. Her face had that same faint greenish tinge like yesterday. "You didn't have to come."

"I want to help. Mornings are rough for you, and since it's getting so warm, I know gardening has to be quite a chore."

Lavina sighed. "Spring in Lancaster County seems shorter and shorter each year."

"I can't agree with you more." She glanced around. "Shall I do some weeding first?"

"That would be *wunderbaar*."

Waneta came out and the three of them got to work, and soon there was a pile of weeds at their sides. David walked over from his work in the fields and looked closely at his wife.

"I'm fine," she told him. "Don't fuss."

He scanned her face, his forehead puckered in concern. "You look warm."

"As long as you don't tell me I look green," she said tartly. She stood, dusting her hands. "I think we've done all we need to this morning. Let's dump the weeds, go inside, and get something to drink."

"Sounds *gut* to me," Waneta said. "My knees are telling me they've had enough."

David hurried over to hold out a hand and she took it gratefully. "You're not old enough to complain about aging," he told her, his eyes twinkling.

"I'm old enough." She glanced around. "Where's your *dat*?"

"Arguing with Sam."

Waneta shook her head. "Those two. Sam's kind enough to come here on Saturdays and help with the farm. Amos should be nicer to him."

"They'll work it out," David assured her. "*Dat* and I did."

"Do you think they ever will?" Mary Elizabeth asked Lavina as they walked inside to clean up and start lunch.

"Like David said, he and his *dat* did and I think they fought worse than Sam and Amos."

Mary Elizabeth looked out the kitchen window as she washed her hands. "Sam's never coming back. He said so the last time we talked." She dried her hands on a dish towel.

The screen door slapped shut. Rose Anna walked in carrying a basket of food. "Sorry I ran late getting here."

Lavina and Mary Elizabeth exchanged a glance. Mary Elizabeth couldn't remember a time when Rose Anna was on time. Their *mudder* even joked that Rose Anna had been born three weeks past the due date the doctor had given her.

They helped Rose Anna unpack the food. Waneta left them to find Amos.

"Mary Elizabeth's got a new boyfriend," she singsonged.

"Oh?" Lavina looked at Mary Elizabeth. "A new boyfriend? Details, please."

Rose Anna smirked as Mary Elizabeth frowned at her. "Really, Rose Anna, we're not in *schul* anymore."

The screen door slammed again. Mary Elizabeth looked over and saw that Sam and David had just walked in.

∽∽∽

There was an old saying that if you eavesdropped you might not hear something *gut*.

Sam figured there was some truth to the saying when he walked in and overheard the Zook women talking about Mary Elizabeth having a new boyfriend.

The only thing he could do was pretend that he hadn't heard, and so he headed down the hall to the downstairs bathroom to wash up.

"I'm sure they were just joking," David said as he crowded into the small room with him to wash his hands.

Sam looked up and met his *bruder's* gaze in the mirror over the sink. "Doesn't matter." Sam picked up a towel and dried his hands.

"*Nee*? The two of you saw each other for a long time before you left home." David took the towel from him and dried his hands.

"Yeah, well that was then. I haven't seen her since then. Well, until recently." He started to walk out of the room but stopped when David put his hand on his arm.

"You know she cares about you."

"Yes, well, it's time she found someone else. I'm not coming back. I told her that." He stared at the door frame rather than meet his *bruder's* eyes. "Listen, I need to leave. I have something to do."

"Have lunch first."

"*Nee*, I need to –"

"If you leave now they'll know you heard."

Sam hesitated. "You're right."

So he stayed for lunch and pretended he hadn't heard the women talking. He kept his head down, concentrating on the cold baked chicken, potato salad, and big glasses of iced tea. Truth was, he was hungry after a long, hot morning working in the fields. And he and John were not only not *gut* cooks, sometimes they had little money for food.

"Have more potato salad," his *mudder* urged. "You look like you've lost weight."

"Don't fuss at the boy," his *dat* muttered. "Maybe he's not *hungerich*."

Sam looked at him and their gazes locked. David had told Sam that their *dat* had changed a lot and he had to a large degree— Amos didn't use to get through a day without shouting or ordering his *sohns* around. But there were times like now when he'd look up and find the old man scowling at him, his thick black brows beetling over his dark eyes, making him feel like a *kind*.

His *mudder* passed him the dish of baked beans and then the bowl filled with corn on the cob.

"I can't eat more," he protested.

"We'll send some food home for you and John so you'll have it for supper."

"Maybe he likes *Englisch* food better," Amos said. "Fancy restaurant food."

"Hardly," Sam said. He hadn't been in a restaurant in ages. Well, he and Peter had gone to a pizza restaurant recently. But Peter had treated him. So he *schur* wasn't spending money on fancy restaurants.

As he ate, he listened to the conversation around the big old kitchen table and thought how different the atmosphere was from when he lived here. His *mudder* had always chattered to lighten the mood, while his *dat* sat at the head of the table and glowered and been as unpleasant as possible.

Lavina seemed to fit in well with his family. His *dat* actually smiled at her and complimented her cooking. He was happy for her and not a bit jealous of her or David. But oh, how he wished a meal had been this pleasant. He never would have left if it had.

"Sam? Mary Elizabeth tells us Leah may have you and Peter help her with the renovations on her new shop."

He glanced up and saw Mary Elizabeth watching him from her seat across the table.

"*Ya*. Peter's working up a bid." He glanced at the clock on the wall. "I should be going. I'm supposed to meet him to help him with it this afternoon." He glanced at his *bruder*. "Don't worry, I'll still be helping you most Saturday mornings."

"I appreciate the help, but if you need to work for Leah to earn some extra money I understand."

"Family comes first," Amos said bluntly.

"Here, Amos, have the first piece of pie," Lavina said, handing him a plate.

How like his *mudder* Lavina seemed at that moment. Back when he lived at home his *mudder* was always trying to avert a blowup between his *dat* and one of his *sohns*.

Amos started to say something, and Lavina turned to Rose Anna. "Would you get the ice cream?"

"There's ice cream?" Amos asked, clearly distracted from whatever he had been about to say.

"*Ya*," Lavina beamed at him. "You know I always have ice cream for pie."

"I'll get it," Rose Anna said, getting up and walking to the refrigerator.

Sam realized that it was the first time Rose Anna had said anything since they'd all taken seats at the table. He wondered if she missed John today...

He hadn't liked making excuses for John not being here today to help. The fact was that John wasn't sick. And when he got home they were going to have a serious talk.

He scraped up the last bite of potato salad, ate it, then wiped his mouth with a paper napkin. "Well, I'd better get going."

His *mudder* jumped up and pulled plastic containers out of a cupboard. "Take some leftovers home for you and John for supper."

Amos scowled but said nothing. Sam rose and put his plate and silverware in the sink.

Lavina sliced two pieces of pie. "Here, Waneta, give me a container so we can send home some of the pie."

"*Danki, Mamm*, Lavina."

Waneta handed him a bag loaded with plastic containers. "Tell John I hope he feels better. Call me if you need me. John always used to get terrible colds this time of year."

"I will, *Mamm*. I'll be here with him next Saturday."

Or else, Sam thought.

He pulled up in the parking lot of the apartment complex just as Peter drove his buggy in.

"Hey, good timing!" he called as he walked over from the visitor parking space. "Whatcha got there?" he asked, gesturing at the bag in Sam's arms.

"Leftovers for our supper tonight."

"Great! When do we eat?"

Sam fumbled his key in the door lock.

Peter slapped him on his shoulder and chuckled. "Relax, I know you meant for you and John."

He breathed a sigh of relief as he unlocked the door and walked inside. "I have some soft drinks in the refrigerator. Want one?"

"*Schur.*" Peter followed him into the kitchen and watched him put the plastic containers inside the refrigerator. "Looks like you've got beer, too."

"They're not mine. They're John's. You can have one if you want."

"Hey, you finally back?"

Sam turned to see John, still dressed in his t-shirt and pajama bottoms, leaning against the kitchen doorway. He yawned then rubbed at the stubble on his chin. "Did you bring back food?"

"Do you think you deserve to eat it when you didn't help?"

"I wasn't feeling good." His voice held a bit of a whine. He muttered a curse word as he banged his toe on a chair in the small kitchen.

Sam grabbed a soft drink for Peter and himself and slammed the door on the refrigerator. "Yeah, well, maybe next time you could party less on Friday night and help out on Saturday. I'm not making excuses for you again. And watch your language."

He turned to Peter. "Let's sit at the dining room table and go over the proposal."

They settled at the small dinette table off the living room, and Peter spread out the papers he carried. "So, was Mary Elizabeth there at the farm today?"

"Yes, how'd you know?"

Peter popped the top on his soft drink. "I didn't know for *schur*. I just remembered that you'd told me she's there on Saturdays helping her sister while you help your *bruder* with the farm."

"Yes, she was there today."

Peter tapped his pencil on the table and regarded him thoughtfully. "If Leah hires us for the work it's possible you're going to come into contact with Mary Elizabeth even more. How are you going to feel about that?"

"Thanks for letting me come along today," Rose Anna told Kate when she climbed into the back seat of her car the next day.

"You're always welcome," Kate told her. "The more the merrier."

"Mary Elizabeth told me I'm never to tell anyone where the shelter's located. So I won't of course."

"Thank you."

Mary Elizabeth climbed into the front passenger seat and set the shopping bag she carried on the floor of the car. "*Mamm* said I could donate some of the quilting magazines we get. There are patterns in some of them for Christmas crafts."

"Terrific! That'll help a lot." She glanced at Mary Elizabeth. "So how are the renovations going on Leah's new shop?"

"She had Sam and Peter there the other day getting some measurements. I'm not sure when the work will start. She does seem to want to use them."

"Not surprised. Sam built some bookcases for us. He did great work. Malcolm is a wonderful husband, but he's not the best around the house. Last time he tried to put a new seat on the toilet he broke the toilet. Said the hinge wasn't opening so he tapped it. With a metal hammer."

Mary Elizabeth winced. "So he broke the plastic seat?"

"He cracked the base of the toilet. Do you know what a plumber charges to come out on the weekend?"

She tried not to laugh. "No, my *daed* is pretty handy."

"I'd have teased him more, but I could see it embarrassed him. Men think they're supposed to be good at stuff around the house." She glanced at Mary Elizabeth as she turned into the driveway of the shelter. "It's a guy thing."

They were early, but as Mary Elizabeth climbed the stairs to the sewing room she could hear sewing machines whirring.

They walked in on a beehive of activity. Women sat at every machine, sewing. Others were cutting material at a table that had been set up. Several of the children sat coloring at a little table set someone had placed in the corner.

"Well, I see we have a lot of early birds," Kate said, pausing just inside the room to grin.

"We're all so excited to be sewing up things for Leah's new shop," Edna Mae said. "I'm making up some potholders out of the quilt blocks we've been doing."

Mary Elizabeth went to an empty table, took the quilting magazines out of the shopping bag, and spread them out. "Kate, when you get a minute, look through some of these. I was thinking some of these holiday table runners would be quick to sew and sell for Thanksgiving and Christmas. They could be more affordable for shoppers than a quilt, too."

Kate set her purse and tote bag down and walked over to flip through some of the magazines. "I think that's a great idea. Ladies, could I have your attention for a moment?" She waited until the machines stopped and all eyes turned to her. "Mary Elizabeth brought quilting magazines in today. They have patterns for some things some of you might want to sew for Leah's shop."

Then she laughed as she had to move quickly out of the way when several of the women jumped up and rushed over to pick up a magazine and take it back to their seats.

"I thought this issue was a good one," Mary Elizabeth said, flipping pages. "See, this fabric is a panel with holiday images and inspirational sayings about believing in hope and dreams and harmony and family and giving. Then you add some simple quilt blocks around it and you have a pretty wall hanging. You can also divide up the panels into smaller sections, make some small wall hangings."

"We should order some of those fabric panels," Kate said thoughtfully. "Let me go back to my friends who've donated money to the quilting class and I'll see what I can get us."

"We might have some more fabric we can donate."

"And Leah said she'll see what she can contribute. I think we'll be fine."

"You know what they say about quilters," Mary Elizabeth said with a grin. "We can make a lot out of scraps."

Kate rolled her eyes and groaned. "I can't believe you said that." She stared at Mary Elizabeth, looking serious. "Are you going to be okay going to Leah's when Sam's working there? I heard she's hiring Sam and Peter to renovate the shop."

"Wow, word gets around faster than the Amish grapevine. I hadn't heard it was definite. They were doing up an estimate for her."

"Leah and I talked last night."

Mary Elizabeth shrugged and walked over to where she'd set her purse and tote bag down on a table.

"I don't expect to see him that often. Besides, I bump into him sometimes at Lavina's house. You have to expect such when you live in a small community."

But she hadn't seen so much of Sam in a long time...that is, until his *bruder* David had married Lavina and David's *bruders* came to help with planting.

She was saved from more questions when Kate was called over to help one of the women with a problem with her sewing machine.

Rose Anna walked around seeming to enjoy what was going on—especially when she saw Ellie sewing on another little quilt for her doll. She crouched down and talked with the girl about her quilt for a few minutes before getting up and wandering around to admire the women working on their individual projects.

Mary Elizabeth did her own walking around to see if anyone needed help and then settled down into a chair at the front of the room next to Kate. She pulled a quilt she was working on from her tote and began sewing, but she found it hard to concentrate. She set the quilt down and just stared at the women sewing.

"Something wrong?"

She turned to Kate. "No, something's right. Things are so different from the time I first came here. Some of the women looked depressed, nervous. Had bruises on their faces. The kids looked scared. Now everyone looks so happy, and the kids have lost that scared look."

"Leah has them excited about sewing for her new shop." Kate set her own work down and smiled as she looked around the room.

"She has a lot to do with it," Mary Elizabeth said slowly. "But if you hadn't volunteered your time here, there couldn't have been a quilting class at all."

Kate shrugged. "It was nothing. I enjoy being here with women who love to quilt."

"I think you know a lot about *hochmut*. About humility," she told her.

And it gave her an idea for a way for all of them to thank Kate.

6

"Mary Elizabeth?" Rose Anna appeared in the doorway of the sewing room.

"Rose Anna. Are you ever going to join us this morning?" Linda asked, a hint of censure in her voice.

"In just a minute, *Mamm.* Mary Elizabeth, Ben Miller is here."

"Here?" She stood. "I wasn't expecting him." She set her quilt aside, stood, and shook the wrinkles from her skirt.

They walked to the stairs, but before Mary Elizabeth could descend, Rose Anna put her hand on her arm. "I'm sorry I teased you the other day."

"When? You tease me a lot."

"I'm trying to apologize." Rose Anna pouted.

"*Allrecht.* I accept your apology."

"You don't know why."

Mary Elizabeth blew out a breath. "Ben is waiting at the door."

"I'm apologizing for teasing you that you have a new boyfriend."

She studied her younger *schweschder.* "Rose Anna, Sam overheard you."

"He said so?"

She shook her head. "I haven't spoken to him. But he came in right after you said it. And he was so quiet at the table. I think maybe it'd be *gut* if you apologized to him."

Rose Anna frowned. "Well, I didn't know he was eavesdropping."

"He wasn't. He was just coming in from the fields. Now, I need to go see Ben."

She went downstairs and found him sitting in a rocker on the front porch. He held his wide-brimmed straw hat in his hands, and the gentle early summer breeze blew his hair, the color of ripened wheat, around his head.

"*Guder mariye.*"

He stood and smiled at her. "*Guder mariye.* I thought I'd stop by and see if I could take you to lunch or for a ride or something. I know it's kind of last minute. I'd have called you, but I don't have your cell phone number." He held his out. "Maybe you'd give it to me?"

"I don't own one. I can give you the number of the home phone in the shanty."

"*Allrecht.*" He punched in the number when she gave it to him. "It's my first cell phone. The bishop back in my district didn't approve."

"Ours does for business and emergencies," she told him as she took a seat in the rocking chair next to his. "We have more businesses and tourism here in Lancaster, less farming since land's gotten expensive. So the bishop realized cell phones were a necessity."

He gazed out at the fields where they could see her *dat* working. "It's a nice life, farming. My youngest *bruder* inherited the family farm, so I apprenticed with a carpenter who was a family friend. Then my *onkel* asked me to join him here."

"So what are you doing not working this morning?"

"My *onkel's* giving me a few days to get settled in."

"He's a kind man. I think you'll like working with him. And living here in Paradise."

"Me, too." He met her gaze directly. "So, Mary Elizabeth. Will you forgive me for stopping by without notice hoping you'd be free today?"

She smiled. "Well, maybe this once. I do happen to be free. Why don't you come back at eleven-thirty?"

"That would be fine."

He stood when she did. "And Mary Elizabeth?"

"*Ya?*"

"Be thinking where you'd like to eat since I don't know the area."

"I will."

He donned his hat and strolled away. She went inside and walked upstairs feeling lighter than she had for a long time. He was interested in her, and that was a heady feeling. Her emotions had taken a beating with Sam leaving her and then his not wanting to renew their relationship when he had to return occasionally to help David with the farm. Sam didn't want her . . . well, it seemed another man might, and she was ready to move on.

The moment she walked into the sewing room Rose Anna's gaze shot to hers. "So, what did Ben want?"

"We're going to lunch."

"You don't seem excited. I'd be excited," Rose Anna told her. "Ben's so cute."

"It's best not to judge a man—anyone really—just on his looks," their *mudder* told her, looking at her over the top of her reading glasses.

"Well, it's nice to have someone cute to look at," Rose Anna said, unrepentant. "And he does seem nice. Not broody and self-centered like Sam."

"Sam's not self-centered," Mary Elizabeth said, coming to his defense.

"Maybe not as bad as John. I heard he's having a fine time on his *rumschpringe*." She frowned and stabbed her needle into the quilt she was sewing.

Mary Elizabeth felt her heart go out to Rose Anna. She wasn't just the youngest, she was the most romantic and the one whose heart was the most easily bruised. She might have enjoyed flirting with another young man at the singing, but it was obvious she was upset about John.

"Maybe he'll get it out of his system," she told her *schweschder.* "Young men seem to need *rumschpringe* more than we women. And he *schur* didn't have much fun growing up with his *dat* the way Amos used to be. If he had, he might never have felt like he had to leave."

"Well, Amos is different now. I don't see why Sam and John can't come back now like David did," Rose Anna said stubbornly.

"Amos and David resolved their differences," Lavina said quietly. "It took them some time, remember? Sam and John haven't done that yet with their *dat.*"

She hesitated, then took a deep breath. "Amos has changed a lot, but I think he feels Sam and John haven't met him halfway." She sighed and shook her head. "But I shouldn't speak for him. He hasn't said that directly. It's just what I'm sensing."

She set the quilt she was sewing down and pulled a tissue from her pocket. "I just wish they'd all work it out. Amos recovering with the grace of God, well, it should show everyone that we need to love each other." She wiped her eyes.

"Lavina, are you *allrecht*?" Linda stared at her, concerned.

"Hormones," Lavina said with a watery laugh. "I've been so emotional since I found out I'm going to have a *boppli.*"

"I was the same way the first couple of months," her *mudder* told her. "At least it seems like your morning sickness is easing. Or is it just that you haven't told me you're still having it?"

"*Nee,* it's better. I just keep having waterworks over the least little thing. This morning I was making *dippy* eggs. David loves it when I fix his eggs that way. Well, I fried one too long and ruined it, and I burst into tears. I scared him. He thought I'd burned myself." She shook her head. "So silly!"

Then she giggled.

"What's so funny?"

Lavina put her hand over her mouth. "I shouldn't laugh. It's not funny. It's actually kind of sweet."

"What are you talking about?" Mary Elizabeth demanded.

"It's kind of private. I shouldn't share."

Mary Elizabeth turned to her mudder. "*Mamm*, make her tell."

"*Ya, Mamm*, make her tell," Rose Anna chimed in.

"Girls, don't squabble." She looked at Lavina. "It isn't fair to tease them, you know."

"Well, it's something David did and a *fraa* shouldn't talk about her *mann*..." Lavina hesitated. "But it's kind of sweet. If I tell you, you can't tease him." She stared at Mary Elizabeth, then at Rose Anna.

"We won't!" they said at the same time.

"Now you're making me curious," Linda told her. She knotted her thread then clipped it with her scissors. "What is this funny but sweet thing David did?"

"Well, you know how I have been having such morning sickness?"

"You said it was better," her *mudder* reminded her.

"*Ya*, I meant before it got better David was feeling queasy in the mornings, too."

"And it wasn't your cooking?" Rose Anna teased her.

Lavina blew out a frustrated breath. "See what I mean? I shouldn't have told you."

Mary Elizabeth shot her younger *schweschder* a disgusted look.

"You're right, it *is* sweet," Linda told her oldest daughter. "And it would embarrass him if anyone said anything to him. So none of us will say anything. Will we, Rose Anna?" she said pointedly, giving her a stern look.

"*Nee, Mamm*." Looking chastened, Rose Anna turned her attention to her quilt.

But when Mary Elizabeth glanced over at her youngest *schweschder* a few moments later, she saw the gleam of mischief in her eyes.

Poor David. She had a feeling that Rose Anna was going to find a way to tease him.

"Let's take a break. We've been going at this for hours."

"In a minute." Sam whacked at a section of wall with his sledgehammer.

"Demo's the most fun, isn't it," Peter said when Sam set the heavy tool down.

Sam grinned. "It's not often we get to tear something down. Leah had a good idea for making a clear passage into her other store."

"Thank you. I thought so." Leah gazed through the hole they made looking like a bright-eyed little bird. "My, you two have gotten a lot accomplished this morning."

"Thanks for giving us the key. Figured it'd be *gut* to do this before your shop got busy."

"*Danki*. I have a sign up warning customers about the dust and noise while the renovation is in progress, but the less noise they have to listen to the better."

"Sam also figured if we could walk over to your shop you might have some of those cinnamon rolls you bake."

"I said no such thing," Sam protested.

Leah chuckled. "Well, as it happens, I did bring some in like I do most mornings. My *grossdochders* can be counted on to show up early to work for them. *Kumm*, the coffee's on and there's iced tea, too. If you hurry maybe they haven't eaten all of the rolls."

They both tried to step through, reminding Sam of how he and his *bruders* had done the same at the farm. Funny how Peter seemed like a third *bruder* more than a friend sometimes. Well, *bruders were* friends most of the time.

Sam stepped back and gestured for Peter to go first. "Age before looks."

"*Ya*, right." Peter preceded him and they followed Leah to the back room of her shop.

Two of Leah's *grossdochders* were working in the shop today. Mary Katherine sat weaving at her loom in the corner. Her eyes were dreamy and far-away looking as she worked rhythmically sending a wooden thing moving through the threads strung on it and adding length to whatever it was she was weaving.

Sam couldn't help thinking of Mary Elizabeth as he passed Naomi teaching a small quilting class. Mary Elizabeth *schur* loved quilting and seemed to enjoy teaching the class at the shelter. He thought it was a shame that women and their children had to have such a place, had to hide to be safe, but it was good that they did have people who helped them.

Was it true that Mary Elizabeth had a new boyfriend as Rose Anna had teased? There had been many times he'd wondered if she was seeing someone while he lived away from the Amish community. He'd never heard any rumor that she was, and he worked with Peter and enough other Amish men to have heard if she had.

Could it be that she'd only started dating once they'd had that confrontation where he'd let her know that he wasn't returning home as his oldest *bruder* had done? Well, things hadn't changed, so it was for the best.

He just wished he really believed it himself.

"Sam, coffee or iced tea?"

"Iced tea, *danki*." He sat at the table in the back room. He waited until she'd served him and Peter and taken a seat before he reached for one of the cinnamon rolls the size of a man's hand.

Leah smiled at them as they ate their rolls. It was obvious she loved feeding such an appreciative audience. Sam drained his glass of tea and was grateful for a second glass from the pitcher she'd set on the table.

"Hot work, eh?"

He nodded. "But not as hot as if we were outside doing roofing, right, Peter?"

"I figure that's why you like to do windows and interior work," he said. "You can't stand the heat."

"You two bicker like *bruders*," Leah told them with a chuckle.

"Look who's eating all the cinnamon rolls." Kate strolled in and poured herself a cup of coffee. "I ran late for the knitting class with Anna," she told them. "Mind if I join you?"

Peter stood and pulled out a chair.

Kate smiled at him and sat.

"There are still some rolls." Leah pushed the plate closer to her. "I think you came in the nick of time."

"You two made a lot of progress this morning," Kate told Sam and Peter as she picked up a roll. "I have two kids who could give you some help with demo today."

Leah clapped a hand over her mouth but couldn't hide her chuckle. "I've met her kids."

"Their daddy's in charge today. I expect an SOS any moment now."

"We might take you up on that," Peter said. "Say, Sam, my nephew might be able to help us a few hours a week. I'll stop by his house later and talk to him."

"Sounds *gut*." Sam stood and carried his glass to the sink. "*Danki* for the iced tea and roll, Leah."

Peter thanked her and followed him back to the job.

"Were you serious about your nephew?" Sam asked him as he donned his safety glasses.

"*Schur.* Why?"

"Aren't you worried about it cutting into your profit margin?"

Peter shook his head. "I planned on a small amount for some help. And if we get finished sooner, it'll give us a chance to take on another job. I'm always planning ahead."

The Amish were hard workers and found ways to survive when farmland grew scarce, but Sam was beginning to think Peter was one of the most ambitious men he knew.

They worked steadily until their lunch break. They ate their lunch as they sat in the doorway of the shop in a couple of old chairs that had been left by the previous owner. It was the perfect place to watch locals and tourists out enjoying the warm summer day.

A group of women carrying shopping bags full of their purchases stopped to ask what was going on in the new shop. Peter appeared to enjoy telling them about Leah's new venture and invited them to walk down to the entrance to Stitches in Time and talk to her about it. They walked on and a few minutes later Sam glimpsed them inside the shop talking with her and strolling through the aisles of fabric and other wares.

An Amish woman walked past, glanced at them, and nodded. She made Sam wonder what Mary Elizabeth was doing today. Was she helping Lavina as she did so often on Saturdays? He'd rousted John out of bed that morning and dropped him off there to help David and their *dat* in the fields.

Sam stared at the cold lunch meat sandwich he was eating and envied John the meal he'd be sitting down to at the farm. He sighed. Well, with luck Lavina would be sending food home with John as she had with Sam the week before.

And he reminded himself that he didn't need to sit at that kitchen table as he had the week before where he had avoided Mary Elizabeth's gaze after overhearing Rose Anna tease her about having a new boyfriend.

Nee, he didn't need that at all.

———

Mary Elizabeth hadn't anticipated feeling a little shy going out with Ben Miller. Of the three *schweschders* she had always thought of herself as the most confident one. But she'd had eyes only for Sam since she was a little girl and had never gone out with anyone else. There was something exciting but at the same time a little scary about being on a date with a man she knew so little about.

Well, except for the fact that he was cute and seemed so nice. He was a gentleman, too, showing up on time to pick her up at the house and help her into his buggy. And he told her she looked pretty in her blue dress.

She told him what road to take to the restaurant, and as they rode there, she worked at not being self-conscious and asked him about himself. She'd heard somewhere that the best way not to focus on yourself was to focus on the other person.

"Beautiful day," he said. "Beautiful country."

If Ben felt any reserve being with someone new he *schur* didn't show it. He was twenty-four and from a family of eight *kinner*— four *bruders* and three *schweschders*—and had visited the area with his family a couple of times. He and his *onkel* Eli got on well so when the older man needed more help Ben had moved here.

So far he liked Paradise and Lancaster County a lot and was glad he'd decided to make the move although he missed everyone back in Nappanee.

Then he turned the table on Mary Elizabeth and asked her about herself. She told him about how she and her *mudder* and two *schweschders* quilted for a living. Though his face was turned away as he watched the road, he didn't look bored.

So she talked about how Kate had persuaded her to volunteer to teach a quilting class with her at a local women's shelter and now the women were busy sewing crafts for a shop Leah, owner of Stitches in Time, was renovating. She and Rose Anna were now helping at the quilting class since Lavina was busy as a new *fraa*. It wasn't polite to mention a woman being pregnant, so she left that out.

"You sound like you're a busy lady."

"It's *gut* to be busy. You know what they say about idle hands."

He chuckled as he turned the buggy into the restaurant parking lot. "*Ya.* So, the food's *gut* here, huh?"

"*Ya.* It's one of the most popular restaurants in the area. Locals come here, not just the tourists."

The restaurant looked like a big, homey Amish kitchen with hand-carved tables and paintings of the local countryside hanging on the walls. Quilts were hung on the walls and available for sale.

They were shown to a table and given menus.

"If you like fried chicken or meatloaf no one makes it better," she told him.

"We'll see if the fried chicken is as good as my *mamm's*." He closed his menu and ordered it when their server came with her order pad.

"I've met a lot of people here in just two weeks," he told her as he glanced around the restaurant. Someone must have waved at him because he waved back.

"That's *gut*. I've lived here all my life, and I love it."

"Well, you were right about the chicken," he said with satisfaction as he finished his second piece and wiped his fingers. "But if you tell my *mudder*, I'll deny I said that."

"Promise. And you have to promise the same thing. I don't want my *mamm* to know I said it either."

They grinned at each other.

"Well, look who's here, Malcolm!" a female voice said.

Mary Elizabeth looked up. "Kate! Malcolm!" She glanced around them. "Where are the kids?"

"At their grandma's. She took pity on Malcolm while I was at Leah's earlier and picked them up for a couple of hours." Kate turned to Ben and stuck out her hand. "I'm Kate Kraft, and this is my husband, Malcolm."

"Ben Miller."

"Ben just moved here from Indiana," Mary Elizabeth told her.

"Great. Hope you like it here. Well, we'll let you get back to lunch. Come on, Malcolm, we need to eat before your mother changes her mind."

Malcolm grinned. "She can handle our two monsters. After all, she lived through my brother and me."

Ben turned his attention back to his meal after they walked away. "So this is the Kate who's a police officer and talked you into volunteering at the quilting class at the shelter?"

So he *had* been listening.

"*Ya*."

"I've only seen one other female police officer," he said as he picked up another piece of chicken. "Is her husband a police officer, too?"

"*Nee,* he's a counselor. He helps a lot of *Englisch* veterans."

Kate and Malcolm had seemed like such opposites when they first met, she thought. Kate was an officer of the law, and Malcolm had problems with drugs and alcohol after he left the military. He'd turned his life around. Now Malcolm was married to Kate, and they had two children.

Mary Elizabeth wondered if she should tell Ben and then decided not to. Malcolm deserved to be judged as he was now, not continually have his past always following him around. She ate and they talked, and she thought about how she was getting to know him. Her *dat* often said that people should be judged by their actions, not their words, so while she enjoyed his easy smile and yes, easy charm, she liked that he didn't attempt to impress her. Instead, he'd stood when Kate and her husband approached the table, and he treated their server politely.

Ya, she thought, she was glad she'd agreed to come out today to have lunch and go for a ride with a man such as this. Maybe he'd be a friend. Maybe he'd be more. She was looking forward to seeing what God intended. For while she'd thought Sam was the man He had set aside for her, that hadn't worked out and now a new man had been put in her path.

They shared a hot fudge sundae, too full from their lunches to do more, and then with a to-go cup of iced tea, climbed back into the buggy. Like most of her friends and family, Mary Elizabeth had never lived anywhere but in her community. So she asked Ben how much he'd had a chance to travel around his new neighborhood and when found it hadn't been much she took him on a guided tour.

Two hours passed before she knew it. There might be more beautiful places in the world, but she'd always felt Paradise was well-named—especially on a not-too-warm summer day.

"I'm glad you could come out with me today," he said, sounding a little formal as he turned into her driveway. "*Danki* for such a *wunderbaar* time."

She gave him a warm smile. "I should be thanking you. So nice to get to know you, Ben Miller."

He drew the buggy to a stop and turned to look at her, his blue eyes intent. "Could I see you again? Maybe after church next Sunday?"

"I'd like that," she said, wondering if she sounded as formal as he had. But it seemed both of them were being very careful since they didn't know each other well. "I'll pack us a picnic."

She saw a movement out of the corner of the eye and glanced at the house. The curtain at the front window moved. Someone was looking out.

"I don't want you to go to any trouble."

"You bought lunch today. I'll pack us a picnic."

"I love picnics."

"I know the perfect spot. I'll see you at church, then. Have a *gut* week."

"You, too."

She got out and hurried into the house, wondering who it was who'd been looking out the front window. She had her suspicions.

Sure enough, Rose Anna pounced on her the minute she opened the door. She immediately peppered Mary Elizabeth with questions.

"So, did you have a *gut* time? Did you like him? Did he kiss you?"

"*Ya, ya,* and of course not!"

She walked into the kitchen to throw away her empty to-go cup. Then she started up the stairs to the sewing room with Rose Anna trailing behind her.

Their *mudder* looked up from her sewing as they walked in. "So did you have a *gut* time? Did you like him? Did he kiss you?"

Mary Elizabeth stared at her. "Rose Anna just asked me those questions."

Linda chuckled. "I know. I have a *mudder's* hearing."

She took her seat and picked up her quilt. "Then you know the answers," she teased as she threaded a needle.

"Well, I'd know the answer to the last one," her *mudder* said, looking at her over her reading glasses. "You'd never let a young man kiss you on a first date."

"Of course not," Mary Elizabeth said in the same prim tone her *mudder* had used.

But she felt a warm blush steal over her cheeks as she thought about what Ben's kiss might be like.

Rose Anna gave her an arch look as if she knew what her *schweschder* was thinking, and Mary Elizabeth felt warmer.

Thank goodness their *mudder* was concentrating on her sewing was all Mary Elizabeth could think.

7

Mary Elizabeth turned on the battery-operated lamp on Rose Anna's bedside table, then leaned over and shook her shoulder. "Rose Anna, wake up."

She muttered something unintelligible and rolled over.

"Rose Anna, get up, *now!*"

"Go 'way!" She tried to pull her quilt up over her head, but Mary Elizabeth pulled it down—all the way down to her toes. "It's *Daed's* birthday, Lazybones, and you're getting up!"

Groaning, Rose Anna sat up and rubbed her eyes. "Don't know why we have to celebrate it in the morning."

"Because it's a surprise. If we do it later today, he'll be expecting it."

Rose Anna muttered, but she got up and pulled on her robe.

Mary Elizabeth handed her a hairbrush. "Here, brush your hair. You don't want to scare him."

Grumbling, she pulled the brush through her hair, bound it back in a bun at the nape of her neck, and put on her *kapp*.

When Mary Elizabeth was certain that her *schweschder* was on her feet and following her from the room she started down the stairs. If left alone Rose Anna was known to sneak back to bed...

They were halfway down the stairs when Rose Anna grabbed her arm and sniffed. "Pancakes. My favorite!"

"*Daed's* favorite," she reminded her.

Rose Anna surged past her and clattered down the stairs.

Their *mudder* took a platter of pancakes from the back of the stove and set it in the middle of the table. A small pile of gaily wrapped presents sat in front of the plate set at the head of the table.

The back door opened and Jacob walked in.

"Happy birthday, happy birthday!" they sang.

He grinned as they finished with a flourish. "Well, well, all my women are up this early!" he said. "Even you, Rose Anna."

"I wouldn't miss it," she told him.

"Which one of you dragged Rose Anna out of bed?" he asked, chuckling as he strolled to the sink to wash his hands.

"That would be me," Mary Elizabeth told him.

"So I'm not a morning person," Rose Anna sniffed. "I got up for your day, *Daed*."

"*Ya*, you did. *Danki*," he said, patting her shoulder before he took a seat at the head of the table.

Lavina walked in just then. She slipped into a chair, and they all bent their heads as Jacob said a prayer of thanks for the meal.

Mary Elizabeth sent up a silent prayer of thanks to God for such a wonderful *dat*. He worked so hard to provide a home for them. She loved the way he showed his love for them by helping her *mudder* take care of them when they were little and sick. And he was always doing little thoughtful things like building shelves for their sewing room instead of grumbling about the stacks of fabric they kept buying.

After the meal of blueberry pancakes, bacon, and juice he opened his presents. New work gloves, a new Sunday shirt all four of them had taken part in sewing, Later, at supper, he'd be treated to his favorite pot roast and a chocolate cake.

But now, there was one more present. He stayed in his seat and enjoyed a second cup of coffee and his *dochders* went out to the barn to do his chores. It was the one day of the year he got a break from them, and Mary Elizabeth and her *schweschders* were happy to relieve him of them.

"So tell us about the date with the new guy," Rose Anna said the moment they got to the barn.

"*Ya*, tell us," Lavina urged, her eyes sparkling with mischief.

Mary Elizabeth shot her an exasperated look. "I expect that out of Rose Anna, but you?"

Lavina just shrugged. "You know I want you to be as happy as me."

"So far only one Zook *schweschder* is," Rose Anna muttered. "So tell us about the new man and make me think he's going to take your mind off Sam. Then maybe I can believe I can find someone to take my mind off John."

"He's nice. He's a gentleman, holds doors open, and listens. Really listens."

"Sounds promising. I like a man with good manners."

"And his eyes are such a dreamy blue." Lavina wrinkled her nose as they mucked out stalls.

Mary Elizabeth looked at her. "Sounds like you were looking at my date."

"I'm married, not dead," Lavina quipped.

"They *are* dreamy, aren't they?" Rose Anna asked with a chuckle.

"You two. As if that's a reason to see a man."

"Not the whole reason," Lavina said.

"But it helps to have someone attractive to look at," Rose Anna agreed. "After all, when we marry it's for a very long time."

Mary Elizabeth glanced over and saw that Lavina had stopped and was just standing there looking dreamy. "You *allrecht*?"

She nodded and began working again. "Just thinking. This time last year I didn't think I'd marry David let alone be having a *boppli*."

"The smell out here isn't bothering you?"

"*Nee*, not more than usual. The morning sickness is gone."

"So when are you seeing Ben again?" Rose Anna wanted to know.

"We're going on a picnic after church next week."

"You're cooking?"

Mary Elizabeth made a face at her. "I'm a *gut* cook!"

"You should have Lavina cook. Or *Mamm*."

"I will not. I'm making fried chicken and potato salad and brownies."

"Be sure to take some Pepto-Bismol."

"Lavina, tell her I'm a *gut* cook!"

"She's a *gut* cook, Rose Anna. Don't tease."

"You just have to hope he never tastes *my* fried chicken," Rose Anna said smugly. She set aside her rake and picked up the handles of the wheelbarrow.

Mary Elizabeth set her hands on her hips. "She's so competitive."

"*Ya.* So make her eat her words. Have a fried chicken cook-off."

"There's an idea," she said slowly. "How did you come up with it?"

"Don't you remember when we were younger she thought she made better mud pies?"

She laughed. "*Ya*, now that you mention it, I do."

"Well, I did," Rose Anna said. "A cook-off..." she mused, pursing her lips and considering it. "You're on!"

John was sprawled in the tattered recliner they'd rescued from trash day when Sam arrived home later that day. A sports program blared on the television set.

His muscles were aching from hours slinging the sledgehammer doing demolition at Leah's store, and here was his *bruder* lazing around looking cool as a daisy in front of a fan and watching sports.

"What are you doing home already?" he asked him as he unlaced his boots at the door.

"We finished a little early."

"How'd you get home?"

"David had to pick up supplies in town so he dropped me off. Lavina sent leftovers home for us for supper. You want to eat now or after you take your shower?"

"After. I feel like I have five pounds of dust on me."

Seeing John looking like he'd had an easy day wasn't bad enough. Running out of hot water one minute into his shower didn't improve his mood. John loved taking long showers, and the water heater in this place was pitifully small. He counted to ten and sent up a thank-you to God that it wasn't the dead of winter or no telling what he'd be saying to John when he got out.

Not that he'd use the kind of words John was using since he left their Amish community. He'd spoken to him about it more than once, but John shrugged him off and told him to "get real" and loosen up. They were in a different world now and an occasional "cuss word" was no big deal.

Clean—and more than several degrees cooler now—Sam got out of the shower, toweled off, and dressed in a pair of jean cutoffs and an old t-shirt that he'd found on the bargain table at the local thrift shop. He and John only had Amish clothes when they left home. The small apartment had a few items of furniture—a sagging sofa, a small dinette table, and beds in the two bedrooms. So they'd kept their eyes out for bargains and even better—for free things like the recliner with orange and brown plaid upholstery and a strip of duct tape holding the stuffing inside.

Sam went into the kitchen and began unloading plastic containers of leftovers from the refrigerator. He'd never envied his *bruder* David for inheriting the farm . . . Sam didn't believe in envy. But it *schur* must be nice to have a *fraa* who was such a *gut* cook. And occasionally because their parents lived in the *dawdi haus* there, their *mamm* cooked or baked something as well.

Today there was enough meatloaf for two, a big container of mashed potatoes with browned butter on top, and another of the first of the summer's tomatoes. He fixed a plate with meat and potatoes and warmed it in the tiny microwave—another thrift shop purchase. The clerk there had been so nice explaining how to work it. Sam had only burned a couple of things in it before he got the hang of it.

Well, so the place wasn't much to look at. But it was a place of their own and the best they'd found for what they could pay.

Sam walked into the living room to tell John supper was ready and found him sound asleep. He hesitated for a moment, wondering if he should just let him sleep. Then he remembered he wanted to ask how things had gone today.

"John? Supper."

His *bruder* woke, blinked. "What?"

"Supper."

He ran a hand through his hair. "Geez, I was having this really good dream. It had this blonde I met at this party—"

"Save it." Sam turned on his heel. He shook his head. John was enjoying his *rumschpringe* a little too much. On the other hand, maybe he was never going back home. Sam still didn't know if he himself ever would.

John stumbled into the kitchen a few minutes later. He gulped down the glass of iced tea Sam had poured. "Feels like you can't get enough to drink on warm days like this."

Sam grunted. He'd drained half of his glass before cutting into the meatloaf. "So tell me about today."

"What? We worked in the fields. *Daed* was actually halfway pleasant." He scooped up a forkful of mashed potatoes and stuffed it into his mouth.

"How was everyone else?"

John shrugged. "All right." He went to the refrigerator for ketchup and dumped some on the meatloaf. Then he looked up, and his gaze sharpened. "Oh, I get it. You want to know how Mary Elizabeth is."

"I didn't ask."

His *bruder* smirked. "You didn't have to." His smirk faded. He ate quickly, avoiding Sam's eyes.

"What?"

"I didn't say anything."

"Just tell me."

"You sure you want to hear this?"

"Yes." His stomach clenched.

"I overheard Rose Anna and Mary Elizabeth talking about her seeing some new guy."

"Rose Anna?"

"No, Mary Elizabeth."

"I see." So what he'd heard when he walked into David and Lavina's kitchen last Saturday had been true. She *was* seeing someone.

Well, that's what he'd expected when he told her they had no future, right? He'd really thought she'd have done that before now. Well, that was that. He didn't need to feel guilty that she was sitting around waiting for a future with him that they couldn't have. He didn't need to feel anything.

So why did he?

"You all right?"

"Yes." He resumed eating. "Why wouldn't I be? I told her I'm not moving back, that we couldn't be together."

"If you really feel that way, then why haven't you been dating?"

"No time. Especially now when Peter and I are taking on extra work."

"You have to make time. You know what they say about all work and no play . . ."

"They don't have bills to pay. Speaking of which, rent's due."

"Geez, trying to eat supper here." He dug in his pocket, counted out bills.

Sam couldn't help holding his breath. They'd had a couple of talks about this when John found it more important to buy new *Englisch* clothes and beer for parties. To his relief, the amount he handed Sam was correct.

"Thank you." He stuffed the bills in his pocket.

"Look, there's a party tonight. Want to come? There're always some single chicks there."

"Don't call them chicks."

"Hey, sometimes they refer to themselves as chicks. It's not an insult."

"Sometimes people call themselves something, but they don't want you to do it."

John rolled his eyes. "I don't need a lecture, bro." He scraped the last of the meatloaf from his plate. "So you want to check out the party or not?"

"Not. And if you need a ride home, don't get in the car with someone who's been drinking."

"I never do." He looked at Sam. "I have more sense than you give me credit for." He rose to put the rhubarb pie Lavina had sent home with him on plates.

Sam pushed his empty plate aside and took the pie John handed him. Since their older *bruder* had gotten married, he felt like he'd assumed that role with John. He wondered if David had ever felt it was a lot of responsibility looking out for his younger brothers.

"I guess you do. If you can't get a ride, find a phone and call me."

"I will. Thank you." He made quick work of the pie. "I'll try not to call you too late. Old men need their sleep."

Sam wadded up his paper napkin and threw it at him. "Smart aleck."

John caught the napkin and tossed it back. "See you later. Chuck's picking me up at six."

He waited until John walked out of the room to get up and get some ibuprofen from the kitchen cabinet. His muscles ached from the exertion of the day. It made him feel as old as John had teased him about being. He washed the pills down with the last of his iced tea, cleaned up the kitchen—John had conveniently forgotten he was supposed to help with such chores—and headed for the recliner his brother had vacated.

An evening in front of the television was about all he could manage tonight.

Mary Elizabeth patted her forehead with a paper napkin. The sun had gone down and a breeze was drifting in the screen door, but it was still hot work frying chicken.

But what was a picnic without it? While it fried she put together a big bowl of potato salad so it could go into the refrigerator to chill overnight. She'd tucked away several slices of buttermilk pound cake she'd baked for the family the day before and had a bowl of nice ripe strawberries sliced up and sugared for dessert.

She hoped Ben would like her fried chicken as much as the chicken he'd eaten at the restaurant on their first date.

"So this is for your picnic with Ben tomorrow?" Rose Anna asked as she walked into the kitchen.

Mary Elizabeth nodded.

Rose Anna leaned against the kitchen counter and smirked. "It's not as *gut* as my fried chicken. Better hope Ben doesn't ever get a taste of mine."

She used tongs to transfer the chicken pieces to a plate lined with paper towels to drain them. Rose Anna picked up a piece of crust that lay on the towel and tasted it.

Mary Elizabeth smacked her fingers. "Stop that!"

"Needs a little salt," Rose Anna told her as she strolled off. "We have to have that cook-off soon."

Their *mudder* walked into the kitchen to pour herself a cup of coffee. "What's Rose Anna teasing you about this time?"

"She thinks her fried chicken is better than mine."

"Your *schweschder* thinks everything is a competition." She chuckled and shook her head. "It's hard being the *boppli* of the family."

"She's hardly a *boppli*."

"Well, she's the youngest, and she has to follow in the footsteps of her older *schweschders*. I was the *boppli* of the family, so I know."

Her *dat* walked in. "Something *schur* smells *gut* in here."

"You can't possibly be hungry after all that supper you ate," Linda told him.

"Which piece do you want?" Mary Elizabeth asked him with a fond smile.

"Maybe a wing?"

She got a plate and placed a wing on it.

"Why are you frying chicken now?" he asked as he blew on it to cool it.

"It's for a picnic tomorrow. Do you want a little potato salad to go with it?"

"Don't mind if I do."

"I'll get it," Linda said. She got the bowl from the refrigerator and doled out a small spoonful.

"Don't be stingy," he said, guiding her hand and making her serve him another spoonful.

She chuckled. "You'll get fat."

"He works too hard for that," Mary Elizabeth told her.

"Don't you go offering him dessert," her *mudder* said.

"There's dessert?"

"*Nee*," Mary Elizabeth said with a straight face.

She watched her *mudder* walk over to the refrigerator to put the potato salad inside, caught her *dat's* eye, nodded, and jerked her head at the plastic container on the counter.

"I know what you're doing," Linda said without turning around.

"Who?" Mary Elizabeth said, trying to sound innocent.

"Woman's got eyes in the back of her head," Jacob muttered as he lifted a forkful of potato salad to his mouth.

Mary Elizabeth had always been a very well behaved *kind*— well, mostly. There was that one time when she and Rose Anna had had words and gotten into a little hair-pulling when they were eight and seven. But her *dat* was right. Her *mamm schur* did know what was going on at all times even when her back was turned.

She gave her *dat* a sympathetic look and he shrugged.

Rose Anna drifted into the kitchen, and her eyes went wide when she saw her *dat* nibbling on the chicken wing. Her glance shot to Mary Elizabeth.

"Are you trying to influence *Daed* about your chicken?"

"What?" He looked at her, puzzled.

"Your youngest is feeling competitive with Mary Elizabeth about her fried chicken," Linda told him. "You can make yours next week, Rose Anna. I'm *schur* your *dat* will be happy to try it."

"Then we'll see whose is best," she said, shooting her *schweschder* a superior look.

"I remember the first time your *mamm* made fried chicken for me," Jacob said, giving his *fraa* a fond look.

She smiled. "Was it the reason you married me?" she asked.

"*Nee*, it was your chocolate cake," he said, his eyes twinkling.

"So the way to a man's heart really is through his stomach?" Mary Elizabeth couldn't resist teasing him.

"*Nee*, it was knowing she was a farmer's *dochder* and *gut* with a plow. And *gut* with a shovel."

"I'll show you a shovel," she said, chuckling.

"*Ach*, now, you know it's your beauty and grace that won my heart," he said, his eyes twinkling.

"Think you can dig your way out of this one, do you?"

He reached for her hand and kissed it. "I know I can."

She shook her head and laughed. "I'm taking my coffee into the living room."

He stood and took his plate to the sink. "I'll join you there."

"Be sure to bring your charm," she said over her shoulder as she left the kitchen.

"I take it with me wherever I go." He winked at his *dochders* as he followed his *fraa* out of the room.

Mary Elizabeth looked at Rose Anna. "I hope we get as lucky finding a *mann* such as *Daed*."

Rose Anna nodded. "Me, too."

She picked up a sponge and wiped the top of the stove. "Ben seems nice. I hope he enjoys the food you made. I tease you, but you *are* a *gut* cook."

"*Danki*. I said we could have a picnic after church. After all, he paid for the meal at the restaurant."

"Well, men *should* pay."

"Not always. It isn't fair."

"Well, I expect them to pay." She tossed the sponge into the sink. "I'm going to bed. See you in the morning."

Mary Elizabeth put the chicken in a plastic container and placed it in the refrigerator. Rose Anna might expect a man to pay for everything, but most of the Amish *maedels* they knew made food for picnics with the men they dated as a way of sharing costs. And showing the men that they were *gut* cooks. The old saying about the way to a man's heart was through his stomach was often true.

She washed up the dishes and cleaned the cast iron skillet from her cooking, wiped down the counters, and said good night to her parents sitting in the living room reading. Then she climbed the stairs to her room. As she undressed and changed into her night-gown, she thought about seeing Ben again.

And wondered what he and other men thought was the way to a woman's heart.

8

That is without a doubt the best fried chicken I've ever eaten." Ben wiped his mouth with a paper napkin and smiled at Mary Elizabeth.

"*Danki*, I'm glad you enjoyed it."

She was glad she'd remembered how he'd eaten three pieces at the restaurant and brought four pieces for him today. He'd eaten every one plus a big serving of potato salad. He *schur* had a big appetite for such a tall, lanky man.

Mary Elizabeth pulled the container of buttermilk pound cake from the picnic basket and placed a slice on each paper plate, then spooned the sliced, sugared strawberries over the top. He took his plate from her, gazing at it appreciatively.

She remembered how her *dat* had eaten the chicken wing the night before and talked about the first picnic he'd gone on with her *mudder*. It was a nice memory and *gut* to think that *wunderbaar* things could come from such simple beginnings.

The day was warm but pleasantly so. A breeze blew over from the small pond at the park she'd directed him to. Butterflies danced among the wildflowers that surrounded the pond. Families sat at tables situated around the pond and enjoyed their lunches.

Mary Elizabeth and Ben had spread a quilt on the soft grass and not missed sitting at a wooden picnic table at all. It was the perfect summer afternoon for a picnic. Even the fanciest of food in a restaurant couldn't match sitting here and enjoying the outdoors. "More lemonade?"

"*Danki.*" He held out his empty plastic cup. "So how has your volunteer work with the quilting class gone this week?"

Surprised he'd remembered what she'd said about her work there, she told him about the wonderful progress the class was making to stock Leah's new shop.

She was careful not to go on too much about it though. She doubted any man really wanted to hear a woman go on about such. So she turned the conversation to his reaction to his new job and his living arrangement with his *onkel's* family.

"I've been saving to build a home of my own for a long time," he told her. "With what I'm making here and saving on expenses living with my *onkel,* I'll be adding to that."

"Land's gotten scarcer and more expensive in Lancaster County," she told him. "Many couples spend the first year living with her parents before they get their own place."

He frowned. "I've heard that about land here. I'm hoping that won't be necessary to live with my *fraa's* family. It's nicer to just be alone together, have some privacy, don't you think?"

Mary Elizabeth thought about how her *schweschder* Lavina had married David after he'd inherited his family's farm, and his parents moved into the *dawdi haus* there. They'd been a lucky couple—they and his parents got along well now. But Sam and John were going to have to find a way to afford their own homes when they married.

"Something the matter?"

"Hmm?"

"You're frowning."

"Oh, *nee,* sorry. My *schweschder* and her *mann* were lucky to have his *dat* decide to retire and give him the farm."

"My family's always been farmers or carpenters," he told her as he ate his cake and strawberries. "Land is cheaper in Indiana than here."

"My *dat's* family has been farmers for generations," she told him.

"But you have no *bruders* to inherit?"

She shook her head. Her *dat* had never made his *dochders* feel he regretted not having *sohns*. She and her two *schweschders* helped him as much as they could around their own work. Two of their neighbor's *sohns* helped him part-time.

But Ben's comment made her think. If she or Rose Anna married a *mann* who wanted to farm when her *dat* was ready to retire, they could take it over. By then her *grosseldres* probably would no longer be living, and her parents would move into the *dawdi haus*.

The last part saddened her. Her *mamm's* parents—were the only ones she had left and each day it seemed they grew more frail and stayed to themselves in the *dawdi haus*.

And the thought of her *dat*, so hale and hearty, not working out in the fields... why, that was a long, long way away. He was only in his early fifties and strong as an ox.

"I think I told you my family's been farming in Indiana for a long time as well," Ben was saying. "I have three *bruders*, so the rest of us went into other lines of work after my *bruder* Marvin inherited."

"This pound cake is very *gut*," he said as he finished it. "Reminds me of my *grossmudder's* pound cake."

There could be no higher compliment than to bake as well as someone's *grossmudder*, she thought as she brushed crumbs from the folds of her skirts. "Do you want to finish mine?"

"*Schur.*"

He finished her serving and sighed happily. "*Gut* meal. *Danki*, Mary Elizabeth."

"Do people go on picnics in Indiana?"

"*Ya*, they're popular when it's warm." He cast a glance at the sky. "It's going to rain soon."

Mary Elizabeth looked up. The sky had been bright blue and cloudless just minutes before. Now the clouds were gray and blocking out the sun. Well, it was summer in Pennsylvania. Such was to be expected.

She packed up the picnic basket and stood. He helped her fold the quilt they'd sat on, and they walked to the buggy.

Raindrops began pattering down on them as they walked. Ben grabbed her hand and they ran to the buggy and climbed inside. Mary Elizabeth shook the drops from her skirt, and Ben took his straw hat off and slapped it against his arm. They watched the rain slide in a silvery sheet down the windshield and the side windows, seeming to enclose them in a world of their own.

"Summer rain is the best," she murmured and when she glanced at him she saw that he was watching her, not bothering to lift the reins and get the buggy moving.

"Have I told you how pretty you look today?" he asked quietly, his gaze intense.

"*Nee.*" The unexpected compliment made her feel shy and she never felt shy. "*Danki,*" she managed.

"I've enjoyed seeing you, Mary Elizabeth. When can I see you again?"

"Would you like to come to supper one night this week?"

"I would love that. Just tell me what night and I'll be there." He lifted the reins and called to his horse. "So, Mary Elizabeth, what is the longest way home?"

She laughed and her shyness vanished. "Let me tell you."

"It's coming along."

Sam stood with Peter at the entrance to Leah's new shop and assessed the work they'd been doing.

All the shelving and fixtures that hadn't worked for her new shop had been demolished and cleared out. New display tables and shelving were nearly done. It had been a good month's work—not easy work adding on time after the day job and working long Saturdays but worth every sweaty, backbreaking hour.

He'd enjoyed working with Peter more than he'd anticipated. They'd been friends for years and worked for the same company during the day, but they were usually in different areas of a worksite. Sam did mostly windows and interior carpentry and such, and Peter was up on the roof.

"Hi!"

They turned and saw Mary Elizabeth standing in the open doorway, a cardboard box in her arms.

"Let me help you with that." Sam walked over to take the box.

"It's not heavy. I can manage," she said, her eyes cool. "Leah said we could put some things in the storage room. I don't want to interrupt your work."

"We're taking a break."

For a long moment she held onto the box, and he wondered if they'd have a tug of war. Then with some reluctance she released it. Rose Anna walked in with a box and Peter rushed to take it from her.

"*Danki*, Peter," she said, giving him a flirtatious smile. "We've got more in the buggy."

Sam registered the smile, shot a glance at Mary Elizabeth, and saw she was looking at him, unsmiling.

He carried the box in his arms into the storeroom, setting it on a newly built shelf, and watched Peter do the same.

"So why's Mary Elizabeth being cool to you?" Peter asked.

He shrugged. "Guess she doesn't want to be friends anymore."

"I know she's seeing someone, but I didn't think I'd see her behave like that."

"Me neither. But you sure got the friendly treatment from Rose Anna."

Peter grinned. "*Ya*. I noticed." He ran his hands through his hair. "Do I look *allrecht*?"

"Fine."

"You didn't even look at me," Peter complained.

Sam met his gaze. "All right, you're real pretty."

Peter smacked his arm, but he chuckled as the two of them left the store room.

"C'mon, let's go help them."

"The boxes aren't heavy."

Peter gave him a look over his shoulder. Sam sighed. His friend and partner was right. They were women, and men were supposed to help them with such things.

Who'd have known the next boxes were indeed heavy?

"It's so kind of you to help," Rose Anna chirped as she followed them inside the store. "Right, Mary Elizabeth?"

Mary Elizabeth didn't respond for a moment. When Sam heard an odd noise come from her, he glanced over his shoulder and saw her nod and quickly say, "*Ya, danki*, Peter and Sam."

A moment later he heard Mary Elizabeth hiss, "You didn't have to elbow me."

Sam glanced back, and Rose Anna gave him a big smile. Mary Elizabeth was frowning until she realized he was looking at her. She pasted a smile on her face.

He couldn't help grinning as he followed Peter into the store room.

"Well, we'll be going now so you men can get back to work," Rose Anna told them. "Unless..." she stopped and smiled at Peter.

"Unless?" he asked.

"Unless you can stop for a cup of coffee. You did say you were on a break."

"Really, Rose Anna, we've taken up enough of their time," Mary Elizabeth said quickly.

"Yes, we do have to get back to work," Sam said.

"Of course we can stop," Peter told her.

Sam gave him a disbelieving look. This was Peter who was all business and all about staying on task.

"C'mon, Sam, let's go." Peter jiggled the keys to the shop in his hand. "There's a great coffee shop right down the street."

"It's our treat, right, Mary Elizabeth?" Rose Anna said. She turned to her. "*Kumm*, these are busy men." She smiled at Peter. "They have the best fruit tarts there this time of year."

Sam looked at Mary Elizabeth. She shrugged and looked resigned before following Peter and her *schweschder* out of the shop. Sam gave up and did the same. Peter locked the door, and the four of them walked the short distance to the coffee shop.

"Rose Anna is something else," he whispered to Mary Elizabeth.

"*Ya*, but I'm not sure exactly what," she responded in the same low tone. "Is it my imagination or is she flirting with Peter?"

He eyed them chatting as they preceded them. "I believe she is. I thought she was interested in my brother John."

Her expression turned cool. "Well, the Stoltzfus men have shown they're not interested in the Zook women—at least, two of them have," she said pointedly. "So we're moving on."

Rose Anna gazed up at Peter as he opened the door to the coffee shop. She appeared to have something in her eye. No, she was fluttering her eyelashes. Sam didn't think he'd ever seen Rose Anna doing that. Certainly Mary Elizabeth hadn't ever. He glanced at her and saw that she was watching her sister with an expression of disbelief.

They entered the coffee shop, and Rose Anna immediately walked over to the case where pastries were displayed and exclaimed over the fruit tarts. Peter stood there with her nodding and smiling. Sam didn't think he'd ever seen Peter looking so interested in someone.

Sam was grateful that there were only two people ahead of them as he stood in line with Mary Elizabeth. He didn't know what to say to her.

Then, as she stood there stiffly, not looking at him, he started feeling defensive. Why did he need to say anything? And why should he apologize to her? He was sorry that she'd been hurt when he moved away, but he didn't know she'd continued to wait for him to return.

And besides, what did he have to offer her? And why should he have to be made to feel badly for it?

"May I help you?"

Mary Elizabeth stepped up to the counter and ordered iced tea. He waited for her to order a cream horn—she had a weakness for them—but she stepped aside, and the clerk looked at Sam.

"The same," he said. "It's too hot for coffee. And I'll have a cream horn." He turned to Mary Elizabeth. "You sure you don't want one?"

"*Nee*," she said very definitely. "*Danki*," she added as if she realized she sounded abrupt. She pulled her wallet from her purse, but Sam stepped closer to the counter and beat her to handing bills to the clerk.

"It's our treat," she insisted, but Sam gave the clerk a big smile, and she was already tucking the bills into the cash register and handing him the change.

"Have a seat and we'll bring your order to the table." She looked past them to the customers in line behind them.

"How about the table by the window?" he suggested, and she nodded. They took seats at the small table, and Mary Elizabeth took the one furthest from him and looked uncomfortable.

"Look, I'm sorry the two of us got roped into coming along," he said.

"It's *allrecht*."

She watched her sister place her order and engage in a laughing, flirtatious play at paying for Peter's drink and pastry. The cashier rolled her eyes but smiled politely as Rose Anna finally gave in prettily and Peter paid for both of them.

"I said we were treating you," she told him as they approached the table where Mary Elizabeth and Sam sat. "Didn't I say that, Mary Elizabeth?"

"Yes, you said that." She glanced at Sam. He'd gotten his way in paying, but she hadn't done the flirtatious struggle over who paid.

"The women at the shelter are getting so excited about having their work displayed," Rose Anna told Peter. "I can't believe how much you've gotten done since the last time we visited the shop."

"It won't be much longer," Peter said, leaning back in his chair as their drinks and pastries were served.

Rose Anna chattered as if oblivious to the tension between her sister and Sam. "How is John?" their server, an Amish woman they'd attended *schul* with, asked Sam. "Is he helping you work at the shop today?"

He looked up at her. "He's good. He's helping David at the farm."

"Tell him I asked about him, will you?"

"I will." He poured sugar into his iced tea. John had women asking about him. He sat at a table with one whose gaze was as cool as his iced tea.

Not all the Stoltzfus men were popular with women. He bit back a sigh and wondered how quickly he could excuse himself from this little party and get back to work.

"What was that all about?" Mary Elizabeth asked as she got into the buggy for the ride home.

"Hmm?" Rose Anna glanced over at her as she settled into the passenger side seat. "What was all what about?"

"Flirting with Peter."

Rose Anna's smile was very female . . . and very smug. "You and I talked about moving on since the Stoltzfus men don't want us, remember?"

"I didn't know you were interested in Peter."

"He's a nice man."

"*Ya*, he is. And it's fine if you're interested in him. But don't use him for practice."

"Practice?"

"Your flirting skills."

Rose Anna laughed. "Oh, stop being a big *schweschder*. Peter's a big boy. He doesn't need you to protect him from me."

Her smile faded and she stared down at her hands clasped in her lap. Then she looked up at Mary Elizabeth. "It felt *gut* to have a man interested in me. I'd think you'd know what that feels like since you and Ben have been going out."

She sighed. "You're right. I—just wasn't sure about what I saw today."

"I flirted with Peter, and Peter flirted with me. We'll see if anything comes of it."

When they arrived home, their *dat* came out of the barn and greeted them. "I hear we have company coming for supper."

Mary Elizabeth had nearly forgotten.

"Go inside and help your *mudder* with supper. Rose Anna and I'll take care of unhitching Bessie and putting her up."

"*Danki, Daed.*" She kissed his cheek and went inside.

"Something smells so *gut*," she said when she walked into the kitchen. She sniffed the air. "Pot roast."

"Your *dat*'s favorite. Thought Ben might enjoy it. Never met a man who didn't like a *gut* pot roast."

"Or a woman for that matter. Give me a minute to put my things in my room and I'll help. I'm sorry, Rose Anna and I stayed in town a little longer than I expected."

Her *mudder* smiled at her. "It's fine. Take your time."

When Mary Elizabeth returned, she washed her hands at the sink and dried them on a dish towel.

"All that's left is a salad. I made a strawberry rhubarb pie earlier."

Mary Elizabeth glanced over at the counter and saw the pie sitting on a cooling rack. "Why don't you make the salad and I'll get us some iced tea?" Linda suggested.

"Nothing better than a strawberry rhubarb pie." Mary Elizabeth said as she washed the fresh lettuce, carrots, and big red, ripe tomatoes they'd picked from the kitchen garden that morning.

She dried them, picked up a wooden cutting board, and sat at the table.

Linda poured them glasses of iced tea and sat down. "So tell me a little about Ben."

She smiled as she sliced the tomatoes. "He's new to town, came here to work for his *onkel*."

"It's been a while since we had a young man come to supper," her *mudder* said.

"David was here just last week with Lavina."

Her *mudder* gave her a level look. "You know what I mean."

Mary Elizabeth grinned as she heard the kitchen door open "Rose Anna, *Mamm* was just saying it's been a while since a young man came to supper. Maybe you'd like to invite Peter."

Rose Anna stuck her tongue out at her and quickly pasted a smile on her face when their *mudder* glanced over at her.

"Peter Beiler?"

"*Ya*." She hung her purse on a peg and walked over to the sink to wash her hands. "What can I help with?"

"Slice some bread?"

Rose Anna nodded and pulled a knife from a drawer. She began slicing the freshly baked loaf.

"We stopped to drop off some crafts to Leah's new store today," she told their *mudder*. "Peter and Sam were working. *Mamm*, you should see what the women at the shelter created so far. There are so many different things. Not just quilts but table runners for Thanksgiving and Christmas, mug mats—little quilted coasters to put under a hot mug, some little stuffed animals and lots of quilted Christmas ornaments. Some of the children made cute little pincushions."

Mary Elizabeth didn't know if Rose Anna was really excited about their work or wanted to deflect questions about Peter. Amish parents gave their *kinner* privacy about dating and Linda and Jacob had done the same, only discussing David when Lavina had shared her concerns about his problems with his *dat*. Later, after they reconciled she'd told them she and David were getting married. Mary Elizabeth hadn't talked about Sam much, but she had the feeling that her *mudder* had guessed how she felt after he came to supper so often before he left home.

Rose Anna finished slicing the bread and set the breadbasket on the table. She poured herself a glass of iced tea and sat at the table with them, watching as Mary Elizabeth arranged slices of tomato in an artful pattern on top of the salad.

They were setting the table when they heard a knock at the front door.

"I'll get it," Rose Anna said, but Mary Elizabeth grabbed her apron sash and pulled at it.

"I'll do it," she told her *schweschder* firmly.

"Of course," Rose Anna said, giving her an impudent grin.

"What's all that about?" she heard their *mudder* asking her *schweschder* as she walked to the door. If she knew their *mudder*, Linda would get Rose Anna to confess.

"*Gut-n-owed*," Ben said, his smile wide and welcoming when she opened the door.

"You're right on time."

"You must be Ben," her *dat* said, walking into the room from the kitchen. "I'm Jacob. This is Linda, my *fraa*," he added as she joined him. "And this is Rose Anna, one of Mary Elizabeth's *schweschders*."

Mary Elizabeth noticed that Rose Anna smiled at him, but the wattage was drastically reduced from what she'd given Peter earlier that day.

They moved into the kitchen and took seats at the table.

"Something smells very *gut*," Ben told Linda. His eyes lit up when she served the platter of pot roast surrounded by potatoes and carrots from their garden.

"You have a fine farm here, Jacob," Ben said as he helped himself to a big serving of the pot roast. "It makes me a little homesick for the family farm back in Indiana."

That led to an animated discussion between the two men over similarities and differences in farming methods and crops and all manner of things. Linda gave Mary Elizabeth a sympathetic smile as she attempted to change the subject twice and then gave up.

"Ben? Strawberry rhubarb pie?"

He groaned. "One of my favorites. I'm not *schur* I have room after two helpings of that pot roast."

"Three," Rose Anna murmured.

He grinned. "Three," he agreed, looking sheepish. "*Ya*, Linda, I would love a piece."

"Be happy to show you around after dessert," Jacob said.

Ben finished the pie in record time, and the two men were out the back door.

"Well," Mary Elizabeth said wryly, watching them leave. "The two of them make a lovely couple. I'm so glad they hit it off."

Linda burst out laughing.

9

I'll be glad when summer is over," Lavina said as she ladled blueberry preserves into jars. "Ben seems nice."

Mary Elizabeth screwed lids on the filled jars. "He is."

"*Daed schur* likes him." Lavina stopped for a moment to wave a small paper fan at her face. "Oh, each summer feels hotter than the last one. I don't mean to question God about why He made harvest the warmest part of the year but..." she trailed off.

Something made Mary Elizabeth look at her, hard. Lavina looked flushed, and her eyes were overly bright.

"Sit for a minute."

Lavina swiped the back of her hand across her forehead. "I'm almost finished. I'll sit then."

Mary Elizabeth took her *schweschder* by the arms and pulled her over to a chair and pushed her into it. "You'll sit now. Take a rest and I'll get you some cold water."

She got the pitcher of cold water from the refrigerator, and when she turned, she saw that Lavina had quietly slid from her chair to the floor in a dead faint. She bobbled the pitcher and nearly dropped it.

"Lavina!" She rushed to put the pitcher on the table and knelt beside her *schweschder* on the floor. She chafed her hands and patted her cheeks. "Lavina! Please, wake up."

She breathed a sigh of relief when Lavina opened her eyes.

"What am I doing down here?" Her face paled and her hands clutched at her abdomen. "The *boppli*! Is the *boppli allrecht*?"

Mary Elizabeth covered her hands with her own. "Stay calm. I'm *schur* he's *allrecht*. You fainted."

"Don't be silly. I never faint," she said indignantly.

She struggled to sit up. Mary Elizabeth stood and helped her to her feet then pushed her back into the chair.

"Then I guess you were just seeing if your floors were clean enough to eat off them."

Mary Elizabeth quickly poured her a glass of water and thrust it into her hands, then reached for a dish towel and soaked it in cool water. She pressed the cloth against the back of Lavina's neck.

"That feels *wunderbaar*," Lavina said with a sigh.

"I want you to go lie down for a while. I'll finish this up." She gave Lavina a stern look. "If you don't do as I say, I'll go call David."

"*Nee*! You'll just worry him."

"Then do as I say."

"Blackmail," Lavina muttered. But she picked up the glass of water and went upstairs to her bedroom.

Mary Elizabeth followed her and made sure she loosened her clothing and lay down. A breeze drifted in the window and cooled things off.

"You stay here for half an hour."

"Bossy," Lavina muttered. But she gave Mary Elizabeth a wan smile. "If I could ask God anything, it wouldn't just be why harvest has to be in the hottest season. It'd be why women have to be pregnant in the summer."

"What's all this about being pregnant in the summer?" Waneta, David's *mudder*, asked from the doorway.

"Just a little complaining," Lavina told her apologetically. "Nothing's wrong."

"I'm making her take a rest," Mary Elizabeth said, giving Waneta a meaningful look. "Maybe you can take over and I can finish the preserves?"

"*Schur*," Waneta agreed, sitting down on the side of the bed. She patted Lavina's hand. "I was pregnant with David in August, you know."

"So like *dat*, like *sohn*."

"Exactly. The Stoltzfus men are demanding for *schur*. Well, you'll forget all about this discomfort when your *boppli* gets here." She sighed. "I'll admit I can't wait. I'm going to be a *grossmudder*."

Mary Elizabeth left them and went downstairs. She finished up the blueberry preserves and cleaned up the kitchen, then started lunch. A quick survey of the contents of the refrigerator revealed most of a baked chicken and a big bowl of boiled potatoes. Cold chicken sandwiches and potato salad would be filling and a nice meal that would help the men to cool off from a hot morning in the fields. She sliced the chicken and arranged it on a plate, then set it in the refrigerator.

She made the potato salad and put the bowl in the refrigerator to keep cold. Now all she had to do was think of something for dessert and she was done. She spied a pail of strawberries on the counter. A check of the freezer revealed a frozen pound cake. Perfect. She set it on the counter to thaw, then cleaned the strawberries, sugared them, and set them in the refrigerator. Now, if her luck held, there'd be cream for whipping or ice cream, and she'd have strawberry shortcake, a summer favorite. She looked in the refrigerator again. No whipping cream but there was ice cream. Probably better than the whipped cream on such a hot day.

A short time later, the men began filing in to wash up. She had the table set and poured glasses of iced tea for them.

"Where's Lavina?" David wanted to know the minute he walked in and didn't see her.

"Taking care of something upstairs," she told him breezily. "It was my turn to make lunch."

He washed his hands and then started for the stairs. Lavina met him and smiled.

"I thought I heard you come in," she said. She glanced over at Mary Elizabeth. "What can I do to help with lunch?"

"Bring your appetite," she told her. "It's all ready."

She got the bowl of potato salad and platter of cold chicken from the refrigerator and put them on the table.

"Are you *allrecht?*" David asked her as he pulled out a chair for her. "You look a little flushed."

"I'm fine," she said, meeting Mary Elizabeth's gaze. "It's summer. It's warm."

"That it is," David said. "I'm grateful for your help today, John." He used a big fork to spear two slices of chicken and heap them on top of a slice of bread, then passed the platter to his *bruder.*

"Sam said to tell you that he should be able to come next Saturday. Figures he and Peter will be finished with Leah's new shop this week."

"*Gut.* I can use the help."

Conversation lagged as the bowl and platter and bread basket were passed around and everyone began eating. Hard work meant big appetites. Mary Elizabeth got up twice for more iced tea and lemonade. A quick glance at Lavina's plate showed she wasn't eating much, but she *was* eating.

David was watching her, she saw. He leaned closer and whispered something in her ear. She smiled and ate a little more.

Lavina had been so blessed to marry David. They'd gone through a lot with him leaving after years of not getting along with his *dat.* She'd persuaded him to return and now he'd not only recovered but Lavina and David had their happy ending: they were married, had taken over the farm, and were looking forward to the birth of their first *boppli.*

The two of them had known each other since *schul,* had only had eyes for each other for years, and had weathered such storms to be together.

Things hadn't worked out with the Stoltzfus *bruder* Mary Elizabeth loved. She'd been convinced that Sam was the man God had set aside for her. But things hadn't worked out for them the way they had for Lavina and David.

Now it seemed that He'd brought Ben into her life. She'd been a little anxious about going out with him since he'd just moved to the community. . . . She hadn't gone to *schul* with him or seen him at church or youth activities. But after just a few dates it felt like they'd always known each other.

They had months to get to know each other before the marrying season—the time after harvest ended. If that seemed too soon, they would wait until next fall to get married.

But as she watched the way Lavina basked in the love and caring from her *mann*, Mary Elizabeth couldn't help wondering if she and Ben would be in the same situation—married and expecting a *boppli*—next year.

Well, it was all up to God, and His will.

She thought about how John said Sam was coming to help David with the farm next week. She hadn't been friendly to Sam the last time they saw each other. Guilt swamped her. She was happy seeing Ben now, wasn't she? Couldn't she forgive Sam and treat him in a more Christian way next time they saw each other?

As she got up to serve dessert, she decided she'd find a way to apologize to him this week.

———

Sam glanced up when a shadow fell over the doorway of Leah's shop.

"May I come in?"

He couldn't see her face with the sun at her back, but he recognized her voice.

Mary Elizabeth.

"*Schur*. Come in. Set the box down and let me clean my hands so I can help you with it."

"It's *allrecht*. It's not heavy. Just more stock for the shop when it opens." She walked into the back room and set it on a shelf.

"Where's Peter?" she asked when she returned.

"He's out doing an estimate for a new job for us," he told her as he finished spreading stain on the newly sanded wood floor in a corner. He sat back on his heels. "In one of my not-so-brilliant moments, I forgot to ask him to get my lunch out of his buggy before he left."

"You're not driving your truck?"

"I didn't today. It's in the shop. I'm hoping the repair won't eat up all the money I made on this second job," He stood. "Well, that's done, and I didn't paint myself into a corner."

Last week he hadn't had his mind on the job, and he'd done it. But she didn't need to know that. He began cleaning his hands on a rag. "I guess I could grab a sandwich from the shop down the street but..." he trailed off as he looked down at his work-stained clothes.

"Tell you what. I haven't had lunch. Why don't I go get us a sandwich?"

Sam stared at her. "That would be nice. But why would you do that? Last time we talked you weren't happy with me."

She looked away. "I'm sorry. I've been thinking about it, and I want to apologize."

He shrugged. "There's no need." But as he watched her he saw that she twisted her hands, a nervous habit he remembered she had. "Thank you for apologizing, but let me apologize, too. I'm sorry I hurt you so much. Maybe we could just leave it at that. Be friends."

"I'd like that. Now, shall I get you your usual? Roast beef sub, mustard, pickle, lettuce, and tomatoes? And a bag of chips and a can of root beer?"

"You still remember?" He thought for a moment. "Turkey sub, provolone, light on the mayo, black olives, tomato, but no lettuce. And Diet Coke. Never Diet Pepsi."

114

She grinned. "I guess we know each other pretty well. I'll be back in a few minutes."

"Oh, here, let me give you the money."

"I offered, so it's my treat."

She was gone before he could object.

While she was off getting lunch, he found a couple of empty ten-gallon buckets for them to sit on and turned a box over for a makeshift table. A clean drop cloth served as a tablecloth. He stood back and viewed the results. Not bad. Then he wondered if he should have gone to the trouble. He'd done the usual things when they dated. Taken her for picnics, drives and very, very seldom, a restaurant, but always an inexpensive one since he had little money.

And Peter had said she was dating some guy who was new to the area...

Oh well, it wasn't like he'd lit candles or anything. It was sandwiches in the middle of the day in the midst of construction.

She was back soon. "The lunch rush was over, so it didn't take long." Her eyebrows went up when she saw the cardboard box table and the bucket seats. "Clever. I didn't much like the thought of sitting on the floor. Even though the job you did refinishing it looks great."

He shrugged. "Leah was happy with it."

"I imagine so. And it sounds like you're going to meet the deadline for finishing." She sat on a bucket and pulled the subs and soft drink cans from the paper bag she carried.

They paused to give thanks for the meal and then unwrapped their sandwiches. Mary Elizabeth looked around. "This shop is going to mean so much to the women at the shelter. They have a way to make money. It's probably not going to be enough for them to support themselves, but it gives them a way to build their confidence, save for their own places. Even the *kinner* have gotten into the spirit of it and made pin cushions and other crafts."

"It sounds like it's been good for you, too," he said quietly.

"Me?"

"You like to help."

"We all do."

"Not all." He bit into his sandwich.

"I just love quilting and showing other women how to do it. And it's hard to turn Kate down. She does a lot for all of us in the community, and if she can find the time I can, too."

She ate her sandwich—a half not a whole like she'd gotten him—and remembered what John had said about Sam helping next Saturday. "David said he'd really appreciate your help Saturday," she told him.

"I've missed helping."

"Do you have more work lined up after you finish here? Part-time work, I mean."

He grinned. "*Schur*, as this is a new, rising business, Peter's scheduling work as we speak. He's very ambitious."

"The two of you have done a *gut* job here. I can't wait to help stock the shop when you finish."

"Maybe I can help."

"You?"

"Well, nothing creative, but I can help lug boxes, put stuff on high shelves, that sort of thing."

"You're right. I'm sure we'd be grateful for any help you can give us." She wrapped up the remains of her sub. She'd eaten her half sub in the time he ate the whole one she'd bought him. He must have been very hungry indeed. Then again, when wasn't a man hungry? She smiled as she got up to put the wrapping in a nearby trash can.

"What's funny?"

She shook her head. "I was thinking of how fast you ate just now. How much."

"I remember a time I got us a pizza and you ate half."

She shrugged. "Half."

"Half of a large pizza. A little thing like you ate as much pizza as a big guy like me."

She colored. "I like pizza. And I hadn't eaten all day."

Minutes ticked by on the wall clock as they talked. He was reminded of countless picnics they'd shared outdoors in the sunlight, Mary Elizabeth sitting on a quilt on the grass in a park, her eyes full of love.

Now she looked at him like a friend, and they only had a short time in the middle of a workday seated here on upturned buckets at a cardboard table in the middle of an empty shop that smelled of paint and turpentine.

A shadow fell over the shop. He looked up and saw a gray cloud obscuring the skylight.

"I should go. It's going to rain soon." She knew she should get on the road but strangely felt reluctant to leave. She forced herself to her feet, took a last sip of her drink, and tossed the can in the trash.

"Be careful on the way home." He got up and followed her to the door. "Looks like you might make it before it starts."

"I will."

"*Danki* for lunch. I enjoyed it."

She looked at him and smiled slightly. "I did, too."

Then she slipped out the door and he was left to stare after her.

Finally, he walked back to the makeshift lunch table and sat on one of the buckets. The sandwich, chips, and drink had filled his stomach. But somehow he felt dissatisfied.

When Peter walked in a few minutes later he was still sitting there, staring at the remains of his lunch.

When Mary Elizabeth pulled into the driveway of her house, she saw that Ben's buggy was parked to one side.

He and her *dat* walked out of the barn to help unhitch the horse.

Ben smiled at her. "Got here a little early for supper."

"I see."

"You're all wet," he said.

"I stopped by to see Lavina on the way from town and got caught in the rain." She glanced around. "You didn't get any here?"

"*Nee*," her *dat* said. "You know how it is. Don't like the weather? Wait five minutes in Pennsylvania and it'll be different."

"Same thing in Indiana," Ben told him as he pulled the buggy over to one side of the barn. He scanned the sky. "I'd say we're going to get some rain here within the hour."

Her *dat* did the same scan, took a deep breath and nodded. "Takes a farmer to sniff out rain."

"I'm going to go in and change," she told them.

They were both still staring up at the sky and didn't appear to have heard her.

She said hello to her *mudder* on the way through the kitchen to go upstairs. "I got wet. I'll change my dress and then help you with supper."

"Take your time," Linda told her.

Mary Elizabeth hung her wet dress in the bathroom, pulled on her favorite cornflower blue dress, and unpinned her *kapp*. She smoothed her center-parted hair before finding another *kapp* and pinning it on. As she placed it on her head and began inserting pins to hold it, she found herself thinking about sitting with Sam in the shop earlier that day as they ate lunch.

It was just lunch with a friend. But it had *schur* reminded her of other lunches, other picnics with Sam. Had it reminded him of the same? She stared into the mirror, her eyes serious. She wasn't sorry she'd gone by to apologize. It was past time she'd forgiven him. Past time that she moved on.

But there had been something about sitting there with him that had felt different. Special. They had so many shared memories of such times.

She shook her head as if to push away those memories. Things had changed between them. She'd never really liked change, but there wasn't much you could do about it, and when there wasn't, she tried to accept God's will.

Taking a deep breath, she left the room and went downstairs to help with supper.

Her *mudder* was the only person in the kitchen. She didn't hear anyone in the living room. Mary Elizabeth glanced at the door. "*Daed* and Ben still outside?"

"*Ya*. They *schur* do talk a lot."

Mary Elizabeth got dishes from the cupboard and began setting the table. "*Mamm*? Do you think *Daed* missed having a *sohn*?"

"Oh, my, *nee*!" she said quickly. "He was so happy when each of you was born healthy."

She glanced out the window and saw the two men talking.

"Why do you ask such a thing?" She came over to touch Mary Elizabeth's face and make her look at her.

"I just wondered. He seems to enjoy talking to Ben so much."

"They share an interest in farming. That's all."

"I guess."

"He talked a lot to Sam when he came to supper, too," Linda reminded her. "You remember that, don't you?"

"*Ya*, I guess."

Her *mudder* moved back to the stove to stir something in a pot. "How was your day?"

"*Gut*. I took some things over to the shop. It's nearly finished."

"How is Leah?"

Mary Elizabeth set the last of the flatware beside a plate. "I didn't see her. I just took the box and put it in the back storeroom."

She bit her lip, then blurted out, "I saw Sam."

Linda turned. "And?"

"I apologized to him. I was angry the last time I saw him, and I said some things…"

"Your heart's been hurting for a long time," she said quietly. Her eyes were kind.

She nodded. "He didn't realize how much he hurt me and he tried to make amends, but I wouldn't let him. I realized that wasn't right."

"Then I'm glad you went to apologize to him." She walked over and put her arms around her. "Do you feel better now?"

"*Ya.* We even had lunch."

"*Gut.*"

"*Mamm,* your pot's boiling over."

Linda rushed back to the stove and stirred the contents with a big wooden spoon. "So, did you stop at Lavina's on the way home?"

"*Ya.* I'm worried about her. The heat and all the work harvesting and canning are too much for her. I want to go over and help her tomorrow. Not just with watering the kitchen garden. With whatever she needs. If it doesn't leave you short with our chores, that is."

"I have Rose Anna," Linda reminded her. "She's getting better with it."

If she said so, Mary Elizabeth couldn't help thinking, then chided herself for such an uncharitable thought. Rose Anna preferred easier chores than working in the kitchen garden in the heat, but she did what was needed. And she seemed to enjoy the canning even though it was hot work.

The men came in then, laughing about something.

"What's for supper?" Jacob asked Linda.

"As if you didn't check that out the last time you came inside for a cold drink," she said tartly. "Don't go opening that oven door and heating the kitchen up more than it is."

He sniffed the air. "Smells like baked chicken to me." He winked at Mary Elizabeth. "Your *mudder's* the best cook there is."

"Now don't be saying that," she told him, trying to look modest. After all, they didn't believe in *hochmut*—pride. But she smiled as she picked up potholders and pulled a big pan with two golden baked chickens from the oven.

"One for today, one for another time," she said, pulling off the potholders and waving her hand to cool her face from the oven heat. "Might as well make the oven do double duty on a hot day." She turned it off and went to the cupboard for a platter.

Ben returned from washing up and took a chair opposite Mary Elizabeth's. "You look pretty," he mouthed and winked at her before responding to her *dat's* quiet blessing for the meal.

Jacob carved the chicken and started the platter moving around the table after serving himself.

"Did you have a *gut* day?" Ben asked her.

"Very *gut*. I had quilting class this morning then dropped off more crafts at the new shop."

She left out how she'd had lunch with Sam.

"Where's Rose Anna?" Jacob asked.

"Having supper with David and Lavina. She took your parents."

He nodded. "It's *gut* for them to get out. I need to remember to make sure their rental home is reserved for them in Pinecraft for the winter."

"My *grosseldres* go there for the winter as well," Ben said. "I'll have to let them know to look yours up, Mary Elizabeth."

She nodded. "One of the things mine love about being in Pinecraft is meeting new people." She smiled as she helped herself to coleslaw. "That and how warm it is. Ever since a friend of theirs sent them a postcard saying she could pick an orange in her front yard, they wanted to go. I wasn't sure they'd come back home last spring."

Just like the first night he'd come to supper, Ben spent most of his time talking farming with her *dat*. Mary Elizabeth exchanged a look with her *mudder* and asked Ben about his job.

He made a brief response and shifted the conversation back to farming. "I miss it," he said simply.

"David could always use some help this time of year," she said. "Would you be interested in helping for a few hours on Saturday?" The minute she said it she remembered Sam would be there . . .

"*Schur,*" he said. "Just tell me where." He grinned when Linda brought a pie to the table to slice for dessert.

Later, after he'd gone, the dishes were done and the kitchen was spic and span, Mary Elizabeth wandered out to the front porch and sat in one of the chairs.

"Nice night," her *mudder* said as she poked her head out the front door. "Want company?"

"Would love some."

"Something bothering you?"

"*Nee*." She looked out at the trees. "Look! Fireflies!"

"Mary Elizabeth?"

She sighed. "I just realized I invited Ben to David and Lavina's on Saturday. And Sam will be there."

"Why is that a problem?"

She shrugged. "I don't know that it will be. I just wouldn't want Sam to be hurt by meeting the new man I'm seeing."

"It has to happen sometime," Linda said practically. "This is a small community. Even if Sam stays in town a lot, they are *schur* to meet sometime."

"I guess you're right."

"I'm going in. See you in the morning." She leaned down to kiss Mary Elizabeth's cheek.

"*Gut nacht*." She lingered, watching the fireflies, remembering past summers when she'd sit here with Sam watching them, not objecting when he'd occasionally steal a kiss.

She sighed and went in to go to bed.

10

Mary Elizabeth's week was long, each day starting with helping Lavina with her kitchen garden, then hours sewing her quilts and spending a few days at quilting class, then delivering crafts to the new shop.

Now she was showing up early on a Saturday to work some more. But tomorrow would be a day of rest after church. Besides, Saturday at David and Lavina's was fun work.

She just hoped Lavina didn't faint on her again. That had been nerve-wracking.

Ben was just arriving as she pulled in with Rose Anna.

"*Danki* for coming," she told him as he walked over to help her unload a basket of food she'd brought to make the day a little easier.

"It was the only way I could see you this week."

She frowned at the faint note of complaint in his voice.

"It's been a busy week." And it wasn't likely that it would be any less so for the foreseeable future, but now wasn't the time to say so.

"Sam! Nice to see you!" Rose Anna said as he walked into the kitchen behind them.

Mary Elizabeth turned. "I didn't see you drive up."

"I'm not surprised," he said, looking at Ben.

"Ben, this is Sam. Sam, Ben just moved here from Indiana. He offered to help this morning."

"I'll take you out to the fields and introduce you. I'm *schur* that's where David and our *dat* are already."

Mary Elizabeth watched them walk outside.

"Are you worried they're going to duel each other for you?" Rose Anna asked her.

She stared at her *schweschder.* "What? Have you been reading historical romances again?"

Rose Anna giggled. "*Ya.* Wouldn't it be romantic, the two of them facing off in the cornfield?"

"What's this about facing off in the cornfields?" Lavina walked into the kitchen carrying a basket of zucchini.

Mary Elizabeth rushed to take the basket from her. "Don't carry something this heavy. Ask for help."

"There was no one around. David was off in the fields. Now tell me what you two were talking about when I walked in."

Rose Anna opened her mouth, but Mary Elizabeth waved her off. "Don't tell her until she gets off her feet."

Lavina sank into a chair. "You don't have to ask me twice. I feel like I went to bed looking like I had a tummy the size of a small apple and today I look like I'm carrying a watermelon."

"You look *wunderbaar,*" Mary Elizabeth told her.

She wanted to say it just looked like there was a cantaloupe under Lavina's apron but didn't know if she'd appreciate that. She was so relieved that her *schweschder* looked better than she had last week. On the other hand, they hadn't started any work yet in the kitchen, and it was *schur* to be as warm as last Saturday.

"So, what are we going to do today?" she asked Lavina.

"Have something to drink first," Rose Anna said firmly. She got a pitcher of tea from the refrigerator and fixed them glasses.

"Mary Elizabeth, grab the cookie jar, will you? I made some oatmeal raisin last night after supper when it cooled off."

She brought the jar to the table and watched as Lavina polished off two of the large cookies.

Lavina gave her a guilty look. "I can't stop eating lately."

"I'm glad to see it. You couldn't eat for so long when you were having morning sickness."

"*Ya*, but now I'm eating so much you'd think I was eating for three, not two."

"You don't think..."

"Think what?"

"*Zwillingbopplin*," Rose Anna said.

"Oh, *nee*, I wasn't even thinking of such a thing," Lavina said, looking horrified. "I can barely think of taking care of one let alone two."

"It would be a gift," Waneta said, coming into the kitchen. "A gift from God."

"Oh, I know, I know," Lavina said quickly. "I just feel overwhelmed having one."

Waneta walked over and took a seat next to her. "Every woman does with her first. But you'll manage. I'll be here to help you, and you have your *schweschders* and your *mudder*."

"And David."

Waneta laughed. "Of course David. He'll make a *wunderbaar dat*."

Lavina finished her tea and stood. "Wait until you see the tomatoes, Mary Elizabeth. All of a sudden a lot of them ripened. I'm thinking we're going to be canning tomatoes today."

"Lucky us," Rose Anna muttered as she followed them outside. "I like doing it, but a day without it wouldn't be so bad."

"We'll be glad of all that we've canned and preserved when winter comes."

Mary Elizabeth wiped the perspiration from her forehead with the back of her hand. "Oh, if I had my way, it would be winter now."

"When winter comes you'll long for the summer." Waneta told her with a smile.

"Just think, when winter comes you'll have a *hoppli* in your arms," Mary Elizabeth told her as they walked the rows of vegetables to where the tomatoes were planted. "Oh, my, you're right. Look at how ripe they are!"

So they gathered the tomatoes. Mary Elizabeth plucked them from the vines, drawing in the rich, ripe scent of them, the pungent odor of their leaves, and placed them in a wicker basket.

"After we deal with the tomatoes, we'll see what we can do with the zucchini."

"There's always too much zucchini," Rose Anna said. "We end up making a million things from them. I think *Mamm* snuck some into fudge last year."

"I doubt that," Waneta said, chuckling. "But the men *schur* don't notice it when I put zucchini in a cake." She glanced around quickly to make sure she hadn't been overheard. "I'm taking these inside and bringing us more baskets."

Mary Elizabeth looked over at the fields.

"Checking to see how Ben and Sam are getting along?" Rose Anna asked her. She grinned.

"Why wouldn't they?" Lavina asked.

"Mary Elizabeth's seeing Ben," Rose Anna reminded her.

"So?"

"So Rose Anna's been reading historical romances again. I think she's hoping they'll engage in a duel."

"It could happen. Joseph Miller and Mark Yoder got into a fist-fight over a *maedel* last year. Remember?"

"*Ya*. But it was hardly a duel."

"Same difference," Rose Anna said with a sniff.

"What?" Lavina stared at her.

"Never mind," Mary Elizabeth told her. "Rose Anna lives in her own little world."

"Oh, you two think you're so superior because you're older. I'm taking these inside, and then maybe I'll fix some cold drinks for the men. I'm *schur* they'll appreciate me more than you two do."

"We do have to stop treating her like the *boppli* of the family," Lavina mused as she watched Rose Anna flounce off toward the house.

"Not yet," Mary Elizabeth said. "It's just too much fun teasing her."

"You're right." Lavina giggled. "Shame on us."

———— ∞ ————

So this was the new guy Mary Elizabeth was seeing.

Sam watched Ben talk to his brother David. There was no need for introductions—the two men knew each other from church. The church Sam no longer attended.

He told himself he wasn't curious about the man. Not at all. He stood to one side as David talked with Ben for a few minutes. The guy seemed nice enough—he sure wanted him to be. He cared about Mary Elizabeth even if they weren't together any more. And Ben was here helping on what could have been a day off. The Amish helped each other all the time. But this man was new to the community, so he couldn't know David all that well.

Sam wondered if Mary Elizabeth had asked him to come since she was here most Saturdays helping Lavina.

He glanced back at the house. "John came with me. Don't know what's taking him so long to come out here."

"You didn't leave the keys in your truck, did you?"

"No way. Besides, he doesn't have a license." He frowned. "What? Why the funny look?"

"He told me he's studying to get one."

"Oh." He wondered why John hadn't said anything to him. "Where's Dad?"

"He hasn't come out yet."

"I hope they're not inside arguing."

"Wouldn't be the first time."

Sam hesitated, wondering if he should go inside and see. Then he shrugged. Time was too valuable to be mediating between the two of them.

The men set to work. David was still farming the way their father had done all his life. Sam knew that wasn't just a way of keeping the peace and being grateful that their father had turned the farm over to him but also because seed had already been ordered and it was too late to change it.

So there was a lot of variety to what they'd been harvesting, and Sam felt it made for more work for David. But he wasn't about to say anything to their father. Not when things were still strained between them. David and their *dat* had made peace with each other, but that still hadn't happened with Amos and his two younger *sohns*.

John sauntered up.

"What took you so long?"

"I carried some baskets into the house for Lavina and Mary Elizabeth."

"*Danki*," David said. "She won't listen to me about lifting, and I can't be in two places at once."

John shot Sam a look that said, "So there."

But Sam couldn't help wondering if that was the real reason John appeared out here at least ten minutes after he had. He didn't think John had been flirting with Rose Anna. That relationship appeared well over. John was enjoying seeing other women— *Englisch* women—and partying.

They harvested corn for hours. It was hot, sweaty work under a blazing summer sun but mindless. Sam could let his mind wander to think about how he and Peter would be finishing up the work in Leah's new shop on Monday.

Mary Elizabeth and Rose Anna brought cold drinks and oatmeal raisin cookies out midway through the morning. He took off his straw hat and used a bandanna to wipe the sweat from his forehead while he waited for them to serve the others. Mary Elizabeth handed him a tall plastic glass of iced tea, and their gazes met.

"Thank you."

She nodded before moving on to serve Ben, and he stood to one side trying to look like he wasn't watching the two of them.

"So is this the new guy she's supposed to be seeing?" John asked in a low tone.

Sam shrugged. "Yes." He gave his brother a sharp look. "How'd you know?"

"I still hear things."

He gulped down the tea and walked over for more. Rose Anna poured it with a cool glance. Mary Elizabeth held out the plate with cookies, and John took two and strolled back to Sam. As soon as he was several steps from them, she whispered something to Rose Anna that had her wiping the sulky expression from her face.

David walked over. "Looks like the rain's going to hold off until later today."

Sam watched their father load corn onto a wagon and straighten awkwardly. When Amos took off his straw hat to fan himself, Sam frowned when he saw how red the older man's face looked.

"Have a look at Dad," he said quietly.

"Time for him to go in."

"You gonna tell him that?"

David sighed. "It's not going to be easy."

Whatever he said got the old man shambling along to the farmhouse.

"What did you say to him?"

"You have to make whatever you want his idea," David said with a grin. "That or convince him that Lavina needs him for something. I told him I needed him to check that she wasn't overdoing. And ask when lunch would be ready."

Together they walked the fields, finishing up. "You planning on trying out some of your revolutionary ideas next spring?"

"Ya."

"It'll be interesting to see what he has to say about that."

"True."

"Old man'll never change," John said as he piled corn into the wagon. "I'll take this into the barn and then go see when we're having lunch."

"Or young ones," Sam muttered and David nodded.

"Seems like we were both more mature at his age."

"I was," Sam said. "Not you."

The next thing he knew he was being doused with a bucket of water. He ripped off his hat, shaking the water from it, and stared at David. "Have you lost your mind?"

David roared with laughter. "That's for saying I wasn't mature at John's age."

Sam shook like a dog, splashing his brother with the drops. "I think that proves my point."

When David started to turn, Sam tackled him. They wrestled in the mud from the water- soaked earth like the two boys they'd been, laughing like maniacs, dodging elbows, and struggling to get the better of each other.

"Get off me, you big oaf!" Sam yelled when David bested him and sat on him,

"Who you calling an oaf?" David asked, bouncing on him for good measure.

Sam laughed and got a mouthful of mud. "Can't breathe!" he gasped with as much drama as he could muster.

David stood and Sam grabbed him around the ankles and dragged him down again.

"What on earth?"

They fell apart and stared up at Mary Elizabeth and Ben.

"Hi!" Sam grinned up at her.

"What are you two doing?" she demanded, her hands on her hips.

"What does it look like?" Sam got to his feet and reached a hand down to David, but his older *bruder* ignored it and scrambled up.

"It looks like the two of you are acting like *kinner!* What if the bishop drove past and saw the two of you?"

David winced. "She's right."

"And I rang the dinner bell!"

Sam slapped his hat on his leg and put it on his head. "David? Hungry?"

"*Ya*. Let's go." He threw his arm around Sam and they walked toward the house.

"Men!" Sam heard her mutter behind them. "Ben, why didn't you stop them?"

"Get in the middle of two guys fighting?" he asked skeptically. "Do I look *ab im kop*?"

"We weren't fighting," David turned to tell her. He swiped dirt from his cheek with his hand. "We were just having a brotherly disagreement. Right, Sam?"

"Right."

"I've never known them to behave this way," she told Ben. "The heat must have gotten to them."

Sam just chuckled. He'd enjoyed tussling with David. It brought back a lot of memories of them growing up. Later, when they'd gotten older, things hadn't been so happy with their *dat* constantly criticizing them when they worked so hard for his approval.

Mary Elizabeth hurried ahead of them and slapped open the kitchen screen door. "Well, Lavina, you'll never believe what I found David and Sam doing!"

"So let me drive you home."

Mary Elizabeth stared at Ben. "You know I came with Rose Anna."

"Can't she drive home by herself?" he asked, giving her a big smile. "Come on, Mary Elizabeth, I haven't seen you all week."

She hesitated. He was right. And she wanted to see him, she really did.

"Ben? I'm glad I caught you," David called from the door. He walked toward them carrying a plastic container. "Lavina wanted you to have a piece of pie to take home since you said you enjoyed it."

"*Danki*. That's very nice."

"It's the least we could do after you helped today. *Danki* again."

"You're welcome. It was my pleasure."

She watched Ben set the container on the back seat with as much care as if it was a small *kind*.

"Let me go ask Rose Anna if she'd mind driving home by herself."

"I'll do that. Why don't you just get inside and rest until I come back?"

"Oh. *Allrecht*."

She climbed inside and sighed. It felt *gut* to get off her feet. While the men worked in the fields, the women had cleaned and canned bushels of tomatoes and tomato sauce. Right now she felt like she smelled like a big tomato and couldn't wait to get home to shower.

A few minutes later Ben reappeared and got into the buggy. Rose Anna drove out and waved to them before she pulled out onto the road.

"*Danki* again for helping today," she said.

He glanced over and grinned. "It was . . . entertaining."

She winced. "David and Sam never behave like that. I don't know what got into them."

"They're *bruders*."

"Do *bruders* behave differently with each other than *schweschders*?"

"Of course. When's the last time you got into a tussle like that with your *schweschders*?"

"Um. Never. Well, just once, with Rose Anna."

He chuckled. "They weren't fighting. They were just fooling around."

"I know. They're just kind of old for that."

"So, this Sam is the one you dated?"

Surprised, she stared at him. "*Ya,*" she said finally. "How did you know?"

"You hear things."

She considered that. It was a surprise. She and Sam hadn't gone out for a long time and like most Amish couples were very private about seeing each other.

"He's working on the renovations on the shop you've been helping with so much?"

"*Ya.*"

"I would like it if you wouldn't see him."

She frowned. "I'm not seeing him. I take boxes of crafts to the shop. Sometimes Rose Anna is with me."

"Still, it wouldn't do for people to talk."

Mary Elizabeth didn't like the direction this conversation was going in. "No one is talking, Ben. And I've done nothing to be talked about."

He glanced back at a car behind them, waved his hand for it to go around as he pulled the buggy over onto the shoulder of the road. He muttered something under his breath that she couldn't understand. "You have rude drivers here. We don't have this kind of thing as much back in Indiana."

Mary Elizabeth squinted to see the tag on the car ahead. "They're from out of state. Tourists, probably. They don't know to share the road with buggies."

"Well, it's not right." He checked for traffic and eased the buggy back onto the road.

She watched him, surprised to see that he glowered at the road ahead for the next few miles. Everyone she knew took such a thing in stride. Well, perhaps it was just that he was new to the area. He'd learn to adjust.

"When is the shop opening?"

"Next weekend."

"*Gut.*"

"*Gut?*"

133

He nodded. "Then there'll be no need to see him after this week."

She opened her mouth to say something and then realized he was entering the driveway to her house. It had been a long, hard, hot day for both of them. There was no way she wanted to get into an argument with him. Perhaps he was a tad jealous, she thought. He didn't know that Sam wasn't interested in her or her in him.

"*Danki* for bringing me home," she said quickly and turned to get out.

He touched her arm. "Mary Elizabeth, I'm sorry if I've offended you."

She turned back to look at him and saw sincerity in his expression. "You have nothing to worry about. Sam and I haven't seen each other—dated—for more than a year. He's left the community and doesn't plan to return."

"*Gut*," he said and he smiled. "Can we have supper one night this week?"

She nodded. "Maybe Wednesday. We'll see."

"*Allrecht*. Have a *gut* night."

"You, too." She got out quickly and strode up the walk to her house. She couldn't wait to get inside and shower.

When she walked in, though, she saw her parents sitting on the sofa. Her *dat* had his arm around her *mudder*, and she was weeping.

"*Mamm, Daed*, what's wrong?"

Her *mudder* glanced up. "Your *grossmudder* has gone to be with God," she said quietly.

Mary Elizabeth sank down onto the sofa and put her arm around her. "*Nee, Mamm*, what happened?"

"She said she was tired and went to take a nap." Linda wiped her eyes with a tissue. "When your *grossdaadi* went to wake her for lunch, she'd passed."

"The doctor—"

"There was nothing he could do, *kind*."

"How is *Grossdaadi*?"

"He's sitting with her."

"Why didn't you call us at Lavina's? We'd have come right home."

"We knew you'd be home soon." Linda looked at Jacob. "We honestly have been so shocked, we haven't done much but call the doctor."

Rose Anna walked in from the kitchen. She stopped and stared at them. "What's wrong?"

"*Grossmudder* is gone."

She grinned. "Oh, *gut*, she got out of the house for a while. She loved it when I took her and *Grossdaadi* out for a drive last week. Where'd she go?"

"She passed, Rose Anna."

Huge tears welled up in her eyes. "Not *Grossmudder*."

Mary Elizabeth rose and went to hug her. Everyone loved *Grossmudder*, but Rose Anna and the older lady had had a special bond. Rose Anna was still the *boppli* of the family, and no one had spoiled her as much as *Grossmudder*.

"Can we go in and see her?" Mary Elizabeth asked their *mudder*. "*Schur.*"

Rose Anna hung back, looking frightened. "I don't want to see her!"

Linda got to her feet and gathered her youngest in her arms. "You don't have to, but *Grossdaadi* could use a hug. He's taking it hard."

Mary Elizabeth walked into the room and teared up when she saw the old man holding his *fraa*'s hand as he sat in a chair beside the bed. She hugged him and looked at her *grossmudder*. She looked so peaceful. "I will miss her smile so much."

He nodded. "So many years and still not enough." He sighed. "We must be content with what God wills."

She knelt at his feet. "Remember how she loved singing her favorite hymn?"

Rose Anna appeared in the doorway, hesitant, and then she walked in slowly, singing the hymn.

11

Mary Elizabeth and her *mudder* gently washed and dressed *Grossmudder* after the funeral home returned her body a day later.

Many Lancaster County Amish used a funeral home although Mary Elizabeth had heard some Amish communities didn't.

Her *dat* took *Grossdaadi* into the kitchen for coffee and a quiet talk.

Rose Anna couldn't handle the task of preparing her *grossmudder* for burial, but after they finished she came into the room carrying a quilt the older woman had sewn her when she was a little girl and tucked it around her. "I know she doesn't need it now to keep her warm," she said, her lips trembling. "But I want her to have it."

Mary Elizabeth hugged her. "It's perfect."

Family and friends came to pay their respects later that day. And then, the following day, they laid *Grossmudder* to rest in the Amish cemetery. Mary Elizabeth placed a bunch of wildflowers tied with a ribbon on the simple wooden casket and then stood with her *schweschders* and *mudder* and *dat* and David as she was laid to rest.

Ashes to ashes, dust to dust.

Ben came and stood at the rear of those attending. Sam, too. Mary Elizabeth was touched by Sam coming and remembered how he'd been fond of *Grossmudder* when he came to supper.

A bright yellow butterfly fluttered over the wildflowers. It reminded Mary Elizabeth of *Grossmudder*, so sunny and cheerful. She'd always been the social butterfly of the family, loving being with people. Mary Elizabeth told herself that it was selfish to want her around longer, to bounce Lavina's *boppli* on her knee, and to bless her own wedding when it happened.

Grossmudder was with God now and how *wunderbaar* was that?

After the funeral service, everyone went back to the house and the mood grew lighter. God had blessed them with Miriam for the time He had and she'd enjoyed a long, happy life with her family and friends around her.

Mary Elizabeth helped make coffee and tea and poured endless cups, served plates of food brought by attendees, and felt comforted by the kind words of many.

Still, she was glad when the door closed on the last of them and the family drew together as one. Home would be short by one person from this day on, one person who had made this house a home before Mary Elizabeth had been born.

Grossdaadi moved like a shadow to the *dawdi haus*, and her heart ached for him to face another night alone, but he gently waved away offers of another cup of coffee, some company, a bed in another room.

"Miriam is still with me," he said gently, touching his heart with his gnarled hand. "I'll be *allrecht*."

As she made her way to her own room, Mary Elizabeth thought about how he and his *fraa* had shared many happy years but many hard times as well. They'd lost two *kinner* soon after they had been born, experienced serious illness, crop failures, and so much more. Yet they had shouldered those burdens together with a strong faith that had had formed the foundation of that of her *dat* and then his *kinner*. Faith that would be passed down for generations to come.

She changed into a nightgown and readied for bed. Exhausted from the emotion of the day, she slid under the sheets and her fingers stroked the quilt that she'd sewn with instruction from her *grossmudder* and *mudder*. Sewing quilts was a legacy that had been passed down to her as well. Smiling at the thought, she drifted off to sleep.

"I dreamed of *Grossmudder* last night," Rose Anna told her the next day as they rode to the quilt class.

"You did?"

"*Ya.*" She smiled as she stared at the road ahead. "It was a nice dream. She was smiling and walking through a field of wildflowers like those you put on her grave yesterday. And Mary Elizabeth? She was walking without her cane, without pain from her arthritis."

She found herself smiling. "That was a *wunderbaar* dream. Thank you for sharing it with me." She glanced at her *schweschder*. "I think you should tell *Mamm* and *Daed*."

"You don't think they'll think my dream was silly?"

"*Nee,* Rose Anna."

"Sometimes the family acts like . . . well, like I'm silly, like I'm a little *kind*."

Mary Elizabeth frowned. "We don't think that, Rose Anna." But sometimes Rose Anna acted so immature . . . well, she supposed everyone had to mature at their own rate.

Kate greeted them with a big smile and hugs when they walked into quilt class.

"I wasn't sure you could come," she said. "I'm so sorry for your loss."

"Thank you. We didn't want to miss class. There's so much to do with the new shop opening."

"How is your family doing?"

"Good."

Kate nodded. "I was sorry to miss the funeral. I got called in for mandatory overtime."

Women began coming in to sew. They greeted Mary Elizabeth and Rose Anna with condolences, touching Mary Elizabeth's heart.

A nearby table was stacked with crafts—quilts, table runners, all sorts of things. After walking around helping the women with whatever project they were working on, she and Rose Anna began packing the goods into cardboard boxes that had been stacked nearby.

"You sure you don't mind delivering these to the shop?" Kate asked, her forehead puckered with worry.

"Not at all. I like seeing the progress."

And last time she'd visited she and Sam had made peace with each other. They wouldn't get to talk much today since Rose Anna would be with her, but that was fine.

Several women helped carry the boxes to the buggy when the class was over.

"I've arranged for a bus to take us all to the shop on Thursday, before opening day," Kate told them. "I think it'll be a fun outing, and they deserve it. They've worked so hard."

She pulled Mary Elizabeth aside. "We're not going to announce it beforehand in the press for security reasons. But I'd like you and Rose Anna to come. And Lavina, if she feels up to it."

"We'll be there."

She took the last box and placed it in the buggy. "See you on Thursday."

Rose Anna climbed into the passenger seat of the buggy. "You *allrecht*?"

"*Ya*, why?"

"You look sad."

Mary Elizabeth told her what Kate had said about taking the women to the shop—but having to keep it private.

"Imagine, some of the women still have to worry about their safety."

They still saw women coming in with bruises and sometimes, with children with wide, frightened eyes. It hadn't gotten easier to see them.... She hadn't gotten used to it, but it was something she'd had to expect to see and know that this place would help them to feel safe and find a way to build new lives.

And the crafts the women made would help fund their new futures.

They drove away with a buggy loaded with the fruits of their labors and their dreams for financial freedom. Mary Elizabeth liked helping in this effort just fine.

<hr />

Sam wiped down the last of the new shelving just as Mary Elizabeth walked in carrying a box. He'd hoped she'd come before he left for the day.

"Let me help you with that," he said and hurried to take it from her.

"*Danki*. Rose Anna is bringing another box in a minute. We're kind of staggering bringing them in since someone stole a quilt from the buggy last year."

The man who'd done it—Carrie's former boyfriend—was now in jail for assaulting her and couldn't steal from them again, but Mary Elizabeth wasn't taking any chances. Not with the hard work of the women at the shelter.

"I'll put this in the storeroom and help you both."

"Where's Peter?"

"Talking to Leah."

She headed toward the front door of the shop. "I'll go get another box."

Sam felt torn. He wanted to go help get boxes from the buggy for her, but couldn't leave the shop open. When he walked over to the entranceway to Leah's other shop, he caught Peter's eye. Peter nodded and strolled back.

"What's up?"

"Mary Elizabeth and Rose Anna are bringing in boxes."

Rose Anna walked in just then. She smiled. "Hello, Peter."

Sam's eyebrows went up as he watched Peter move faster than he'd ever seen him move. Peter took the box from Rose Anna and chatted with her as they walked to the storeroom. Rose Anna's eyelashes fluttered like butterfly wings as she smiled up at Peter.

He shook his head. The three Zook *schweschders* were so different. He'd never seen Lavina or Mary Elizabeth flirt so openly. They were more serious than Rose Anna. More mature. Well, Rose Anna was still young...just eighteen.

Leah bustled into the shop, her faded blue eyes alive with excitement as they brought in the last of the boxes.

"All ready to set up?" she asked Mary Elizabeth.

"I *schur* am," Mary Elizabeth said. "Kate said she'll stop by after her shift to help."

"*Gut.* Then she can offer some suggestions. Sam, Peter, if you could help getting boxes out of the storeroom and set them on the tables and shelves where I'm going to display them."

"Just tell us where," Peter said with a grin. "It's great to see everything coming together."

"Let's start with the less expensive items and as we move into the back of the shop do the more complicated, more expensive items. I want to put seasonal things—for Thanksgiving and Christmas and holidays—on the big table at the rear. The crafts made by the *kinner* at the shelter should have a special table of their own with a sign that says that they made them. I think people will like that."

Sam liked that idea just fine. Leah was known for her good business sense.

She moved about, assigning tables, watching Sam and Peter set the boxes where she wanted them. Then she asked them to hang some quilts on the walls to brighten the space and show off the patterns.

Kate came after she finished work and brought her husband and several large pizzas to sustain the workers. Sam heard Peter's stomach growl and watched him head for the pizza the minute the last quilt was hung.

Leah's *grossdochders* wandered over after Stitches in Time closed and worked on the window displays. No one who stopped to look in the Stitches in Time windows could resist going into the shop to look over its quilts, woven goods, and all manner of fabrics and kits to make things.

Kate smiled at Sam and Peter when they stopped to help themselves to pizza and soft drinks. "It's so nice to see so many helping us with this shelter project."

Sam knew she meant the Amish—Leah and her *grossdochders*, Sam and Peter after they'd completed their paid work on the shop, as well as Mary Elizabeth and Rose Anna.

"We all help each other," he said. "The *Englisch* are so supportive of our mud sales and other things."

"Don't you be talking to Kate about mud sales," her husband, Malcolm, said as he came over to get some pizza. "I had to drag her away from the last one before she spent all our money."

"Oh, hush," she told him, laughing as she elbowed him. "As I remember, you bought some things at the last mud sale."

"It was for a good cause," he said loftily.

"Yeah, now our garage has so much stuff stored in it we don't have room for our cars."

Sam put a second slice of pizza on his paper plate and watched Mary Elizabeth approach the table with the food. He'd wondered how long it would take her to do so. She loved pizza and could eat as much of it as him.

She lifted the lid to one of the boxes. "Oh, pepperoni! My favorite!"

"Uh-oh, better hurry and get more if you want it," Sam told Peter. "Pizza Monster is here."

She wrinkled her nose at him. "Not funny."

"I do remember the two of you fighting over the last piece that time I went for pizza," Peter said.

"Any plain cheese?" Rose Anna asked as she opened a box.

"What's the point of pizza with no pepperoni?" Mary Elizabeth asked as she raised a slice and eyed it with appreciation.

"I agree." Peter watched Rose Anna choose a slice of plain cheese and shook his head sadly. "Oh, well, leaves more pepperoni for us."

"Maybe not," Sam told him and gestured with his slice at Mary Elizabeth. She was already on her second slice.

He loved her expression when she realized others were staring at her. Saying she looked embarrassed was putting it mildly. "I guess I'm being selfish," she said and started to put it back in the box.

"Don't be silly," Kate said. "No one eats one slice."

"That's for sure. Kate's had three," Malcolm told them with a grin.

"Hey, I missed lunch, and I had to chase a bad guy down two blocks to make an arrest," she said as she popped the top on a can of diet soda.

"You didn't mention that earlier."

"Missing lunch is no big deal."

"Having to chase a bad guy."

She shrugged. "All in a day's work." She jumped up. "Say, Leah, what do you think of putting the lap quilts on a separate display table?"

Malcolm stared at the retreating back of his wife. "We'll talk about that later," he murmured.

Sam wondered how he handled having a *fraa* who did such a dangerous job.

"You okay?" he finally asked him quietly as he watched the other man looking so worried.

He nodded. "I know she can take care of herself. And it's work she loves." He sighed. "I'd never ask her to stop working as a cop because it worries me. That would be selfish. She makes a difference."

"Naomi Hershberger was killed when she was working in the fields with her husband," Mary Elizabeth said. "Remember, she was struck by a hay baler that was being pulled by their mules.

And an Amish woman in Ohio was hurt when her dress was pulled into a conveyor belt."

"Good point," Malcolm said. He stood and patted his stomach. "Well, I'm going to see what else I can do and leave some pizza for the rest of you."

"That was nice of you," Sam told her quietly.

She shrugged. "Sometimes people focus on the obvious— Kate's a police officer and that's dangerous work. But we don't know what will happen in any one day. It's God's will after all. We should do what we feel led to and for Kate, that's the job she's doing."

They returned to work and as dusk was falling Leah came to thank Mary Elizabeth. "You came in your buggy, right? Then you and Rose Anna should be heading home before it's dark. Tell Lavina we're sorry she couldn't come."

Mary Elizabeth nodded. "I will. I can't wait until the women at the shelter see the shop tomorrow. We'll be back then."

"*Danki* for your help."

"It's been such fun."

She went to find Rose Anna who was standing a little closer than was proper to Peter in the storeroom. They jumped apart, and Peter's ears reddened. Mary Elizabeth knew from having gone to *schul* with him that this was a sign he was embarrassed.

"We need to go home now. See you later, Peter."

"*Ya*, well, *gut-n-owed* to you both." But Mary Elizabeth saw he was looking at Rose Anna, not at her.

"I'll walk you out," Sam said.

"*Danki*, but that's not necessary."

"Humor me." He held open the front door to the shop and they walked outside.

He escorted them to their buggy and then, after Mary Elizabeth drove off, followed them home to make sure they arrived safely. There were so many tourists on the road this time of the year. Some of them were curious and followed too closely or passed them in an unsafe way. When automobiles and buggies collided, few in the fragile buggies survived.

So he followed them and fortunately Mary Elizabeth didn't notice.

Mary Elizabeth sat in the bus Kate had chartered to take the women from the shelter to the new shop.

Everyone chattered at once as they boarded the bus. The noise level and excitement rose during the short time it took to drive there.

And then, as the bus drew closer, silence fell. Mary Elizabeth glanced over at Kate, and with a tilt of her head, Kate indicated she should look at Pearl, the woman who ran the shelter. Pearl dabbed at her eyes as the bus made the last turn to town.

The driver parked in front of the shop and opened the door. The women filed off the bus, some of them holding the hands of their *kinner* tightly. They crowded around the display windows and gazed at their work.

"Look! That's my baby quilt!" Edna Mae exclaimed, pointing at it. "Carrie, that's your set of mug mats!"

Several of the women stepped aside so Carrie could see.

Leah herself opened the front door and beamed at them. "Our special guests have arrived! Welcome!"

The women surged inside. They swarmed the display tables and looked awed at the crafts that had been artfully arranged on them.

There were more than a few tears shed and hugs exchanged as the women roamed around. Leah mingled, patting a shoulder here, speaking a few encouraging words there.

The *kinner* loved their table and stood, hands behind their backs as if they'd been told not to touch, even though these were the things they'd made. Anna, one of Leah's *grossdochders*, invited them to visit the refreshment table and sample cookies supplied

146

by an Amish bakery down the street. Mary Elizabeth loved how they showed off their good manners by taking only one cookie and not spilling their little paper cups of fruit punch.

"I don't know who loves the shop more—the women or the children," Pearl said as she came to stand next to Mary Elizabeth.

Kate brought a young woman over and introduced her as a reporter for the local paper. She'd been invited to do a story on the shop and was talking to some of the women but had agreed she wouldn't take photos of the women or their children because of security concerns.

Pearl had trouble holding back tears as she spoke about how Kate had come to her offering to teach a quilting class to the women at the shelter.

"She recruited other volunteers like Lavina Stoltzfus and Mary Elizabeth and Rose Anna Zook," she said, gesturing at them, then turned to smile at Leah. "And Leah here has donated a lot of fabric and supplies. Then one day Leah approached Kate and me about the women sewing crafts for a new shop Leah was thinking of opening next to her Stitches in Time shop. And now we have this."

She stopped and had to mop her eyes. "This is a place for the work made by women who need hope, need a place to call home. Some of them didn't even know how to sew when they came to the shelter, but they learned and had fun being creative and grew proud of their efforts."

Pearl glanced around. "Life beat them down, but they were brave and came to the shelter and learned how to start looking out for themselves and their children and break the cycle of abuse." She took a deep breath. "And now they have a place to sell their work so they can become independent and one day use what they've earned to get an apartment and get themselves jobs to support themselves and their children."

Turning to the reporter, she smiled self-deprecatingly. "I'm sorry, I've gone on and on. I just am so grateful to Leah and Kate and Mary Elizabeth and Rose Anna and Lavina for making this shop possible. I hope everyone in the community comes in to see what wonderful crafts are displayed here."

The reporter turned to Leah. "So tell me why you decided to open another shop and one that features crafts made by *Englisch* women."

"The community has been so good to my family, buying quilts and other things made by my granddaughters and others," she said quietly. "They've supported our Amish community for many years as well as through mud sales and such. This is just our small way of helping others. We have some wonderful crafts here for bargain prices. I'm looking forward to our official opening later this week and hope we have a great turnout."

She waited until the woman finished writing and closed her notebook then invited her to help herself to refreshments.

Kate rushed in a few minutes later. "I wasn't sure I was going to make it in time. Got held up at work." She glanced around, nodding and smiling hello at the women and children from the shelter. The reporter waved to her, and Kate waved back. "Excuse me, I promised to give her a few minutes." She hurried over, spoke with the reporter, and had her picture taken with Pearl in front of a display.

"Such a busy woman," Mary Elizabeth told Leah. "I don't know how she does all she does."

"It's not easy for anyone to balance a family with work," Leah said. Her eyes were on her *grossdochders* working in the Stitches in Time shop they could see through the entranceway Sam and Peter had made between the shops. One of their *kinner* slept in a cradle near them.

Some of the women had noticed the entranceway as well. "Is it all right if we walk over there?" one of them asked.

"Of course!" Leah responded. "I have some fabric set aside I thought I'd see if any of you would like."

"I need some thread," Rose Anna said, and she deserted them.

The word spread that they could visit the other shop—fabric! sewing supplies!—and the women drifted over until Mary

Elizabeth and Kate and Pearl were the only ones left in Sewn in Hope.

"We may not get them back on the bus," Pearl said with a chuckle.

But the time came that they had to board the bus and return to the shelter. "Maybe we can come back again one day," she said and walked over to round everyone up to leave.

The ride back to the shelter was surprisingly quiet. It wasn't an unhappy silence, though. The women just looked a lit tle . . . stunned was the best way Mary Elizabeth could describe it.

"Are they okay?" she quietly asked Pearl, who sat in between her and Rose Anna. "No one's talking."

"Some of these women haven't had enough reason to be proud of themselves," Pearl said. "They've had husbands and boyfriends beat down their confidence and self-esteem for so long. Today showed them they could be productive, could make some money, not just enjoy sewing or anything else as a hobby." She patted Mary Elizabeth's hand. "It was a very good thing."

"I remember the first time I saw my quilts displayed for sale in Stitches in Time," she said slowly. "I was . . . awed."

Pearl opened the bag with the Stitches in Time logo. "Look what I bought in Leah's shop."

The framed sampler was of a tiny quilt with stitching that read, "When life gives you scraps, make a quilt." She grinned. "I thought I'd hang it in the sewing room."

Mary Elizabeth had enjoyed a comfortable life with loving parents, a home that provided security, and a job getting to be creative and work at her own pace at home. She sent up a prayer of thanks to God as the bus pulled into the shelter parking lot. Then she turned to Rose Anna.

"Come on," she said. "Let's go home."

12

I wonder why Peter and Sam weren't there today."

Mary Elizabeth glanced over at Rose Anna. "I expect they had to work."

"But it was a special day."

"For the women. For Peter and Sam it was more a job."

Rose Anna shrugged. "I still thought they'd be there."

"Maybe they will be for opening day." Mary Elizabeth hesitated, then plunged ahead. "About the other day—"

"I know what you're going to say," Rose Anna burst out.

"You do?" She kept her tone mild and stared straight ahead at the road.

"*Ya.* Now I'm going to get a lecture about whatever you think you saw when you walked in on Peter and me in the storeroom."

"What do I think I saw?"

"We weren't kissing."

"That's *gut.*"

"We weren't touching either."

"*Allrecht.*"

"I do know how to behave." Rose Anna folded her arms across her chest. "And you're not my *mudder.*"

"*Nee,* I'm not. I'm your *schweschder,* and I'm just concerned about you."

"Are you going to say something to *Mamm?*"

151

Mary Elizabeth took a deep breath and then shook her head. "It's all John's fault."

A car passed the buggy. Mary Elizabeth concentrated on it until it was safely past and ahead of them on the road. "It is?"

"I could be so happy if John would just cooperate with God's will."

"Oh?"

"If he'd just realize he's the man God set aside for me, I wouldn't have even looked at Peter."

What could she say to that? Their street was coming up soon. She only had a few minutes. "If John doesn't believe he is, if he doesn't want to be with you, then you can't do anything."

"You think I don't know that? Why do you think I decided to start seeing someone else?" She glanced out her window at the passing scenery.

"As long as you're not just seeing Peter as a substitute for John."

Rose Anna turned in her seat to look at her. "I'm not. I've always liked Peter."

Mary Elizabeth hoped she was telling the truth. Rose Anna had certainly flirted with him the last few times they'd been together. She hoped her *schweschder* wasn't using him as salve for her ego. Rose Anna's ego had taken a beating when John told her he didn't want to be with her.

Mary Elizabeth saw a buggy parked in front of their house when she pulled into the driveway of their house.

"Who is it?" Rose Anna asked, craning her head to see.

Mary Elizabeth's heart sank when she saw Ben sitting on the front porch with their *dat*. "Ben."

"Did you know he was going to be here?" Rose Anna asked as they got out of the buggy at the barn and began unhitching their horse.

"*Nee*."

"You don't look happy."

"I wasn't expecting him. I'm just tired. It's been a long day."

"Why don't you go on in? I'll finish here."

"You're *schur*?"

"*Ya*."

Mary Elizabeth smoothed the skirt of her dress and went in the back door. "Hi, *Mamm*. How long has Ben been here?"

"About half an hour," she said, turning from the refrigerator with a bowl of butter. "He looked so disappointed you weren't home yet that your *dat* invited him to supper."

"That was kind of you." She set her purse down on the counter.

Her *mudder* took a bowl of butter from the refrigerator and set it on the table. She studied her face. "Is there a problem? Should he not have invited him?"

Mary Elizabeth realized she was too easy to read since both her *schweschder* and her *mudder* had guessed how she felt about Ben's unexpected visit.

"*Nee*, I'm just tired."

"Did you have fun going to the new store with the women from the shelter?"

"I did. I'll have to tell you about it later."

"Go let the men know supper's ready."

She walked to the front of the house, opened the door, and summoned a smile. "*Daed*, *Mamm* says supper's ready. *Gut-n-owed*, Ben."

He stood and walked toward her. "*Gut-n-owed*. Hope you don't mind my stopping by."

"Of course not." Now that he was giving her his charming grin and looking happy to see her, she realized she was glad he'd stopped by.

"Your *dat* was kind enough to invite me to supper," he said as he stepped into the house. He took a deep appreciative sniff as they approached the kitchen. "Something smells wonderful."

"Just a simple baked chicken," Linda said, setting a platter on the table. "It's cooling down a bit, but it's still too hot to cook much."

She turned to Rose Anna who'd come in from unhitching the buggy. "Would you go tell *Grossdaadi* supper's ready? And don't let him say he's not hungry. He needs to eat."

Rose Anna returned with *Grossdaadi*. He said hello to everyone, took a seat, and ate. Not much but he ate. It just seemed to her that he was a pale shadow of himself, still going through the motions.

Well, no one expected him to get over the loss of his *fraa*. There wasn't any "getting over" someone anyway. She knew that from watching others and from what she'd gone through with Sam.

Bowls of potato salad, corn on the cob, and cole slaw went around the table. Mary Elizabeth had enjoyed cookies at the shop so she wasn't that hungry, but Ben's appetite more than made up for hers.

Once again, Ben and her *dat* talked so much about farming that the women found themselves having their own conversation. *Grossdaadi* didn't contribute much to the conversation, but he was eating, Mary Elizabeth noted with satisfaction. Several times her *mudder* quietly urged him to have a second helping of his favorite—the potato salad.

And several times, she noticed *Grossdaadi* watching Ben, but he didn't engage him in conversation.

"Baked chicken's my second favorite way to eat chicken," Ben told her when they walked outside to sit on the porch after dessert.

"Oh?"

"Fried's best."

Maybe he didn't mean it as a criticism of her *mudder's* cooking. But she didn't figure you should eat supper at someone's table and act like what you were eating was somehow second.

"Men don't realize how hot it is standing over a stove in the summer," she told him, trying to keep her voice level. "It's a lot easier on the cook on a hot day to put the chicken in the oven and walk away while it bakes."

He stopped rocking and took a long look at her. "I'm sorry, I didn't mean to offend."

She shrugged.

"So I guess I better not ask when we can go for a picnic and have some of your *wunderbaar* fried chicken," he teased.

"*Nee*," she said shortly.

Then she felt bad. "I'm sorry, I'm just really tired. It was a long day. Long week. Harvesting the kitchen gardens here and at Lavina's, my quilting work, and the new shop opening."

"You didn't have to help at the shop," he said. "Was Sam there?"

She stood. "I need to help Rose Anna with the dishes."

To her relief, he left. She returned to the kitchen. Her *gross-daadi* still sat at the table, finishing a piece of pie.

He looked up. "Whatever happened to Sam? I miss playing checkers with him."

She sat down. "He moved away from the community, into town, *Grossdaadi*. You remember I told you."

"Oh, *ya, ya*." He sipped his coffee. "Well, if you ever see him, tell him I miss playing checkers with him."

"I will." She glanced over at Rose Anna standing at the sink. Their gazes met and Rose Anna nodded. Getting up, Mary Elizabeth fetched the checkerboard. "I'll play a game with you."

He grinned and pushed his empty pie plate aside.

⸺⸺

Sam didn't know what he liked better—depositing another check for the second job or going with Peter to do an estimate for another renovation.

Both meant money in the bank, money he was saving for a place of his own. Oh, it would probably be one he shared with John until one of them got married. But it would be for a home, not a dingy little apartment they didn't own and where the rent might go up every six months.

He just didn't know yet where that place would be...he'd left the Amish community when he and his *dat* couldn't get along, but he hadn't embraced the *Englisch* community like John and used the time for *rumschpringe*. Instead he'd lived the same kind of life as he had when he'd lived at home—working long hours, staying home most evenings.

And he'd found himself increasingly being pulled back to the Amish community by friends like Peter and work for other Amish like Leah.

"I have something to show you after we look over this place," Peter said as Sam drove them to the location.

"What?"

"It's a surprise."

"I hate surprises," Sam reminded him as he pulled into the driveway of the house Peter pointed out.

"Tough."

"So where are the owners?"

"Be patient. We're a little early." He relaxed against the seat. "So I wonder how it went at Leah's shop yesterday. With the preview for the women from the shelter."

"Haven't heard. Are we still going to stop in for a few minutes today? It's the official opening day?"

"*Schur.* Wouldn't miss it."

Sam drummed his fingers on the steering wheel and considered the house. It looked...sad like it needed someone to help fix it up. The porch sagged, paint was peeling, and from what he could see of the roof, there was definitely a new one in its future.

"What time is it?"

"Five minutes later than the last time you asked. What's your hurry? You got a hot date or something?"

He snorted.

A car pulled up, and a young *Englisch* couple climbed out.

"I'm Randy Smith and this is my wife, Becky. And this is our new house we're hoping we won't come to refer to as the 'money pit,'" he said, sticking out his hand to Sam, then Peter.

Becky smacked him on his arm. "Don't you dare call the house that." She gave them a big smile. "I love this house. It just needs some love." Turning, she climbed the stairs to the porch.

Randy rubbed fingers together in a gesture to indicate spending money and quickly turned it into a wave when Becky jerked her head around. "We're coming, honey," he called.

The four of them went into the house, a two-story that looked almost as bad inside as it did out. The husband walked around pointing out things that needed to be addressed and both Peter and Sam made notes. The wife drifted around and asked if a window seat could be added here and a French door out to the garden there.

Sam figured this was what people meant when they said someone had stars in her eyes. She was in love with the place, and her husband regarded her indulgently but clearly had his mind set on the dollars they would have to spend.

After they'd gone through the house, the man turned to Sam. "You've been quiet. What do you think?"

"House has good bones."

He laughed and slapped Sam on the back. "A man of few words. I like it." He turned to Peter. "Can we do this without breaking the bank?" he asked him, looking worried.

"We'll give you an estimate in a couple days, see what you think," Peter told him. "You could take it in stages, fix the most urgent things you need to do to have a safe, comfortable place to live and work on the cosmetic things as you go."

"That would be great," he said. "We're staying with her parents while you do the work so if we could do the most important first . . ." Becky nodded and wandered off into the kitchen.

"I want to make Becky happy," he told them quietly. "You know, 'happy wife, happy life' like my dad used to say. But it's taking a lot of money to buy the place."

"Property's expensive in this county," Sam agreed.

"Tell me about it. Honey, time to go!" he called to his wife.

157

She came into the room, a drift of cobwebs on her hair, dust on her hands. He brushed his hand over her head without remarking on the cobwebs, and they walked outside.

Sam and Peter followed them out. The men shook hands. Becky reached into her purse and found a tissue for hers before she responded.

"Glad we called you," Randy said. "We'll look forward to hearing from you."

"Don't forget my window seat and those doors out to the back yard," she reminded Sam and Peter.

"We won't," Peter assured her.

Just as they drove off Sam saw a buggy coming down the road. When it drew closer, he thought he recognized the driver as she pulled over onto the grass in front of the house.

"This is a surprise," Mary Elizabeth called out.

Sam walked over to her. "*Gut-n-owed*. Going home?"

She nodded. "I was at the shelter for a couple of hours."

Peter joined them. "How did it go yesterday?"

"Oh, I wish you both could have been there," she said, visibly moved. "The women couldn't believe it, and the *kinner* were so excited. It was such a joy to see them."

"That's *gut*," Sam said.

"We're stopping by for an hour or two now that we're finished here," Peter told her. He turned to Sam. "I'm going to get in the truck and make a call on my cell. Take your time."

"I'm glad I saw you here," she said. "*Grossdaadi* asked about you. Said he missed playing checkers with you."

He grinned. "Really? I always liked him. How is he doing?"

"Maybe you could stop by and see for yourself? Play a game or two after supper?"

"Just tell me when."

"Is tomorrow too soon for you?"

"As it happens I'm free."

"*Gut*. Then we'll see you at the usual time."

"I'll be there. And Mary Elizabeth? Thanks for asking me."

"You're *wilkumm*. And don't let *Grossdaadi* cheat."

His eyes widened. "Cheat?"

She laughed at his dry tone. "You know he does. *Gut-n-owed*, Sam."

"Good night, Mary Elizabeth."

He watched her check for traffic and then pull back onto the road before he walked to his truck and climbed inside. Peter sat jotting notes on his clipboard as he spoke on his cell.

Sam started the truck and drove Peter home. Tonight he would be eating some scraped-together meal with his brother John, but he could look forward to a delicious meal with Mary Elizabeth and her family tomorrow.

The day had been long, one that sent you home with muscles that ached a little from hard work at the day job. Then he and Peter had met with a couple who'd probably give them their next job if he was any judge of character. And then he'd run into Mary Elizabeth and had her smile at him and invited him to supper and a friendly game or two of checkers with an old man who remembered him.

It had been a *gut* day.

And Peter made it even better when he had him stop at a small farm.

"The Fisher place," he said. "Did you hear Elias died?"

"I did."

"His *fraa* moved to Ohio to be near her *dochder*. Sam, the farm is up for sale. The bishop is helping arrange things for her. He gave me the key so we could look at it. So *you* could look at it, Sam."

Feeling a little dazed, Sam shut off the engine, got out of the truck, and followed him up the walk to the front door.

"I *schur* wish cold weather would get here," Mary Elizabeth said as they sewed on their quilts in the sewing room. "Even sewing holiday quilts isn't helping me feel cooler."

She got up and walked over to the window. "I know I complain about the cold, but right now I'd take a blizzard."

"You want to go for ice cream?" Rose Anna asked, looking up with a distracted air. She'd been trying to piece a new quilt pattern for hours. "Go get *Grossdaadi*. He's always ready for ice cream."

"*Nee,* no ice cream now," their *mudder* said with a chuckle. She glanced at the clock on the wall and set down a quilt she'd been sewing. "It's time for lunch."

"I'll help," Mary Elizabeth said. She was nearly done with her quilt.

They went down to the kitchen. Linda made sandwiches and Mary Elizabeth cut up peaches, strawberries, and melon for a fruit salad. Who wanted something hot on such a warm day?

That reminded her that Sam was coming to supper.

"What shall I make for supper?" she asked her *mudder*.

Linda looked up from the sandwich makings and smiled. "Whatever you like."

Mary Elizabeth went to the refrigerator and examined the contents. "I'd love just a big salad, but I don't suppose the men would be content with that," she mused.

She remembered Ben's comment about fried chicken and frowned. There was chicken and hamburger in the freezer behind big packages of vegetables and fruit they'd chosen to freeze rather than can. Hmm.

"What do you think of using the hamburger for haystacks with a big pan of baked beans and corn on the cob on the side? I don't know about you, but I can't get enough corn on the cob this time of year."

"Sounds good. We have plenty of ripe tomatoes and some lettuce for the haystacks."

Mary Elizabeth set the ground beef out to thaw, got out a couple of cans of pork and beans and a package of bacon. She stirred some brown sugar and mustard into the beans and poured them into a baking dish. Then she topped them with several slices of bacon. She'd have to heat the oven, but they were going back upstairs to sew after lunch. Blackberry cobbler could bake toward the end of the time for the beans. Done.

Her *mudder* set the table, then called upstairs for Rose Anna. She turned to Mary Elizabeth. "Why don't you get *Grossdaadi* while I pour some iced tea?"

She nodded and walked over to knock on the door to the *dawdi haus*. When he didn't answer, she opened the door and ventured inside cautiously. He was known for napping during the day, but she heard him talking. Was it possible a friend had stopped by to see him? The *dawdi haus* had a separate entrance. She found him sitting in the recliner he loved in the small living room, sound asleep, his wire-rimmed glasses half-on, half-off his nose. He was talking in his sleep and gesturing with his hands as if he was eating.

"Miriam, you make the best pot roast in Lancaster County," he was saying, as he appeared to be eating. "I hope there's pie for dessert. I love your pie. Doesn't matter what kind. Any kind of pie my *fraa* makes is the best."

Tears welled up in her eyes. In his dreams he was sharing a meal with the woman he'd been married to for so long. She turned and went to get her *mudder*.

"*Mamm*, come see."

Linda paled. "Oh no, don't tell me something's wrong with him."

"*Nee, nee*, he's fine. Look." She watched as her *mudder* stepped into the room and saw *Grossdaadi* talking in his sleep. They both listened for a few minutes. He was still "eating" and complimenting his *fraa* in his dreams.

"Let's not wake him," her *mudder* said, taking her hand and leading her from the room. They tiptoed out, and Linda shut the door. "Let him sleep a while. It's his chance to be with Miriam."

Mary Elizabeth pulled two paper napkins from a holder on the table and handed her one. She wiped her own eyes. "He misses her so."

Rose Anna walked into the room and frowned. "What's the matter?" Her gaze went to the door to the *dawdi haus*. "Is *Grossdaadi allrecht*?"

Linda nodded. "He's fine." She told her what they'd just witnessed, and Rose Anna's expression turned sad. "Maybe we can take a ride later and get him some ice cream."

"Sam's coming for supper. *Grossdaadi* mentioned him and said he missed playing checkers with him. Sam said he'd love to come and play a game or two with him."

"He liked Sam." She glanced at the table. "I'll go get *Daed*."

They were halfway through lunch when the door to the *dawdi haus* opened and Abe shuffled out.

"*Grossdaadi*, we didn't want to wake you," Mary Elizabeth said.

"I was just resting my eyes," he told her as he took a seat at the table.

Linda chuckled. "You were sound asleep."

"Just resting my eyes." He bent his head to say a blessing for the meal then took a sandwich and placed it on his plate. His expression brightened when Rose Anna handed him a small bowl of the fruit salad.

"*Grossdaadi*, Sam's coming to supper tonight," Mary Elizabeth said. "He said he'd love to play checkers with you."

"*Gut, Gut.*"

"I told him not to let you cheat."

He pretended to look offended. "I never cheat."

"You always cheat," her *dat* said with a grin.

"Only because you do," he retorted. His eyes twinkled behind his glasses.

"Just for that I'll play a game with you before I go back to work."

"You're on!"

But *Grossdaadi* seemed in no hurry. He chewed his sandwich slowly, and her *dat* was rolling his eyes as Abe then savored each bite of fruit salad with a pleasure that seemed exaggerated. Finally Jacob got up, fetched the checkerboard, and put it on the table.

The women cleared the table, leaving the two men having a mock argument over the board, and returned to the sewing room to work.

"Wonder who'll win?" Rose Anna said as she went back to piecing her new quilt pattern.

"*Grossdaadi* will," Mary Elizabeth told her as she studied the pattern. "He always does."

Rose Anna grinned. "Only because he cheats better than *Daed*."

Mary Elizabeth laughed. "Well, Sam knows about *Grossdaadi*."

13

Mary Elizabeth heard the knock on the door and went to answer it. She said a silent prayer hoping it was Sam.

The last thing she needed was Ben stopping by unannounced.

Schur enough it was Sam carrying a bunch of daisies. "I brought these for your *mudder*."

"Why, Sam, that was so sweet!" Linda said behind Mary Elizabeth.

"Just a thank-you for all the meals you've cooked and invited me to share over the years," he told her as he stepped inside.

"Actually, Mary Elizabeth cooked tonight, but I'll share," her *mudder* said.

Jacob stood and dropped his copy of *The Budget*, the Amish newspaper, into his recliner, shook Sam's hand, and followed them into the kitchen.

Grossdaadi was already seated at the table, and his grin was wide when he saw Sam. "There you are!"

"Good to see you," Sam told him as he rounded the table to shake his hand. "I hear you want a game of checkers."

"*Ya*. You think you can beat me?"

"I *schur* do."

"We'll see about that. I trounced Jacob here in both games today."

"He cheats," Jacob mouthed behind the old man's head.

Linda beamed at Sam as she arranged the daisies in a white ceramic pitcher and set it in the middle of the table.

Sam took a seat after the women did. Jacob asked Abe to bless the meal, and Sam thought about how he had faltered for a time, thinking God had turned His back on him when he had to leave his home.

Rose Anna peppered him with questions about his life outside the community until her *dat* frowned at her.

"I missed this!" Sam exclaimed when he realized what they were having for supper. Haystacks were an Amish favorite at all sorts of gatherings, especially fundraisers. A bowl of crushed soda crackers made its way around the table. Each person dumped a handful or two on his or her plate, then a mound of browned hamburger mixed with taco seasoning, chopped lettuce and tomato, and green pepper and onion fresh from the garden. A couple spoonsful of rice, grated cheddar cheese, and Sam's favorite—homemade salsa—and it was a haystack of edible delight.

He sighed happily as he dug into it. What could have been better on a hot summer night than this dish he remembered eating at so many special occasions in his youth?

His *dat* had growled at his *mudder* once when she served it. "Man doesn't want a salad after working all day in the fields," he'd complained. But the dish was hearty enough with all the ground beef and such. And his *mudder* had helped them harvesting in the fields and had hardly had time to come inside and slave over a hot stove afterward.

"Is it *allrecht*?" Mary Elizabeth asked him, and he realized he'd been frowning.

"Perfect," he said, looking up and smiling at her. "I remember having this at so many youth gatherings. Remember when Naomi Rose's *mudder* added too much taco seasoning in the hamburger?"

She laughed and nodded. "We drained two pitchers of lemonade that day."

Their gazes locked, held as they both remembered that day. The clink of silverware, the family talking as they ate, faded away.

Mary Elizabeth didn't know how long they might have sat there staring at each other. Her *mudder* tapped her on her arm. "This was such a *gut* idea. Look how your *grossdaadi* is cleaning his plate."

They looked at him and he grinned and wiped his mouth with a paper napkin. "Miriam and I had this in Pinecraft last year when we went there for the winter. Hundreds of people showed up. Don't remember what they were raising money for, but everyone *schur* did like having a taste of home." He paused and looked thoughtful. "She *schur* did like being in Florida and visiting the beach when it was cold and snowing back here."

He set his fork on his empty plate and craned his neck to see what was on top of the stove. "Is that blackberries I smell?"

Mary Elizabeth smiled at him. "*Ya.* Blackberry cobbler."

"Do we have ice cream?"

Linda laughed. "Of course."

"I'll get it," Rose Anna said.

Mary Elizabeth rose, pulled on oven mitts, and carried the still warm baking dish to the table.

Sam cleaned his plate and watched as she scooped up generous servings of the cobbler and passed the bowls to Linda so she could top them with vanilla ice cream.

The taste of the warm berries on his tongue brought back another memory. He and Mary Elizabeth had gone blackberry picking after a picnic once. They'd seen the wild berries growing alongside the road, and he'd stopped his buggy so they could climb out and pick them. The two of them had eaten more of the sun-warmed berries than they'd put in a bucket he got from the buggy.

That day he'd dared to kiss her. They'd both been so young, and the kiss had been innocent. The taste of her lips had been sweeter than the ripe berries.

Once again, their gazes locked, and he watched a blush creep up her cheeks.

She remembered.

Suddenly the room felt too warm, too close. Sam wanted to pull his collar away from his neck. He concentrated on the cooling ice cream and told himself he couldn't do this again. This family, this home, had been his family and his home away from the troubled one where his *dat* berated everyone and his *mudder* pretended nothing was wrong.

And Mary Elizabeth belonged to someone else now. He'd practically thrust her into Ben's path. He'd been crazy for sure.

Finally the meal was over, and the family went their separate ways: Rose Anna to do more work on a quilt pattern she said was challenging her, Linda and Jacob to sit on the porch and talk, Mary Elizabeth to wash the dishes and clean up the kitchen. Abe grinned at him.

"You ready for that game?" he asked.

"Sure."

Mary Elizabeth pressed a hand on her *grossdaadi's* shoulder. "I'll get the board."

In the end, Sam played four games with Abe and overlooked his cheating. He was just not able to hold it against him when he was such a friendly old man who remembered him and asked if he'd come play a game with him.

He lingered, accepting another glass of iced tea from Mary Elizabeth, until Abe nodded over a game. "I win," he said, and Abe woke and blinked at him. "What?"

Then he glanced down at the checkerboard and chuckled as he stroked his snowy beard. "Guess it's time to go to bed," he said and got to his feet a bit creakily. "*Danki* for coming to play checkers with me, Sam."

He turned to Mary Elizabeth. "So glad you're seeing him again."

Mary Elizabeth's cheeks flamed as she watched him walk to the *dawdi haus*. She turned to Sam. "I'm so sorry, he misunderstood. He's half asleep—"

Sam plucked a daisy from the vase on the table and handed it to her. "I'm not sorry he said it. I'm sorry I walked away from you. I wish there was a way to turn back the clock and change everything. Good night, Mary Elizabeth. Thank you for inviting me to supper."

He saw the expression of utter shock that flashed over her face before he walked out of the room.

On the way home, he passed the Fisher place, the farm that Peter had shown him after they met the new homeowners at their house. Dusk was falling. The Fisher farmhouse was small and the fields around it lay fallow. But it was a good, sturdy house, and the soil was rich.

There had been Fishers there for generations but no more. Sarah Fisher had packed up and moved to Ohio to be closer to her *dochder* and *grossdochders* who lived there. The Amish stayed planted where they were most times, but the *dochder* had fallen in love with a distant cousin in Ohio, and after her *dat* died, her *mudder* had decided to move there to be closer to her, Peter had told him.

The thought of buying the place was a temptation Sam was afraid to even think about. Land was a precious commodity here in Lancaster County. But he'd promised Peter he'd talk to the widow by phone the next day. He'd learned not to underestimate God. Hadn't his *mudder* often told him that God's plan for him was better than anything he could envision?

He'd never thought he'd be invited into Mary Elizabeth's home again and then she'd come to him and asked him to supper. As he drove home he thought about what it had felt like to be near her and be a part of a family again tonight. And as he took the familiar road he prayed for guidance for the one true path for his life.

⸺⊙⸺

Mary Elizabeth sank into a chair at the table and stared at Sam's back as he left the kitchen.

Had she lost her mind? Had he really just said he wished there was a way to turn back the clock and change everything? Maybe she was asleep, as *Grossdaadi* had been over the checkerboard.

Maybe she was dreaming. She pinched herself and winced. *Nee,* she was awake.

"What are you doing?" Rose Anna asked, frowning with concern at her.

She glanced up, surprised that she hadn't heard her walk into the kitchen. "I have to break up with Ben."

"*Gut!*" she said as she got a pitcher of tea from the refrigerator.

"I thought you liked Ben."

"Not really. And it's obvious from the way the two of you were looking at each other tonight that you and Sam still love each other."

"He didn't say he loved me." She stared down at the daisy he'd handed her, telling herself that she would *not* pull off petals. *He loves me, he loves me not.*

Rose Anna got glasses from a kitchen cabinet and poured them both a glass of iced tea. "What did he say?"

She related the conversation and shook her head. "I didn't know what to say. But he didn't wait around for an answer."

"So what are you going to do about Sam?"

"I have no idea." She looked at her *schweschder.* "He said he was sorry, but he didn't say he wanted to get back together." She took a deep breath. "But whether I think we'll get back together or not, I don't want to see Ben anymore. I . . . well, I'm sorry to say that the more I know him, the less I like him."

"Then you shouldn't see him anymore," Rose Anna said with the wisdom of someone much older. "Are there any more chocolate chip cookies?"

Mary Elizabeth stared at her, unable to absorb the lightning switch in topics. "What?"

"Never mind, I'll see," she said, jumping up to check the cookie jar. She pulled out a cookie and crunched into it. "Want one?"

"*Nee, danki.*"

Their *mudder* came into the kitchen and shook her head at Rose Anna. "Into the cookie jar again?"

"First time today." She took another bite. "Well, second. It's my last."

Cookies were Rose Anna's downfall. Fortunately, she never gained an ounce from them.

Mary Elizabeth looked at her *mudder*. "*Mamm*, if Ben comes around again, don't invite him to supper, *allrecht*?"

Linda nodded slowly. "And what about Sam?"

She smiled. "Definitely invite Sam."

"*Gut*. I'll tell your *dat* so he doesn't invite Ben again." She poured herself a glass of cold tea and left the room.

"I'm going to bed."

"We're going to the open house at the new shop, right?" Rose Anna grabbed another cookie from the jar and followed her up the stairs.

"*Ya*, of course."

"Peter told me he and Sam'll be there."

Mary Elizabeth thought about that as she climbed the stairs to her bedroom and got ready for bed. Well, so she'd be seeing him sooner than she'd thought she might. That was fine.

She didn't know if this was leading anywhere, but that was fine. Maybe she'd decided Sam wasn't the one God had set aside for her and looked in another direction—Ben—and shouldn't have. Time would tell.

Sleep was a long time coming. The moon shone full tonight, lighting the room, but she didn't want to get up and draw the shades. Instead, she lay there looking at the daisy sitting in a little dollar-store vase on her bedside table. And when she finally slept, she dreamed of Sam and picking blackberries on a bright summer day.

The next day she found herself distracted as she sat in the sewing room and tried to work.

Usually sewing relaxed her, even when she had a lot of it to do on a deadline for Leah. Which was most of the time. Christmas orders were continuing to come in, stronger than usual, perhaps because the *Englisch* stores in town had recently run Christmas in July promotions. But her mind kept wandering, and she felt restless. All she could think about was the shop open house. And seeing Sam there.

"It's about time to leave, isn't it?" her *mudder* asked. "Rose Anna went to her room to primp half an hour ago."

Mary Elizabeth smiled as she set aside her quilt. "Are you saying I should have done that?"

She chuckled. "*Nee,* Rose Anna loves to primp. No one spends as much time doing it as she does. Lavina and you never have done as much."

But today, maybe she should, she thought, pulling her favorite church dress, a blue one, from the closet and changing. She smoothed her hair and pinned on her best *kapp* and slipped on her best Sunday shoes. And then, she looked at the daisy and plucked a petal. *He loves me.*

Her *dat* had hitched their horse to the buggy and had it waiting in the driveway. "What will I do without you this afternoon?" he asked, looking at his *fraa.*

"Work, like you'd do if I was here," she responded tartly, but she was smiling as he helped her into the buggy. "Oh, I almost forgot. I left cold chicken salad for sandwiches in the refrigerator, and there's leftover blackberry cobbler for you and Abe."

"We'll manage," he said with a grin.

"I'll bring you a treat from town."

"No need," he said as she picked up the reins. "Just bring yourself back home. Drive safe."

"What about us?" Rose Anna wanted to know.

He winked at her. "You two also. Have fun and drive safe."

"It's not us who don't," Rose Anna said. "We watch out for cars more than they do for us."

"*Ya.* So drive safe," he said again.

Mary Elizabeth watched him set his straw hat on his head and start off toward his beloved fields. Her *mudder* drove the buggy in the direction of David and Lavina's farm.

The seasons were so visible here. Farmers were gathering the last of their crops, and women were harvesting their kitchen gardens. Soon there would be bare fields and haystacks—the real ones—and pumpkins and other fall vegetables and fruits sold in the roadside farm stands.

Right now, they made so many things with the always bumper crop of zucchini: zucchini bread and muffins and casserole with cheese and bread cubes and even zucchini cake. Her *dat* had peered suspiciously at a piece of chocolate cake just the other night and inquired as to whether it had zucchini in it. Her *mudder* had retorted that he didn't taste it in half the things she made them so hush. But as usual she'd had a smile on her lips and a twinkle in her eyes.

Soon everything would be made of pumpkin and butternut squash. The *Englisch* coffee shop in town did a brisk business in pumpkin coffee in the fall. Mary Elizabeth had been doubtful it was *gut* until she tried it herself.

They picked up Lavina, and Rose Anna gave up her passenger seat in front without complaint.

"How are you feeling?" Linda asked her as Lavina smoothed her dress over her abdomen.

"*Wunderbaar* since the morning sickness passed. But now I'm hungry all the time." She pulled a plastic bag of apple slices from her purse and offered them to everyone. "I'm trying to stick with fruit between meals."

Rose Anna sighed as they rode. "It's so nice to take a day away from kitchen duty. I think we've canned twice what we did last year."

"You always say that," Lavina said, turning to look at her.

Rose Anna pouted. "Well, it feels like it."

"We'll be grateful for our bounty when winter gets here and there are no fresh vegetables and fruit."

"You always say that," they chorused and laughter filled the buggy.

There'd been little laughter in Sam's house, Mary Elizabeth couldn't help thinking. He'd told her about the fights he and his *bruders* had at home. That's why he had enjoyed being invited to supper at their house so often, just as his *bruders* David and John had. She'd seen the way Sam behaved last night, seen him staring at each of them, felt that he lingered over the checkerboard for so many games with her *grossdaadi* before he left. He couldn't hide the emotions from a face she knew so well. There had been contentment, peace, a sense of belonging... and yearning on it, carefully masked and yet visible to her when he caught her watching.

His red truck wasn't in the parking lot behind the shop when they arrived. She told herself she shouldn't have expected it when he was undoubtedly working.

The shop was filled with friends and shoppers who were a mixture of Amish and *Englisch*. Carrie manned the cash register with some help from Rachel Ann, who worked in Stitches in Time as well as the bakery and had volunteered that afternoon. Mary Elizabeth had seen such a change in Carrie during the time she'd been at the shelter. Carrie had worn bruises on her face and thought the whole idea of a quilting class wasn't worth her time. Kate had been patient with her, and gradually Carrie had come around.

And something Carrie had said had in a way led to the shop. What good would it be to know how to sew quilts, she'd demanded. People wouldn't want to buy a quilt made by an *Englischer*. Tourists would only buy quilts made by the Amish here. That had led Kate to thinking of other things they could sew and to a conversation with Leah... and so had begun the seed that became Sewn in Hope.

Now the old-fashioned cash register rang merrily with sales, and Carrie beamed as she worked the first job she'd had in months since she arrived at the shelter bruised and without hope.

Mary Elizabeth tried not to watch the door for Sam as she mingled, but she caught Rose Anna's teasing smirk and realized she wasn't doing a good job of hiding her attention to it.

She wandered over to the table of coffee and tea that had been set out. Choosing between a snickerdoodle and a miniature cinnamon bun became a big decision. She'd just picked up a little bun when the bell over the shop rang and she turned to see who'd walked in.

And saw Sam.

Sam figured there was no way Mary Elizabeth would be in the new shop when he walked in with Peter after four-thirty.

But there she was, standing near the refreshment table and looking cool and pretty on one of the last days of a hot summer. It wouldn't do for him to walk right over to her—there were too many members of the Amish community here, and nothing was faster than the Amish grapevine. After all, he knew she'd been seeing Ben and even though dating was kept very private, some people might have paired them.

For all he knew, she didn't care that he was sorry he'd walked away from what they'd had as he said the night he'd had supper at her house. It was possible the next time they talked she'd say too bad, you had your chance.

But he didn't think he was wrong about the way she looked at him now . . . as if she was happy to see him.

Could it be he'd get a second chance?

So he strolled around, greeting Leah and Kate and Carrie, the *Englisch* woman who'd been hired to work at the store.

Then casually, ever so casually, he found Linda and Rose Anna and greeted them and stood making small talk about the work he and Peter had done on the shop before making his way to Mary Elizabeth.

Judging by the wink Rose Anna gave him as he left them, he realized he probably hadn't fooled mother or daughter.

"I didn't think I'd see you today," he said, trying to look casual as he helped himself to a cup of some pinkish punch and a cookie. "I thought you'd come earlier."

"We were about to leave," she said. "*Mamm* wants to fix supper and make sure *Grossdaadi* ate today while we were gone. Sometimes *Daed* gets busy in the field, and if she's not there to call *Grossdaadi*, he ends up forgetting to since *Grossmudder* passed on."

She frowned. "I know she's worried about him. *Grossdaadi*, not *Daed*. The doctor warned her that sometimes when one half of a couple that's been married a long time dies the other—" she stopped, unable to finish.

He wanted to touch her hand, to reassure her, but an unmarried man wasn't supposed to do that with an unmarried woman.

"He seems to be handling it well, doesn't he? I know I haven't been around him but those few hours the other night, but he didn't seem overly sad or depressed."

"*Nee*, you're right. Still, we worry." She eyed him. "So how's the punch?"

"Have you tried it?"

She shook her head.

"Don't. I think it's got some grapefruit juice in it." He glanced around to see if anyone was watching and dumped the cup in a trash can.

"How's the cookie?" she asked when he took a bite, chewed, then got a funny look on his face.

"Did you make it?"

"Rose Anna did."

"Anybody looking?"

She glanced around. "*Nee*."

He took a paper napkin and swiftly disposed of the bite in his mouth. "Reminds me of some of Jenny Bontrager's early efforts cooking and baking."

"Hi, Jenny!" Mary Elizabeth said, looking over his shoulder.

He froze, then glanced behind him. Jenny was nowhere in sight.

"Very funny."

She grinned. "You should have seen your face."

Peter joined them, so Rose Anna wasn't far behind. "Is this guy hogging all the cookies?" he asked her.

"There's still some left for you."

"I made the snickerdoodles," Rose Anna said, proudly holding out the plate. "Snickerdoodles are my specialty."

He reached for one immediately. "Mmm," he said appreciatively after he'd taken a bite. "Sam, we need to get going if we're to meet— "

"I'm ready when you are," Sam said, frowning at him.

"Then let's go. Nice to see you, Mary Elizabeth. See you Sunday, Rose Anna." He picked up a cookie to go, then a second, giving Rose Anna a grin.

Mary Elizabeth watched Sam leave the shop with Peter.

That was odd. It seemed like Sam hadn't wanted Peter to say who they were going to meet. She shrugged. Men weren't the easiest creatures to understand sometimes. Except about food. They always wanted food and lots of it and often weren't that particular about it.

Take for example Rose Anna's snickerdoodles. Mary Elizabeth hadn't needed to try her *schweschder's* latest attempt after seeing Sam's reaction.

For Peter to eat one and take another was a sure sign he was as infatuated with her as she was with him.

Kate wandered over and checked out the cookies. "Did you make them?"

"Rose Anna."

Kate shrugged philosophically and picked up one. "Can't be any worse than mine."

"No?"

She bit into one. "Uh, I was wrong."

177

Mary Elizabeth handed her a paper napkin. "Sam spit his out. No one's looking."

Kate disposed of the cookie. "What about the punch?"

"Sam said it tastes like it has grapefruit juice in it."

"Oh, I happen to like grapefruit juice." She helped herself to a cup and stood sipping it. "Nice turnout." She studied Carrie. "Never saw her so happy. And she's so good with the customers." She sighed. "In my line of work you can get cynical about people, but I had a feeling she'd pull herself out of the abuse cycle. It's early days still, but I think she'll be okay."

Neither of them had to say it helped that the man Carrie had been involved with was in jail, so there was no way she could go back to him even if she wanted to.

"Well, I guess I should be heading home." Kate cast a longing glance at the Stitches in Time shop visible through the entranceway between the shops. "Malcolm bet me I couldn't come home without new fabric and I'm not letting him win this one."

Mary Elizabeth took a second look. "Maybe I'll browse in there for both of us. We can always use new fabric for the quilting classes."

Kate grinned. "I like the way you think. See you later."

She and her *mudder* and *schweschders* left not long after Kate did.

A few blocks from the turn-off to their road, Rose Anna leaned to look out her window. "Say, isn't that Sam's truck?"

It was red and it looked like it, but Mary Elizabeth couldn't be sure. She craned her neck to get a better look, but it didn't help.

"It might be. Maybe he and Peter are looking at a home they're renovating for someone."

All the way home, she wondered when she would see him again.

14

A week passed before she saw Sam again.

Mary Elizabeth wasn't sitting around waiting for his call. To do that she'd have to sit out in the hot phone shanty and not get anything accomplished. This was the busiest time of the year on an Amish farm. She had too much to do helping her *mudder* and Lavina with harvesting the kitchen garden and canning and preserving, and many orders were pouring in for quilts Leah's customers wanted for Christmas gifts.

And she had to find time to talk to Ben. She had a feeling it might not be pleasant. He hadn't been happy when she'd last seen him, complaining that they didn't get enough time together.

"It's Sam, isn't it?" he said, sounding bitter when he came by the house and sat on the porch with her to talk. "I knew you were seeing him, too."

"I haven't been seeing him," she said patiently. "Sam left our community and lives in town."

"I saw his truck here one evening last week."

A chill ran down her spine. Was he watching her house? She knew someone who'd been stalked by a man. It didn't happen often, but it wasn't unheard of. Maybe it was a *gut* thing she'd asked him to stop by and was sitting here on the porch with him. Her *dat* could be seen in the distance working in his fields, and her *mudder* was inside the house.

"My *grossdaadi* wanted to play checkers with him," she told him. "So he came to supper and played checkers with him." Then she told herself she didn't have to explain. "I just don't think you and I are well suited."

His eyes were hard as he tapped his fingers on his knee. "There are other *maedels* interested in me, you know."

In a way, she'd hoped he'd lost interest in her when they had trouble finding time to see each other and found someone else. She'd seen those *maedels* he mentioned at church.

"I know. I think you'll be much happier with someone else."

He got to his feet and slapped his straw hat on his head. "I was going to ask you to marry me."

"I'm sorry, Ben. Truly I am."

"You're the one who'll be sorry. I'll be married as soon as harvest is over, and you'll be sitting here pining for a man who has nothing."

He stomped off the porch and got into his buggy, calling angrily to his half-dozing horse so that it started abruptly and pulled onto the road. Fortunately, there weren't other vehicles on the road.

She'd been hurt by things not working out with Sam, so she certainly understood Ben's disappointment. Well, he didn't seem so much disappointed as angry, but certainly she knew that emotion as well. She wasn't proud of how angry she'd been with Sam and how she'd let him know it. It had cleared the air, though, and they seemed like they could at least be friends. She didn't think Ben wanted to be friends with her. At least not for some time.

Before she went back into the house and picked up her work she walked around the side of the house to the phone shanty. She checked the answering machine in the airless little addition to the house, and there was a message from Sam saying he'd stop by after work.

Neither of them owned a cell phone. Many Amish did in Lancaster County; the bishop here allowed their use for business calls. The income of many Amish depended upon business, often tourism, far more than in other Amish communities where farming was still the prime source of income. Mary Elizabeth didn't want a cell phone because she didn't feel the need for it or want the expense. She went back inside and gave her *mudder* a message from a friend and told her Sam might drop by for supper.

But when he arrived he asked if they could go for a drive, and she accepted. She let her *mudder* know she'd be gone for a while with Sam and climbed into his truck. It still felt strange to be in such a vehicle after years of riding in a buggy.

"Do you want me to turn on the a/c?"

"A/c? Oh, air conditioning. *Nee,* there's a nice breeze coming in the window."

"Good. Saves on mileage. Gas isn't cheap."

"More than oats?" she teased.

"Yes."

"Hungry?"

"A little. We could eat supper at the house."

He shook his head. "I wanted to talk to you. What would you like?"

"How about a sub?" She knew from the direction he was driving that they were coming up on a little store that sold them.

"I can do better than that."

"You can't do better than their subs. And they always fill you up."

He pulled into the parking lot. "You want your usual?"

She nodded, and he went inside for them. While she waited in the truck, she enjoyed looking at trees around the store. Nights were getting cooler and leaves were starting to change color. Fall was her favorite time of the year.

"You won't believe it. They have stuff for Christmas on some shelves," he said, sounding disgusted as he climbed inside the truck with his hands full of bags with sandwiches and soft drinks.

"Tourists like to shop for Christmas while they're here," she reminded him. "We put up a lot of crafts for the holidays at Sewn in Hope, remember?"

"Just seems like people rush things along so fast." He stuck his key in the ignition.

"If you like slow, why aren't you driving a buggy?"

He glanced at her. "The horse would have to share John's room. He wouldn't like that."

"John or the horse?"

He chuckled. "Either. You're in a good mood."

She took a deep breath and sighed. "Fall's coming. You know it's my favorite season." Then she frowned. She shouldn't say such things. It reminded them both of all they'd shared in the past.

"I thought we could eat the sandwiches in the park like we used to."

So if she wasn't reminding him of the past he was doing the same thing, she couldn't help but think. "*Schur.*"

The park was empty. Families were probably at home having supper and then getting their *kinner* ready for baths and bed. They took their subs and drinks and picked a wooden table under the shade of a big tree.

Mary Elizabeth checked the wooden bench for splinters before sliding onto it. She didn't want to risk tearing her favorite everyday dress.

"You got me a foot-long," she said, glancing at his sandwich to make sure she had the right one. But his was a foot-long roast beef and hers was the turkey she favored.

"I can always finish it off for you," he said, grinning before he took a huge bite of his sub. "Or I can take it home to John. It's his night to cook so I'm sure he won't mind having it as a snack later."

"So you're eating with me rather than eating his cooking?"

He pretended to shudder as he opened his bag of potato chips. "He's on this kick of making things with ramen noodles. Apparently one of his *Englisch* friends told him about them."

She'd seen the square, cellophane-wrapped packages in the store. "I've never eaten them. What do they taste like?"

"The way he makes them? Soggy and tasteless. Kind of like spaghetti. That's what he serves them with sometimes—spaghetti sauce. Then other times he mixes in chicken or vegetables. It's the only thing he seems to know how to cook. At least it's fast. And cheap."

A thought struck her. It was his second reference to saving money—he'd mentioned the expense of gas in the truck. "I meant to give you the money for my sub. My purse is in the truck."

"Don't be ridiculous. I can afford this." He frowned and lapsed into silence.

They ate and put the half of the sub in the truck and walked around the park. Once they would have held hands. Today they didn't.

And then Sam took her hand and drew her closer and touched his forehead to hers in a familiar gesture. "Mary Elizabeth, I know it's asking a lot, but do you think we could see each other again?"

"See each other?" she repeated, uncertain what he meant.

"I don't know where my life is going," he said. "I don't think it's supposed to be in town. But I don't know what it is. I can't offer you anything—"

She pulled back a little. "I never asked you to."

"Oh, a man can't help wanting to when he looks at you."

Ben had said he was going to offer marriage. She'd had the feeling he might want to, but she just hadn't been interested.

She'd loved Sam for years, and it didn't look like she was going to stop anytime soon.

"We could be friends," she offered.

His eyes were full of emotion as he stared at her. "*Gut*," he said, reverting to the *Pennsylvania Dietsch* he'd used all his life. Lately, she'd noticed he hadn't spoken it around her.

He reached for her hand. "Friends can hold hands, *ya*?"

She smiled. "*Ya*."

Sam drove by the farm on his way home. He supposed some would call it stalking. Every chance he'd gotten since Peter had shown it to him, he'd driven past it. He knew the place well, but he felt compelled to see it one more time.

He still didn't see how he could buy it, but he was trying not to be negative. Peter had let him use his cell phone to call the widow who owned it, and when he reached her answering machine, he left a message that he'd like her to call back one afternoon when he knew he'd be with Peter. Not having a cell phone made things a little harder sometimes, but he didn't want the expense right now. He was saving every cent he could.

And miracles could happen...somehow he had a second chance to see Mary Elizabeth. It might only be friendship, but he'd missed her so.

He'd missed so much. Living in town felt like exile. Even with John. Maybe especially because he was living with John. His younger *bruder* had turned his time away from family and community into his *rumschpringe*. And Sam just didn't feel like exploring the world of the *Englisch* even while he lived in the midst of them.

He was jerked from his thoughts when Peter's cell phone rang as they were driving to the new job of renovating the Smith house.

Peter answered it and then looked at Sam. "Just a minute, I'll have Sam pull over and talk to you."

Sam pulled off the road and took the phone. It had been quite some time since they'd seen each other but Sarah Fisher remembered him. It was a tight-knit community, and they'd seen each other at church and *schul* activities. He expressed condolences for her *mann's* passing, and she asked how his *mudder* was doing. She didn't ask about his *dat*. He'd always gotten the impression people didn't like his *dat* as much as his *mudder*. He asked about her family and how she liked Ohio.

He listened as she chattered happily about her *grosskinner*.

The Amish seldom rushed when they talked about family with each other...or about any subject for that matter.

Peter sat patiently waiting, scribbling notes in the small notebook he always carried with him on a side job.

"So you're calling about the farm?" she asked when she ran down. She named the price she was asking, and Sam tried not to gasp. "Can you meet that price?" she wanted to know with her usual brisk manner. An Amish *fraa* was as good at business as her *mann*.

"I—haven't got that in cash," he said, his heart sinking.

"Have you talked with the bank?"

"Not yet. We just saw the farm up for sale the other day."

"So you're still living in town? How is your *dat*?"

"The doctor says he beat the cancer."

"Like he did his *sohns*." She paused for a moment. "I'm sorry, I shouldn't have said that."

"He only did once," Sam felt compelled to say. But it wasn't true.

"Because some of us spoke to the bishop." He heard the righteous indignation in her voice.

"He turned the farm over to David. He and Lavina—they got married before you moved away, remember—live there now."

He heard her gasp of surprise. "So does John live with you in town?"

"Yes. We share an apartment." He looked at the clock on the truck dashboard. They'd been talking ten minutes, and he and Peter needed to get to work on the Smith house.

"It's *gut* you have each other. Well, you go to the bank and see what you can arrange. And remember Jason, at the agriculture office? Heard he was very helpful with explaining financing farms and such. He's *Englisch* but very helpful with the Amish farmers."

"I hadn't thought to talk to him." Sam reached over and took Peter's pencil and notebook from him. He jotted down the man's name. "I'll call you in a couple of days."

"It was *gut* to talk to you. Say hello to your *mudder* for me."

He said goodbye and hung up.

"How much does she want?"

When Sam told him, Peter winced. He went on to say she'd suggested contacting the agricultural agent.

He started the truck and drove to the Smith house, and the two of them continued the measurements and notes they'd begun the day they'd met the couple. Randy had left a key hidden on the porch for them since he wasn't sure he'd be there in time to let them in.

Sam worked methodically and tried not to think of the widow's asking price.

The Smiths arrived a short time later, and Randy flicked a switch and lights came on inside the house.

"Wasn't the electricity on when you got here?" he asked. "Power company said they'd have it on this morning."

Sam and Peter looked at each other. "We didn't think to try it."

"Guess you're not used to having it, huh?" Becky asked. "I couldn't live without it. Or my car." She wandered off into the kitchen.

"We'll let you get back to work," Randy said. "I'm going to poke around in the basement. Hoping to use part of it for a man cave."

Sam looked at Peter. "Man cave?"

Peter shrugged. "Never heard of one. But whatever the customer wants, we'll give him."

Becky came and got them to answer some questions about the kitchen. She had a notebook in her hands and it was stuffed with magazine photos of what she called her dream kitchen. They looked at cabinets and backsplash tiles and countertop materials. She wanted granite, but Randy had told her it might be too expensive. Was it too expensive? What about less expensive materials that looked like granite? She wanted to know. Did she have to settle for something cheaper?

Sam listened to her, nodded now and then, and let Peter answer her questions. He knew more about the cost end of things.

And his thoughts kept drifting back to the conversation with the widow. He thought about what he wanted. The farm. Mary Elizabeth. A home and *kinner* and a future.

And wondered if he was getting his hopes up just to get them dashed.

Ben had complained that she didn't have enough time for him. Mary Elizabeth found Sam had even less time for her in the weeks to come.

Working two jobs wasn't easy. He and Peter had their day jobs, and when they were through there, they spent many evenings and Saturdays working on a renovation for an *Englisch* couple named Smith.

When they were able to get together, he told her funny stories about how the work was done and how Becky, the wife, was obsessing over her kitchen.

"It's nice you told her the kitchen's the heart of the home," she said as they shared a dessert and drank coffee in the little shop they loved. "My *mudder* always says that."

"Mine, too." He used his forefinger to trace a pattern in a spill of sugar crystals on the table. "She wants her dream kitchen, and he wants a man cave. He told me that's a place where a man hangs out with his friends."

"Man cave." She laughed. "That's a new one. Although if I think about it, isn't a barn a man cave for an Amish man? They love to hang out there."

"They work there."

"I don't know . . . I catch my *dat* spending time out there when he isn't doing chores. He reads—"

"Seed catalogs."

"Other things, too."

"Farming magazines."

"Books, too. I caught him reading a book out there once, too."

"Oh my, call the police," he said in a mock, horrified voice.

"Stop!" She giggled.

"Anyway, the other day when we were working on her kitchen, Becky told me that she and her husband agreed Peter and I should get the work because we understood what they wanted, how they needed our help to make the house the home they want for their family."

He grew quiet then, seemed to draw within himself. Then he looked at her with a serious expression. "What is it you want, Mary Elizabeth?"

"What I've always wanted. I'm a simple woman, you know that. I want a loving *mann*, some *kinner*. However many God sends. Work I love. Family and friends. Oh, I guess after seeing your *dat* so ill this year, I'd add in *gut* health. Sometimes we take that for granted."

Mary Elizabeth paused and sipped her coffee. "I guess that's quite a list."

"I didn't hear many *things* in that list."

She shrugged. "A place of our own." She colored. "I mean, when a woman marries, she just hopes to have a place of her own with her *mann*. It doesn't have to big and fancy or new. So many couples we know live with the bride's parents for a year or so after they marry until they can afford to buy or build their own place. That works most of the time, but every once in a while you hear that there's some . . . tension between the women having to share a kitchen, that sort of thing. There's just not as much privacy." She hadn't thought about the privacy thing until Ben brought it up.

The shop clerk came over to ask if they wanted their coffee topped off. Both of them nodded and thanked her.

"You said the Smiths are staying with his parents until their house is renovated."

He nodded. "Peter asked them to make a list of what was most important to them, you know, what they wanted done first. Then they can move in, and we can work on the other stuff. They picked the kitchen, the master bedroom and bathroom."

She grinned. "Not the man cave?"

He chuckled. "No. He told us if she's happy, he's happy, so the man cave can come later." He yawned. "Sorry. Long day."

Mary Elizabeth nodded and finished her coffee. "Let's go. Your days start early."

They drove home in his truck. As they passed the farm, he seemed to slow the vehicle and look at it.

"I thought I saw your truck parked outside this place one day when *Mamm* was driving us home from town."

"Really?"

"*Ya.*"

"I heard it was for sale. Sarah Fisher moved to Ohio to be closer to her *dochder*, you know."

"Yes, I heard that."

"I guess news gets around even when you don't live in the community," she said.

"They were a nice family. I was sorry when she moved after her *mann* died. But now she's in Ohio and has *grosskinner* to spoil." She was silent for a moment. "I wonder how much she wants for it. The farm, I mean."

"Too much."

"Oh? How do you know?"

"Land's expensive in Lancaster County."

"True." He sounded so noncommittal, and yet his tone had been so decisive about the price. She decided she was just imagining things. Why would he be interested? He'd helped David with the farm but didn't seem to love it as much as his older *bruder*.

Or was that because their *dat* had criticized them so much, had driven the *bruders* from their home?

He yawned again and looked so tired in the dim light of the truck she didn't have the heart to ask him.

She wanted to reach out and hold his hand but driving the truck seemed to take so much more attention than driving a buggy where the horse knew the direction and your attention could wander.

Too soon, he was pulling into the drive of her home, and they were saying good-bye. That was the trouble with trucks, she couldn't help thinking as she stood on the porch and watched him drive away. She stood there until the red taillights winked out and then she walked inside slowly.

Her parents were sitting in the living room reading. They looked up and greeted her. "Did you have a *gut* time with Sam?"

She nodded and sat on the arm of her *mudder's* chair. "We just went for coffee and dessert."

"Have either of you heard how much Sarah Fisher is asking for her farm?"

"*Nee*, why?" her *dat* asked.

"I don't know. I got the funniest feeling that Sam is interested in it. I'm probably just imagining it. Don't say anything to him or anyone."

"We wouldn't. A man's business is his own."

"Oh, speaking of a man. You'll never guess what Sam and Peter will be doing at that house they're renovating." She told them about the man wanting what he called a man cave. "I told Sam Amish men use their barns for a man cave."

"Nonsense," her *dat* said.

"You do, too," Linda spoke up. "I've caught you stealing some time to yourself out there many times, Jacob."

That led to some good-natured bickering between them. It reminded Mary Elizabeth of the way she and Sam had debated the topic earlier. She realized they'd probably sounded a lot like a married couple then.

On that note, she decided to go up to bed.

"Home already?" Rose Anna called as she passed her bedroom.

Mary Elizabeth walked into the room and sat on the other bed. "*Ya.* Sam was tired. He'd worked his job and then a few hours at the Smith house."

"John said they asked him if he wanted to work some hours for them. He's thinking about it. He said he could use the money."

"Do you think they're hurting for money?"

Rose Anna nodded. "John said Sam's been complaining about money and turning out lights and such, fussing at him about the electric bill and wasting food and things. So John's been trying to save on groceries and cooking cheap things."

"I heard about the ramen noodles."

Rose Anna laughed. "Me too. He said they're not bad."

"So you saw him recently?" she asked casually as Rose Anna picked up her hairbrush from her bedside table and began giving her hair its nightly hundred strokes. After it, she'd use a length of silk to rub over her hair to make it shine. It was one of her *schweschder's* little vanities.

"I bumped into him one day when I was in town. We talked for a few minutes." She frowned. "A woman walked up to him and acted a little too friendly with him like I wasn't even there. Asked if he'd be at a party later. She works in the coffee shop."

Mary Elizabeth knew who she meant. The woman had asked about John once when she and Sam visited the shop.

"So, did Sam say anything about Peter?" Rose Anna asked with studied casualness.

"As in how?"

Rose Anna shrugged and continued to brush her hair. "You know, about how the renovations are going."

"*Nee*, sorry. See you tomorrow." As she walked to her room she wondered if Rose Anna would be able to forget about John. She hadn't been able to forget about Sam.

15

Mary Elizabeth stood on the back porch with a basket of eggs she'd gathered and drew in a deep breath. There, she could just catch a hint of fall in the air. Her *dat* came out of the kitchen door and stopped beside her.

"You smell it, eh?" he asked, settling his hands on his hips and inhaling deeply.

She nodded. "Fall."

He grinned. "You're a farmer's *dochder.*"

That she was. Once she'd thought she'd be a farmer's *fraa,* but now who knew?

He turned back and held open the door. "Let's have breakfast."

She carried the eggs to the sink and washed them before placing them in a bowl and handing it to her *mudder* who had a cast iron skillet heating on the stove. She dropped several pats of butter into it and it sizzled. "*Dippy eggs*?" she asked her *mann.*

He nodded, sat at the table, and sipped his coffee.

Soon there was a platter of bacon and eggs and fried potatoes along with a basket of piping hot biscuits. A hearty breakfast always started the day even when it was still warm. After they'd prayed, Jacob split two biscuits and made a kind of breakfast haystack, placing bacon, then potatoes, the *dippy eggs*, and finally, some grated cheese atop it. Today, he ate it with a fork and knife, but some mornings when he was in a hurry he made a sandwich of it, wrapped it in a napkin, and ate it while he worked.

After they cleaned up the kitchen, he went out to his fields and Mary Elizabeth, Rose Anna, and their *mudder* went upstairs. Mary Elizabeth had delivered the last batch of completed quilts to Leah, and now it was time to sift through the sheaf of new orders and decide who would sew what.

Lavina would join them later, after she took care of cooking breakfast for David and doing her morning chores. She'd asked if she could sew some baby quilts because her mind was on the *boppli* she carried. Then, too, they were smaller projects, and she felt they were something she could manage right now. So those would be set aside for her.

As Mary Elizabeth looked through the orders Leah had given her the last time she delivered a box of quilts, she felt her heart race as she read them off to *Mamm* and Rose Anna: a nine-patch in holiday colors, a Dutch spinning star, a wedding ring quilt, an around-the-world quilt, a log cabin, and a patchwork sampler.

She asked to make the log cabin quilt. It would be the perfect way for her to welcome the new season. And the spinning star quilt, a great way to anticipate Christmas.

Rose Anna wanted the wedding ring quilt. She was such a romantic. And their *mudder* wanted the nine-patch to be made of autumnal colors and a patchwork sampler, a way to show off her knowledge of many Amish patterns. There were several baby quilts for Lavina and lap quilts for all of them to do after they finished the regular size quilts. A bounty of work indeed.

They began with a search of their shelves for the fabrics they'd need, and Mary Elizabeth knew that despite her *dat's* teasing that they owned enough fabric to fill a shop, there would be at least one trip to Stitches in Time to choose more. The morning went quickly in a flurry of cutting material and discussing a plan of action for each.

As always Mary Elizabeth said a prayer of thanks to God for work she enjoyed in such pleasant surroundings. As she worked, she wondered what Sam was doing. She knew he loved his job as well, but for his main job the work involved working outside when the weather wasn't so pleasant. Pennsylvania summers could be so hot, the winters so cold. And spring was so short its delightful temperatures were a fleeting memory. Almost ephemeral. She'd read that in a book once.

Now that the shop was up and running, she and Rose Anna would be going to the quilt class twice a week, so it was important to work productively. No daydreaming about Sam, she told herself. When she glanced at Rose Anna, she wondered if she had trouble concentrating since she'd become interested in Peter.

When it came time for a break, she hurried out to the phone shanty to check for messages and then chided herself for being disappointed that there weren't any for her. She was acting like a lovesick *maedel*, and all that Sam had asked was to be friends again.

She walked back inside and gave her *mudder* a message that a friend of hers had called. "Peter didn't call?" Rose Anna wanted to know.

"*Nee*. Sorry." She poured herself a glass of iced tea, drank it, and headed back upstairs.

Lavina joined them a short time later. She'd had an appointment with the midwife that morning and was happy to report all was well with the *boppli*. She chattered about the visit as she studied the orders and then began choosing fabric.

Work went quickly. It was always fun to start a new project. Sometimes by the end of a long and complicated pattern, she was glad to complete it and move on.

Still, the excitement of the new quilt didn't keep Mary Elizabeth's mind from wandering as she sewed. The scent of fall in the air made her think about the big event of the season: weddings.

Ben had said he'd thought of asking her to marry him. She didn't regret telling him she didn't want to see him anymore, but the subject of marriage made her remember that this would be another wedding season that she remained a *maedel*...that she wouldn't become a *fraa*.

She almost sighed but caught herself. A glance at the clock showed her it was nearly time for lunch. Maybe a break would help her forget about what wouldn't be and concentrate on how *gut* her life was right now.

And she reminded herself there would be a *boppli* in the family at Christmas this year. It was so special to think that Lavina and David's first child would be born in the month of the Christ child. She smiled, thinking of it.

"What are you smiling about?" Lavina asked her as they walked downstairs to have lunch.

She told her about her thoughts, and now Lavina smiled.

"It'll be a special Christmas for *schur*."

"It's a lot to think about, isn't it?"

Sam glanced at Peter as he drove them home. "Thanks for going along to see that agricultural agent. My head is swimming with facts and figures and financing strategies." He sighed. "It sure is."

Peter patted his ever-present notebook sitting on the front seat in between them. "I took notes for you."

Sam chuckled. "I noticed. Thanks." He'd taken his own but was sure Peter's were superior.

They drove past the farm on the way to Peter's house. Peter didn't remark on how it was the longer way to get to his house. He knew Sam drove by the farm often.

"Jason certainly had an interesting idea about talking to the widow about her holding the mortgage."

The very idea had struck Sam speechless for long moments. "But she wants to sell and when she can get cash, why wouldn't she?"

"I don't know. But it's something you should discuss with her."

Sam thought about it as the miles sped past.

"Have you told Mary Elizabeth?"

"Told her what? About a dream that might not go anywhere?"

"Maybe you won't get this farm," Peter said reasonably. "But I think Mary Elizabeth would be encouraged to hear that you're interested in it, in returning to the community."

Sam pulled into the drive of Peter's home and sat there with the engine running.

"That's what it means, doesn't it?"

"Yeah," Sam said finally. He shut off the engine and rested his head on the seat.

"That's a *gut* thing."

"I know." He sat up. "Gotta go home, fix supper."

"No ramen noodles, huh?"

"No."

"Think about coming to church on Sunday."

"I will."

Peter gathered up his trusty notebook and lunch box and got out. "See you tomorrow."

"Thanks again for meeting with Jason with me."

"You're welcome. Pray about it."

"I will."

Sam wasn't sure if tiredness or discouragement weighed heavier on his shoulders. Maybe they were both one and the same. He could handle long days of hard physical work whether it was construction or farming, but this trying to figure out how to buy the farm was wearing him down.

He found himself driving past Mary Elizabeth's house. He didn't often do it. In the past he'd stayed in town. The Amish community he'd left had been *verboten*. Now, when he often dropped Peter off after they worked their second job together, he often found himself driving past her house and wondering what she was doing. They saw each other as often as possible, but it couldn't be every night since he and Peter were putting in so many hours on the Smith house.

As he passed it, he saw someone sitting on the front porch. He slowed. It was Mary Elizabeth. When she saw his truck, she waved, so he took it as an invitation to pull into the driveway and get out.

"What are you doing out here?" he asked her as he climbed the steps to the porch.

"Just smelling fall."

"Huh?"

She laughed and drew her shawl around her shoulders. "Can't you feel it? Can't you smell it?"

He lowered himself into the rocker, set it to moving with his foot, and took a deep sniff. "You're right. I've been inside much of the day."

It was on the tip of his tongue to tell her about the farm. But he had nothing to tell her. She didn't need to know about this dream that might never happen.

"Fall was always your favorite season."

She nodded. "Cooler than summer, warmer than winter. And lasts longer than spring in Lancaster County. Of course, nearly everything lasts longer than spring here."

Sam chuckled. "True."

"It won't be long before Christmas. We've been sewing quilts for customers to give for Christmas gifts for months, so it's been on my mind."

"The Smiths have asked us to have the first repairs to their house done before Christmas so they can spend it there," he told her. "Then we'll be doing the other work in stages. This way they can move out of her parents' house and be in their own."

"There'll be a first for David and Lavina this Christmas, too."

It took him a moment to remember. "Their first *boppli*." When she stared at him in surprise, he stopped rocking. "What?"

"It's been a long time since I heard you use *Pennsylvania Dietsch*."

He shrugged. "Don't have much need to use it around the *Englisch* when I work."

"I guess not."

They sat in a silence that was comfortable.

"Did you eat?"

"Peter got us subs for lunch. There're some leftovers in the refrigerator at home for supper."

"Men *schur* do love their subs."

"Quick and cheap," he admitted.

"There's some pie left from supper."

"Wouldn't turn down pie."

She got to her feet. "You didn't even ask what kind."

"Since when did it matter?"

She slapped at her arm. "Maybe we should have it inside. Mosquitoes are still hanging around here."

He followed her inside. Jacob sat reading *The Budget* in his recliner while Linda knit a small blanket in a pale green yarn. For Lavina's *boppli?* he wondered. They nodded and said hello as Mary Elizabeth and Sam walked through the room to the kitchen.

Abe sat at the table cutting himself a large wedge of pie.

"*Grossdaadi!* You're eating another piece?"

He looked up guiltily and dropped the knife. "It's really *gut* pie."

"You had two pieces at supper. *Mamm* will be fussing at you if she finds out."

"Now who's going to tell her?" he asked craftily.

Mary Elizabeth shook her head. "She has a way of finding these things out."

She walked over, picked it up, and set it in the sink. Then she got a clean knife from a drawer, cut the slice for him, and set it on a plate. "Maybe you should take it into the *dawdi haus* and eat it."

"You *schur* you don't just want to be alone with Sam here?" he asked, and his eyes twinkled behind his wire-rimmed glasses.

Sam watched her blush as she poured coffee for the three of them.

When they heard footsteps approach the kitchen Abe quickly slid the plate of pie before Sam.

"What's this? More pie?" Linda asked as she came into the room. She looked directly at Abe.

"Just having a last cup of coffee," he said with an innocent expression. He poured sugar into his cup and stirred it.

"That'll keep you up tonight," Linda warned him. "It'd be better if you had some chamomile tea before you went to bed." She put the teakettle on the burner and turned up the gas flame.

He wrinkled his nose. "Don't want to drink flowers, *danki*." He drank his coffee and watched Sam eat the pie.

Linda fixed her cup of tea and walked out of the room. Mary Elizabeth quickly cut a piece of pie and put it before her *grossdaadi*.

"I know what you're doing."

Mary Elizabeth dropped the knife as her *mudder's* voice drifted back into the room.

"Did she develop that ability after she had us *kinner* or did she always have it?" she asked him.

He chuckled. "After she had you *kinner*." He ate the pie quickly.

"All *mudders* have it," Sam said.

Abe nodded. "Well, I'm off to bed. Stop by early enough for a game of checkers some night, Sam."

"I will."

After the older man shuffled off to the *dawdi haus* and shut the door, Sam turned to Mary Elizabeth. "I'm coming to church Sunday. Could we go for a drive, maybe a picnic afterward? I'll stop at the store and get some food."

"That would be *wunderbaar*. Church and the picnic, I mean. I'll make some fried chicken, though. It's my turn. You got us subs last time."

"It's not about turns."

"*Nee*, but I'd like to make the fried chicken."

"I've missed it, so I'll let you." He smiled and stood. "*Danki* for the pie and coffee. 'Til Sunday, then."

"'Til Sunday."

She walked with him out to the front porch.

"Stars are out," he said, looking up. "Don't see as many of them in the city. Too many lights." He turned back for one last look at her. "I'm glad I stopped on the way home after I dropped off Peter."

"Me too. Drive careful."

This time he felt lighter, less tired and discouraged as he headed home.

It felt *gut* to see Sam in church on Sunday.

Men and women sat in separate sections for church so he didn't sit next to her. But all though the three-hour service she could think about how they'd go for a drive and a picnic afterward. Well, she tried to keep her thoughts off afterward and concentrate on the church, but it was hard.

There was speculation as to why he was there today after his absence of more than a year. But when church was over, members greeted him and spoke to him. Some of the men slapped him on the back in the way of men. Some of the *maedels* said hello and gave him flirtatious looks even as they slid their glances toward Mary Elizabeth. No matter how couples tried to keep others from knowing, word got around when they were seeing each other— that they were "taken."

Mary Elizabeth did her stint in the kitchen helping serve and clean up after the light meal while Sam helped setting up the tables. When she was finished, she went looking for him and saw he was talking with the bishop out on the front porch. She lingered at the door for a long moment, wondering what was being said, then had to step aside when someone wanted to leave.

She wasn't being nosy. She wasn't. Part of her felt protective of Sam. What if the bishop wasn't being nice to him. What if he was asking Sam if he intended on returning to the church and Sam wasn't ready yet. She'd heard stories of how sometimes those who had left were pressured much too hard to return. Those who'd pushed too hard defended themselves by saying they were trying to save the person.

Mary Elizabeth took a deep breath and walked back to the kitchen. Sam was a grown man capable of taking care of himself. He didn't need her to do that.

A few minutes later when he appeared in the doorway looking for her, she was able to smile and join him in leaving the house and walking out to where Peter was hitching up his buggy.

Peter had brought Sam to church so he took him and Mary Elizabeth back to his house for Sam's pickup truck. He'd told her he didn't want to offend anyone by driving up in the truck to the home where church was being hosted.

"Everything *allrecht*?" Peter asked, looking closely at Sam. "I saw you talking with the bishop on the porch."

"It's fine."

So she wasn't the only one who'd been concerned. Peter was a *gut* friend to Sam.

Sam took the picnic basket from Mary Elizabeth and helped her into the buggy. He put the basket in the back after making a joking sniff of it.

"Fried chicken?"

"Of course."

The two men talked about plans for work the following week and then Peter was pulling into his driveway and Sam and Mary Elizabeth got out, retrieved the basket, and headed for his truck.

"Mind if we go someplace new?" Sam asked her as they drove.

"No."

"I saw a nice park outside town one day when I took a drive. I think you'll like it."

He was quiet on the drive. Not that he talked a lot. None of the men she knew did . . . not just Sam and his *bruders*. Her own *dat* didn't talk much, either. Today, though, when she glanced at him now and then, she felt that his mind was elsewhere.

"Something bothering you?"

He looked over at her. "No, I'm sorry. I'm just a little tired. Been a long week."

"How's the work coming on the Smith house?"

"Good. They're a nice couple to work for."

He pulled into a pretty little park she'd never visited in town, and they spread a quilt on the grass. Mary Elizabeth pulled out containers of fried chicken, macaroni salad, baked beans, and deviled eggs. The family had eaten so much of the popular summer favorites, but she figured Sam probably hadn't. He had seconds of everything—three of the *eggs*—and two brownies.

She waited until they were relaxed and drinking lemonade from plastic glasses before asking the question that had been bothering her.

"Sam, can I ask you a personal question?"

"Since when have you ever needed to ask such a thing?" He leaned back on his elbows and frowned at her. "You know you can ask me anything."

She bit her lip. "Why are you working two jobs? Do you need money so badly?"

He sat up and poured himself another glass of lemonade. "I have more bills than when I lived at home."

"I'm *schur.*" She couldn't help gazing at the pickup truck parked not far from them.

"Peter and I wanted to start our own business. That way we can work for ourselves."

"I see. So you like doing construction better than farming like you did when you lived with your family?"

He shrugged. "I like both. But I can't farm without having one."

She brushed crumbs from her dress. "*Nee*, I guess not."

"I'm glad David got the farm," he told her. "He deserved it for all he did for *Daed* and *Mamm* when *Daed* was sick."

"I know you feel that way. You've never acted like you resented him. If you did, you wouldn't have helped him so much with the work." She flicked at a little parade of ants that walked across the quilt. "Maybe someday you'll have a farm of your own if you want one."

He started to say something and then stopped.

"What?"

"Nothing." He stared at a couple of children who played on the swings in the distance.

"It isn't nothing. You started to say something."

"It's not important."

Frustrated, she started to press him. But he was loading the plastic containers back into the basket and avoiding her eyes.

"If you need some money I can help—"

"*Nee!*" he said sharply. When he saw her recoil, he took a deep breath. "No, thank you," he said in a quiet voice. "Look, a little extra work never hurt anyone. And it's helping me pay bills and build up some savings in the bank. Everyone should have some savings."

"True."

"Look, I'm sorry if my working so much has meant I haven't had a lot of time to see you."

"I'm not likely to complain about that. I've been busy, too."

"So I guess you haven't seen—" again he stopped.

"Go on."

"So you haven't seen much of Ben?"

He acted casual, but there was a tenseness about him, a wariness as he watched her.

"I'm not seeing him anymore."

"Can I ask why?"

"Because you're the only man I want to see," she blurted out. She found herself holding her breath.

An expression of pure joy swept over his face. He reached for her hand and then pulled his back. "I don't know what's going to happen."

"I know."

"You're all right with that for now?"

She nodded.

He reached for her hand and clasped it. They sat there, gazing at each other, not needing words. The wind picked up, sending a cooling breeze.

Fall was coming. And with it came the end of harvest and the beginning of weddings. She wouldn't think about that now. Sam hadn't joined the church, so even if he suddenly wanted to get married, he'd have to attend a lengthy number of classes first.

And today was the first time he'd even attended a church service in well more than a year.

Well, it was a start, wasn't it? As much as she'd always wanted to marry him, she wanted him to join the church and be a part of the Amish community again. Be with her and his family. Be the man who loved God as he'd done in the past.

For now, she enjoyed the afternoon with him and hoped she'd see that day sometime soon.

16

They were driving through town when it suddenly occurred to Mary Elizabeth that she didn't know where Sam lived.

"Where's your apartment?"

"My apartment?" He glanced at her, then back at the road. "Why?"

"Just curious."

He slowed, signaled, and pulled over. "I could take you there, but you know the bishop would have a fit if he knew."

Mary Elizabeth glanced around. "I don't see him."

"When did you become a smart aleck?"

She laughed. "Always have been."

Sam hesitated. There were strict rules about a single man and woman being together unchaperoned—particularly inside the home of one of them. But maybe John was there. And as Mary Elizabeth said, the bishop wasn't there.

So he checked for traffic and pulled out onto the road again. "It isn't much. Best I could find for what I could afford."

"I'm sure it's fine."

The apartment was in a drab building without a lot of personality.

"David found a room to rent in a house an elderly woman owned," he explained. "But that wasn't big enough for John and me."

Sam pulled into the parking place for his unit and they got out and walked up to it. "It's not much," Sam said again.

"What are you worried about?"

"John's a slob."

"I'm not going to judge you."

"*Schur*," he muttered as he unlocked the door and opened it.

Her first thought was that everything was beige—the walls, the sofa, the carpet. It had no pictures on the wall, nothing of the personality of the two men who lived there. It was clean but not neat. The door to one room was open, revealing an unmade bed and clothes strewn everywhere.

"John's room," Sam said as he closed the door.

The door to another room stood open. The bed was made and nothing was out of place. "Yours?" she asked with a grin.

He nodded.

She glanced curiously at a small room off the living room. He gestured at it, inviting her to take a look. It was the tiniest kitchen she'd ever seen with a small refrigerator, stove, and barely enough room for a rickety wooden table and two chairs. A stack of cellophane packages of ramen noodles took up much of the space on the kitchen counter. Two plates, two forks, two knives, and two glasses sat in a dish drainer.

"So this is how single men live?"

He grinned. "Well, it's how these two men live." He looked around. "It's not so bad."

"It's not bad at all," she rushed to say. "You've made a home for the two of you. And there's no strife."

"Well, sometimes John and I get into it."

"Of course. You're *bruders*."

"Do *schweschders* argue?"

"Not so much anymore. Not since Rose Anna grew up a little."

He rummaged in the refrigerator and handed her a soft drink. "It was her who caused disagreements between you then?"

"Of course. It wasn't ever me."

"No," he said trying to keep a straight face. "Of course, it wasn't ever you."

She lifted her chin and regarded him as haughtily as she could. "I'm very mature and easy to get along with."

"You are."

"You're laughing at me."

"No." But his laughter spilled out and even after she smacked his arm, he couldn't stop.

Mary Elizabeth glared at him. And then she started laughing, too.

He stopped laughing and a serious expression swept over his face. "I missed this. Laughing with you."

She sobered. "Me, too."

Something intangible passed between them. Sam stepped forward one step, then two. Only inches separated them.

Then the door to the apartment opened and John walked in.

They sprang apart.

"Hey, Mary Elizabeth! What a surprise!"

He stepped into the kitchen and then stepped back. The room was too small for two, let alone three.

"Hi, John." Mary Elizabeth felt warmth rush into her cheeks. She looked down at the soft drink in her hands, popped the top, and tried to look casual as she took a sip.

"Are you staying for supper?" John asked her.

Mary Elizabeth shook her head. "*Nee*, I can't, but *danki*."

"I told her about your specialty," Sam teased him.

"Hey, ramen noodles are good. They're not just cheap."

Sam gestured for Mary Elizabeth to precede him from the kitchen and rolled his eyes as his back was to John. "They are," Sam agreed.

"I notice you always clean your plate," John retorted.

"I need to get going," she told Sam.

He nodded. "I'll be back soon."

"Are you eating here?" John called after him. "I need to know how much to cook."

"You're welcome to have supper with us," she told Sam when they got into his truck.

"Thanks, but I have some paperwork to do. And I've taken up a lot of your day."

"I enjoyed it," she told him.

He turned to look at her before putting the truck into gear. "I did, too."

When he sat there staring at her, she wondered what was on his mind. It was clear that something was . . .

Then he put the truck in gear, checked for traffic, and exited the parking lot. The drive home was silent as they thought their own thoughts.

"You should have let me know you were going to bring Mary Elizabeth here."

Sam looked up from his plate of spaghetti sauce over ramen noodles. "She wanted to see the apartment while we were in town. That's all that was happening."

"Okay, you don't need to jump down my throat."

"I didn't. But I would never do anything inappropriate with her. You should know that."

John twirled noodles on his fork. "Just bringing her here could cause talk if anyone Amish saw her. You know how the bishop is about that sort of thing."

"I know that." He pushed his plate aside and picked up his glass of water. He hadn't missed the strict rules of his old community, but the new bishop today had seemed less stern than those in the past. And even a strict bishop wouldn't keep him from returning to be with Mary Elizabeth, to buy the farm and marry her and make a home with her.

"You gonna finish that?" John asked him as he eyed his plate.

Sam pushed the plate toward him. "Mary Elizabeth made too much food for a picnic today."

John paused, his fork halfway to his mouth and a dreamy expression came over his face. "That's one thing I miss about going out with Amish *maedels*. The *Englisch* women I date don't seem to cook."

"Food's not everything."

His *bruder* grinned. "Nope. Matter of fact this woman I met at a party—"

"Spare me." He stood and put his plate in the sink.

"Hey, where are you going? It's your turn to wash up. I cooked."

"I'll do them later. I have some paperwork to do."

But when he got to his room he couldn't seem to force his attention to it. Instead, he found himself thinking about his time with Mary Elizabeth today.

He tossed down his pencil and lay back on his bed. The long, hard week caught up with him. That, and the huge picnic Mary Elizabeth had prepared. He fell asleep.

"You're late again!" his dat thundered as he walked into the barn.

Sam jerked, spilling the pail of horse food onto the barn floor. He hadn't heard him come in.

"Now you're throwing around money!" Amos scowled at the pellets on the floor.

"I'll pay you for it." Sam drew himself up and looked his dat straight in the eye. The old man got worse when you cowered from his harsh voice and his swift hands.

"Where you getting money, huh?"

"I'll help Saul at the store on Saturday. He always needs someone to do stuff around the store for him."

"Just clean it up and don't dawdle. If you're not at the table on time you can go without supper."

Sam watched him stomp off toward the house. It was tempting to go without supper just so he wouldn't have to sit at the table with him. But his stomach was already growling. He quickly finished feeding and watering the stock and hurried to the house.

His dat wasn't sitting in his usual place at the head of the table. He looked over at his mudder standing at the stove stirring something in a pot, "Where is he?"

"Your dat?"

"Ya."

"He's out on the front porch talking with Abe Zook."

Sam quickly washed his hands at the kitchen sink. "What can I help you with?"

She smiled at him. "Everything's done." The oven timer dinged.

"Let me get that for you," he said, rushing over to the stove. But she already had pot holders in her hands and was pulling a big roasting pan from the oven. She set the pan on top of the stove and winced.

"You shouldn't be lifting something that heavy. The cast hasn't been off your arm all that long."

"I'm fine," she said. "Hand me that platter."

He did as she asked and watched her transfer a perfect pot roast and vegetables from the pan to the platter. "How was the job today?"

"Gut."

"You're schur you want to do your apprenticeship in carpentry rather than learn farming right here at home?"

He gave a short bark of laughter. "Have a day getting praised for doing a gut job instead of being yelled at by my dat because he doesn't think I can do anything right?"

She sighed. "The two of you butt heads because you're so alike."

Sam took the platter from her and set it in the center of the table. "I'm nothing like that mean old man."

Waneta flicked a dish towel at his arm. "Don't talk that way about your dat."

He walked over to pick up the basket of bread and set it on the table. "I'll call David and John."

"David's having supper at Lavina's house."

"Lucky him," Sam muttered. He went to the stairs that led up to the bedrooms and called John, then got the butter from the refrigerator and placed it on the table. It was then, as he stood by the table, that he saw how exhausted she looked. Harvest time was the hardest time of the *year for an Amish* fraa. *All that gathering fruit and vegetables from the kitchen garden, preserving and canning in the late summer heat. Cooking after days in a hot kitchen for a* mann *who insisted on meals like this...*

"Sit down, Mamm, have some iced tea," *he said, drawing out a chair for her.*

She sank into it. "You're such a gut sohn."

"Don't go filling *the boy with prideful compliments," Amos snapped at her.*

John came clattering down the stairs. "Mmm, something smells good, Mamm." *He skirted around his* dat *and took a seat at the table.*

Amos took his seat and the family bent heads for the blessing.

Sam lifted his head as he finished and stared at John, then his mudder and his dat. *They'd grown older while their heads were bent. He stared at his hands. They weren't the hands of a gangly teenage boy but the wide, hard-callused ones of a man. He scraped back his chair, stumbled to his feet.*

"Excuse me," *he said as he rushed from the room to the downstairs bathroom. There, he stared at his reflection in the mirror over the sink. A man in his late twenties stared back at him. He touched his face as if he'd find it didn't match the reflection, but felt his skin and knew it was the face he saw in the mirror.*

He made his way back to the kitchen, not sure what was happening. The family sat at the table calmly eating supper.

"Still here?" *his* dat *demanded, glaring at him.* "Always was a failure. Guess you'll be living here, eating us out of house and home, forever."

Sam opened his mouth and screamed.

"Hey, Sam, wake up!"

He shot up in bed. John was leaning over him looking concerned.

"Bad dream?"

He scrubbed a hand over his face and nodded. "Must have been the spaghetti," he muttered, embarrassed at having a nightmare like a little *kind*.

"Hey, no more comments about my cooking," John snapped.

Sam grabbed his arm. "Sorry."

John nodded. "Must have been a doozy."

He swung his legs over the side of the bed and stood. "I was still living at home, and *Daed* was his old self."

His *bruder* shuddered. "Man, that's a horror movie."

"*Ya.*"

"How about a beer and something on ESPN?"

Sam thought about how he hadn't embraced much of the *Englisch* world during his time away from their Amish community . . . and how soon that things might change when he returned to it.

"Let's take a ride," he said. "There's something I want to show you."

"Maybe I can drive?"

Sam gave him a healthy slap on the back. "Not a chance, *bruder.* Not a chance."

The leaves were changing on the trees, bright splashes of gold and scarlet. Pumpkins and gourds and Indian corn were featured in roadside stands in the community. Shawls and jackets came out as the weather had a real nip to it. Warm quilts for sale were draped over porch railings and clotheslines. Fall had officially swept into Pennsylvania.

And many of the stands featured jars of jewel-toned preserves and jellies with little signs beside them suggesting they'd make great Christmas gifts.

Mary Elizabeth pulled into the driveway of her home and watched her *dat* come out of the barn wiping his hands on a rag. He greeted her and Rose Anna and shooed Mary Elizabeth inside with her market bags while listening to her younger *schweschder* chatter as she helped him unhitch the buggy.

The air outside was cool but when she opened the door into the kitchen, Mary Elizabeth felt the welcome warmth of the oven spill out carrying the scent of bread baking.

When she and Rose Anna had left the house earlier, *Mamm* was cleaning up the kitchen after breakfast. Now she was preparing to serve lunch. There was such a comfortable rhythm to the days here, Mary Elizabeth mused as she set the market bag down on the counter. Days revolved around work and meals, measured by the seasons and work and obligations. Living on a farm, of course, meant that with each season there could be surprises—unexpected storms and crop failures and such. You had to trust in God's will so much. But there was a comforting rhythm to life on a farm in an Amish community. Maybe farms anywhere, really.

Still there was change here . . . the season, her relationship with Sam. But when she walked into her home, she felt the continuity. The unity. The welcome and the love.

"Back from class already?" her *mudder* asked as she stirred a pot of soup on the stove.

"*Ya*. I'm starving."

"Where's Rose Anna?"

"Talking with *Daed*. They'll be right in." She walked over to put her arms around her *mudder's* waist.

"What's that for?"

"Just because I love you."

Linda chuckled and turned to hug her. "I love you too, *kind*."

"I got a surprise for *Grossdaadi*." She pulled the gallon of apple cider from the bag and set it on the table.

"Oh, he loves cider. Why don't you go call him for lunch?"

She pulled off her shawl, hung it up, and walked over to the door to the *dawdi haus* and knocked. No answer. She glanced over at her *mudder*. "Maybe he's taking a nap."

"He needs to eat. Doctor said he was losing weight when I took him in for a checkup last week."

Mary Elizabeth did as she asked and walked in and found *Grossdaadi* lying on the floor and groaning as he clutched his chest. She yelled over her shoulder for her *mudder* and rushed to kneel at his side.

Her *mudder* rushed in and knelt beside him.

"Chest—hurts," he gasped.

"Go call 911," Linda told Mary Elizabeth.

She ran for the phone shanty, made the call, and then raced to the barn to alert her *dat*. A short time later she stood with Rose Anna in the drive and watched the ambulance leave with *Grossdaadi* and *Daed*.

"I called the driver, and he'll be here in a few minutes," Linda came to stand with them. "I'll call you later. There's soup on the stove for lunch and—"

"Don't worry about us," Mary Elizabeth said. "We'll pray for *Grossdaadi*."

"He looked in so much pain," Linda said, pulling a tissue from her purse to wipe away her tears. "But the paramedics said he's breathing on his own and that's a *gut* sign."

"He'll be back before we know it, drinking his cider," Rose Anna assured her as she rubbed her *mudder's* back.

Mary Elizabeth smiled at her *schweschder* for her reassurance.

Linda clapped a hand to her mouth. "Oh my, I don't remember if I turned off the stove!"

"I'll go make sure. If the car comes for you before I get back, remember to call us when you hear how *Grossdaadi* is," Mary Elizabeth said. "And don't worry, *Mamm*. I'm sure he'll be fine."

"I've never seen *Mamm* scared," Rose Anna said a few minutes later when she walked inside.

"I know. That was nice, what you said to *Mamm*."

Rose Anna looked at her, surprised. "I just told her not to worry."

Mary Elizabeth didn't know how to tell her that it had been *gut* to see her look past herself to someone else's feelings. "Want some soup?"

"*Nee*. Not hungry."

"Me either." Mary Elizabeth searched in a kitchen cupboard for plastic containers and then ladled the soup into them. She'd keep one big container in the refrigerator for her parents to have when they came home from the hospital and freeze the others. It would be *gut* to have soup that could be defrosted and warmed up now that the weather was cooler.

The wait seemed to last forever. They got the quilts they were working on from the sewing room and sat in the living room and sewed. Then they took turns checking for messages on the answering machine in the phone shanty. This was one day when Mary Elizabeth wished for a cell phone like other Amish she knew.

Sam dropped by after work. "You look surprised to see me. Did you forget I was coming by?"

She grimaced. "Sorry, I did." She explained what had happened to *Grossdaudi*.

"Do you want to go to the hospital? I can take you."

Mary Elizabeth and Rose Anna exchanged looks. "*Ya!*" they said at the same time.

"We just need to get our purses," Rose Anna told him.

"Wait, we could take some sandwiches and coffee," Mary Elizabeth said. "*Mamm* and *Daed* didn't have a chance to eat lunch and it's almost suppertime."

"I'll wait in the truck." He turned back. "Should I go feed and water the stock?"

She hadn't thought of that yet. "*Ya, danki,* Sam."

They hurried to the kitchen. While coffee was percolating on the stove, they made ham and cheese sandwiches for all of them, including Sam, and wrapped cookies. When the coffee was ready, they poured it into a Thermos and packed everything in a canvas tote.

Sweaters went on, purses were grabbed along with the tote, and after locking the doors, they were off.

Sam dropped them at the entrance to the emergency room and went to park the pickup truck. Mary Elizabeth and Rose

Anna hurried inside. Their parents were surprised to see them and grateful for the food and coffee. They hadn't been willing to leave the emergency room waiting area until they heard about *Grossdaadi*. "They're still running tests," their *mudder* explained.

Sam appeared and at first tried to refuse a sandwich and some coffee and then relented when he saw they had plenty. "I missed lunch today. Had to make an important phone call." He bit into his sandwich and didn't elaborate.

Finally the doctor, a tired looking man, came out. He was the youngest looking doctor Mary Elizabeth had ever seen. He told them that *Grossdaadi* most likely had experienced an angina attack—an episode of heart pain, he explained. They'd keep him that night for observation and if everything went as he thought it would, *Grossdaadi* could go home the next morning.

"You know, we see this often when an elderly person loses a spouse," he said kindly. "They truly do feel their heart is broken. They feel pain and it feels physical, not just emotional to them." He paused. "Sometimes, quite honestly, they want to go on and be with that spouse. But I think he's going to be fine. You should go on home and we'll call you if there's any change. Otherwise, we'll see you in the morning when you come to pick him up."

Relieved, her parents thanked the doctor who told them that a nurse would be out to take them to see *Grossdaadi* for a few minutes before they left.

"I should call the driver," Linda said.

"I could take Mary Elizabeth and Rose Anna home then come back for you," Sam offered.

"Oh, but that's too much trouble," her *dat* said.

"No trouble at all," he assured them. "I'll be back soon and see you at the emergency entrance."

"That's awfully nice of you," Mary Elizabeth told him as they walked to the parking lot.

"No trouble at all. I'm happy to help."

He drove them home and touched her arm as she went to slide out of the truck when he pulled into the driveway and stopped. "Can I stop by tomorrow evening after work?"

"Of course," she said, frowning as she looked at him. "Is something wrong?"

He shook his head quickly. "I just want to talk."

"Come to supper."

"*Danki*, but I just want to be with you. We can go for a drive, get something to eat somewhere where we can talk without anyone around."

"*Schur.*" She wanted to press him now, but he needed to get back to the hospital for her parents. "See you tomorrow. And Sam? *Danki.*"

17

I had no idea that people could die of heartbreak," Rose Anna said as she made herself comfortable in the chair in Mary Elizabeth's room.

Mary Elizabeth undid her bun and brushed out her hair, feeling almost too tired to perform the nightly ritual. Rose Anna still bubbled with energy. She'd changed into a nightgown, brushed her teeth and hair, and now sat there talking up a storm like usual instead of going to her own room.

"The doctor didn't say they actually die of heartbreak," Mary Elizabeth reminded her. "They feel pain in their heart like it's real."

"Same difference."

"Huh?"

"You know what I mean." She rolled over and stared up at the ceiling. "Did you feel that way when Sam left?"

Her hand halted midstroke. "*Ya*," she said slowly. "Exactly like that. Like my heart stopped beating, like something was sitting on my chest." She put the brush down on her bedside table.

"Me, too. I thought I was going to die when John left." She sighed melodramatically. "Now I'm still upset. But it's pretty nice having Peter interested in me."

"You're not just flirting with him?"

"*Nee,* I like him." She sat up. "Was that the front door? I think it was the front door." She swung her legs over the side of the bed and was out of the room like a shot.

Mary Elizabeth slid under her quilt. Her parents would stop by her room to say good night so she didn't have to summon up the energy to go downstairs like Rose Anna. She grimaced. Was she tired or getting old? She smiled at the thought. No, just tired from the strain of the day. She knew all was in God's hands. Phoebe, Jenny Bontrager's *grossmudder* and one of Mary Elizabeth's favorite people in the community, often said worry was arrogant . . . that God knew what He was doing. But sometimes it was hard not to worry and stress while something like *Grossdaadi's* scary time was going on.

She lay there thinking about what Rose Anna had said. Yes, she had thought her heart was broken when Sam left the community with his *bruders.* Amazingly, it had kept beating, and she'd put one foot in front of the other and gotten through the first few days, then the first few months. She'd gone on when she hadn't thought she could, but the days passed with the speed of molasses being poured. The year had felt endless.

Then he'd come back to help David with the farm and gradually they'd started seeing each other. She still didn't know where it might lead, but she realized that she was feeling more hope these past few weeks. And now, in the quiet of her room, she wondered what he wanted to talk to her about tomorrow. He'd been so serious, so intent about asking her to go out with him, away from family.

She couldn't wait for the next day to come.

Her *mudder* came in the room a few minutes later to tell her how *Grossdaadi* was doing. He'd grumbled about staying but agreed it was for the best. Her *mudder* and *dat* would be picking him up the next day, and he said he was looking forward to sampling the first cider of the season. Mary Elizabeth smiled at that. Simple things were pleasures at times.

Her *dat* stopped in to say good night and said he was grateful for the help Sam had been, driving them all home and best of all, taking care of the evening feeding and watering of the stock. It was a worry off his mind, he said.

"Sam's a *gut* man."

She smiled. "I know."

He looked like he wanted to say more, but he wasn't one to do that, especially if it was about something personal. So he said good night and with her *mudder* went off to their room.

Mary Elizabeth snuggled under her quilt and listened to the sound of the wind rustling the bare branches of the tree outside her window. She felt tired, but her mind was awhirl with questions about what Sam had to say. Reading didn't help. Turning off her bedside battery-powered lamp darkened the room but didn't summon sleep.

So she turned the lamp on again and got out of bed to fetch the gifts she was making for Christmas. It was so hard to find uninterrupted time to sew or knit in a busy house, so often she had to retire early to her room and work on them. She had decided to make a nice navy woolen muffler for her *dat*. It would keep him warm when he did chores on cold winter days.

She left the gifts she was making for her *mudder* and *schweschders* in the wooden box for now. Lavina was getting a new sweater in her favorite color—a dark hunter green. She'd cut out the fabric for a tote for Rose Anna to carry her sewing project to the quilt class. It was safely tucked under her mattress. Several times Rose Anna had been caught looking for her gifts before Christmas.

David was a dilemma. She'd have to do some more thinking about what to make for him, maybe ask Lavina for suggestions.

Her favorite gift, one she hadn't started yet, was easy and going to be so much fun. She was going to make a quilt for her very first niece or nephew.

She couldn't wait.

The house was so quiet. The only sound was the clacking of her knitting needles as the muffler grew and grew. When she dropped several stitches, she finally had to acknowledge it was time to give up and hope she could fall asleep. She put the gifts back into the box and hid it in her closet and padded back to her bed. As she snuggled under the warmth of her quilt, she said a prayer of thanks for the good news that *Grossdaadi* wasn't ill as they'd thought. They'd be bringing him home tomorrow and hope that with their love and reassurance he'd grieve less for *Grossmudder*. They'd all always miss her but believing she was home with God helped when she missed her. She had to hope that *Grossdaadi* wouldn't continue to miss her so much he'd want to go home and be with her and God, too.

Maybe it was because she'd worked on gifts for her family she dreamed of Christmas that night.

She woke at dawn. Christmas Day! She might be grown-up now, not a kind, but she felt the same excitement that the day was here just as she had all her life.

She pulled on her robe and slid her feet into her slippers. A quick brush of her hair and she was flying down the stairs to join her family. Her mudder and dat were in the kitchen enjoying a cup of coffee. Rose Anna was slow to get moving nearly every morning and so far today Christmas wasn't an exception, but as Mary Elizabeth poured herself a cup of tea, she heard her schweschder's *footsteps in the bedroom above the kitchen.*

Sometimes Englischers *said the Amish didn't celebrate Christmas very much. They didn't put up trees, didn't have electric lights strung on the outside of the house, and oh my, no Santa? But the inside of their house smelled of evergreens draped on the mantel of the fireplace and Mamm loved lighting candles with the scents of bayberry, cinnamon, and vanilla. And no Santa? There was always Grossdaadi with his snowy hair and beard, his glasses perched low on his nose, sitting in the chair by the fireplace reading the story of the night Jesus was born, and that was better.*

Mary Elizabeth had always thought the celebrations of both Amish and Englisch *were just perfect for each of them.*

And this year, the Christmas of some women at the shelter was going to be brighter because of the new shop.

She smiled in her dreams and snuggled deeper under her quilt as the cold wind rattled the panes of her bedroom window.

———

Today was the day.

Sam had decided he couldn't keep seeing Mary Elizabeth and not tell her what was going on in his life—not if he wanted to have a life with her.

When he pulled into her driveway, he found his hands were damp on the steering wheel. He knew he was being silly. But it wasn't every day a man told the woman he loved that he wanted a life with her.

Mary Elizabeth walked out immediately, so she must have been watching for him. She gave him a shy smile as she climbed into the pickup truck. "*Gut-n-owed.* Did you have a *gut* day?"

He nodded. "You?"

"The best," she said as she fastened her seat belt. "*Grossdaadi* came home. He's feeling much better."

"I'm glad. Tell him I'm ready to beat him at checkers whenever he's ready."

"I will."

He pulled out onto the road and drove in the direction of the farm. "I have someplace I want to show you. I've been meaning to for a while."

"*Allrecht.*"

When he pulled into the driveway of the Fisher farm a few minutes later, she glanced at him curiously.

"What do you think of it?" he asked, sure she could hear his heart thumping in his chest as he waited for her answer.

"It looks sad."

225

"Sad?" That didn't sound good. "I know it needs paint and fixing up. It's sat empty since Sarah moved to be with her daughter in Ohio."

"Sad because the family's no longer there," she said quickly. "It needs a family to love it and care for it."

"Could you love it?" he asked, looking at her. "Could you care for it?"

"I don't know what you mean." She stared at him, puzzled.

"I've talked to Sarah about buying it. I asked her if she could hold the loan and I could pay her each month, with interest, instead of me trying to get a loan from the bank. It would help me, and she'd earn the interest so she'd make more money. She just wouldn't get it all at once. This agricultural agent with the county helps Amish farmers figure things out. He suggested it."

He wiped his palms on his pants. "She said she'd think about it. I wasn't going to talk about it with you until I found out, but Peter said I should."

"I see," she said slowly. "What are you telling me, Sam?"

Taking a deep breath, he reached for her hand. "I love you and I want to marry you, have a family with you. Live out our lives here on this farm. And if I can't buy this one, then I'll find a way to buy another or a house and keep doing construction."

He watched her eyes widen and her mouth fall open in surprise as he talked, and he almost lost his nerve.

"I spoke to the bishop that day I went to church weeks ago," he went on. If he didn't get it all out right now, he was afraid he'd lose his nerve. "I've been taking classes to join the church."

Mary Elizabeth pressed her fingers to her mouth, then dropped them. "I had no idea. This is a lot to take in."

He squeezed her hand. "I'm coming home." He paused. "What do you say?"

"*Ya*, of course I'll marry you!" she cried. "I've loved you for so long, Sam Stoltzfus. I wondered if this day would ever come."

"We can get married after harvest if that's not too soon for you."

"It's not too soon."

"*Gut*. I don't want to wait until next year."

They sat and stared at each other. Sam knew he wore a silly grin, and Mary Elizabeth couldn't stop smiling even as tears poured down her cheeks. They were happy tears, he knew, and he wished he'd never been the cause of sad ones since he'd left the community with his *bruders*.

After a time he started the truck up again and drove them to a nearby restaurant they liked. Sam ordered his favorite meatloaf, but later he'd barely remember eating it he was feeling so happy. Mary Elizabeth had her favorite broiled chicken but ended up asking for a take home container when she couldn't finish it. Mostly they just sat there talking and staring at each other.

"I've been thinking about the farm," she said as they drank their coffee. "I remembered what it says in the Bible about a place for us. 'In my Father's house are many mansions: if it were not so, I would have told you. I go to prepare a place for you.' If that's not the home for us, I truly believe God will provide for us."

He studied her dear face. Yes, this was the woman he wanted by his side as his helpmate, as the mother of his children. He smiled at her and nodded. "I do, too."

"Do you want to come in?" she asked when he took her home. "We don't have to tell the family tonight if you don't want to." She looked up into his face. "You're not nervous, are you? You know my family has always loved you."

"I know. I think we should tell them," he said after a moment. "When you think about all that's happened these past few months with your family . . . and your *grossdaadi* getting sick yesterday and all."

"You're right." She smiled. "I'm not *schur* anyone will be surprised since you've been coming here so much lately."

"Maybe we should wait on telling them about the farm until I know more."

She nodded. "*Allrecht*."

"Mary Elizabeth."

"*Ya?*"

"I love you."

Her smile was the most beautiful smile he'd ever seen. "I know. I love you."

There were second chances, he thought as he started up the steps to the porch with her.

Mary Elizabeth stopped suddenly, midstairs, and looked at him. "Are you going to tell your parents?"

He frowned. "I haven't seen them for a couple of weeks. Been too busy to help David."

She squeezed his hand. "There's time."

"I'll tell John tonight."

They started up the stairs again and went inside. Mary Elizabeth's parents and her *grossdaadi* sat at the kitchen table having an evening snack. Sam smelled apple cider warming in a pot on the stove.

Linda glanced over, saw him, and smiled. "You two are just in time for some hot cider and gingerbread."

Mary Elizabeth bent to kiss her *grossdaadi's* cheek. "How's the cider?"

"*Wunderbaar. Gut-n-owed*, Sam. Join us."

He took off his jacket and hung it on a peg by the back door. "*Danki.*"

"Where's Rose Anna?" Mary Elizabeth asked her *mudder* as she took off her jacket and hung it beside Sam's.

"Up in her room."

"Be right back." She winked at Sam as she headed for the stairs to the bedrooms.

When she returned, Sam saw that Rose Anna followed her. They sat at the table, and Mary Elizabeth smiled at Sam and nodded.

Suddenly Sam's throat felt dry. He took a sip of his cider then looked around at the faces of Mary Elizabeth's family. They had always felt as much—maybe more—his family than his own. "Mary Elizabeth and I are getting married."

Rose Anna squealed and jumped up to hug Mary Elizabeth. Abe thumped his mug on the table and grinned. Tears welled up in Linda's eyes, and Sam saw Jacob's Adam's apple bob before he rose and shook his hand.

"Have you set the date with the bishop yet?" Linda asked as she wiped away tears with a paper napkin from the basket on the table.

"*Nee.* Sam just asked me. He hasn't told his parents yet."

The family lingered over the hot apple cider and hot chocolate and gingerbread. But finally Jacob stood and excused himself. The day started early on a farm. Sam had to leave and get to bed early since a day working construction started almost as early.

Mary Elizabeth walked Sam to his truck to say good-bye, and they shared a kiss before he left.

As he drove home, Sam thought about how well the day had gone. He'd been nervous. What man wouldn't be. Oh, not about the decision to ask Mary Elizabeth to marry him. He knew that was a good decision. But even though she had forgiven him for leaving her, he wasn't sure she was ready to trust her heart to him enough to agree to marry him—and this season, not the next fall after a long engagement.

He'd grown up with the belief that God set aside one woman for a man, and it had been the hardest thing he'd ever done to leave the community with his *bruders*. But living with his *dat* had become unbearable and—he stopped. That was done. Over. He had to forgive his *dat,* forgive the decision to leave. He was coming home to the place he'd missed more than he thought he would.

He didn't know if he'd be able to buy the farm. All he could do was pray and if he was meant to, his heavenly Father would provide. He remembered what Mary Elizabeth had said earlier as they'd sat in the truck parked in front of the farm and looked at it, about mansions and God preparing a place for them.

The road was dark in the country and he could only see a short distance ahead with the truck's headlights. But he was determined to step out in faith.

Mary Elizabeth stepped into her bedroom that night and realized someone was there, poking in the closet. She tiptoed up to it and saw her *schweschder* poking around items on the top shelf. "Boo!" she cried, startling Rose Anna.

Rose Anna shrieked and spun around, clutching a pile of blue fabric to her chest. "You scared me to death!"

"Haven't you outgrown looking for your Christmas presents?" She took the fabric from her.

"I wasn't looking for my Christmas present," Rose Anna said, looking indignant. "I haven't done that for years. Well, not for a year or two," she amended. "Look at what you have in your hands."

Mary Elizabeth glanced down and saw that she held several yards of a smooth, beautiful fabric. Her heart leaped up into her throat and she swallowed.

"I bought this last year for my wedding dress," she whispered, remembering. "Then, after Sam left I couldn't bear looking at it so I hid it in the closet so I wouldn't have to see it."

Rose Anna smiled. "I know. I was thinking it's time to get it out and get started sewing your wedding dress. I'll help." Then she stopped and pressed her finger to her mouth. "Oh, unless you've changed your mind about using it."

"Why would I do that?"

She shrugged. "Maybe it brings back bad memories of Sam leaving and you not getting to use it last year for your wedding dress."

Mary Elizabeth shook her head. "It's not the fabric's fault." She stroked it. "I can't wait to cut and sew it. I love this."

"Then we'll start first thing tomorrow."

They hugged and then Rose Anna went to her own room to get ready for bed.

She started to put the fabric back in the closet and then something made her spread it out on her bed and gaze at it. The design would be simple, but the material, while not silk, held a luminous quality like a summer sky just before dusk. As she changed into a nightgown, unpinned her *kapp*, and brushed her hair, Mary Elizabeth thought how she'd look wearing the dress to marry Sam.

She couldn't wait to make it into her wedding dress. She folded the fabric lovingly and put it back on the top shelf of her closet.

They began cutting out the dress the next day—she and Rose Anna with help from *Mamm*—and began stitching it up. Rose Anna found a small notebook in her room and began helping with planning. Amish weddings might look simpler than *Englisch* ones, but the bride's family cooked all the food for two meals–midday and supper–for what could be a couple of hundred church members. Since their home was the location for both the ceremony and the reception, there was a lot of cleaning and organizing that would have to be done.

Lavina came about an hour after breakfast to sew on quilts as usual and was thrilled to hear Mary Elizabeth's news.

"I knew it would work out," she said as she hugged her *schweschder*. "I prayed for you."

"Are you praying for me?" Rose Anna wanted to know.

"Of course," Lavina said, holding out an arm to enfold her in a hug. The three of them stood there for a long moment. "The Stoltzfus men can't hold out against the Zook *schweschders*."

"Or God," *Mamm* said mildly as she stitched on her quilt.

Mary Elizabeth set the dress aside before they went downstairs for lunch. She needed to stay on schedule with her current quilt, after all.

A short time after lunch, Lavina gave them a scare when she started having contractions. Mary Elizabeth got her to lie down in her old room, and their *mudder* went to call the clinic. When she returned, the contractions had stopped.

"Doctor said they might be Braxton-Hicks," Linda said as she sat on the side of the bed and patted Lavina's hand.

"What's that?"

"The *boppli* wants to come early. You just rest for a while."

"I don't think I'll argue with you," she told her *mudder*. She rubbed her baby bump.

Mary Elizabeth got her quilt and sat sewing on it as she told her *schweschder* about how Sam had proposed. She didn't mention the farm since she and Sam had agreed to wait until they heard whether he'd be able to buy it.

Lavina smiled as she listened to Mary Elizabeth talk and then she frowned. "Where will you live?"

"We'll stay here until we get our own place. Most couples live with their parents until they do."

"I know but it doesn't seem fair David got the farm and Sam has nothing," Lavina fretted.

"Sam and I talked about that," Mary Elizabeth said slowly. "Sam felt David made a big sacrifice returning to help his *mudder* take care of his *dat* when he was going through chemotherapy and reconciled with him. He feels David deserves the farm. So don't go worrying about that any more. You need to stay calm and think about the *boppli*."

She watched her *schweschder* shift on the bed and walked over to adjust pillows under her head. "Any more contractions?"

Lavina shook her head. "I think I'll get up in a minute and get back to sewing."

"*Nee*."

"Are you bossing me around?"

"*Ya*. And you better listen or I'll call *Mamm*."

She laughed. "I guess I have that coming. I did boss you around every once in a while, didn't I?"

"That's what big *schweschders* do."

"What will happen to John? When Sam moves out of the apartment?"

"I don't know. I guess he'll get a roommate if he can't afford the apartment on his own. I wonder if he'll get Sam's truck?"

Lavina grinned. "I bet he's hoping to. Sam *schur* did when David joined the church and we got married."

Rose Anna popped in to ask if they wanted some tea and after she left, Lavina frowned. "Do you think she and John will get together?"

Mary Elizabeth shook her head. "I don't think so. The last time Rose Anna and I talked about him, he'd hurt her feelings when she saw him. And she said he was enjoying *rumschpringe* a little too much. I don't know if he'll ever come home."

"We should pray for him."

So that's what they did. And then they had tea and some cookies Rose Anna had arranged on a plate on the tray, and they sewed and laughed and talked about weddings for the rest of the afternoon.

And Mary Elizabeth reflected on how blessed she was to have such a loving, happy family and work she loved and the comfort of her home.

Soon she'd marry the man she'd loved for years and begin a new life as his *fraa*, and they'd have a home of their own and hopefully, raise their *kinner*.

God was *gut* indeed.

18

Mary Elizabeth had to admit that Sam's idea of sharing the news with her family that they were going to get married was a *gut* idea when she saw how *Grossdaadi* perked up.

"It'll be nice to have another man in the house," he told her one day when she was doing the dishes. He was having a cup of decaf coffee before retiring to the *dawdi haus* to read before bed. "My *sohn* and I have been outnumbered in this house for too many years."

"And you've loved every minute of it," Linda said as she walked into the room. "Every one of the women in this house has spoiled you. Don't think I don't know Mary Elizabeth slipped you another slice of pumpkin pie after I left the room."

"Don't know what you're talking about," he harrumphed.

Linda picked up a paper napkin from the basket on the table and wiped at the corner of his mouth, then showed him the whipped cream on it.

He looked at his second-oldest *grossdochder* and winked at her. "Guess I forgot to wipe my mouth after supper."

"*Ya*." Linda said as she poured herself a cup of coffee. She gave Mary Elizabeth a stern look. "No more giving him double desserts."

"I won't."

"*Gut* food's one of God's pleasures for us on earth," *Grossdaadi* said. He sipped his coffee. "I was hoping Sam would stop by for supper."

"Me, too," Mary Elizabeth said, and she sighed as she dried the last dish and put it into the cupboard. "He had to work late."

"Maybe tomorrow night?"

"He's going to David and Lavina's house. He hasn't seen them or his parents in a long time."

Lavina had said she'd tell David about the engagement and promised they'd keep the news to themselves until Sam shared it with his parents—if he did. Sam and his *dat* didn't get along at all, and he might not want to tell him. Anyway, couples often didn't share such private matters with their parents or other family until they were ready to have the announcement made in church, so it was a little out of the ordinary to have told her family last night.

"It's nice to see you looking happy again."

She stopped and stared at him, surprised. "I didn't know I'd been looking unhappy."

"Been looking more cheerful lately," he allowed, taking a sip of his coffee. "But you lost your sparkle for a long time. *Gut* to see you got it back again."

"Why *Grossdaadi*, I didn't know I had any sparkle," she teased.

"You remind me of my dear Miriam. Had such a kind heart, such a big smile. Able to talk to anyone about anything."

"That's so sweet," she said. Tears welled up into her eyes. "People always said she could light up a room." She walked over and hugged him. "We were very lucky to have her in our lives, weren't we?"

He nodded and patted her hand. "*Schur* were. Well, guess I'll be going off to read before bed. I don't suppose—"

"I put some cookies in the *dawdi haus* earlier when I changed the sheets on your bed. Don't you dare tell *Mamm*."

"I won't breathe a word," he said, chuckling. "Did I ever tell you that you're my favorite?"

"Because Lavina and Rose Anna don't slip you sweets?"

His eyes twinkled behind his wire-rimmed glasses. "Well that, and because you look like my favorite *fraa*."

His only *fraa*. She watched him shuffle off and close the door to the *dawdi haus*, thinking about how she hoped she'd have the kind of marriage he'd had with her *grossmudder* for so many long, happy years.

She climbed the stairs to her room and thought about sewing on her wedding dress, but her hands were tired. She'd spent many hours that day sewing on her latest quilt, then had helped with supper and the dishes. Rose Anna had been invited to a friend's, so both chores had fallen on her tonight. She didn't mind. There was nothing she liked better than cooking and keeping house. A *maedel* learned all about such so that she could be *a gut fraa,* but Mary Elizabeth just plain loved taking care of those she loved, feeding them and making *schur* home was comfortable. It was she who'd helped *Grossmudder* take care of the *dawdi haus* when housekeeping became difficult, so she'd simply continued after *Grossmudder* died.

Mamm didn't need to know she kept the cookie jar filled on the kitchen counter there for *Grossdaadi*.

She got ready for bed and climbed in, tucking the quilt around her before reaching for the small notebook she and Rose Anna were keeping to write down plans for the wedding. Rose Anna had made a list of the things they needed to buy and when they had to be bought or ordered. *Mamm* had taken the list for the food items needed—a familiar one since Lavina's wedding hadn't been that long ago. Tomorrow, after quilt class, Mary Elizabeth and Rose Anna would be visiting Stitches in Time to buy the fabric needed for the dresses her *newehockers* would wear to her wedding. It was all coming together.

It wasn't a dream. Just weeks from now she'd be walking down the aisle with Sam to get married before all her family and friends and fellow church members right here in her home.

She fell asleep with a smile on her lips, dreaming of her wedding.

Leah kept smiling while she cut the fabric the next day. Their eyes met, and Mary Elizabeth knew that the older woman figured out why she was buying so much fabric—a dressy one at that—in one color. But the soul of discretion, she cut it quickly, rang it up, and had it in a shopping bag before anyone else in the store could remark on it.

"She knows," Rose Anna said as they walked over to Sewn in Hope.

Mary Elizabeth grinned. "Of course she knows."

Carrie jumped up from the stool behind the cash register. "Hello! It's good to see you!"

"There's no one here," Rose Anna said, looking disappointed.

"First chance I've had to give my feet a break all day," she was told. "The traffic is pretty much nonstop."

"That's good to know," Mary Elizabeth said. "I think we'll be bringing more things to you later in the week from the shelter."

"So, did you hear the good news?"

Mary Elizabeth and Rose Anna exchanged glances. "No, what?" Mary Elizabeth asked.

"I'm getting my own place. It's just a little studio apartment. But it'll be mine!"

"That's wonderful!"

Carrie nodded. "I've been saving my salary. It comes furnished. Pearl at the shelter said she can give me some sheets and a bedspread for the bed and a few towels, so I'm all set."

They chatted for several minutes, enjoying her excitement, and then a customer walked in and needed her attention so they said good-bye.

"Seems like everyone's going through change," Rose Anna said a little sulkily as she got into the buggy to go home. "Lavina, you, Carrie..."

"And what about you seeing Peter?"

"I haven't seen much of him lately." She folded her arms across her chest. "He's been working too much."

"He and Sam. But it's *gut* that they found extra work. Sam said Peter hopes he'll have his own business and work for himself."

Rose Anna turned to look at her. "I thought Peter and Sam were going into business together."

"Oh, *ya*, that's what they said," Mary Elizabeth said quickly. If Sam bought the farm she wasn't *schur* if he'd still do construction. Sometimes farmers did part-time jobs part of the year.

Sam had said he was having supper at David's tonight but he'd stop by later to see her. She wondered if he'd talked to Sarah about the farm and what her answer had been. The hours couldn't pass quickly enough until she saw him.

"So the truck knew its way here, huh?" David joked when Sam arrived at his farm. He leaned in the window and looked over the interior. "You've been keeping it clean, I see."

"Sorry I haven't been able to get by lately."

"No problem. I know you've been holding down two jobs." He glanced at the house, then looked at Sam. "Congratulations. Lavina said we're to keep your engagement quiet until you decide if you want to tell *Mamm* and *Daed* before the official announcement at church."

"*Danki*. I'd like to tell *Mamm*, but with the way *Daed* and I get along who knows what he'd say."

"He's always liked Mary Elizabeth—all the Zook *dochders*—but *ya*, with the way the two of you are getting along, you do what you feel is best." He sighed. "All I can say is things didn't get better overnight between *Daed* and me. Give it some time."

They went inside. Lavina was moving awkwardly around the kitchen, so big Sam was afraid she was going to deliver any moment.

"Sam! *Gut* to see you!" she cried the moment she saw him.

"You look *wunderbaar*," he told her. "You're *schur* having me over isn't too much?"

"Lavina knows what's best for her," Amos said as he walked past him. "Do you need any help getting something out of the oven, Lavina?" he asked, ignoring Sam. "Smells like pot roast."

"Your nose is right," she told him, handing him the pot holders. She grinned at Sam and David.

Sam watched his *dat* pull the roaster from the oven and set it on top of the stove. His eyes nearly fell out. He couldn't remember Amos ever helping his *mudder* in the kitchen in all the years he lived at home.

Lavina transferred the pot roast and the potatoes, carrots, and celery to a platter and again, Amos was there to carry it to the table.

Sam glanced at David and he shrugged as if to say that if it made Amos happy, he was fine with it.

His *mudder* came out of the *dawdi haus* with a basket of rolls. "Sam! I didn't know you were here!" She set the basket on the table and reached up to hug him. "So *gut* to see you."

Sam heard his *dat* mutter something, but he ignored him and took a seat at the table. He was glad to see his *mudder* looking so well, so animated. His *dat's* battle had been hard on her in spite of all David had done to make things easier.

She wanted to know how his two jobs were going. He told her about the second job he was doing with Peter and heard his *dat* snort. "Should be helping David, not a friend," he said as he scooped up another helping of pot roast.

"Sam's helped me a lot," David said calmly. "He needs the extra money from the work he and Peter are doing."

"Wouldn't if he wasn't living in some expensive apartment."

Sam started to say that the apartment was the cheapest he could find but what was the point? His *dat* was just trying to get a rise out of him. Besides, even if he disagreed with him he didn't have to let the man draw him into an argument.

No, better to use his mouth to eat more of the excellent meal Lavina had prepared. It was miles above the ramen wonders John cooked and food that he himself made. He knew how to cook a bare half-dozen meals.

His *mudder* handed him the basket of rolls and he used one to mop up the meat juices on his plate. She patted his hand, clearly happy with his appetite.

"Take some supper home to John," she said.

"He's probably out at some *Englisch* party," Amos grumbled. "Can't be bothered with family."

"He's working with Peter this evening," Sam told him, meeting the old man's gaze levelly. John had actually asked Peter if he had any work for him.

"Sam, are you going by Mary Elizabeth's on the way home?" Lavina asked.

"I hadn't planned on it. Why?"

"I wanted to tell her I'd like to go with her and Rose Anna to the quilting class tomorrow."

"Do you think you should?" David asked her. "You've been so tired lately."

"I'm fine."

"I could drop by and give her the message," Sam said. The thought of seeing her, even for a few minutes, sounded pretty good.

"Some man's going to come along and take her out from under your nose," Amos said suddenly.

He'd tried to rile Sam with such talk before. Sam looked at Lavina. "Is that pumpkin pie I smell?"

"The Stoltzfus men *schur* have *gut* noses," she said, laughing. "I made apple dumplings one day to take to a friend's house, and David found where I'd hidden them."

"A *gut fraa* never hides food from her *mann*," he said.

"She does if she wants to take it to a friend and not have her *mann* eat it all."

He got up, walked over to the bread box on the counter, and pulled out the pie. "Found your latest hiding place," he told her smugly. He set the pie down in front of her on the table.

"David! You ate a piece!"

He grinned. "Anyone want ice cream on their pie?"

"You don't," she told him sternly. "You already had your pie."

"Don't listen to me," Amos told Sam. "You'll wake up one day, and Mary Elizabeth will be married to someone else."

"That's not going to happen." Sam turned to Lavina. "I'm going to skip the pie if you don't mind. I'll stop by and give Mary Elizabeth your message. *Danki* for supper." He got up, snatched his jacket from a peg by the back door, and walked out.

"Sam?"

He turned and saw his *mudder* had followed him out.

"Have you and Mary Elizabeth gotten back together?"

"*Mamm*, go back inside. It's cold out here."

"Answer me, Sam. Have you?"

"Such things are private." He was still smarting from having his *dat* ride him about Mary Elizabeth during supper.

"It would mean so much to me to know you were," she said quietly, shivering as she stood there. "I've prayed and prayed she'll bring you home. Lavina got David to come home."

Now it was he who shivered, remembering his nightmare. "I'll never come back here, *Mamm*."

Her shoulders slumped. "I know you'll never come back to this house. I meant the community."

So that was why his *dat* and *mamm* adored Lavina . . . they considered that she'd brought David back into the fold, so to speak. The Amish felt that those who left went to hell, and they shunned the person in an effort to get them to return to the church.

He couldn't tell her. If he did she'd share the news with his *dat*, and he just wasn't giving the old man the satisfaction.

"*Gut nacht, Mamm*." He strode off to his truck.

Hopefully, John would be home and still awake when he got there after he gave Mary Elizabeth the message from Lavina. John deserved to know that he'd be marrying Mary Elizabeth in the next month. John would need to find a roommate or a smaller apartment—if there was such a thing.

He'd just have to swear him to secrecy. He snorted. There was no worry that John would tell their *dat*. John didn't want to be near the old man either.

Sam came to the back door not long after supper was over.

Rose Anna was helping Mary Elizabeth clean up the kitchen and she let him in. Mary Elizabeth smiled as she wiped her hands on a dish towel. "I wasn't expecting you tonight. Did you go to David's for supper?"

He took off his hat and nodded. "Lavina asked me to come by and give you a message. She'd like to go with you and Rose Anna to the quilt class tomorrow."

"*Danki* for stopping by to tell me. Can I get you a cup of coffee? Some pie?"

"No, *danki*. I have to get home."

She searched his face, trying to read his expression. He looked stiff. Remote. "Sam? What's the matter?"

"Nothing."

But something was wrong. She glanced at Rose Anna and saw her *schweschder* was frowning as she stared at Sam. So she, too, felt it. They looked at each other, and Rose Anna nodded and left the room.

"Is it your *dat*?"

He laughed but it wasn't a sound of mirth. "When isn't it?"

"He's not ill again?"

"No. Just his usual irritating self."

"I'm sorry."

"It's *allrecht*. I should have expected it."

She wished the two men didn't rub each other like two pieces of sandpaper.

"You're *schur* you don't want some coffee?"

He shook his head. "I want to talk to John before I go to bed. He deserves to know we're getting married. He's going to have to find a roommate or a smaller place."

"Or he could come to live with us when we're married."

"That's nice of you to offer, but I don't think he wants to come back to the community. And if I can't buy the farm or find someplace for us, then we'll have to ask your parents if we can live here for a time."

"And they would love to have us if we need to do it," she said quickly. "You know that, don't you, Sam?" She touched his arm. "They love you like a *sohn*."

"I know." He ran a hand through his hair. "I didn't tell them our news, Mary Elizabeth. I couldn't."

"*Allrecht*."

"It's not because I thought they wouldn't like to hear it."

"Sam, most of the couples we know don't share such until the announcement in church."

He stared at her, the expression in his eyes fierce. "*Dat* would be overjoyed!" he blurted out.

She blinked, shocked at his vehemence. "I—see."

"No, you don't." He paced the room, his steps agitated. "I wondered why he was practically goading me about you, saying some man was going to snatch you up. Then *Mamm* told me why he'd be happy if we were together." He stopped, stared at the window, then spun around to look at her. "It's because if I marry you, I'll return to the community."

"If?" she managed to say.

"When," he said, gentler now that he could see the word had bothered her. "When."

She let out the breath she hadn't realized she'd been holding. "I'm sure it's because he loves you."

"Is it that? Or is it that it made him look bad that his *sohns* left?"

244

She heard the bitterness in his voice and didn't know what to say. They stood like that, the only sound the ticking of the clock on the wall.

Finally, he looked at the clock. "I should go."

"Sam, don't leave while you're so upset. It's not *gut* to drive like that."

He sighed. "Fine. I'll have some coffee." He paused, remembered his manners. "Please."

She smiled. "You *schur* you don't want a piece of pie before *Grossdaadi* sneaks in here for some?"

"I didn't stay for dessert," he said, wavering.

"Then sit. Have some pie with your coffee."

She fixed his coffee, set it before him and cut a piece of pie, adding a big scoop of ice cream. Then she joined him and sipped a cup of tea as she watched him relax.

In the quiet, the sun going down and sending its last rays in the kitchen window, she found her imagination wandering down a path she hadn't dared to dream of . . . the day winding down, the two of them married and sitting together in their own kitchen, idly talking and enjoying a last cup of tea or coffee. Then they'd climb the stairs to their bedroom, and someday, if God willed, they'd have *kinner* and the house would be filled with joy and love and laughter.

"Where did you go?" he asked quietly, reaching across the table to touch her fingertips with his.

"I was just thinking how it will be when we're married and we can sit together like this at the end of the day."

"It won't be much longer that we have to be apart."

She swallowed and nodded. "I love you."

"And I love you. But I have to go now. I have to work with Peter tomorrow evening, but the day after?"

"That would be nice. Drive careful."

"Always. So I can come back to you."

His kiss was brief, but her lips tingled as she walked him to the door and watched him get in his pickup truck.

He said he had to talk to John. She wondered what his *bruder* would think of them getting married. John seemed to like her, so she wasn't worried about that. But Sam and his *bruder* David before him had been a mature influence on John, the *boppli* of the family. She knew Sam worried about John and loved him for that. She'd grown to love all the Stoltzfus men as *bruders* and hoped John would consider coming back to the Amish community and living with them. It wasn't just because Sam had said it was expensive for a single man to live in the *Englisch* community. She wanted John to return to his family and friends, to his church, to his community.

"Is he gone?"

Mary Elizabeth turned and saw that Rose Anna had come downstairs. She'd been so lost in thought she hadn't heard her. She nodded. "*Danki* for giving us some time alone."

"He looked so upset. Did his *dat* say something to him? I know he went over there for supper tonight."

She sighed as she cleared the table and put the dishes in the sink. The water had grown cold and the suds were gone. She let the water out then filled the sink again, squirting in dish soap. "I'm afraid so. I wonder if they'll be able to heal the rift between them."

"David and his *dat* did. So maybe there's hope." Rose Anna picked up a dish towel, waiting for Mary Elizabeth to hand her the cup she was washing.

"I'm worried about John."

"Why?" Rose Anna grabbed her wrist. "Has something happened?"

"*Nee*, John's fine," she said quickly, squeezing her *schweschder's* hand. "But it'll be hard on John to afford the apartment on his own. I hope John will move in with us if we get our own place."

"I don't think John will do that. He likes his *Englisch* life a little too much." Rose Anna frowned and set the mug she was drying down with a thump on the counter.

"Maybe. But I want Sam to ask him."

Rose Anna nodded. "It's the right thing to do." She reached over and hugged Mary Elizabeth. "You have a kind heart, *Schweschder.* Some newly married couples want their privacy."

She shrugged. "Well, I don't even know if we'll have our own place, so who knows."

Sam had asked her to keep the fact that he was trying to buy the farm to herself and she had to honor that promise. She lifted the sink drainer and watched the water swirl down, her own thoughts spinning around and around. So much to think about, so much still uncertain. All she knew for certain was that soon she'd be making her vows before God and her family and her church and who knew what else He planned.

She looked out the window. Night had fallen. The day was done. No more thinking, no more planning or worrying. Time for sleep, to rest in His arms and let His will be done.

19

I'm so glad fall is here!"

Mary Elizabeth glanced over at Lavina and smiled. The summer heat had been awful on her *schweschder*. She'd never forget the day they'd harvested Lavina's kitchen garden and the kitchen had been like an oven as they canned and preserved fruits and vegetables. Lavina had fainted and scared her so. Lavina was the oldest Zook *schweschder* and was always so hardy.

She'd scared them again recently having fake contractions. Braxton-Hicks, their *mudder* had called them. Apparently, they were the *mudder's* way of getting her body ready for childbirth.

So Mary Elizabeth had some qualms about taking Lavina to town today. What if she suddenly went into labor? Oh, she knew she should take her to the birth center or a hospital. She wasn't a dummy. But she'd heard of women delivering very quickly. What if Lavina went into labor and they didn't make it to the hospital in time, and she and Rose Anna would have to deliver the *hoppli*?

The reins slipped in her hands. She pulled a handkerchief from the pocket of her skirt and wiped her hands, hoping Lavina didn't notice.

But Lavina was staring out the window and chatting with Rose Anna in the back seat. She was so happy to be getting out and seeing women at the class. She'd been the first Zook *schweschder* Kate had asked to help with the class, and she'd loved doing it until she'd become pregnant and her housework and pregnancy had consumed her time.

Maybe, if Lavina wasn't too tired and felt like it, the three of them would treat themselves to a nice lunch someplace before they headed home.

"Stop it," Lavina said.

"Stop what?"

"You're watching me like I'm going to have the *boppli* at any moment."

It was on the tip of Mary Elizabeth's tongue to say that Lavina looked huge but she had enough sense to keep that to herself.

"I have a month left. The midwife said so."

David had made Mary Elizabeth promise she'd watch his *fraa* like a hawk but that was something else she wasn't about to tell Lavina. He was worried that she seemed so tired lately.

"It would be nice to have a Christmas *boppli*," Rose Anna chimed in, leaning forward to look at Lavina. "Born on Christmas Day, I mean. Is the midwife still *schur* you're not having *zwillingbopplin*?"

"Rose Anna! Are you saying I look big enough to be having *zwillingbopplin*?"

"*Nee*! Of course not!" she stammered quickly. "It's just sometimes they don't know until you get farther along and—and— you know what I mean."

"*Nee*, I don't. Do you, Mary Elizabeth?" Lavina asked, her voice frosty.

"I think Rose Anna's just hoping, aren't you?" she asked, looking back at her. "We'd all love to have a set of twins in the family."

"Then one of you have them," Lavina said dryly.

She laughed and then glanced over and smiled at Lavina. "I think it's just starting to sink in that you're going to have a *boppli*. My big *schweschder* is going to be a *mudder*."

"All three of us could have been *mudders* by now if the Stoltzfus men hadn't left home," Rose Anna said bitterly.

Mary Elizabeth and Lavina exchanged looks in the front seat.

"Rose Anna, they just couldn't live at their home anymore," Lavina told her. "You know that. It doesn't do any *gut* to think what might have been. We have to think about what lies ahead."

"Easy for you to say," she muttered. "You have a *mann* now and a *boppli* on the way. And Mary Elizabeth's getting married."

"You've been seeing Peter, haven't you?"

"*Ya*, he's nice," she allowed. "And John was…exciting." She sighed.

Mary Elizabeth parked the buggy at the front of the shelter and Rose Anna helped Lavina out. The stairs up to the porch weren't a problem, but by the time Lavina climbed the ones to the second-floor classroom, she was clearly winded. She didn't argue with them about sitting down. Mary Elizabeth sent Rose Anna for a glass of water. Several women hurried over to say they'd missed her and asked when the baby was due.

Kate walked up, all smiles. "So good to see you again."

"I missed you and the class."

"The first baby's always so special," Edna told Lavina. "Oh, you love them all equally, but there's just something about that first one."

"It's true," Pauline, another resident, said. "And then, when I had my last, there was something about knowing I wouldn't have any more. My hubby and I had decided three was all we could afford. But sometimes I wish we'd had another one."

"What about you, Kate? Do you ever think about having another baby?" Pauline asked her.

"No. I did briefly when mine were smaller. But now they're almost out of elementary school and with Malcolm and I having jobs and volunteering…well, I think we're happy with the family we have."

The women drifted back to their sewing and after Lavina appeared to get a second wind, she rose and wandered the room admiring what they were doing and offering help when needed.

Kate motioned for Mary Elizabeth to join her at the back of the room. "When is she due?" she asked quietly.

"She has another month to go."

"I don't think she's going to make it. Do you?"

"David said she's been looking tired and asked me to make sure she doesn't overdo while we're out today." She watched her *schweschder* for a moment. "But you know, she's perking up some. Maybe it was good for her to get out today. She always loved helping with the class. You know that. If she keeps on like this, I'm thinking we might have lunch on the way home. Would you like to join us?"

"Thanks, but after I leave here I have to attend my son's soccer practice."

"Maybe next time."

"That would be nice."

Halfway to the restaurant, Lavina doubled over.

Alarmed, Mary Elizabeth touched her arm. "Are you *allrecht*?"

"Contraction," Lavina gasped.

"Are you having the *boppli*?" Rose Anna wanted to know. She leaned forward to look at Lavina.

"It's not due until next month."

Mary Elizabeth pulled the buggy over. "A *boppli* decides when it wants to come. Not the midwife, not the *mudder*. What do you want to do?"

Lavina straightened. "It's over."

But they were no sooner back on the road than another contraction hit. Mary Elizabeth checked for traffic and pulled off the road again. "I think we should stop by the clinic. What do you think?"

"It's probably just Braxton-Hicks. I just want to go home."

"But if it's not..."

Lavina sighed. "*Allrecht*. We can stop there. And if it's just Braxton-Hicks, you promise you'll take me home?"

"I promise."

"Lavina?"

She glanced over her shoulder at Rose Anna. "*Ya*?"

"Promise me you won't have the *boppli* now and Mary Elizabeth and I have to deliver it."

Now it was Mary Elizabeth's turn to gasp. "Promise me that, too!"

It was the first time Mary Elizabeth could remember envying the driver of a car. How she wished she could just press the accelerator and speed them to the clinic.

Sam stared at the cell phone Peter had loaned him since Sarah had promised to call him today with her answer and it hadn't been good news.

She'd said no. She couldn't sell him the farm and hold the mortgage. She was sorry, but she and her daughter had decided it wasn't a good idea.

His heart sank as she'd talked, as she wished him well, and he'd thanked her and ended the call. He shoved the phone into the pocket of his shirt and sank down on the bottom step of the porch of the Smith house. What was he going to do now? He'd wanted to start a life with Mary Elizabeth in a place that was their own.

He knew the two of them were welcome to stay at her house just as many young Amish couples did with the bride or groom's parents. But he wanted so much for them to have their own place.

It wasn't the end of the world. He knew that. Knew that God would provide. Knew that His timing wasn't always—often wasn't—what he or others wanted. But hadn't the past year or more been hard enough for them? There was an *Englisch* expression John had used last time he'd lost a job. Couldn't he catch a break?

Chiding himself for thinking such, he shook his head and tried to snap out of it. He had the love of Mary Elizabeth, had his health, and not one, but two jobs. He'd figure out something. No, he'd try to let go and let God lead him where he was supposed to go. Too often he'd decided what God's plan was for him instead of allowing Him to show him the way.

He didn't know how long he sat like that. Thunder rolled overhead, stirring him from his depression. He got up, went inside, and climbed the stairs to the master bedroom where he'd been repairing some water damage to the ceiling. There'd been a leak in the roof and quite a bit of damage had occurred to the ceiling while the house had sat empty. A roofer had been out to make repairs the week before but now, as Sam crossed the room to close the windows he felt a drop of water, then another, fall on his arm.

He looked up. Sure enough, the roof was leaking again. The repair hadn't been enough. That was the trouble with just repairing a leak. You never knew where it started...sometimes you just had to rip the roof off and do a new one.

He wasn't the only one who was going to get bad news that day. The Smiths would have to be called. Hopefully, the roof could be repaired without too much additional expense and before the ceiling showed more damage.

With a heavy sigh, Sam picked up his tool box and walked to the second floor landing. His thoughts dark and heavy, he didn't notice the small puddle of water at the top of the stairs.

He slipped, and his feet shot out. His toolbox flew out of his hand, crashing down the stairs. He reached for the banister but couldn't grab hold and tumbled down the stairs. He felt a jabbing pain in his thigh. Then his head smacked a stair at the curve and everything went black.

When he woke, he didn't know what he was doing at the foot of the stairs. His head throbbed like a truck had hit him, and his leg was wet. Then he remembered he'd slipped in a puddle from the roof leaking and he'd fallen down the stairs. He tried to sit up but the world tilted so he waited for it to settle. His leg hurt. Had he broken it? He looked at it, blinked as something trickled into his eye. When he swiped his hand across his face it came away wet—and red. He stared at the leg that hurt and saw two of them. Well, of course he saw two. He had two legs, didn't he? He blinked hard and the double vision cleared.

His leg was feeling wet because a splinter of wood was stuck in it—a big splinter—and a thin stream of blood was spurting from it like a mini-fountain. Sam knew what that meant. He wasn't taught science in Amish *schul,* but he knew enough about the human body to recognize he'd bleed to death if he didn't get help quick.

He crawled toward the cell phone, inch by painful inch. It slipped from his blood-slick hand like a slimy fish, sliding a few more inches from his grasp. He wiped his hand on his shirt sleeve and managed to grasp it. It took several tries to punch in 911.

"I need an ambulance," he said. His address? It took precious seconds to remember the address of the Smith house. "I fell down the stairs," he said and his voice sounded loud to his ears, but the dispatcher urged him to speak up. "I'm bleeding. Bad." Then he passed out again.

He woke to the sound of a siren fading, to boots clattering on the wooden porch and into the house. Voices rang in his ears. He looked up into the faces of paramedics.

"We're here to help, buddy," one said as he leaned over him.

"Don't pull out the wood," someone said sharply. "He'll bleed out if you do. Strap his leg to a board, and let's get him to the hospital."

He grabbed the sleeve of the man leaning over him as they put him on a gurney. "Lock—lock up the house. It's not mine."

"Don't worry, we'll take care of it. You just stay calm."

Stupid, stupid, stupid not to have noticed the puddle. That was what he got for letting his attention slip for just a moment. He prayed as the men strapped a board under his injured leg, then his head and wrapped restraining bandages around both. What if he'd messed up his leg and he couldn't work for a long time. He wouldn't be able to make his rent or his truck payment. And he wouldn't be able to marry Mary Elizabeth. That would mean they couldn't get married for another year . . .

The ride in the ambulance was a blur of noise and pain, a terrible cold, and slipping in and out of consciousness. Two paramedics worked on him, strapping on a blood pressure cuff, inserting a needle in his arm, managing to keep their balance in the swaying vehicle as they snapped out terse questions. Sam? Sam? Do you have any allergies? Are you on any medications? Who should we call for you?

Then they were talking to each other, their voices urgent. He heard them in a kind of bemused, detached way. His BP's falling. Hospital wants our ETA. They're standing by.

They pulled into the hospital parking lot—the same one he'd come to so recently. Why had he come here? he wondered, searching his memory. His *dat*. He'd been here with his *dat*. No, he'd been here with Mary Elizabeth and her family when her *grossdaadi* was brought here.

They opened the doors of the ambulance and pulled out the gurney. Despite their care, there was still a bump as the transfer was made from vehicle to the pavement. It sent a shaft of pain from the leg, and he felt it seeping blood. He stayed awake as nurses and doctors swarmed over him, and then he felt himself slipping away.

"Just put something in your IV to knock you out," a nurse with kind eyes told him, leaning close to get his attention. "Sending you upstairs to take that little splinter out of your leg and stitch you up."

"*Danki*," he said, and he blinked at using his old language as he hadn't for a long time.

"*Wilkumm*," she told him with a smile. "*Ya*, I know some Pennsylvania *Dietsch*."

When he woke next, he found himself in a hospital bed, one leg wrapped in a bulky cast and raised in some sort of pulley thing, and he had the worst headache of his life.

"So you're awake."

He turned his head, wincing, and saw two of his *bruder* John sitting in a chair beside the bed. He blinked, squinted, blinked again. No, there definitely were two Johns.

"Why are you looking at me like that?"

"There are two of you."

"That can't be *gut*. I'll get the nurse."

"No, wait a minute. Tell me how I am. The truth."

"Peter called me. One of the paramedics found his cell phone in your hand and tracked him down. Said you fell down the stairs and probably had a concussion and maybe a broken leg. You lost a lot of blood when a piece of the stair got stuck in your leg. I'm gonna have to clean that up before the Smiths see it."

"Sorry."

"Hey, I was just teasing. I'm glad you didn't break that hard head of yours." He opened his mouth and then shut it.

"What?"

"I called *Mamm* and *Daed*. I had to, Sam."

He shifted, trying to get comfortable. "I know." He sighed. "Thanks."

"They should be here soon. Anything I can get you?"

"Something to get rid of the double vision. I'm not sure I can handle seeing two of *Daed*."

John laughed. "Oh man, that's scary!"

A nurse walked in and smiled at Sam. "So you're awake. How's the head?"

"Pounding."

"He says he's seeing double." John told her.

"It's tough to see two of him," Sam complained.

She pressed her lips together as if she was trying to hide a laugh. "I'm going to check your vital signs and then I'll call the doctor, tell him you're awake and having double vision. And feeling good enough to joke about it."

"Maybe I'll get to go home today?" he asked hopefully.

"Not likely," she told him and stuck a thermometer in his mouth.

257

"Mary Elizabeth," he said the minute she left. "Did you call her?"

"I left a message on the answering machine."

"I need you to call Peter. I need to talk to him right away."

"He was here until I got here and said he's coming back. But I'll find a phone and call him if you want."

"Please."

"Be right back."

The doctor came in some time later, introduced himself, and examined him. He waved his hand in front of Sam. "How many fingers am I holding up?"

"Four."

He frowned. "Some people get double vision from a concussion, some don't. It can take a few days, up to a week or more for the double vision to wear off. How bad's the pain on a scale of one to ten?"

"Maybe an eight."

"You're due for some pain meds. You're a pretty lucky guy. Lost a lot of blood before you got here. They gave you two units in the operating room. The surgeon said he took out a doozy of a piece of wood and stitched you up, put a cast on your leg. It's broken in two places."

"When can I go home?"

"You're here for a couple days. I'll look in on you later."

"Man, that's rough," John said when he returned and heard the news. "You sure I can't get you anything?"

"Mary Elizabeth."

"I'm sure she'll be here as soon as she gets the message. Say, look who's here."

Sam looked expectantly at the door. His *mudder* rushed in, his *dat* just steps behind her.

Great, he thought. Seeing two of his *dat* had to be the worst nightmare ever.

Mary Elizabeth pulled into the driveway of Lavina's house and breathed a sigh of relief. David came rushing out looking worried.

"She's all yours," she said as he opened the passenger side door and helped his *fraa* out.

"False alarm," she told him. "These Braxton-Hicks are getting old. What happens if I go into labor and we think it's just another false alarm?"

"You'll go in to see the midwife if you get hiccups," he said fervently. "*Danki*, Mary Elizabeth."

"*Ya, danki*," Lavina told her. "I'm sorry I was so much trouble."

"You weren't any trouble. Call me if you need anything. Both of you."

David put his arm around Lavina and led her into their house.

Mary Elizabeth headed home wondering if she'd find Sam waiting for her. It was an hour past suppertime.

But Sam wasn't there. Her father came out of the back of the house and stopped her as she unhitched the buggy. "Your *mudder* has a message about Sam."

"You mean from Sam?"

"*Nee, kind*. Go on in and talk to your *mudder*."

Her heart sank as she climbed the stairs to the back door.

"Mary Elizabeth!"

She turned to see her *dat* hurrying toward her with her purse in her hands. "You left this in the buggy."

"*Danki*." She rushed into the house and found her *mudder* cleaning up the kitchen. "Mamm? *Daed* said you have a message about Sam? What's happened?"

Linda hurried over and took her hands. "John called. Sam had an accident. He's in the hospital."

"Is he going to be *allrecht*?"

"John said he has a concussion and a broken leg. Sam's asking to see you."

"I need to go."

"I'll call a driver. You might be there a while, and I don't want to worry about you driving home after dark in the buggy."

Mary Elizabeth wanted to argue, but her *mudder* was firm. "I'll go make the call. I made you some sandwiches and put them in the refrigerator."

"I couldn't eat."

"You'll take them for later. John's there with Sam, and maybe he hasn't eaten."

She nodded and sighed. *Mamm* was always practical. She found a soft fabric tote bag, tucked the sandwiches and some bottled water in it, and set it by her purse on the counter.

Linda walked her out to the van when it arrived and handed her money for the fare. Mary Elizabeth didn't argue. She felt so rattled she couldn't remember if she had any cash in her purse. She prayed the whole ride to the hospital and had to stop herself from jumping out before the driver stopped the car at the entrance.

"Wait, you gave me too much," he said and handed back a twenty.

She looked at the bills in her hand and exchanged them for the bigger bill. "Thank you, Phil."

"You call when you need a ride home. Doesn't matter how late," he told her kindly.

She'd memorized the room number *Mamm* had given her and found it, but stopped for a moment just outside, drawing in a breath to calm herself and say a quick prayer. Sam wouldn't need her to be hysterical when she saw him.

Still, it took her breath away when she walked into the room and saw big, strong Sam looking pale and in pain, one of his legs encased in a cast and hanging in some contraption.

"Good. You're here," John said. He stood. "He's been driving me crazy asking when you were coming."

Sam opened his eyes. "Mary Elizabeth? There you are. Both of you." He grinned.

"Both of me?" She glanced at John.

"Concussion's giving him double vision."

"Two of you beats two of my *dat*."

She reached for his hand. "Well, I guess that's *gut*. How are you feeling?"

"Like I fell down a flight of stairs."

John nudged her toward the chair he'd vacated. "I'm going to let the two of you have some privacy and get something to eat in the cafeteria."

"*Mamm* packed us each a sandwich," Mary Elizabeth told him. She handed him the cloth lunch bag. "There's bottled water in there, too."

"Thank you. You're a lifesaver."

"*Mamm* is."

"Right. Back in a while."

She sat and looked at Sam. He was being so quiet. She supposed he was in a lot of pain. But it was more than that. He looked . . . depressed.

"I'm sorry" he said at last. "I've messed everything up."

"How did you do that? It was an accident."

"I was upset, and I wasn't careful," he told her, sounding disgusted with himself. "I didn't see there was a puddle of water from the roof on the floor near the stairs. I know better than to not pay attention when I'm working."

"It was an accident," she said again and she squeezed his hand. "Anyone can have an accident." She thought about what he'd said. "Sam, what were you upset about?"

"Sarah said no. She doesn't want to hold the mortgage for the farm. We're not getting the farm."

"I'm sorry, Sam. I know you wanted it."

"I wanted us to start our life together there."

"I know. There must be something better God has in mind."

"But how am I going to buy something else if no one wants to hold the mortgage?"

"I don't know. But Sam, it's not our job to know, to figure everything out. We just have to trust God."

261

"I think He's forgotten me."

She winced at the bitterness and the pain in his voice. But before she could say anything, a nurse came in and gave him medication. Soon Sam's eyelids were drifting shut.

"Sorry," he said, his voice slurred.

She gathered up her jacket and purse. "It's getting late. I'll be back first thing in the morning. Is there anything I can bring you?"

"Just you. Both of you."

She smiled, leaned down, and kissed his cheek. "Maybe the double vision will be gone in the morning when you wake up. One of me is enough for anyone."

"One of you is more than I deserve."

"Don't talk like that. Tomorrow's going to be better."

"Promise?"

"Promise." She truly believed God had a plan for everyone but sensed Sam was in too much pain, feeling too much despair to hear such right now.

John joined her in the hallway and handed her the lunch bag. "Give me a minute to say good night to him and I'll walk you out."

When he returned, he looked worried. "I hate to leave him here by himself. He's in a lot of pain, and he's really bummed out."

She studied him as they rode down in the elevator. He looked so *Englisch* with his haircut and clothes and had even picked up the slang they used. She could see why Rose Anna had said he was enjoying his *rumschpringe* and was unlikely to return to the Amish community.

"See you tomorrow," he said as they arrived in the lobby.

"Where are you going?"

"Home."

"But you haven't called for a driver."

He reddened. "I can walk. It's not that far."

What if he didn't have the money for a ride home? John was a lot like Rose Anna—both were absorbed with self but had kind hearts.

"Share a ride with me. Keep me company for part of the way. You'll do me a favor. I've had a day, John. Lavina acted like she was in labor earlier today, and I'd just gotten home after dropping her off at her house when *Mamm* told me about Sam."

She handed him the driver's card. "Call Phil for us? He said he'd be happy to come back for me."

John hesitated and then he walked to a nearby courtesy phone. She sat on a bench and closed her eyes, willing away the tension of the day.

She opened her eyes when she heard footsteps approach.

"Phil says he's on his way." He sat beside her on the bench. "Sam told me the two of you are finally getting married. I'm glad, Mary Elizabeth."

"*Danki.*"

"So what do you think Sam's going to say when he finds out I got my driver's license and I'll be driving him around until he gets his cast off?"

A laugh bubbled up, the first all day. "Oh my, John, wait until he hears that!"

She laughed until tears ran down her cheeks and then she was crying and she couldn't stop. John put his arm around her waist and pressed a bandanna into her hands.

20

Sam's color was a little better the next morning.

But although he said he was happy to see her—and said he only saw one of her—he looked as depressed as he had the night before whenever he thought she wasn't watching him.

She was his sole visitor. He said John had come by to see him, but he'd insisted his *bruder* go to work.

"I don't know when I'll be able to go back to work," Sam told her quietly. "You know what this means, don't you?"

She found herself holding her breath. "What, Sam?"

"We can't get married."

"That's crazy, Sam. Have you forgotten we have a place to stay? We can live with my parents, same as other newly married couples do."

"But I don't have a job."

"Well, I do, and we'll get along fine until you're able to work."

"I won't live off my wife." He stared at his hands on the blanket covering him.

"What if I'd been the one hurt, Sam? Are you saying you wouldn't take care of me?"

"I'm the man, I'm the one who is supposed to provide."

"Oh, so you're invincible—you're supposed to take care of not only yourself but your *fraa* no matter what? And are you the only one who gets to honor the vows of 'in sickness and in health'?"

A doctor came in then and she had to step outside while he talked to Sam. She walked out and shut the door quietly behind her. Then she decided it was best if she kept walking until she could calm herself. It was too much, just too much to handle. She could have lost him forever and here he was being stiff necked about getting married and staying at her house until he went back to work and they got their own place.

She felt a little calmer by the time she returned to the room and found the door open and the doctor gone.

"I won't let you do this to us because of pride," she announced before he could say anything. "We're getting married and that's that."

A nurse started into the room and then she backed out again. "Mary Elizabeth—"

Another nurse—a man—came in pushing a cart with glass tubes. "Excuse me, folks, gotta get some blood."

"I'll come back later when you've had a chance to recover your good sense," she told Sam, and she stalked out.

"Wow," she heard the male nurse say.

She got into the elevator and punched the button for the lobby with a little more force than was necessary. Fortunately, it went straight down without stopping because she felt she would have had trouble being polite to anyone.

The doors opened with a swish. She walked out and got as far as a few feet outside. And then she turned around and went back up to Sam's room. He was alone and looked miserable as he stared up at the ceiling.

She walked in and sat down in the chair beside the bed. "I'm sorry I got angry with you. But I'm not going away, so you can just forget that."

He turned his head and winced at the effort. "Oh, yeah?"

"*Ya.*" She folded her arms across her chest.

"You can do better."

"Maybe. But you're the one I love, and we've lost enough time to your pride."

He winced again, but this time she could see it was because her words hit home.

"So you need to get better fast and get out of here so we can get married."

"Bossy," he muttered, but she heard the humor under his complaint.

She lifted her chin and gave him a direct look. "I can be if needed. I want a life with you, Sam. It seems to me we got yet another chance at it. God didn't promise us easy, but we can make it something special."

He held out his hand, and she put hers in it. "*Danki* for reminding me."

⁂

"Where are you going? You were supposed to turn back there."

David glanced at him as he drove his buggy. "I know where I'm going."

"Oh?" Sam felt a sinking in his stomach. "And where is that?"

"Home."

"My apartment's in the opposite direction."

"We're going to my house. You can't take care of yourself right now. And have you forgotten you live on the third floor of your building and the elevator's broken half the time?"

He had, but he wasn't about to admit it. "So what? It's not like I'm going to be going anywhere for a while."

"What about food? Medicine? Doctor visits?"

"John—"

"Agrees with me."

Sam managed to turn in his seat in the front of the buggy to stare at his younger *bruder*. John had been so strangely silent in the back seat that Sam had almost forgotten he'd come with David to bail him from the hospital.

John sat slumped in the back seat. "David's right."

"Have you forgotten that nightmare I had a couple weeks ago?"

267

"David said *Daed's* changed."

Sam turned to stare ahead. "He's changed toward David. He hasn't blessed us with a kinder attitude yet." His headaches had faded some in the past week in the hospital, but now he felt the pain returning. "*Daed* couldn't have agreed to this."

"He did," David told him. "And even if he hadn't, it's my *haus*, my farm now."

"If it makes you feel any better, you won't be suffering alone." John's tone was disgruntled.

"What do you mean?"

"I'm coming with you."

"Why?"

"I can't afford the apartment on my own."

"You could get a roommate."

"Not fast enough."

The headache was pounding now. His accident was forcing John back into the home the three of them had fled...nothing could make him feel worse.

He felt a hand on his arm and looked over to see the sympathy in David's eyes. "It's going to work out."

"I don't see how," he said bleakly.

"Trust."

Sam sat there staring ahead at the familiar road he'd traveled so many times, depression deepening as they grew closer to the farm. "It's too much work for Lavina with the *boppli* coming," he said, casting desperately for a way out.

"*Mamm's* there to help. *Daed*, too. And me. Relax, you're going to get well and in no time you'll be getting married and living at Mary Elizabeth's with her."

"That's the first positive I've heard so far."

David grinned. "You're welcome."

"I'm sorry, I should be thanking you for helping me out."

"No thanks necessary."

"Does Lavina still make that great pot roast?" John leaned forward to ask.

"You bet. Sometimes once a week now that the weather's cooled off."

"That'll beat ramen noodles," Sam said.

John gave Sam a playful punch to his shoulder.

"Another positive," David agreed and earned a punch as well.

"What'll we do with our things?"

"John and I'll take care of it this Saturday."

It seemed there was nothing to do but make the best of it.

"Oh, how could I forget?" Sam burst out. "My truck's still parked at the Smith house." He looked at David. "I have to get it moved."

"Don't look at me. I don't have a driver's license as you well know."

John leaned forward and pushed his face close to Sam. "Look at me. I have a driver's license now."

Sam stared at him, horrified. "You have a driver's license? When did you get it?"

"Couple days ago. After you told me you were getting married."

"What's my getting married got to do with a driver's license?"

John grinned at him. "You're passing the truck down to me like David did to you, bro."

"I bought the truck from David, bro."

"I'll pay you for it. 'Course you know it should cost me less. Has another year of depreciation. Anyway, it's parked at the farm, so you don't have to worry about it."

Sam clutched his head. The day was just getting weirder and weirder.

"You *allrecht*?" David asked him.

He leaned back. "The hospital doesn't seem so bad anymore."

"Hey, we can take you back. Let them stick a few more needles in you, draw some more blood. Feed you whatever that was on your tray this morning when we came."

There were few times Sam had felt like crying in his adult life but now was one of them.

"Relax. It's going to be *allrecht*," David said. "We'll get you home, put you in bed with one of your pain pills, and let Lavina or *Mamm* make you a meal and you'll feel a lot better."

They were treating him like he was a child that had to be babied, like he couldn't make his own decisions.

As David pulled the buggy into the driveway of the farm, Sam saw Mary Elizabeth sitting on the front porch.

She stood, walked down the steps, and opened the buggy door. "Welcome home."

He grimaced. "Were you in on this? Deciding they should bring me here?"

"Everyone wants to help you." She held out her hand to help him get out of the buggy.

John emerged from the back seat with a pair of crutches. Sam took them and carefully maneuvered his way to the stairs. It wasn't easy even with the help of a brother on each side. By the time he got to the top of the short flight of porch stairs, he was out of breath, sweaty, and shaky.

He'd never have made it up the three flights of stairs to his apartment.

"Here, sit down for a minute and catch your breath," Mary Elizabeth told him.

He sank into the chair she pushed over and watched his brothers return to the buggy and drive it back around the house to the barn. John would probably sit in the truck for a while if he knew him. He remembered how he felt when David turned over the pickup truck. Bliss.

"How are you feeling?" Mary Elizabeth asked him. "The truth."

"Like I fell down a flight of stairs. Like I had to move back into my parents' home."

He felt her take his hand and squeeze it.

"You'll get better. You'll move out."

"I don't know if I can walk down the aisle without these." He gestured at his crutches.

270

She shrugged. "So you'll use crutches. Or a wheelchair. It doesn't matter."

He sighed. "No, it doesn't." He lifted her hand and kissed it. "I love you."

"And I love you." She hesitated for a moment. "Sam, I told them about us when you were in the hospital."

"How did they take it?"

"They're delighted."

"Especially my *dat*."

She looked at him, surprised. "How did you know?"

"I told you, my *mudder* said he felt you'd bring me back to the community like Lavina did David."

"God brought you back."

He nodded.

"Let's go inside. It's cold out here, and you need to get to bed and rest. Your *mudder* invited me to have supper with all of you."

"Just a few more minutes." He couldn't get enough of looking at her.

"A few more," she agreed with a smile.

His *mudder* came to the door a little later, peeked out, smiled, and went back inside. And then, just as Sam realized he was wearing down, his *dat* came to the door.

"Time to come in."

He'd been gearing himself up to standing but now, perversely, didn't want to move. "I'll be in in a minute."

"Your *mudder's* worrying."

"Go," said Mary Elizabeth. She squeezed his hand, then released it. "I'll see you later."

His *dat* held open the door. Their gazes met, held. Sam saw no welcome in his eyes, but when his crutch tip caught on a board on the porch and he lurched, his *dat* stepped forward and grasped him by the arms.

"Careful," he said gruffly.

He walked Sam inside and called David.

"I'm *allrecht* now," he told them, but both men stayed close.

"*Mamm* and Lavina fixed up the downstairs bedroom for you."

"*Gut. Danki.*" That would solve the problem of climbing the stairs. And hopefully he wouldn't have that nightmare in a different room than the one he'd had all his life.

Who was he kidding? As if location had anything to do with it.

Mercifully, his *dat* left the room and David helped him undress and slide under the quilt. He'd no sooner gotten settled than his *mudder* came in with lunch and a pain pill.

"Welcome home," she said, beaming as she put the tray on his lap. "I made you your favorite. Eat and get some meat back on those bones. Then take a nap and before you know it it'll be suppertime and Mary Elizabeth will be back."

"Sounds like the perfect prescription to get well," David told him.

Sam hadn't had much appetite in the hospital, but the hot meatloaf and gravy sandwich smelled incredible. He devoured it to his *mudder's* delight.

"Where's Lavina?"

"Taking a nap."

Sam yawned.

"Stop fighting it," David said with a chuckle. "C'mon, your little boy's all settled in."

"Very funny," Sam said, and then he was sound asleep.

The uneasy truce between Sam and his *dat* lasted a week.

Mary Elizabeth walked into the kitchen one afternoon and found the two men seated at the kitchen table. Tension was so thick she felt she could cut it with a knife.

Waneta looked at Mary Elizabeth. "I'm glad you're here. I need your help." She took Mary Elizabeth's arm and led her from the room.

"But—"

"Help me strip the bed," Waneta said when they walked into the front bedroom.

She did as she was asked. It was a job that didn't need two women, but Waneta had taken on extra work with Sam back home.

They made the bed with clean sheets and covered it with a quilt. Still, Waneta lingered in the room.

Finally, Mary Elizabeth could stand it no longer. "Don't you think we should get back to the kitchen? They looked like they were about to have an argument."

Waneta sat on the edge of the bed. "I spent years trying to keep the men in the family from arguing. Sometimes I should have said more. But now? This is the last chance for Amos and Sam to heal what's between them. I—" she broke off as they heard shouting.

Mary Elizabeth turned and ran. Were they killing each other?

When she got to the kitchen, she saw Sam lying on the floor. His *dat* stood over him.

"He wouldn't listen to me," Amos said, sounding disgusted. "Insisted he could walk without his crutches. Help me get him up."

"No, call David," Sam told Mary Elizabeth. "I don't want you hurting yourself."

Amos stalked to the back door and rang the bell that was used to summon someone in the fields.

"What's all the racket?" Waneta asked as she came into the room.

"Sam fell," Amos said. He slammed the back door. "Trying too hard to take care of himself. Wouldn't let me get him a glass of water."

"I can take care of myself." Sam rolled to his side and tried to lever himself up but couldn't.

David rushed in, looking frantic. "What is it? Is Lavina having the *boppli*?"

"*Nee*, it's Sam. He didn't want me to help him up off the floor."

"Let *Daed* and I do it."

Sam looked like he was going to object, but he let his *dat* help David get him up and to a chair.

"If you don't need me, I'm going to check on Lavina."

"I'm fine, thanks."

"Always so stubborn," Amos muttered as he looked at Sam. "Acting like everything's my fault. Well, it takes two to have an argument."

"Not if one man wants to keep trying to pick one." Sam took the glass of water Mary Elizabeth handed him. He pulled a prescription bottle from his pocket, shook a tablet out, and swallowed it with some water.

"I'm not trying to pick one." Amos sat down in a chair at the opposite end of the table and glared at him. "I did the best I could raising you three *kinner*. Didn't do any different than my *dat* did and seems to me I turned out *allrecht*."

Mary Elizabeth held her breath as Sam raised a brow.

"Seems to me my *sohns* did, too."

"All of us? Not just David?"

"Not just David," Amos said a little grudgingly. "Don't go telling John I said that, though. We don't want him thinking it's *allrecht* to live with the *Englisch*."

"Amos, there's something I need your help with," Waneta said.

"What?"

"Something in the *dawdi haus*."

He hesitated and then he must have gotten the message from her. He hauled himself to his feet and followed her there. The door shut behind them.

"Well," Sam said. "That's as close to an apology as I'll probably get for the way he treated us."

"*Ya*, it is," she agreed.

"I'll take it."

She smiled.

Mary Elizabeth stood with Sam at the back of the living room.

She'd sat on the porch of his old house one day when he came home from the hospital and told him time would pass quickly and soon they'd be married.

Time had flown by. Now they stood together about to walk to the minister and say their vows.

Their day had finally come.

She looked at him, thinking he'd never looked more handsome in a new suit and white shirt. And he'd never looked happier.

"Are you sure you don't want your cane?"

"Don't need it."

"If you need to you can lean on me."

He smiled. "I know. I have these past weeks, haven't I, *lieb*?"

"*Ya*, you have. That's what people who love each other should do. Right?"

The minister looked back at them and nodded. They walked toward him, past the rows of friends and family gathered here in her home to watch them marry.

Once again, time seemed to fly by. Amish weddings were long, filled with so many traditions: the verses from the Bible, the songs the congregation sang a cappella, the testimony of another lay minister who spoke of his own long, happy marriage blessed by God. Three hours passed in a happy, happy blur.

The men of the church turned the pews around to tables for guests to sit at the reception. Mary Elizabeth and Sam accepted congratulations as they moved to sit at the *eck*, the corner of the wedding table.

"Feels *gut* to sit down," he murmured. He inhaled the aromas of the food the women began laying on the table: the baked chicken, *roasht,* mashed potatoes with browned butter on top, so many vegetables you could almost hear the table groan. And, of course, the celery that was a feature of Lancaster County Amish weddings.

After the midday meal there'd be games and visiting and, before the guests left, another meal. Marriages lasted a long time in the Amish community and started with lengthy celebrations. Mary Elizabeth couldn't stop smiling as the hours passed.

"Have I told you how beautiful you look?" Sam asked her, squeezing her hand under the table.

She smoothed the skirt of the wedding dress her *mudder* and *schweschders* had helped her sew of the material she'd stored so wistfully in her closet while he lived in town. "A dozen times," she said, smiling. "But I'll be happy to accept the compliment one more time."

Finally, the last guest departed and Mary Elizabeth and Sam turned to each other. They smiled and walked without speaking to climb the stairs to her room. Sam opened the door to the room for the first time.

A new quilt covered a new bed—a double bed had been quietly moved into her room one day by her parents while Mary Elizabeth and Rose Anna were at quilting class. Now a wedding ring quilt in colors of blues and golds that her *mudder* and *schweschders* had sewn as a wedding gift covered it. She and Sam would spend their wedding night and their honeymoon and the months before they moved into their own home in this room where she'd grown up.

And they were both grateful for the welcome her parents had given them to stay as long as they needed.

She couldn't ask for more, she thought as she closed the door and looked at her new *mann*.

Except to ask for Christmas to come quickly. She'd dreamed so long of spending Christmas with Sam as his *fraa*.

21

Mary Elizabeth never understood why the calendar year didn't start with December—December 25 to be exact.

What was a more important date to remember than the birth of the Christ child?

But the rest of the world followed a calendar that started with January 1 and ended with December 31. She sighed. Well, it was finally December 1. She was a new *fraa*—how she loved that term—and she was sitting here in a nice warm home stitching on one of the last Christmas themed quilts of the season. There'd be a break to do others and then, perhaps only a month later, they'd begin on new ones for the next Christmas.

It was a comforting thing to have work you loved and that kept you thinking about Christmas through the year. Oh, not the one of trees and Santas and the like but the heart of Christmas—the giving of love and good will for your fellow man. At no other time of the year did people think about giving of heart and hand as they did at this time of year.

Amish Christmases were simple but deeply felt. Gifts were seldom luxury items or even store-bought. A gift made by hand with thought and care was the best, to her mind. So when she had an hour here and there, she sewed or knitted the gifts for her family.

And locked the bedroom door to keep out her new *mann* so he wouldn't walk in and catch her sewing the first shirt she'd make for him. Hopefully, there would be many shirts she'd sew in the many years she hoped God would give her with him.

Lavina shifted in her chair and Mary Elizabeth glanced over at her. "Just can't get comfortable," her *schweschder* said ruefully.

"Maybe you should get up and walk about a bit," Mary Elizabeth suggested. "That usually helps."

"Then I'll have to climb the stairs again." But she got up, and they went downstairs.

"It won't be much longer," she reminded her as they walked into the kitchen.

"I know."

"Tea?"

"Love some."

Sam limped in. "I thought I heard voices." He settled into a chair at the table.

Mary Elizabeth pulled a chair over and put his injured leg on it. "Doctor wants you to keep it elevated," she chided him gently.

"*Danki.*"

"Coffee?"

"That would be nice."

She checked the percolator on the back burner of the stove and found it still warm. She poured him a mug of coffee and turned the gas flame up under the tea kettle.

Lavina brought the cookie jar over and set it before him. "*Daed* always has to have a cookie about this time of day."

Sure enough, he came in a few minutes later, bringing cold air with him. He took off his jacket and hung it on a peg by the back door. "We're getting some snow flurries."

Mary Elizabeth set a plate before Lavina so she could pile the cookies on it. All the women had baked up a storm the past week. Fruitcake cookies sparkled like jewels with their cubes of candied pineapple, maraschino cherries, and ginger. Candy cane cookies and German *lebkuchen* had taken extra time, but they were expected year after year.

Sam chose a sugar cookie cut in the shape of a reindeer. Mary Elizabeth picked a gingerbread man and smiled. Amish *maedels* often ate gingerbread men and thought about the man they wanted to marry. Now she had hers. God was *gut*.

She poured mugs of hot water and, before she sat, knocked on the door of the *dawdi haus* to see if *Grossdaadi* wanted to join them.

Soon the table was full of family. The Stoltzfuses did love snack time. It was too bad John was in town working and David was at the farm or the family would have been complete.

When cookies and hot drinks were consumed and the women got to their feet, Sam reached for Mary Elizabeth's hand. "Do you have to go now?"

"In a few minutes," she said. "After I clean up the kitchen."

Rose Anna winked at Mary Elizabeth as she left the room.

"I wish I had something to do," Sam said as he watched her clear the table.

"You could take up quilting," she suggested tongue in cheek. "We could use some help with the orders this time of year."

"Men don't quilt."

"*Schur* they do. Why, I have a quilting magazine upstairs with an article about men who quilt."

"I'm not going to learn to quilt. Maybe I could walk out to the barn and help your *dat* with his seed order or repair some bridles or something."

"It's too slippery out there for you to walk that far. If you fall you could set yourself back even more." She stared at him. He'd always had trouble sitting still. Recuperating had proven hard on him. "Tell you what. I'll walk out and ask *Daed* if he has something he needs help with. Maybe the two of you could look over the seed catalogs in here. It's getting cold for him to be out there anyway."

"*Danki*. Be careful."

She smiled as she pulled on her jacket. "I will. Be right back."

Her *dat* jumped in surprise when she slid the barn door open. When he quickly put his hands behind his back, she raised her eyebrows. "What's going on?"

"None of your business," he said, but he grinned.

Christmas secrets, she decided, and she walked toward him and tried to see what he was hiding. He dodged her each time she moved toward him and finally he laughed. "If I show you, you'll have to promise you won't tell your *mudder*."

"I'm not the one who can't keep secrets," she reminded him. "That's Rose Anna." Not only did her younger *schweschder* do her best to find out what she was getting for Christmas—she'd always blabbed what others were getting when she found out about gifts in progress.

He brought out what he'd been holding—a pretty spice rack for her *mudder*. "Think she'll like it?"

"She'll love it. *Daed*, Sam's bored. I told him maybe he could help you with the seed order or something."

"It's done. I'm concentrating on finishing my gifts this afternoon."

"Maybe I can drop him off at David's when I go to town."

Jacob hid the spice rack. "*Gut* idea. I'll hitch up the buggy for you."

Sam nearly jumped out of his chair when she told him she'd take him to his *bruder's haus*.

But when they got there, Lavina answered the door and told them that David had just left to help a neighbor with something.

"I should have called," Mary Elizabeth said.

"*Kumm*, have some tea with me," Lavina invited.

"I can't. I have errands to run for *Mamm*. But Sam can."

Lavina smiled at him. "That would be nice. I'm feeling cooped up. Doctor said it could be any day now."

Sam stiffened and turned to Mary Elizabeth. "I could go with you. Maybe Lavina would like to rest."

Mary Elizabeth hesitated, but when she saw her *schweschder* rub at her lower back she felt a little uneasy. "David should be home soon. And Lavina shouldn't be left alone."

"I'm not a *kind*," Lavina told her, frowning.

"*Nee,* you're about to have one, and you shouldn't be alone."

"I could run the errands," Sam offered.

"You don't need to be sliding around in the snow," Mary Elizabeth said.

The oven timer dinged. "Cookies are done." Lavina headed for the kitchen.

"Cookies?" Sam followed her. "What kind?"

"Gee, see you later, Mary Elizabeth," she said, her lips quirking in a grin.

Sam turned and gave her a quick kiss. "Oh, sorry, *lieb.* Have fun and I'll see you soon."

"Don't let the door hit you on the way out," she murmured and left.

Sam thoroughly enjoyed helping Lavina. He set his cane aside, pulled the trays of cookies from the oven, and was invited to have several. They smelled so *gut* he couldn't resist blowing on one and popping it into his mouth.

"Ow."

"You're as bad as a *kind*. You need to wait 'til they're cool."

He grabbed a glass of water to cool his mouth. It was worth it. "That was *wunderbaar. I might* be able to wait until another one cools."

Lavina smiled as she used a spatula to move the cookies to a big plate. "We have enough to make about two dozen more cookies. You can take some home with you."

He watched her rub at the small of her back again. "Let me put the next batch in the oven. Your back is hurting."

"It's been aching all day."

"Then sit."

"Neither of us should be on our feet," she said. But she sank gratefully into a chair.

"I'll sit, too." They worked dropping spoonfuls of dough and when they were finished, Sam slid them into the oven and set the timer as she instructed.

A few minutes later, she suddenly uttered a cry, and he heard something splashing. She slapped a hand on her mouth and stared at him with horror in her eyes.

"What is it?" he asked, his heart leaping up into his throat.

"My water just broke."

He jumped to his feet and felt a twinge in his injured leg at the sudden movement. Then he was grabbing at the back of her chair as his feet slid in the water on the floor. Not water, he told himself. The water that surrounded a *boppli* in the womb. Amniotic fluid.

The *boppli* was coming.

"Stay there," he croaked when she started to rise. "I don't want you slipping."

He grabbed a couple of dishtowels from the kitchen counter and threw them down to absorb the liquid.

"We need to call David."

Sam reached into his pocket for the cell phone Peter had insisted he get after the accident. He hit speed dial and handed her the phone.

"David? You need to come home. The *boppli's* coming. Really coming this time."

She pulled the phone from her ear and stared at it.

"What's the matter?"

"He hung up."

"What can I do?" He hoped he could do whatever it was. Right now, he was feeling the kind of terror he imagined all men felt when confronted by the prospect of being around a woman who might give birth at any minute.

How he wished he could call Mary Elizabeth. But she didn't have a cell phone.

"Shall I call your *mudder*?"

"*Ya*, please."

But the phone rang and rang until the answering machine in the phone shanty picked up, and he listened to the message her *mudder* had left on it. He gave the phone to Lavina so she could say what she wanted and awkwardly tried to wipe up the dampness on the floor.

She finished the call and handed him back the phone. "Can you call the midwife for me? The number's over there in the address book on the kitchen counter."

He got the book for her and pressed it and the phone into her hands. She made the call and then looked at him.

"I need my suitcase from our room upstairs. Maybe a clean dress?"

Then she waved her hand and shook her head. "*Nee*, let's wait until David's here. I don't want you to hurt your leg climbing the stairs."

"I've been managing the stairs at home."

Suddenly the color drained from her face and she doubled over. "Oh my," she exclaimed when the pain passed. She glanced at the clock on the wall. "Remember the time for me so we'll be able to time the contractions."

He noted the time and then dumped the damp towels in the sink, trying not to shudder as he washed his hands. Contractions. Where was David?

The oven timer dinged. He picked up potholders, took the baking pans out of the oven, and set them on the top of the stove.

"You need to turn the oven off," she reminded him.

He stared at the controls. *Allrecht*, he figured it out. He didn't know much about operating an oven.

The back door slammed open and David rushed in looking frantic. He rushed to her side and took her hand.

"Are you *allrecht*?"

She nodded. "I called the midwife, so she's expecting us. Can you get my suitcase and my green dress?"

"*Schur.*" He glanced at Sam. "Watch her until I get back?"

"I'm not going anywhere."

David was back in seconds with the suitcase and a dress.

"You brought blue," Lavina told him.

"Huh?"

"You brought my blue dress not my green one."

"Lavina, you're only going to wear it for a little while and we're kind of in a hurry here."

She bent over with another contraction. Sam looked at the clock. "Ten minutes since the last one."

When the pain passed she looked at her *mann.* "The green one."

"Get it," Sam said. "It's faster than arguing."

So David ran upstairs and brought back the green one. Sam excused himself so she could change in the kitchen. Then, when David called him back in they helped her into a jacket and grabbed her purse and suitcase. They walked her out to the buggy and helped her inside between contractions.

Sam watched them leave and realized his knees were shaking. He made his way back into the house, careful not to slip on the stairs, and sank down into a chair in the kitchen.

That's where Mary Elizabeth found him when she returned. Sitting there half-sick from too many cookies and cups of coffee. And nerves.

"Where's Lavina?" she asked, glancing around.

"Having her *boppli,*" he said, grabbing his cane. "Come on, I'll tell you all about it on the way there."

A new member of the family joined the celebration of the birth of the Christ child when the family gathered the next week.

Grossdaadi had the seat of honor next to the fireplace in the Zook living room. He held his great-grandson Mark in the crook of one arm as he read the story of the birth of the Christ child

284

from his Bible. One child who had changed the world, thought Mary Elizabeth. She loved watching Mark studying the flames with his big, serious blue eyes while *Grossdaadi* read about a *boppli* born so long ago who had taught so many about love.

Lavina quietly told her that *Grossdaadi* had looked sad when she walked in like he was missing *Grossmudder*, so she'd handed Mark to him. So the oldest member of the family held the newest. There was something so special about that, Mary Elizabeth thought.

She sat next to Sam and sent up a silent prayer of gratitude for her first Christmas with her new *mann* and wondered if next year *Grossdaadi* might be holding her first *kind* as he read the Bible.

It was sad that *Grossmudder* wasn't there with them, but Mary Elizabeth felt she must be happy to be with her Father and Jesus.

Tonight they gathered to hear about the birth of Jesus, and they basked in the glow from the fire and the candles set on the mantel. It was cold and snowy outside, but gathered here on this holy night all was well.

Amos and Waneta Stoltzfus had been invited, and Mary Elizabeth didn't think she'd ever seen him so relaxed. So peaceful. Oh, he'd cast a disapproving glance at John when he walked in wearing *Englisch* clothes, but there hadn't been any comments. Waneta glowed with an inner happiness and couldn't keep her hands off her first grandson.

Mary Elizabeth and Rose Anna set out the huge supper they'd spent the afternoon cooking. Lavina was only allowed to sit and do things like slice loaves of bread and arrange cookies and slices of cake on a plate since she was a new *mudder*.

"Amos is behaving tonight," Rose Anna said in a low voice as she helped Mary Elizabeth arrange slices of baked ham on a platter. "Maybe things are going to work out and John will stay."

"It's Christmas," Mary Elizabeth warned her.

"She's right," Lavina said, giving her youngest *schweschder* a sympathetic look. "It takes time."

"Besides, I thought you decided to give up on him and see Peter."

"I like Peter but..." she trailed off and walked over to stand in the doorway and look out at John sitting in the living room.

Linda walked in carrying Mark and held him out to Lavina. "Someone wants you."

"I'll take him up to my old room and nurse him."

"We'll wait until you come down to eat."

"*Nee,* don't wait."

Linda just smiled and set the percolator on the stove. Sam wandered into the kitchen and swiped a cookie from the plate Lavina had arranged. Mary Elizabeth fussed at him for disturbing the artistic arrangement Lavina had made, but he just grinned at her and asked when they were going to eat.

"Soon," she said. "Go ask who wants coffee and who wants hot chocolate."

"I know what he's giving you for Christmas," Rose Anna told Mary Elizabeth after he left the kitchen.

"Rose Anna!"

She looked at her *mudder.* "I said I know. I didn't say I'd tell."

"Why don't you pour the coffee when it's done?"

Rose Anna shrugged and started setting out cups and saucers. Sam returned to say everyone wanted coffee, no hot chocolate. *Grossdaadi* wanted hot cider if there was any otherwise he'd take coffee, *danki,* so she poured some cider in a small pan and heated it on the stove.

Jacob wandered in and snatched a sliver of ham when his *fraa's* back was turned. "Stop that," she said without turning.

"Eyes in the back of her head," he muttered as he grabbed another piece. "Are we eating soon?"

"After Lavina takes care of your grandson."

"Bet he'd like some of this ham."

Linda laughed and shooed him out of the room.

Lavina came down a few minutes later, but she didn't have Mark with her. "He was ready for a nap."

Mary Elizabeth frowned. "Have you been crying?"

"I was just thinking about *Grossmudder*. She loved Christmas."

"And she would have loved Mark. She loved *bopplis*. Bet *Grossdaadi's* missing her even more right now than usual."

She was glad Lavina had put Mark in his arms when he sat in the big chair by the fire with his Bible.

"Maybe next year Mark will have a cousin to play with," Lavina said.

Mary Elizabeth smiled. She'd been thinking earlier that it would be *wunderbaar* if she and Sam had a *boppli* next Christmas.

"That would be the only thing better than tonight."

"I can't wait for tomorrow," Rose Anna said. "Wait until you see what Sam got for you, Mary Elizabeth."

"Rose Anna—"

She held up her hands. "I told you I'm not telling her!"

Later, as she drifted off to sleep, Mary Elizabeth smiled as she remembered how Rose Anna had been so excited about Sam's gift. He didn't need to give her a thing. She had everything— everyone—she wanted.

Second Christmas was the day they had always exchanged gifts. David had made a beautifully carved cradle for Mark and a rocking chair for Lavina. He loved his knitted woolen muffler she made to keep him warm as he worked outside in the winter. Linda delighted in the spice rack Jacob had made for her. An avid reader, he exclaimed over the books she'd found him and wanted to start reading right away. *Grossdaadi* immediately put on the warm navy sweater the women in the family had taken turns knitting for him.

Sam loved the new shirt she made him for church. And then he handed her the present he'd made—a hand-woven basket filled with new thimbles, sewing scissors, and all manner of things to use when she sewed. Linda had picked up the supplies at Stitches in Time. Then he handed her another gift. He'd made a second basket and filled it with packets of flower and vegetable seeds.

She pulled a card from the basket and tears began slipping down her cheeks as she read it: "For your first kitchen garden. Believe that with God's help you'll have it soon." She hugged him. It was the perfect gift.

The house soon filled with friends stopping by to bring holiday wishes and gifts. Mary Elizabeth wasn't surprised to see the bishop and his *fraa*, but he seemed unusually ebullient today. After visiting for a time, he said something to Sam and the two men went into the kitchen. The bishop came out a few minutes later, nodded at her, and then left with his *fraa*.

Sam walked out of the kitchen looking stunned. He sank down onto the sofa next to her, and she felt him trembling.

"Is something wrong?"

He smiled at her, and she saw then that he had tears in his eyes. "*Nee*, something is very right." He glanced around at the family and stood.

"We just had the most wonderful gift. I've been trying to buy Sarah Fisher's farm. The bishop just came to tell me that she's changed her mind and agreed to hold the loan. Mary Elizabeth and I will be buying it and moving into it soon. God is so *gut*."

He sat again and looked at her. Mary Elizabeth barely heard the excited exclamations of her family as she stared into Sam's eyes. "Is it true?"

Sam nodded. "She heard about my accident from a friend who still lives here and called the bishop to talk. Then she and her family in Ohio discussed it. They felt they wanted the farm to stay in the Amish community, not be sold to *Englischers*. And they wanted us to have it."

Her hands still clutched the basket of seeds for her first kitchen garden. She set it on the floor at her feet and threw her arms around him.

"Merry Christmas, Sam."

"Merry Christmas, *lieb*."

Recipes

Haystack Supper

1 ¾ cups soda crackers, crushed
3 pounds hamburger, browned
3 tablespoons taco seasoning
4 cups lettuce, shredded
3 medium tomatoes, chopped
2 cups green peppers, chopped
1 large onion, chopped
Spaghetti, rice, or both, cooked
Shredded cheese or cheese sauce, optional
Salsa, optional
Ranch dressing, optional

Brown ground beef. Drain and add taco seasoning. Layer some of each ingredient on your plate. Top with shredded cheese or cheese sauce. Salsa or ranch dressing is also a good addition.

Serves six, but amounts can be adjusted to suit your taste and other vegetables can be added.

Buttermilk Pound Cake

1 cup shortening
1 stick butter or margarine
2 ½ cups sugar
4 eggs
1 tablespoon vanilla extract
1 teaspoon butter flavoring
1 tablespoon hot water
3 ½ cups all-purpose flour
½ teaspoon soda
½ teaspoon salt
1 cup buttermilk

Preheat oven to 325 degrees F. Cream shortening, butter, and sugar until light and fluffy. Add eggs, beating after each. Add flavorings and water. Beat well. In a separate bowl, combine flour, soda, and salt. Mix into creamed mixture, alternately with buttermilk. Pour into greased and floured pan. Bake for 1 hour and 5 minutes. Cool and remove from pan.

Serves 16 to 20

Bread and Butter Pudding

1 teaspoon ground cinnamon
¼ cup sugar
4 tablespoons butter or margarine, at room temperature
5 slices white bread with crust
½ cup raisins
2 cups milk
2 eggs

Preheat oven to 350 degrees F. Add cinnamon to sugar and mix well. Set aside. Generously spread butter on one side of each piece of bread. Cutting diagonally, slice each in half. Arrange triangle slices in pan, slightly overlapping, with butter side up and cut edges facing the same direction, making a spiral. As you add the bread, sprinkle with sugar-cinnamon mixture and raisins. Pour milk in small bowl, add eggs, and using whisk or fork, blend well. Pour milk mixture over bread and raisins in baking pan. Let sit for about 15 minutes for bread to absorb liquid. Bake for 30 minutes, or until top is golden brown. Serve the pudding while still warm in individual dessert bowls. It can be eaten plain or with cream.

Serves 4

Blueberry Zucchini Cake

2 cups finely shredded and drained zucchini
3 eggs, lightly beaten
1 cup vegetable oil
3 teaspoons vanilla extract
2 ¼ cups white sugar
3 cups all-purpose flour
1 teaspoon salt
1 teaspoon baking powder
¼ teaspoon baking soda
1 pint fresh blueberries (you can reserve a few for garnish if so desired)

Preheat oven to 350 degrees F. Butter and flour two 8-inch round cake pans. Place grated zucchini in a clean dish towel. Squeeze until most of the liquid comes out. You want 2 total cups of shredded zucchini draining. Set aside. In a large bowl, beat together the eggs, oil, vanilla, and sugar. Fold in the zucchini. Slowly add in the flour, salt, baking powder, and baking soda. Gently fold in the blueberries. Divide batter evenly between prepared cake pans. Bake 35 to 40 minutes, or until a knife inserted in the center of a cake comes out clean. Cool 20 minutes in pans, then turn out onto wire racks to cool completely. Frost with lemon buttercream.

Serves 10 to 12

Lemon Buttercream

1 cup butter, room temperature
3 ½ cups confectioners' sugar
$^1/_8$ teaspoon salt
2 tablespoons lemon juice, about 1 lemon
1 teaspoon vanilla extract
zest of 1 lemon

Beat butter, sugar, and salt until well mixed. Add lemon juice and vanilla and continue to beat for another 3 to 5 minutes or until creamy. Fold in zest.

Makes approximately 4 cups frosting

Unstuffed Cabbage Rolls

1 tablespoon olive oil
1 large onion, chopped
1 ½ to 2 pounds lean ground beef or turkey
1 clove garlic, minced
1 small cabbage, chopped
2 cans (14.5 ounces each) diced tomatoes
1 can (8 ounces) tomato sauce
½ cup water
1 teaspoon ground black pepper
1 teaspoon sea salt

Heat the olive oil over medium heat in a big skillet. Sauté the onion until tender, and then add the ground beef or turkey until the meat is browned. Add the garlic, cook an additional minute before adding the remaining ingredients. Bring to a boil, reduce heat, and cover. Simmer about 25 minutes or until the cabbage is fork tender.

Serves 6 to 8

Glossary

ab im kop—off in the head. Crazy.
ach—oh
allrecht—all right
boppli—baby
bruder—brother
daed—dad
danki—thank you
dat—father
dawdi haus—a small home added to or near the main house to which the farmer moves after passing the farm and main house to one of his children.
Deitsch—Pennsylvania German
Der hochmut kummt vor dem fall.—Pride goeth before the fall.
dippy eggs—over-easy eggs
dochder—daughter
eck—the corner of the wedding table
Englisch—what the Amish call a non-Amish person
fraa—wife
grossdaadi—grandfather
grossdochder—granddaughter
grosseldres—grandparents
grosskinner—grandchildren
grossmudder—grandmother
grosssohn—grandson
guder mariye—good morning
gut—good
gut-n-owed—good evening
haus—house

hochmut—pride

hungerich—hungry

kapp—prayer covering or cap worn by girls and women

kind, kinner—child, children

kumm—come

lebkuchen—traditional German cookie

lieb—love

liebschen—dearest or dear one

maedels—young single women

mamm—mom

mann—husband

mudder—mother

nacht—night

nee—no

newehocker—wedding attendant

onkel—uncle

Ordnung—The rules of the Amish, both written and unwritten. Certain behavior has been expected within the Amish community for many, many years. These rules vary from community to community, but the most common are to have no electricity in the home, to not own or drive an automobile, and to dress a certain way.

roasht—roast

rumschpringe—time period when teenagers are allowed to experience the *Englisch* world while deciding if they should join the church.

schul—school

schur—sure

schweschder—sister

sohn—son

verboten—forbidden, not done

wilkumm—welcome

wunderbaar—wonderful

ya—yes

zwillingbopplin—twins

Group Discussion Guide

Spoiler alert! Please don't read before completing the book as the questions contain spoilers!

1. In the beginning of the book Mary Elizabeth is still grieving over Sam, the man she loves, leaving the Amish community—and her. Have you ever grieved over losing a relationship with someone you loved? How did you cope?

2. Mary Elizabeth decides she must move on and start seeing someone else. Have you done this? What advice would you give her?

3. Do you believe God has a plan for your life? What is it? How do you know when it's His plan or the one you think you should have?

4. Amish young people get to experience *Englisch* life during a period called *rumschpringe*. While some youth use it as a chance to break out of the strict rules of the Amish community, most do not. Do you think teens of either culture need a period of unrestricted time to mature?

5. Many Amish believe God has set aside a marriage partner for them. Do you believe this? Do you believe in love at first sight?

6. Sam finds himself regretting his choice to leave the community. But Mary Elizabeth is seeing someone else. Do you think he deserved a second chance with her?

7. Home and family mean different things to different people. Sometimes family is made up of our mother, father, and siblings. What is home to you? What is family to you?

8. Sam and Mary Elizabeth get a second chance at love after Mary Elizabeth forgives him for leaving her and the community. Have you ever gotten a second chance at love?

9. The family rejoices when Mary Elizabeth's sister becomes pregnant with her first child. Have you had children? What was your experience?

10. Sam hopes to buy a farm before he and Mary Elizabeth marry. Many Amish couples live with her parents until they get their own home. If you're married, did you and your husband have your own home or did you stay with his or your parents first? How did this work out?

11. How do you feel the struggles Sam and Mary Elizabeth experienced helped them grow as a couple?

12. *Englisch* Christmas celebrations are different than those of the Amish. How do you celebrate Christmas?

Want to learn more about author Barbara Cameron?
Check out www.AbingdonFiction.com
for more information on all of Barbara's books
and the other fine fiction from Abingdon.
Be sure to visit Barbara Cameron online!
www.BarbaraCameron.com

and on Facebook at

https://www.facebook.com/pages/Barbara-Cameron
-Reader-Page/359763767479635

And now for a sneak peek at *Home to Paradise*, book 3 of the Coming Home series.

1

Snow fell quietly, cold and white. Inside the big old farmhouse where Rose Anna had lived all her life it was warm. A fire crackled in the hearth, the only sound in the room.

Rose Anna glanced around the sewing room. Usually she and her two *schweschders* sat chatting and sewing with their *mudder*, sometimes singing a hymn as they worked. Today it was just her and her *mudder*. She sighed. "So here you sit with your old *maedel dochder*, Mamm."

Linda laughed. "I hardly think you're an old *maedel* at twenty, Rose Anna."

She knotted a thread, clipped it with scissors, and squinted as she rethreaded her needle. Her *schweschder* Mary Elizabeth had once confided she felt like making an Old Maid's Puzzle quilt.

"I feel like one," she said, pouting a little. "Both of my *schweschders* are married and so are lots of my friends. I have been a *newehocker* at so many weddings!" She made a face as she began stitching on her quilt again.

"*Gut-n-mariye!*"

Rose Anna glanced up. "*Ach,* here comes my newly married *schweschder.*"

"Mary Elizabeth, it's *gut* to see you. *Kumm*, sit by the fire and get warm. You look cold."

She leaned down and kissed her *mudder's* cheek. "Lavina's on her way up."

Linda brightened and turned to look in the direction of the door. When Lavina walked in a moment later her face fell. "Where's Mark?"

Lavina laughed and shook her head. "You're not glad to see me?"

"Well, *schur*," Linda said quickly. "But I thought you were bringing my *grosssohn*."

"He was fussy and stayed up most of the night so now he's sleeping." Lavina sank into a chair. "Waneta said she'd mind him so I could get out for a bit. She told me she wouldn't let him sleep all day so he'd keep us up again."

"You look like you need a nap," Rose Anna told her.

"It's tempting, but I need to stay to my goal of finishing this quilt," she said as she threaded a needle.

"Could he be teething already?"

Lavina shuddered. "I hope not. He's not three months old yet. I've heard about teething from my friends."

Soon it was like it had been for so long, everyone chattering and sewing, the mood as bright and cheerful as the fire.

But Rose Anna felt a growing restlessness. She put her quilt aside, went downstairs to make tea for their break, and found herself staring out the kitchen window. The trees were bare and black against the gray sky. Snow had stopped falling, coating everything with a white blanket that lay undisturbed. She found herself pacing the kitchen as she waited for the kettle to boil water.

Finally she knew she had to get out and burn off her restless energy.

"I'm going for a walk," she announced when her *mudder* and *schweschders* came downstairs. She pulled on rubber boots and her bonnet, then shrugged on her coat. "I won't be long."

"But *kind*, it's cold out there," her *mudder* protested.

"I need to walk. 'Bye."

"She'll be fine, *Mamm*," she heard Lavina say behind her before she closed the back door.

Funny, her older *schweschder* reassuring their *mudder*.

She started off down the road, watching for cars and staying well to the right. Smoke billowed from chimneys as she passed farms. Fields lay sleeping under the snow. The only sound was her boots crunching snow.

Usually she loved this time of year when life was slower, easier. All the planting, harvesting, canning was over. Farmers spent time in their barns repairing harnesses and equipment and planned their spring planting. Women occupied themselves with sewing and knitting and mending clothes. *Kinner* grew restive being cooped up and begged to go outside and build snow men.

The Stoltzfus farm came into view. Lavina had married David, the oldest *sohn* and lived there now. Mary Elizabeth had married Sam, the middle *sohn*. And she, the youngest Zook *schweschder*, had hoped to marry John, the youngest.

John's truck, a bright red pick-up, was parked out front. She wondered what he was doing home during a work day. Her feet slowed as she frowned and worried. Was his *dat* ill again? Surely Lavina would have said something. Amos had been cured of his cancer for quite some time now.

John came out of the farm house carrying a box and walked toward the truck, then he saw her. "Need a ride?"

"*Nee, danki*," she said, lifting her chin and walking past him. She might have to be pleasant to him in front of family, but she'd never forgive him for not wanting her any more.

She heard the engine start and the next thing she knew he was pulling up beside her. He stopped and the window on the passenger side slid down. "You're sure you don't want a ride?"

"I said *nee, danki*," she repeated, and her words sounded as cold as the air she was breathing. She'd rather freeze to death than get into his truck.

His driving the *Englisch* vehicle was a source of friction between himself and his *dat*. John was the last of the Stoltzfus *bruders* who had moved to town after not getting along with their *dat* and the last to reconcile with him and rejoin the Amish community. The only reason he was living here now was because Sam and Mary Elizabeth had married and John could no longer afford the apartment he'd shared with Sam.

Mary Elizabeth had confided to her that she and Sam had asked John to move in with them. She supposed that was why John had carried the box out to the truck just now.

It was nice that they had offered when they'd only been married a few months and moved into their own farm down the road.

But it meant that she was going to have to see him more often and that rankled.

Rose Anna glared at the truck. Later she'd chide herself for childishness. She found herself reaching down to a drift of snow at the side of the road, packing some into a hard ball in her hands, and throwing it at the truck as he accelerated away.

It hit the glass window of the truck cab, dead-on—no surprise since she was great at softball. He slammed on the brakes then got out and stood staring at her, his hands on his hips.

"Why'd you do that?" he demanded.

She turned on her heel and began stomping back toward home.

And that was when she felt something thump her on the back. She turned and saw him forming another snowball in his hands.

Lowering her eyebrows, she bent, quickly scooped up snow in her hands, formed another ball, and hit him in the center of the chest before he could lob another at her. She took off running toward the Stoltzfus farm and made it to the front door just as he got her with another ball of snow. Doors weren't locked in the middle of the day. She slipped inside before he could hit her again and found herself staring at Amos sitting in his recliner reading the newspaper.

"*Guder-n-mariye,*" she said politely. "Is Waneta home?"

He closed his mouth that had fallen open at her abrupt entrance and nodded. "In the kitchen."

Rose Anna brushed the snow from her coat and wiped her feet before walking there. Waneta stood at the big kitchen table kneading bread.

"I was just out and thought I'd stop by," she said brightly. She spun around when she heard footsteps behind her.

John strolled in just then. "I think you forgot something," he said, pushing a handful of loose snow in her face.

"John! Whatever are you doing?" his *mudder* cried, looking appalled.

"She started it," he told her as he strolled out, chuckling.

Rose Anna wiped the snow from her face and grinned at Waneta as the older woman hurried over with a dish towel to dry her off. "He's right. I did. I don't know what got into me."

She did know, but she wasn't going to tell the woman she'd hoped would be her mother-in-law one day. It just hurt too much to share with her how badly her *sohn* had hurt her when he turned his back on their relationship and left the Amish community.

2

If there was anything Rose Anna loved more than quilting it was teaching the twice-weekly quilting class at the women's shelter in town.

She'd started volunteering there with her *schweschders* and now whether or not they were able to come she continued because she enjoyed it so much.

The shelter was a big, rambling house just outside the town proper. There was no sign in front. People passing by wouldn't know it was anything but a family home. That was because the women and *kinner* inside wouldn't be safe if the husbands and boyfriends the women fled from knew where they were.

She knocked and Pearl, the woman who ran the shelter, answered the door herself and greeted her with a big smile.

The shelter should have been a sad place. Actually it had been at times when she first came with Lavina. She'd never seen women with bruised faces or *kinner* with eyes full of fear who hid behind their *mudder's* skirts. It wasn't that abuse didn't happen in the Amish community, but it wasn't something that she had come into direct contact with like here.

Gradually she'd seen the women's shelter as a place of hope. Because the place itself had changed.

The quilting classes Kate Kraft, a police officer and quilting enthusiast, had organized had made a difference.

One by one, women climbed the stairs to the second floor of the shelter to a room Pearl had converted into a sewing room with long tables and donated sewing machines. Kate had volunteered to teach quilting classes and, being Kate, she'd convinced others to join her.

Lavina hadn't believed she could contribute anything, but Kate showed her that she could. And then Lavina had gotten Mary Elizabeth to come.

So of course Rose Anna had to see why her two older *schweschders* took time off from their work and daily chores to teach quilting at a women's shelter.

And she'd been hooked.

Kate had made a difference and then Leah, an Amish woman who owned Stitches in Time shop in Paradise, had seen a way to help the women even more. The two of them had come up with the idea for Leah to open a second shop called Sewn in Hope to sell the crafts they made.

Now the room was filled with women who happily sewed a way out of despair and financed a way to build a future for themselves and their *kinner*.

Today many of the women were sewing Thanksgiving and Christmas crafts. They were the most popular items offered at Sewn in Hope at any time of the year.

Rose Anna stopped by the table near the window where a new resident sat staring at the quilt block that had been handed out at the beginning of the class. The woman looked small, her chin-length brown hair falling forward over her thin face. She wore a faded T-shirt with an Army slogan and camouflage pants.

"Hello, I'm Rose Anna."

The woman jerked and stared up at her with frightened green eyes. "I—hi. I'm Brooke."

"Would you like some help with your block?"

"No, I think I can handle it."

She bent over it again, and Rose Anna couldn't help wondering if she was intent on working on it or trying to hide the yellowing bruise around one eye.

And Brooke kept glancing nervously at the windows at her side as her fingers plucked at the fabric block.

"Just let me know if you need anything," Rose Anna said quietly. "And welcome to the class. I hope you enjoy it."

Brooke nodded jerkily and kept her eyes focused on the block.

Rose Anna walked a few steps away and suddenly something bright and round whirled at her like a child's Frisbee and chucked her on the chin. She grabbed at it and frowned at the fabric circle. "Why, it's a yo-yo."

"Sorry, Rose Anna."

She grinned at Jason, a little boy who'd come to the shelter last month with his *mudder* and two *schweschders*. "It's okay. It didn't hurt me."

"That's not a yo-yo. Yo-yos are toys."

"My grandmother made these," Edna told him. "I thought about making a quilt with them but then I came up with something different." She waved a hand at her table and Rose Anna saw that she'd made various sizes of them, stacked them from largest at the bottom to the smallest at the top. Then she'd sewed a fabric ribbon at the top to hang them. They were little trees of fabric.

"They're darling," Kate said as she stopped at the table and held one up. She smiled at Edna "I think they'll sell well at the shop."

"They're easy to make and don't take much fabric."

"Speaking of fabric." Kate announced as she walked in. She held up a shopping bag in each hand.

"I thought you had court this morning."

"I did. We finished early and Leah's shop was on the way here."

"Hah!" said Edna. "You know you find every excuse you can to stop by there."

"Guilty!" Kate laughed. "So I guess this means you don't want to see it?"

Edna jumped up. "You guessed wrong." She turned to the other women in the room. "Kate's got new fabric!"

Sewers swarmed over, eager to check out the new fabric. Kate stepped closer to Rose Anna.

"I see we have someone new," she said quietly, jerking her head in the direction of a woman who sat at a table near the windows.

"Her name's Brooke. She didn't want to talk much," Rose Anna told her. "So I told her to let me know if she needed any help and just let her be. Sometimes it takes a while for a person to feel comfortable."

Kate nodded. "I'll put my things down and say hello."

A woman walked up to ask her a question, and after she left, Kate turned to Rose Anna.

"Where'd Brooke go? I didn't see her leave the room."

Rose Anna glanced around. "I don't know."

"Could I have this piece, Kate?" Edna asked, her eyes bright with excitement. "It'd go great in a lap quilt I want to make."

"Sure. Take whatever you want." She smiled at the women milling around the table admiring the fabric. "Malcolm said if I brought any more fabric home he'd have to build an addition onto the house."

Rose Anna laughed. My *daed*'s always saying things like that. But I noticed that he always smiles when he says it, and he keeps building more shelves in our sewing room."

There was a tug on her skirt. She glanced down and saw Lannie, a little girl who was two, clutching at her skirt.

Lannie popped her thumb out of her mouth. "Lady," she said, pointing at the table by the window. "Lady," she repeated and pulled at Rose Anna's skirt to indicate she should follow her.

She let the child lead her over to the table, wondering what she could be trying to tell her. "Lady," she said again. She pointed under the table.

So Rose Anna obliged and looked under the table and into Brooke's terrified gaze. The woman had her arms wrapped around herself and was shaking.

She knelt down. "Brooke? What's wrong? Are you feeling unwell?"

"Window," she managed. "I can't. The window."

Rose Anna turned and gestured to Lannie. "Get Kate, Lannie. Get Kate."

———

"So how are things going?"

John dumped the shovel of manure in the wheelbarrow and grimaced at his older brother.

"Couldn't be better. It's the weekend and here I am helping my brother clean out a stall. As if I don't shovel enough of this on my job."

David laughed and slapped him on the shoulder. "Well, Lavina'll make it up to you. She's fixing us lunch, and you know she'll give you enough leftovers to feed you for a week. I heard she made an extra pie."

"Apple?"

"*Ya.*"

John paused and considered. "That makes me feel a little better."

"Still eating a lot of ramen noodles?"

He laughed. "My specialty."

"Sam must be missing them now that he's married to Mary Elizabeth."

"The two of you are getting to be soft old married men," John jeered.

"Marriage is great," David told him as he set his shovel aside. "You should try it."

"Not me. Not for a long time. It's up to me to keep up the Stoltzfus reputation now." He grinned. "It's hard for one man to carry the load, but I'll try to do the job."

David frowned. "Sounds like you're enjoying your *rumschpringe* a little too much."

"No lectures, big brother." John picked up the handles of the wheelbarrow and started out of the barn. No way was he going to admit that he didn't have the time—or the money—to enjoy the single *Englisch* guy lifestyle.

He dumped the contents of the wheelbarrow and returned to the barn.

"Seriously, you and *Daed* couldn't get along? It would have saved you from having to get your own place."

"I tried."

"Did you?" David asked quietly.

John felt his defenses leap up. "It's not me!"

"*Nee?*"

"No." John refused to use Pennsylvania *Dietsch* since he'd left the community. "I just seem to . . . irritate him. Nothing I do, nothing I say is right."

"Yeah, I always felt that about you."

"Gee, thanks."

"I was joking, John."

He stared off into the distance and sighed. "I know Mom was happy that I was here, but I just can't handle it any more. And if I stayed I'd just be pressured to join the church. You know that. So I found myself a place."

"Something you can afford on your own? I thought you and Sam looked before he got married."

"A friend of my boss has a caretaker's cottage he hasn't been using. It needs some fix-up, so I'll be doing that to reduce the rent."

"Well, I guess that's *gut*," David said doubtfully.

"Why wouldn't it be?"

"I'd hoped you'd work out the problems with *Daed* if you stayed here."

"Well, I couldn't." He pinched the bridge of his nose. "I think it's for the best. I appreciate you and Lavina having me here."

"Anytime." David laid a hand on his shoulder. "Anytime. I mean it. And I know Sam and Mary Elizabeth asked you to stay with them."

"Yeah, just what a newly married couple needs. A brother hanging around so they have no privacy."

"You're forgetting *Mamm* and *Daed* live with us and they don't intrude on our privacy."

John shuddered. People always said that things could be worse. And they could. He could be an old married man like his brothers and have his parents living with him. He was just twenty-three. He wasn't ready to be a married man anytime soon.

"Look, I'm glad you and Sam are happy being married. But I'm not ready. I'm not sure I'll ever be ready."

David paused shoveling and regarded him. "I thought you were interested in Rose Anna for a long time."

John shrugged and shoveled up more manure. "That was a long time ago. And I can safely say we're not going to get back together now."

"Now?" David straightened. "What happened?"

"You mean *Daed* didn't tell you?"

"*Nee.*"

He stopped and propped his arm on the shovel handle. "She has quite a temper, that Rose Anna." He told David about the snowball fight.

"You didn't! Right there in the kitchen?"

"She started it!"

"*Ya*, and you didn't have any trouble finishing it, did you?"

John looked hard at him, trying to see if David was judging him. But David was grinning.

"She's sure holding a grudge," John said as he went back to shoveling.

"The Zook *maedels schur* never held back on letting us know how they felt."

"But Lavina forgave you. Mary Elizabeth forgave Sam."

"*Ya*. But we met them halfway."

"You know Rose Anna. She wants all the way—and everything her way."

"She reminds me a lot of you."

"I don't have to have everything my way."

"*Nee?*"

"No!"

They went back to shoveling and didn't speak. When the wheelbarrow was full David stood with his hands resting on his shovel. "Lavina forgave me. And then she saved my life. She persuaded me to come home. It was hard at first. *Daed* was as miserable as he ever was when I first came back. He'd always been hard. But he was angry at getting the cancer."

"I know all this."

"*Ya.* But maybe you're forgetting that things changed for the better. And it's because of Lavina leading me back home, back to church, Back to God."

"I'm happy for you," John said quietly. "But I don't need the same things."

"*Nee?*"

"No. And I don't need you trying to bring me back to the church. I know that's what you and everyone in the church is supposed to do to save me. I don't need saving."

He propped the shovel against a wall, pushed the wheelbarrow outside and dumped the contents. Turning, he started back and then stopped. He took a deep breath to steady himself, then another. It was no good getting mad at David. They'd both gone to church since they were babes in their mother's arms. They were taught that if someone strayed from the church you had to try to save them or they couldn't go to heaven.

By the time he went back inside David had spread bedding in the stalls for the horses. "I gotta go," he told him. "I promised to put in a couple hours with Peter."

"Eat first. Please. Lavina will be so disappointed if you don't."

John hesitated.

"Please."

He nodded. It was tough to say no when he brought up Lavina. "I can't stay long."

"I'll tell her you have to eat and run."

"Well, that doesn't sound very gracious."

"She knows how you are." David grinned at him and slung an arm around his shoulders.

"Think you're pretty funny, don't you?" John grabbed him in a headlock and they tussled for a few minutes before David managed to throw him off.

"I'm not so soft, am I, *bruder*?" he asked, chuckling.

"I let you go," John said. "I'm hungry."

But just to make sure David didn't try to prove him wrong he took off to the house.

"How are the quilting classes going at the shelter?" Mary Elizabeth asked as they sat working on their quilts in the sewing room of the Zook home later that week. "I was so sorry to miss them the past two weeks."

"We had some excitement the other day."

"Not an angry ex-husband—"

"*Nee*, nothing like that." Rose Anna knotted her thread, clipped it with scissors and looked at her *schweschder*. "We have a new resident who came to the class and had an anxiety attack."

"Quilting class made her anxious?"

"Kate says she has PTSD as well as being abused by her ex-husband. She hadn't been out of her house in months then she had to leave when he beat her."

She frowned. "She came to the class and couldn't handle sitting by the window. She was hiding under her table. It was so sad."

"What's PTSD?" their *mudder* asked.

"Post traumatic stress disorder. Kate said Chris Matlock had it after he served in the military. You remember, he used to be

Englisch before he came here and married Hannah, Matthew Bontrager's *schweschder*."

"So this woman was in the military?"

Rose Anna nodded. "Kate said she served in Afghanistan."

"Imagine, women in the military," Linda said.

"Kate was in the Army before she came here to work as a police officer," Rose Anna reminded her.

"I forgot. Seems like she's been here so long she's always been a part of Paradise." Linda got up and put another log on the fire.

"So what happened?" Mary Elizabeth sat, needle suspended over her quilt, looking at her. "Kate got under the table and talked to her awhile and got her to come out. Then they went downstairs. When Kate came back she told me that when Brooke returns we should find her a table away from the window."

"Sad."

"I think it's time for a cup of tea," their *mudder* announced a few minute later. "I'll go put the kettle on."

"We'll be right down." Mary Elizabeth watched her leave the room then turned to Rose Anna. "So, how's Peter?"

"He's fine."

"Just 'fine'? That doesn't sound so *gut*."

Rose Anna stared at the quilt in her hands. "I like Peter. I really do."

"But?"

"But I don't feel the same way about him that I do about John."

"Well, from what I hear, Peter might be happy about that."

"What?"

Mary Elizabeth tried to fight back a smile. "You've got really good aim."

It took a moment and then Rose Anna realized what her *schweschder* was talking about. She rolled her eyes. "How did you find out? *Nee*, let me guess. Waneta told Lavina and she told you."

Mary Elizabeth just grinned.

"Are you going to tell *Mamm*?"

"Do I look like a tattletale?"

"*Ya.*" She paused then shook her head. "*Nee.* That would be our older *schweschder.* She was always telling on us."

Mary Elizabeth laughed. "Well, if I don't, there's no guarantee Lavina or Waneta won't, you know."

"I don't know what got into me," Rose Anna said, remembering, "He was getting into his truck, and suddenly I just saw red. Before I knew what was happening I was making a snowball and throwing it at him."

She sighed. "And you know John. He didn't just keep going on his way. He got out of his truck and started firing snowballs back at me."

Mary Elizabeth shook her head. "The two of you have always gone head to head."

"Hey, I'm not the one who does that."

Her *schweschder* just looked at her.

"Anyway, I ran inside his *haus* and he followed me. He actually followed me into the kitchen and rubbed snow in my face. In front of his own *mudder.*"

"Bet he's going to be getting a lecture from her," Mary Elizabeth muttered.

Rose Anna grinned. "And hopefully his *dat* heard about it from her and he'll have something to say to John."

"Now that's just mean! You know he and his *dat* don't get along. I bet Amos is burning his ears off right now."

"I know." She giggled. "I wish I could be there for that."

"Shame on you." Mary Elizabeth tried to look stern. Then she giggled, too.

"Are you going to tell *Mamm*?" she asked her again.

Her *schweschder* stared at her for so long Rose Anna felt apprehensive. "If she asks me I have to tell her," she said finally. "But I won't go telling her. That would be gossiping."

Rose Anna nodded. "*Danki.*" She sighed. "But like I said, Lavina or Waneta could." She set her quilt down. "That's what I get for my behavior. It's just that John makes me so mad sometimes."

"Now he doesn't make you anything," Mary Elizabeth chided as she put her quilt down. "It's how you choose to react."

"Look out," Rose Anna told her as she narrowed her eyes. "I'm feeling like reacting right now."

Laughing, Mary Elizabeth ran for the stairs. "You'll have to catch me first."

Linda looked up as they clattered down the wooden stairs. "Well, well, there's two dainty, ladylike *maedels*."

She turned to her *mann* sitting at the kitchen. "Do you know these hooligans, Jacob? They look like our *dochders* but I'm not schur."

He chuckled. "Sounded like heifers coming down the stairs, but *ya*, those do look like our *dochders*."

Their *mudder* shook her head and smiled as she poured boiling water into mugs. "I wasn't *schur*. *Kumm*, have your tea."

Rose Anna pulled out a chair and sat primly. "Mary Elizabeth was chasing me."

"Really?"

She stared at Mary Elizabeth, then her *mudder*. She'd learned her lesson about impulsive behavior, hadn't she? "*Nee*," she said after a long moment. "I was teasing her."

The four of them shared a break with cookies and tea—well, her *dat* was having his usual coffee. He never drank tea.

After a few minutes he got to his feet, saying he had to get back to his chores. He shrugged into his jacket and grabbed up another cookie before heading out the back door.

Linda went upstairs shortly afterward leaving Rose Anna and Mary Elizabeth alone at the table.

"You're being awfully quiet."

Rose Anna stared down into the contents of her tea cup wishing she could find an answer there. "I can't—Peter—I can't—" she lifted her hands, let them fall as she shook her head. "I tried to fall in love with Peter. I wasn't just flirting with him the way you and Lavina thought."

She shook her head. "Well, I did flirt with him, and he flirted with me. It felt *gut* to have a man want to be with me after John didn't want me."

Mary Elizabeth just sat listening.

"But I don't feel Peter is the *mann* God set aside for me."

"And who is?" Mary Elizabeth asked her cautiously.

"John."

"If he is—and I'm not saying he isn't—don't you think things would have worked out before now?"

"Sometimes it takes more time," Rose Anna said firmly. She got up and put her cup in the sink.

Then she turned to face her *schweschder*. "And sometimes God needs a little help."